THE GREAT MANN

THE
GREAT
MANN

A Novel

Kyra Davis Lurie

CROWN
NEW YORK

CROWN

An imprint of the Crown Publishing Group
A division of Penguin Random House LLC
1745 Broadway
New York, NY 10019
crownpublishing.com
penguinrandomhouse.com

Library of Congress Cataloging-in-Publication Data
Names: Lurie, Kyra Davis, author. Title: The great mann: a novel / Kyra Davis Lurie.
Description: First edition. | New York City: Crown, 2025. |
Identifiers: LCCN 2024045546 | ISBN 9780593800867 (hardcover) |
ISBN 9780593800874 (ebook) Subjects: LCGFT: Novels.
Classification: LCC PS3604.A972 G74 2025 | DDC 813/.6—dc23/eng/20250103
LC record available at https://lccn.loc.gov/2024045546

ISBN 978-0-593-80086-7
Ebook ISBN 978-0-593-80087-4

Editor: Shannon Criss
Editorial assistant: Austin Parks
Production editor: Patricia Shaw
Text designer: Andrea Lau
Production: Heather Williamson
Copy editor: L. J. Young
Proofreaders: Rob Sternitzky, Robin Slutzky, and Janet Renard
Publicist: Dyana Messina
Marketer: Kimberly Lew

Manufactured in the United States of America

1 3 5 7 9 8 6 4 2

First Edition

The authorized representative in the EU for product safety and compliance is
Penguin Random House Ireland, Morrison Chambers, 32 Nassau Street,
Dublin D02 YH68, Ireland, https://eu-contact.penguin.ie.

To my late big brother, Charles Trammell III
I carry you

Spacious, well-kept West Adams Heights still had the complacent look of the days when most of Los Angeles' aristocracy lived there. But the look was deceiving.

—*Time*, December 1945

I've learned by livin' and watchin' that there is only eighteen inches between a pat on the back and a kick in the seat of the pants.

—Hattie McDaniel, *Denver Post*

Author's Note

Like most Americans, I first read *The Great Gatsby* in high school. I fell in love with the story. But while I was drawn to the optimism of Jay Gatsby, the brazenness of Tom, the clear-sightedness of Nick, and the aloof pragmatism of Jordan, there were three other characters that made an even deeper impression on me. Three characters to whom F. Scott Fitzgerald didn't give a single line of dialogue, who were only featured in the bottom half of one paragraph, and whom he described in dehumanizing terms:

> As we crossed Blackwell's Island a limousine passed us, driven by a white chauffeur, in which sat three modish negroes, two bucks and a girl. I laughed aloud as the yolks of their eyeballs rolled toward us in haughty rivalry.
>
> "Anything can happen now that we've slid over this bridge," I thought; "anything at all . . ."
>
> Even Gatsby could happen, without any particular wonder.

To Fitzgerald, the idea of African Americans having wealth and a white driver was evidence of a world that has become so fantastical, it has entered the arena of comical absurdity. This despite the fact that *The Great Gatsby* was published only four years after what had been known as Black Wall Street, a highly prosperous Black community in

Oklahoma, had been burned to the ground, many of its most successful Black residents murdered.

If you are born into a marginalized minority group, you come to accept that you will be hated by many of your heroes. And while I've seen no evidence that Fitzgerald's feelings about African Americans ever rose to the level of hate, his manuscripts and professional correspondence evidence an acute disdain for us as well as for other minorities. Yet he continues to be an author I love. I've read every single one of his books and all of his short stories. I've learned from him as a writer and I'm incredibly grateful for that.

But those three African Americans in the limo have haunted me. Because to me they represent not absurdity but a forgotten history. Within the Great American Novel, they represent a Great American Story that is rarely told.

I wanted to tell it. I wanted to write a story inspired by a novel created by a brilliant but bigoted man, a story that featured characters based on very real, brilliant Black pioneers.

THE GREAT MANN

Chapter 1

"Wake up, I said it's the end of the line."

My eyes fly open, my hand automatically reaching for my weapon. But instead of metal, I find paper.

This isn't Bastogne. I'm not in the middle of a battle-scorched forest. And the words aren't coming from a Kraut. Instead, it's the old Chicano who's been sitting next to me since he boarded the train back in Texas, his heavy jowls draped over a frown as he shakes me awake. In my other hand is a folded-up copy of the *Chicago Defender,* a newspaper, not a grenade. The ink's been smudged at the top so all that you can see of the date is the *45*. But I know it's October. I know the war's over. The place I was just in while sleeping . . . that was just a nightmare's retelling of a memory. Guess that's why those Nazis were wearing white hoods.

"Son, we've reached Los Angeles," the frowning man says. "You're blocking my way."

I grab my duffel and join the line of all the folks deboarding, making way for the white ones as a precaution. Got to figure out the rules of this place before deciding if they're worth breaking.

On the platform, I stop to read the giant clock hanging over a newsstand across the way before being startled by a sudden impact. I'm being pushed . . . no, more like bumped out of the way by some careless white man in a rush. He presses past toward some destination, cheerily using his shoulders and elbows on everybody blocking him, no matter their color or sex.

Something's different about this place.

Maybe it's the air, unseasonably warm for autumn. It pours into your lungs, thick, like this crowd. All these white folk looking hurried.

But there're a few folks here with skin like mine. Negroes dressed like they're ready for church.

I'm dressed for war.

I changed into my uniform somewhere 'round Arizona.

Margie says they respect uniforms out here. Not like back home where any Negro in uniform is a target. Maybe I shouldn't put so much trust in my cousin's assurances, seeing as I haven't seen her since we were both half the height of a tobacco plant. What do I really know of her now? In those two decades since her family fled our hometown, she may have written me half a dozen letters in total—most of them filled with nothing more than exaltations over the latest romantic Hollywood movie that made her laugh or cry. She rarely ever wrote about anything real.

I didn't get around to watching most of what she recommended because the nearest theater open to Negroes was forty miles from my home. Instead, I used my letters to describe the books I loved although reading had never been her passion. Then three years ago, I got to see *Casablanca* while training at Camp Hood and I wrote to tell her how much I liked it. When she wrote back, she suggested I come out to L.A. after the war, where I could both find a good job and occasionally accompany her to the movies that her husband didn't have the patience to sit through. At the time, I wasn't sure I'd take her up on it.

Yet here I am.

Maybe it was foolish to assume the girl who had always made me laugh had grown into a woman who could guide me right. But looking around . . . I don't think so.

It's different here.

I see it in the way these people ain't seeing me. I'm accustomed to white folk sizing me up, trying to work out if I'm a predator they can beat down to prey.

Invisibility feels clean.

Except I do feel one pair of eyes. A Negro girl, dressed like she's headed to a lily-white country club, her skin walking the line between copper and gold. That girl's smiling at me like she knows me.

I'd like to know her.

My train arrived early, so I got time to kill before Margie shows to fetch me. I navigate through the maze of people, heading toward those seeing eyes until I'm close enough to smell just a hint of perfume. "Somethin' I can help you with, miss? I'm new 'round here, but I can work out a train schedule if you need it."

"Why, don't you recognize me?"

Her voice. Light, sweet . . . familiar.

And the laughter bubbling out of her, I know that, too.

"Charlie, it's me, Marguerite!"

Can't be. I've never met this woman before me.

"Margie, that really you?" When her smile gets bigger, I see it. The undeniable spark of mischief her mama was always trying to slap out of her. "Damn, girl, you changed! You out here looking like a movie star!"

"Hush, I'm the same girl you knew from Miss Peesly's class."

Now she's got me laughing. The idea of this woman, in her tailored jacket and unscuffed shoes, that she could have anything to do with the one-room schoolhouse where lil' Margie and I used to spend our days! A girl we called Margie 'cause she was too tiny to bear the weight of that foreign-tongued name Uncle Morris brought back from the Great War. A cheap, expensive gift for his next-born daughter.

But then, overnight, four days before her ninth birthday, Margie and her family picked up and left.

Seems she used all those years to expand into the rest of those French syllables.

"I think you're the one who's changed the most," she says, taking a step back to get a better look at me. "Tall, handsome, and . . . oh, you have medals!" She gestures at the ribbons on my chest. "You never mentioned them in your letter! How thrilling! Did you get them saving a damsel in distress?"

I force a smile even though I'm also gritting my teeth. "Don't think they give out medals for saving pretty girls." I can't hold her flippancy against her. All she knows of the Nazis is what she's seen in the movies. Hollywood makes them seem like genteel villains, not the swastika-wearing sadists I encountered on the battlefield.

"No, I suppose not, there are other awards for that." She gives me a playful wink. "Anyway, you always were my hero. Ever since we were babes." I don't move as she reaches to touch my face, so tender you'd think we ain't cousins and she ain't married. "Is it my imagination, or are you one tooth short?"

Shouldn't have smiled so wide. Don't like thinking about things others knocked out of me.

"I happen to know a marvelous dental surgeon, Dr. John Alexander Somerville. Graduated top of his class at the University of Southern California. They say he's the best in the whole state. I do believe he could give you a smile that all the pretty girls would feel compelled to return."

"I don't got money for nothin' like that."

"Oh, John's a friend. Perhaps he'll do me this favor." She turns and starts walking, her confidence a clear sign I'm meant to follow.

"This must be some kind of paradise." I direct the words to her shoulder blades, moving with rhythm as she leads me out of the station. "Even in Europe, I can't imagine a white man doing that kind of favor for a Negro."

"He's not white. He's one of us." There's a line of freshly waxed automobiles up along the sidewalk. Few of them got Negro drivers, looking sharp in their black suits and caps. And they're looking at Margie with the same kind of wonder I'm feeling. The cloth her clothes are cut from looks too expensive for our kind. Her hands look like they never washed a dish, and the diamond sitting on her finger is either fake or looted from the goddamned Louvre.

I look up at the distant hills that press against the skyline. I can just barely make out the white letters mounted on the closest one. "That's the Hollywoodland sign!"

"That old thing?" She briefly tilts her head in the far-off direction. "It's a bit of a wreck, but the city says they're going to spruce it up. Maybe remove the *land* so it just says *Hollywood*, which would make more sense. Speaking of Hollywood, I saw that flick you liked so much, *Casablanca*? You didn't tell me how sad it was! Bogart doesn't even get the girl! He sends Ingrid Bergman away!"

"Yeah, but you gotta remember, in the movie, Bergman's married to another man. That's who she ends up with," I point out.

"Paul Henreid? Please, Bogart is much more dashing." Margie shakes her head, as if disappointed by the whole affair. "I'm done with sad movies. Now that the war is over, perhaps there will be more fun films in the theaters for us to see next year." She stops in front of a Lincoln Continental. "Hop on in!"

"Girl, you're pullin' my leg, this ain't your car!"

"I'm afraid it is." She laughs, dangling the keys in front of me. "I promise I haven't run over a single thing."

Negroes don't drive cars like this. Not in Virginia, not here. I can see the truth of it on the faces of the Negro drivers still checking her out.

She takes my arm, brings her singsong melody down to a volume just north of a whisper. "My husband would prefer I have a driver. But we can't quite afford it. Not yet."

She releases me, unlocks the door, and gets behind the wheel.

"I hope you don't mind, but I'm going to avoid the freeway," she says as she pulls from the curb. "I simply don't trust myself on it. If I let myself go too fast I might never slow down!"

I let her do the talking as we drive. She's going on about how, after they left the tobacco fields for the paved streets of Richmond, her brother Willie took up with a colored girl so light she could disappear into the white world, taking him with her. Margie hasn't heard from Willie in years.

It's hard to focus on the words, though. The people on these streets are a whole mix of races, most of them looking like they haven't had a bath since Hoover was running things. The men are all stumbling and yelling, their sentences scrambled by dope, drink, or some other kind of misfiring of the mind. And there's no missing the five Black and brown men lined up against that storefront, hands against the wall as white officers pat them down. Everything outside is filthy and ugly, everything inside this chrome is neat and beautiful. It's got me off balance.

"Where are we?"

"Hmm? Why, this is Skid Row. Isn't it a horror? Don't worry, we'll be out of it soon," she says before going back to her family saga.

Sure enough, it only takes a few minutes for things to get better.

There're apartment buildings, boxy and utilitarian but well maintained, and the people walking on the sidewalks are all colored and it looks like they got work. But there's too many of 'em. Everybody's crammed together like they were at the station. In a city the size of Texas, it don't make much sense.

Margie keeps talking as she takes a corner, moving the car up an incline.

She tells how, after Willie took off with his white-passing girl, Uncle Morris took the rest of them briefly to Maryland before changing course and trying out the urban centers of Georgia, where her two other brothers found good work and nice wives. Georgia's also where her mother's family heralded from, so while they were there Margie got to know aunts, uncles, and cousins she hadn't met before.

As she talks the streets get better.

Whiter.

Spanish-style homes with tile roofs. Manicured lawns. White folk playing with their dogs, sipping on what could be iced tea and lemonade. Saturday afternoon being treated like the day of rest it is meant to be.

Margie keeps chattering, telling me about how her younger cousin Daryl was lost in the early days of the war. Telling me how he led the charge in a heroic battle only to catch a bullet in the heart while raising the victory flag, and how his death was that elusive trifecta we all hope for—quick, proud, and painless.

It's the kind of myth Margie always weaves for the loved ones she's lost. But I can pick out the pieces of truth. The killing. The death. Been way too much of that in our family.

She's taking me through her history while driving me through a city. We're high enough now that we can look down on where we've just been.

The houses grander, the spaces between them wider, the cars in the drives got a sheen on 'em. The women got porcelain skin and scrawny hips, the men sporting button-downs tucked into pleated pants. I spot one Negro face: a woman wearing a maid's uniform so pristine you'd think she was hired for decoration, not dusting.

Margie presses on, talking about her nomadic family adventures. Telling me how at first it was just her and her parents in California. The three of them came out on the rumors of better opportunities and bluer skies.

We're driving up into that sky right now, the whole city laid out beneath us. We reach the top of the hill and the streets get different.

Real different.

What I'm seeing ain't possible.

Houses replaced by mansions, fancier cars, the men and women as fashionable as Cary Grant and Rita Hayworth.

Except Cary and Rita ain't colored.

Everybody here's a Negro.

A Negro woman wearing a mink stole as she strolls down the pristine street. A colored man stepping out of a brand-new roadster. Black children playing on the lawn of a manor as a few women watch over them while chatting and sipping what might be iced tea from sparkling glasses.

Like they own the place.

"Charlie, if you don't close your mouth, you're bound to catch flies."

"Am I dreamin'?"

"I certainly hope not!" She lets out that charming little laugh. "I'm about to introduce you to my husband and son and I expect you to be fully awake for the occasion."

"But where are we?"

"Why, this is West Adams Heights"—she waves at our surroundings as she takes another corner—"but anyone who's worth talking to knows it as L.A.'s very own Sugar Hill. Isn't it heavenly?" Her ring catches the light and throws it back with a flare. "God willing, I'll live here 'til I die!"

Chapter 2

I'm still reeling from the tour Margie and her husband, Terrance, just gave me of their home.

I'm struggling to make sense of what seems impossible.

This house of Margie's has two stories, a giant lawn, and a gazebo out back. I've been standing in the middle of the living room with her and her husband for the last twenty minutes drinking wine that's as good as anything I had tasted while serving in France. Margie's sitting in an upholstered armchair that don't got a single rip or stain, her foot wiggling to the sound of some old-time melody coming out of their mahogany radio.

"Do you mind the music?" she asks. "I always tell Terrance a room simply isn't complete without music."

"The music's fine . . . You're in insurance?" I ask Terrance for what might be the fourth time. I don't know much about insurance, but I never would have guessed working with it could buy a man all this.

"I'm a VP at Golden State Mutual, the most successful Negro-owned insurance company in the nation." Terrance's grin lets me know he doesn't mind repeating himself, at least not while talking about himself. "Technically I'm second in command behind our president, Norman Houston. But between you and me? I'm often the one in charge." He pauses, making real sure that last part sinks in. "Rumor has it the *California Eagle*, L.A.'s foremost Negro newspaper, will be naming me businessman of the year. I was one of the first Negroes to graduate with a business degree from the University of Southern California. They don't allow many of us in, but they're savvy enough to make exceptions for the truly exceptional." He leans back, sizing me up. "Marguerite tells me you have some education yourself."

Terrance reminds me of the East Coast Negroes I dealt with in the army. The ones who thought any colored man with a slow, Southern drawl also had a slow, docile mind. All my life I'd been combing through dictionaries, collecting words like baseball cards. I had welcomed the excuse to pass the expensive ones out among the other Southern Negro soldiers. Whenever those Northern boys came 'round we'd toss words like *perspicacity* and *evanesce* into our sentences just to get 'em gawking.

"I've been trained in accounting by those who know the field. Fair to say I've also read more literary classics and history books than your average professor. I was invited to enroll at Virginia Union," I tell him. "But all those plans got sidelined on account of the war."

"Why, when we were children you couldn't stop Charlie from learning," Margie chimes in. "Six years old and he'd pull old newspapers right out of the trash just so he could read them!"

"'Fraid that's true." I lay heavy into my drawl and give Terrance a down-home smile. "If a book got somethin' to teach me, I'm gonna read it. I'm just one curious, autodidactic son of a bitch."

Gives me some pleasure to see this "exceptional Negro" silently trying to work out what *autodidactic* means without lowering himself to ask.

"Oh . . . oh, they're playing the Charleston!" Margie leaps to her feet and starts to dance. "I was born too late, I would have been a wonderful flapper!"

"Flappers were hussies," Terrance retorts. "That's not you."

"Oh, don't be such a drip and dance with me!" She laughs, throwing her arms and feet around. "Why, if I was born twenty years earlier,

I would have gone to all the most cosmopolitan speakeasies and danced the night away Monday through Sunday."

What's this woman talking about? I remember being with Margie when her mama, my aunt Henny, returned from the tobacco fields, the sap making her hands five times blacker than the rest of her. Her back would ache so bad she could barely handle standing for the time it took to make supper. And the few freewheeling fools we did have in our family didn't make it to twenty. That's the stock we come from. This halcyon history Margie's going on about ain't ours to claim.

The door bursts open and a little boy, somewhere under five, runs on in. His face is just two shades darker than Margie's and one shade lighter than Terrance's. They've got him dressed up like a lil' British lord. "Mommy, guess what? I had cake!"

A blue-black Negro woman follows him, smiling down at the boy in a way that makes me think she's one of his aunties.

"Charlie, this is my son, Art!" Margie says, still dancing. "Art, this is your cousin Charles."

"Hello, Art." I bend down to greet him. His face gets serious as he shakes my hand, his little fingers stretching out, as if he thinks he might somehow get them around my palm. I turn to the woman who entered with him. "Charlie Trammell," I begin, but then Terrance breaks in.

"That's our nanny," he says, real dismissive and haughty, before turning to the woman. "I assume Art behaved himself?"

"He minded his manners the whole time," the nanny assures him.

"Oh, let the boy have a little mischief!" Margie pulls her son to her to teach him a few dance steps. "I do wish I could have come with you today, Art, you know how much Mommy loves parties."

"There was cake and ice cream and balloons and a clown with bright red hair!" He's trying hard to match his mother's rhythm. But when she goes into the knocky-knees move he gives it up. "What are you doing, Mommy?"

"This? Why, it's the Charleston!"

Art looks around the room, his smooth forehead creasing. "Cousin Charles has a son?"

Margie and Terrance crack up at that, the nanny does, too. "It's a dance," Terrance explains.

Art blinks at his father, still not understanding but not interested enough to ask for further explanation. He turns back to his mother. "Can I play outside?"

"Gertie, do you mind?" Margie asks, smiling kindly.

"Not at all, Mrs. Lewis."

"Nice to meet you, Gertie," I call out, which gets me a quick nod of appreciation in return before the woman and Art disappear into the backyard.

Margie collapses, pink-cheeked, into her chair. Terrance observes her fondly before turning back to me. "Have you ever had a job that required more of your head than your hands?"

"I did the books for a man named Alvin Flynn. He had a small general store for the colored folk."

"Oh, I remember the Flynns!" Margie exclaims, still slightly breathless. "His daughter was just a few years older than us . . . Brenda, wasn't it?"

"Barbara," I say.

I won't add that the last time I saw Barbara was in her coffin. She'd been found naked, beaten, and lifeless along the banks of the Potomac. No one bothered investigating. We all knew the white boys who did it. I won't add that years after the murder Mr. Flynn refused to remove his hat while passing one of her killers on the street, that he failed to step off the curb to make way, a clear violation of the Jim Crow laws. It was enough to get that grieving father a night in a cell. When he got out there was nothing left of his general store but ash.

"Well, there's a lot more to insurance work than numbers," Terrance tells me. "The challenge is Negroes are used to operating without insurance. We need it, but most don't have it because white insurance companies won't write us policies, at least not ones you can count on them honoring. My company can give members of our race the very thing this country has worked so hard to deprive us of. We solve their greatest problem."

"Are you sayin' the Negro's biggest problem is not a lack of human rights," I ask, working hard not to chuckle, "but a lack of insurance?"

"Don't be dense," he snaps as Margie uses her hand to hide her smile. "Insurance is more than a policy."

"I'm not following."

"It's a sense of security!"

The veracity of his response pulls down the corners of my mouth.

"To the Negro," Terrance goes on, "a sense of security is worth all the money in the world."

"Which is why it's not such a big thing to ask them to part with just a little of their money to have it," Margie adds with a giggle.

"You think this is a joke?" Terrance's glare doesn't cow her one bit, robbing him of a certain satisfaction.

"Oh, darling, no." Her tone's sweet, but her eyes are narrowed. "A man taking pains to keep his family and *home* protected, why, that's the most serious of responsibilities! Why, any man who can't manage that isn't much of a man at all!"

Is that a tremor I detect under the syrup of her voice? And as for Terrance . . . something she said has got him agitated. He gets up and starts pacing. "My company—"

"*Your* company?" she interrupts.

But he pays her no mind. "We're not just selling policies, we're providing our clients with dignity and well-deserved respect—"

"And fidelity," Margie breaks in again, putting an odd emphasis on the word. She pats her hair, making sure nothing's mussed. "Isn't that what your boss, Norman, was going on about at dinner the other night?"

"Stop calling him my boss! He doesn't oversee me!"

"Didn't he say that along with respect those you serve deserve *fidelity*?"

Terrance positions himself so that he's towering right over her. "I don't serve," he corrects. "I provide."

Margie doesn't even blink, just sits up straighter, looks him dead in the eye.

Just then their son hurls himself into the room, Gertie at his heels. "Mommy, we saw a gopher! He stuck his whole head out of the ground just to look at us! He had the biggest front teeth you've ever seen!"

Both his parents seem a little flummoxed by the announcement. Gertie gently pulls the boy away. "Maybe I'll just get him bathed and ready for supper."

"Yes, that would be best," Margie agrees, and watches the two disappear again, this time up the stairs.

"Didn't I tell the gardener to exterminate those rodents?" Terrance asks.

"You did," Margie confirms. "Of course you did."

"I knew I shouldn't have hired him. You know who recommended him to us?" Terrance asks me.

Did Negroes in these parts have gardeners? And nannies? And . . .

"Your white-ass-kissing landlady, that's who. I shouldn't have trusted her. People like her are the reason Les and his ilk think so lowly of us. She's sold out our entire race at every turn, why should this be any different?"

"Wait a minute, I have a landlady?" I could ask who Les is, too, but Terrance said too many confusing things at once for me to inquire about all of 'em.

"Darling, I hardly think recommending an incompetent gardener is on par with selling out the race, or . . ." She pauses, giving the matter more thought. "Oh, could there be a metaphor in there? What might the gopher stand for?"

"Uncle Toms maybe," Terrance replies, his lip twitching with humor.

"Or white trash perhaps?" Margie offers.

"All the ugly that burrows under the surface of America," I suggest.

Margie and Terrance exchange looks and then fall into a fit of laughter. "Ah," Terrance says, once he's caught his breath, "you do have a brain in there after all. You're what, twenty-six?"

"He's twenty-five," Margie corrects, "eleven years your junior and a year younger than me. Although I swear I still feel like I'm twenty."

"Twenty-five, old enough to be taken seriously, young enough to give a company decades of work," Terrance muses. "Okay, come with me to work on Monday morning . . . no, wait, I have a meeting . . . make it Tuesday. I'll introduce you to some people, get you an interview. We'll see if you can continue to impress. But keep your smiles small," he adds, chuckling again. "That missing tooth gives you the look of a field hand."

I let the barb slide. "I'd appreciate that. But . . . I have a landlady?" I press. "Or is that a metaphor, too?"

"Oh, yes." Margie's got the sense to at least look abashed. "Seeing as we only have three bedrooms and there's four of us, when you include Art and Gertie, that is, well, we thought it might be better for you if you stayed elsewhere, quite nearby, of course," she adds quickly as she reads my face. "Really, it's just a short walk from here. Louise always has a few boarders. And we've paid your first month's rent, so don't worry about that one little bit. You'll be more comfortable. Her house is much grander than ours."

"Tell him how she paid for that house!" Terrance demands with a good-natured bellow.

Margie sits up properlike and announces with exaggerated seriousness, "The house is paid for with Black shame!" Then the two of them fall into another laughing fit.

I might as well be back in France for all the sense I'm able to make from the words coming outta these two. "If I'm not staying here, should I be headed out? When am I expected by this Louise . . . Louise . . ."

"Beavers," Terrance supplies.

That can't be right. "Louise Beavers . . . like . . . the actress?"

"Actress?" Terrance scoffs. "More like Hollywood shill!"

"Louise Beavers lives here? In your neighborhood?" It's not possible . . . is it?

"Oh, dear." Margie shoots me a teasing wink. "I fear our Charlie has a bit of a crush!"

"Give me a break." Terrance snorts. "She barely qualifies as a woman."

Louise Beavers. Mama had been so excited to see Miss Beavers in the movie *Imitation of Life*. The word was that her character, Delilah Johnson, had as many lines as the white lead. Finally, a studio film with a colored woman in a major role.

We had found the time to make a special trip into Petersburg for that movie. We walked into that theater feeling as proud as can be.

We walked out feeling different.

"It *is* nice they gave her such a big role," Mama had said. And I nodded, not willing to voice what we were both thinking.

White folk gonna love this movie.

It wasn't Delilah's servility. Lots of us gotta bow our heads to eke out a living.

Ain't no shame in it. But her love of her servility . . . the way she wouldn't give it up even when independence was on offer . . . that just didn't sit right. Delilah was the kind of Negro the white boys who burned down Mr. Flynn's store thought we should all be.

I'm not exactly a fan of Louise Beavers. But she *is* a bona fide movie star!

Terrance is still ranting like a preacher outside a whorehouse. "It's not just the parts they play. The way these actresses behave off set is just as bad. Going through husbands like they're tissues. Sleeping with any man who whistles at them. They have no idea what it means to be a lady. Not like my Marguerite here."

"But they do seem to throw good parties," Margie says wistfully.

"We're not going to lower ourselves by attending some sordid bacchanalia! Not that any of them are educated enough to know what a bacchanalia is—"

I'm having a hard time focusing on what he saying. Partly because he ain't saying nothing interesting. But also . . .

. . . *I'm gonna board with a bona fide movie star!*

"Should I go now?" I ask.

Margie's laugh makes me blush, and I stare down at my feet. "Well, I was hoping you'd stay for dinner," she says. "But after dessert, I promise to take you right over."

Chapter 3

"So you're my new boarder," Louise Beavers says. She's standing before Margie and me, her artfully carved wood front door thrown open wide enough for me to get a good look at the light-filled anteroom with a coatrack. There's a dark wood sideboard fine enough to be called a credenza. The only time I've seen such splendor before . . . was in some of the homes my mama cleaned.

"Uh . . ." I begin, but no words come. It's too much. The place, the wealth, the celebrity. How the hell are you supposed to greet a movie star? Should I mimic her greeting to me? *So you're the actress* . . . no . . . *So you're my new landlady* . . . That sounds mighty familiar, probably more than appropriate . . . Maybe *I've seen your films* . . . no . . . How about *It's an honor* . . . But is it an honor? I've got mixed feelings. Maybe just *howdy*? Can you say *howdy* to famous people?

"Damn, I've heard more talking in Charlie Chaplin movies." She turns to Margie as my face heats up. "You coming in, Marguerite?"

"Oh, no, I just wanted to show him where the place is," Margie says. "Terrance is waiting for me."

"I thought you were the one always waiting on him," Louise shoots back. "He still taking joyrides every day after work?"

"Oh, come now, it's never been every day . . . just when he needs to clear his head."

It's my head that clears as I hear their exchange. "You ain't plannin' on walkin' home alone?" I say. "Margie, you got a child, you can't be actin' reckless like that."

"Silly! It's not even eight and we're barely three blocks away!"

I grab her arm before she can leave. "The kind of white men who prey on colored women don't wait 'til midnight to do it."

Louise Beavers's soprano laugh is so loud it almost pops my ear-drums. "And here I was thinking I was going to be living with a mute! Where'd you come from, anyway? Mississippi?"

"Virginia."

"The rural part? Probably just as bad. The Negroes who live in *these* parts have too much fame and money to be vulnerable to the kind of nonsense you're fretting about."

"Louise is right." Margie removes my hand from her arm and kisses it like I'm a lady and she a gentleman. "There *are* a few nasty white men around here, but even those knuckleheads are too posh to resort to anything beastly."

I give up and let Margie leave even as visions of Barbara shoot cracks and splinters through her assurances.

"Are you coming in or are you planning to sleep on my doorstep?"

I follow Louise Beavers into the anteroom. The chandelier looks like damn expensive crystal, too. "This a real nice home you got here."

"Thank you, I plan on keeping it."

By her tone you'd think I was threatening to put the whole house in my duffel and slink off into the night.

But then everybody always says actresses are crazy.

WHEN WE GET to the salon there're two young women sitting and talking on a love seat, one dressed for a night out, the other looking like she's done for the day. "Girls, meet Charles Trammell III. Charles, these are my other boarders. Anna Caldwell." She points to the dressed-up girl. "Anna's also my publicist. And this," she says, turning to the other, "is Patricia Jackson. Patty's trying her luck as an actress, although if she wants to make any real headway in the movie business, she's gonna need to put on some pounds."

Louise slaps me on the back and Patricia rolls her eyes. "The studio's been force-feeding me since I landed my first role and I still gotta wear padding to be round enough for 'em. Speaking of which, have you eaten? We've just finished up, but there's some dinner left if you want it. My husband, Robert, makes a mean meat loaf."

"Your husband cooks?" I didn't even know she was married.

"He's got to, because I'm allergic to kitchens and brooms."

In every single one of her films, Louise Beavers plays a maid. It's disorienting. This woman's got the same face as her characters, but a completely different spine.

"I just had dinner with the Lewises. I'm fine."

"All right, then. Bob's upstairs, but you'll meet him soon enough. Anna, you'll show Charles to his room?"

"I can manage it," Anna replies, although I can tell by the way she keeps glancing at her watch she's in a hurry.

Louise is headed toward the stairs, but she pauses right before climbing. "Say, Charles—"

"Everybody calls me Charlie."

"Charlie, do you play poker?"

"On occasion. Can't say I'm any good."

"Well, then, you're more than welcome to join me for my poker night. I host it every Sunday, up on the third floor." The smile she gives me is downright Machiavellian. "Pleasure to have you here, Charlie."

Patricia places her hand on her stomach and looks down at it with sad eyes. "She keeps going on about my weight. But surely there will be some roles for us colored gals that won't require me to look like a mammy."

"Let's save the optimism for the press releases," Anna advises. "The reality is you should've had another slice of Bob's meat loaf." I like Anna's smile. It's got some intelligence to it. "That bag looks heavy. Let me show you to where you can leave it."

I follow her through the house toward the back, keeping up with her clipped pace. The dress Anna's wearing hugs her waist and pads her shoulders. Her hips have just enough swing in 'em to make walking behind her a pleasure.

"Patty and I have rooms on the second floor, you have this room on the first." She opens the door to a bedroom that in any other Negro residence I might go as far as to call fancy. But compared to the rest of the place it's pretty modest.

I try to put my duffel down gently, but it makes a thud when it hits the floor.

"You packing bricks?" she asks.

"Nah, just the regular. Clothes, razor, toothbrush, couple of books . . ."

"Which books?"

I dig them out and hold them up for her inspection, hoping she won't be put off by the worn bindings, the brittle pages.

She takes them and I wait for her to act astonished that a country boy like me could ever be inspired to read a book that doesn't have the word *almanac* in the title.

"We have similar tastes," she says.

A simple response that makes her a little more gorgeous. "You really a Hollywood publicist?"

"Ha, you think Louise is making up stories? Journalism's my first love, but it's not always steady and stars pay more than publishers." She gestures to my uniform. "You really a soldier?"

"Until a few weeks ago." I cross the room and pull the drapes, blocking out whatever the night's hiding.

"And that hardware on your chest? I assume you earned that through an act of heroism."

I look down at my medals. Part of me thinks that if I wear them long enough, I'll start to believe I deserve them. But then the ghosts of all my fallen brothers sidle up to me, placing cold, envious fingers against my still-beating pulse. "I just served my country is all." I'm repeating lines I've said before. "Just like my pa did in the war before this one."

"And what did the country give your pa in return for that service?" I can tell from her tone she already knows the answer.

I shape my bitterness into a laugh. "Not even the medical treatment to properly heal his wounds."

Anna's leaning against the doorframe in a way that brings attention to her curves. "Everyone in this neighborhood has done better than their parents ever dreamed. They've all figured out the secret."

"And what's that?"

"Bold," she says with a playful smile, "but I need to know a man for a lot longer than ten minutes before I start whispering Sugar Hill secrets in his ear." She points to my bag. "Is there anything in there that you can wear to a party?"

If she had asked me that question at the train station, I'd have said yes. I packed a shirt, slacks, and a tie I had thought would be respectable enough to wear to either a sermon or an interview.

But that was before I understood what kind of environment I'd be walking into, one where the clothes were made of the finest cloth and were replaced instead of mended. "They call this a dress uniform," I say. "As in it's better for dancin' than killin'."

"Mmm, the jitterbug may very well be tonight's weapon of choice. It's just over a six-block walk if you're up for it. The host is . . . he's a very interesting man."

"Lots of interesting Negroes in these parts."

"Not interesting like him."

Uncertainty tugs at my confidence. She might have a crush on this fella. But then, the way she's smiling at me . . . like I got possibilities . . .

"Will you come?" she asks.

I let my eyes lose focus until Anna blurs right into the walls of this house, which blurs into the streets of this neighborhood. I feel like I'm standing somewhere between heaven and earth where nothing's clear . . .

. . . but nothing's out of reach.

Chapter 4

"My God."

The words hiss through my teeth, so soft Anna doesn't hear them.

Whoever our host is, he don't live in no house.

This here's an estate. You'd need a crane just to touch the ceiling of the ground floor.

There's a live band playing out by a giant swimming pool.

The number of guests is in the hundreds. The air is flavored with flowery perfumes and earthy cigars. All around me diamonds glitter from brown earlobes, gold watches flash against brown wrists. The only things white are the walls.

Generations of warnings regurgitate inside me, burning my throat like bile: *Keep your voice quiet, your head down.* The rules of survival.

In the crowd I see a midnight-colored man throw back his head, his loud scratchy laugh lancing through the hubbub like a sword.

I can hear Mama's teachings from my boyhood days: *Don't let the white man see you reachin' for things they don't want you havin'.*

Ten feet to my right, a bronze beauty with a flamingo neck reaches for a glass of champagne balancing on a servant's tray.

Champagne. One of the luxuries that disappeared after the Nazis invaded France. Yet here it is. The unattainable served right up in a glass.

And all these Negro servants serving it . . . so many of them I can't count. When white folk want to show off their money, they get themselves some colored folk and dress them up to be butlers and maids.

But what does it mean when those butlers and maids are used to show off the wealth of people who look like them?

Like me?

"Our host . . . what the hell does this fella do for a living?" I ask.

"He says he's in international trade, but who knows what that means." Anna's voice takes on a breathy quality, like a woman with juicy gossip to share. "He's rather shadowy. A little over a year ago, before anyone around here had even laid eyes on him, he had some European—Italian maybe?—act as his proxy to buy two properties, had them razed, and built this in their place." She pauses as a server holding a tray of hors d'oeuvres skillfully sidesteps a gal who has just tripped on her own dress. "Nobody even laid eyes on Reaper until he showed up with the moving vans."

"Wait a second, the guy who owns all this is named *Reaper*?"

She shrugs one shoulder as we squeeze through the horde. "His name is James Mann. But around the time he was moving in, someone overheard some cagey-looking fella calling him Reaper. It stuck . . . Of course, no one calls him that to his face." I almost lose Anna as we work through this clinquant crush of revelers. We brush against silk, mink, the occasional scratch of a gem.

Once we've got ourselves a few inches of space, I look up at a regal staircase that leads to the next level. Positioned at the top is a man, dark-skinned, broad, muscular build, wearing a suit that fits so well it must have been made just for him. He stands alone, his hands crossed low behind his back. There's an urgency in the way he's scanning the crowd like he's looking for something important. "Anna, is that him?" I ask.

"Hmm? Who?"

I try to point her gaze in the right direction by subtly tilting my head to the side, but before I succeed, someone else catches her eye. "Oh, look who decided to come after all!" she says. "Charlie, this is Dr. John Somerville and his wife, Dr. Vada Somerville."

A tall, distinguished-looking gentleman with ruler-straight posture and hooded, downturned eyes smiles at Anna. The woman on his arm is just as stately, her gray hair straight and styled just so, her broad nose and full lips telling a story of African ancestry that her light complexion might otherwise hide.

"You're the dentist," I say to the man before I can stop myself, then turn to his wife, "or is it you?" I had never met a woman doctor before, that'll take some getting used to. "My cousin Margie mentioned you," I say, directing my words to both of them.

"I don't believe I know a Margie." He's got a tone that sounds extra proper. Like he's a Brit who's only starting to lose his accent.

"Marguerite," Anna clarifies.

"Oh!" Mrs. Dr. Somerville exclaims. "You're Charles Trammell the third!"

I shift my weight, feeling awkward. "I see it more as being a junior two times over." I steal a glance up the staircase again. The man once there is gone. "Anyway," I add, bringing my attention back to the Somervilles, "people call me Charlie."

"Then you must call me Vada!"

"The Lewises are good friends of ours," Dr. Somerville says. Unlike his wife, he doesn't invite me to use his Christian name. "Your cousin's husband and I share the same alma mater."

"Marguerite phoned us just minutes before we left the house," Vada explains. "She says you might be in need of my husband's services."

"Ah, I don't wanna impose . . ." A splash of alcohol hits my shoe as a woman walking past us gesticulates wildly with a full martini glass in her hand.

"Are all his parties like this?" Dr. Somerville asks, his eyes following the offending spiller.

"He spares no expense," Anna replies.

"Garish." Dr. Somerville sniffs.

Vada glances around at the crowd, her eyes wary. "Normally I'd be bemused by all this, but if there's true debauchery here—or God forbid criminality—it could undermine us, Anna. Particularly now with our situation being so . . . tenuous."

"What is it that's tenuous?" I ask. Maybe I'll ask about this supposed debauchery next.

Dr. Somerville places an arm around his wife and pulls her closer. "Nothing at all. Everything is going to be fine. Better than fine, in fact. I anticipate a historic victory." He looks down at her with a reassuring smile as she continues to scan the room. "Speaking of things to look forward to, Anna, please tell me you haven't abandoned journalism entirely for the sake of your fame-hungry clients. I haven't seen your byline in the paper since . . . July, was it?"

"May," Anna corrects. "My last article was published in May. I'm trying to get an opinion piece in the *Eagle*, but the editor isn't sure of it."

"Sorry, what kinda victory are we talkin' about? Who are we fighting?" I press, but Vada's attention is elsewhere, distracted by something or someone in the crowd.

"Lena!" Vada calls out across the room as she tugs on her husband's arm. "Look, it's Lena. We must go say hello before we leave." Vada reaches out and squeezes Anna's hand as a way of saying goodbye.

As they start to walk off, Dr. Somerville says over his shoulder, "Have Anna give you the address of my office and I'll see what I can do about your tooth on Monday."

Once again, I'd smiled too widely.

I'm about to ask Anna what the Somervilles had been alluding to with all that tenuous-situation-victory talk, but then I spot the person they've gone over to greet and all thoughts drain from my head. That woman's so stunning she doesn't seem real.

"Lena Horne," Anna says before I can ask. "She's been in a few films."

"The *Stormy Weather* gal!"

"Come," she says.

I let Anna drag me to another room, breaking my trance.

"Reaper only moved in three months ago, but since then he's had a party at least every other week. Each one attracts a bigger crowd than the last."

I gotta concentrate to hear her over the din. As we pass through rooms, the revelers get increasingly rowdy: laughter ricocheting against crystal tumblers, conked hair shining under sparkling chandeliers, colored beauties in fancy gowns talking jive.

We make it out onto the patio. It's got a view of what could be the gardens of Versailles. You can hear every note the band is playing now, the bass vibrating through clothes and skin like an electric charge.

As Anna accepts a glass of wine from one of the servers, I look up and see there's a smaller balcony attached to a room on the second floor. The same man I had seen at the top of the stairs is now there, his very presence lording over the crowd beneath him.

Anna leans into me, her glass pressed to her chest. "Let's be naughty," she says in a purr.

Did she just say that? Immediately the man on the balcony loses my interest. "Um, how so?" I ask, trying to keep the hope out of my voice.

Her smile is mischievous and my heart speeds up to an embarrassing level. How long has it been since I've been with a woman? Two years? No, longer. There were women who made themselves available to the troops overseas, gals so desperate they traded favors for food. When I could, I shared my rations, but I didn't touch a single one of 'em. It had been the right thing to do. But being honorable can be damn lonely.

And to get a shot with a woman like Anna? This place really is too good to be true.

"I mean we should break a few rules and"—she takes a deep breath, leans in even closer; I don't dare move an inch—"sneak around and explore the rest of the house."

I feel myself blink. She looks up at me expectantly, then with confusion as I break out in a raucous laugh.

"What's funny?" she asks, but I shake my head, unwilling to confess how badly I misread the moment.

I look back at the manor. "You suggesting we check out the rooms that aren't open to the guests?" Her grin is her answer. "And why would we do that?" I press. "For the sake of . . . what, snooping around to see if we can find a spare sitting room? Count the bathrooms maybe? The risks don't seem worth the reward."

"Oh, it's not a real risk, I know a few others who've done it, one who was caught by the butler and even then he was barely chastised. Come on." She tugs at my arm. "I understand Reaper has an amazing library."

A library. I've seen people in the movies with rooms they called personal libraries, filled with so many old books they lined multiple walls. But that was just in the movies, right? No one could actually have their own library.

"Come on." She's pulling me again. I look up to get one more glance at the man on the small balcony, but he's gone once again.

Beginning to think he's some kinda ghost.

More people have arrived in the short time we've been here. Weaving and dodging revelers as we walk through the main rooms is much like trying to cut a path through an overgrown jungle. Finally, we come to a less populated hallway. "I think there's another bathroom this way," Anna says loudly, in case anyone is watching us as she ushers me forward. When she's sure no one's looking, she discreetly tries a doorknob of a closed room. It's not locked. Quickly she pulls me inside and closes the door behind us.

It's an office, with a tapestry on the wall that looks to be from the Middle Ages. The desk and chair are made of a dark, shiny mahogany.

"You think this is where he conducts business?" I ask.

"Of course not, it's much too small. I bet he lets his staff use it, maybe the butler."

"A butler gets to work from a mahogany desk?" I ask. I can't imagine such a thing. But she's already pulling me back into the hall and into the next room. A small study or maybe a meeting room? There's a bar on one side with a crystal decanter and on the other a settee and chair that look like they come from another era.

"Not interesting," Anna declares, and pulls me back into the hall.

The next room's door is already open a crack. We step inside to find a pool table, a poker table made of what looks like oak, and a game table complete with a chessboard with pieces that are more like small works of art than rooks, pawns, and bishops. There are active flames in a grand fireplace warming the space. I spot a large gray-winged moth flitting around it, protected from its self-destructive impulses only by the screen.

"Perhaps Reaper expects guests to find their way here," Anna says, standing before the flames. "Otherwise, why light this?"

But my attention's on the chessboard. "The pieces on both sides are the same color, they're all white." I pick one up: the king looks like an actual king, sitting on his throne with a crown and a scepter. But on the other side of the board, the king is altogether different, wearing robes that hint at a different culture . . . maybe Arab? Indian? The rooks are carved into the shape of ships and the bishops are elephants. Each side's pieces have their own distinct characteristics; the European-looking ones are slightly bigger than their counterparts to help differentiate them on the board. "They're beautiful," I say, in awe of the craftsmanship.

Anna places her hands on her hips and raises an eyebrow. "Are you up for a game of chess? I warn you, I'm quite good."

She walks to the opposite side of the board and moves a pawn that is carved into the shape of a soldier.

I suppose all frontline soldiers are pawns in one way or another.

"Your move," she says as she caresses the carved white hair of her queen.

"Anna, I barely know how to play—" I say, but stop as her eyes leave mine and move to whatever's behind me.

"Mr. Mann!" she exclaims.

I whip around to see the face of our host.

It's the same man I saw at the top of the stairs and on the balcony. But now he's standing in the doorway. "I . . . I'm sorry," I stammer, "we probably shouldn't be in here . . . I . . . well, we . . ."

But he waves his hand in a swift dismissive motion. "It's fine." His voice is a deep baritone. "I always leave this room open during my parties for my guests who may seek quieter amusements."

He walks over to join us. There's something shocking about him. Dark skin, aristocratic clothes, and the stalking gait of a boxer.

I don't like that he's smiling at Anna.

"That's an interesting first move," he says, pointing at her pawn. "I suspect you know the game well."

Anna bites her lip and gives a one-shoulder shrug. "Not to toot my own horn, but it's true. I rarely lose."

Our host nods, seeming to appreciate her confidence. "It's perhaps the most noble game in the world," he says. "There's no luck in chess. There's no cheating, and perhaps most important, there's no hiding." He makes a slow, sweeping gesture over the board. "Everyone can see everything."

"So you're a good player as well?" Anna asks.

He hesitates and then chuckles. "I'm all right, but nothing close to a master." He pauses, then adds, "I'm better at poker."

"You ever play poker with Miss Beavers? I think she has a game every week." Those are the words that come out of my mouth. Not hello, not an introduction. As with Louise Beavers, I'm not sure how I'm supposed to start. All I know is that I need to find a way into the conversation before I become a third wheel to Anna and this Reaper fella.

"Does she?" he replies. "I wasn't aware."

Anna makes eye contact with me and gives a very subtle shake of her head. Might have been out of line of me to broadcast Louise's private games to a stranger. I try to bring the conversation back to the chess set. "I've never seen pieces like these," I say.

"It's a Russian set," he responds, "made sometime in the late 1700s from walrus ivory." He gives me a wry smile. "I tried to find an all-black chess set, but c'est la vie."

Anna and I both laugh at that. Again, he turns to Anna. "You've been here before, yes?"

She nods and offers her hand. "Anna Caldwell."

"Oh!" His voice warms in recognition. "I've seen your byline in the *California Eagle*."

Anna's mouth drops a little and then she beams with pride. "Yes, thank you . . . um . . . it's been a while since I've had anything published. And this is Charlie Trammell. He's just returned from the war and will be boarding with Louise Beavers. He's originally from . . . Oh, dear." She laughs. "Where are you originally from again?"

"Virginia." We shake and his palm swallows mine. Maybe they call him Reaper 'cause he can strangle a person with his bare hand.

"I've been to Virginia," he says, his tone friendly but his gaze disinterested. The moth temporarily abandons the fire and flutters up by his ear, maybe drawn to a different kind of energy. "There's a lot of history there," he adds. He places one hand in his pocket and again nods at the board. "I'll let you get back to your game. Miss Caldwell, be sure to introduce your friend to some more people here. It's hard to move to a new city without knowing anyone."

"I know a few people," I say. "My cousin Margie lives nearby . . . although it seems everybody calls her Marguerite around here."

The moth changes course and starts to fly between us. Reaper, overcome with a sudden violent impatience, swipes at it, sending the stunned creature crashing to the ground. He studies me, as if seeing me anew.

"That's a Silver Star, correct?" he says.

"It is," I confirm, surprised he can name it.

"You earned this through your service in Italy?"

"No, I was with the 761st, we were in France and Belgium mostly."

He cocks his head, leans back on his heels. "Come out fighting."

I'm impressed and more than a little surprised that he knows our motto.

"Were you part of the Battle of the Bulge?" he asks.

An involuntary shudder shoots through me. I hate that feeling. "Yes, sir, I was."

"So, you were there for the worst of it. All those soldiers lost. Our men, *your* friends." He bows his head as if thinking, maybe praying. "Bloody business, being a hero."

Anna lets out a shocked little laugh; she thinks he's being offensive.

But that's not it. He understands the brutality of war in a way she doesn't.

"What did you say your name is again?" he asks.

"Charles Trammell. Friends call me Charlie."

"Then I'll call you Charlie." He hesitates. "Are you two really planning to play a full game?"

"No," I say definitively, then give Anna a wink. "One thing you learn as a soldier is that when you're truly outmatched, there's no shame in a strategic retreat."

"Good," he says jovially. "Then I'll start off our friendship by giving you a tour and getting you a glass."

———

We're outside in his gardens. The music is gone.

The band's packing up, the crowd's reduced to a few handfuls of drunken stragglers . . . and us. Anna and me.

Reaper has been glued to our side for hours.

He introduced me to all the guests whose names he knows, which is surprisingly few. At some point he switched out the champagne Anna and I were drinking for some one-hundred-year-old cognac that he took from his private collection. Anna had no taste for it and switched to water. But me? Those smoky notes of status went down smooth.

It was like I was drinking somebody else's history, swapping out my red blood for blue.

"Do you come from a big family, Charlie?" he asks now. We're relaxing by the side of his pool. Only Reaper sits in a chair, which he's angled so he can face our profiles as Anna and I sit on the pavement, dangling our feet in the water. Our shoes sit right alongside two neatly folded towels a servant brought us at Reaper's request.

"Shouldn't you see off your remaining guests?" Anna interrupts, sounding a little uneasy. "We didn't mean to monopolize your time."

This gotta be at least the sixth time she's asked some version of that question. It gives me hope that she's trying to get a little alone time with me.

"Everyone here has been well tended to by the staff," he says. He turns his attention back my way. "It must have been hard on your family to have you away at war. Do they know what you went through?"

"They know enough." I don't want to go into the details. "My mother said she knew I'd be fine 'cause she had a bunch of people praying for me or some such nonsense. Still, I'm glad it gave her comfort."

Anna's brow creases, but she doesn't say anything. Maybe she's religious. Hopefully, not so much that she'll reject a man who's not.

I turn back to Reaper, hoping to change the subject. "How 'bout you? Did you see much action over there?" My vision's gone a bit fuzzy and I'd be hard-pressed to say if he had five years on me or ten. But I do know he's still of fighting age.

"I wasn't in the military," he says, his words coming slow, measured.

I shake my head in disbelief, too fast apparently, and for a second, I think I'm gonna pitch forward and drown. "But you know so much about it," I finally manage after regaining some balance.

"I wasn't in the military, but I was in France . . . on business, when it was invaded."

"What kind of business are you in, James?" Anna asks, and gives me a wink when he looks away.

"International trade. I was in France right as Hitler had his monsters march into the place."

"Not a great time to be a tourist," I say with a humorless laugh. "Did you have any trouble getting back home to the States?"

"I didn't try," he says breezily. "My business wasn't done."

"Hold on a minute, you stayed in France after the occupation? To do business?" Anna asks, incredulous. "Wouldn't you stick out . . . to the Nazis?"

"I didn't stay in France the whole time . . . I also wasn't the only colored person in the country."

"Josephine Baker!" I announce, more loudly than I intend. A group of three remaining revelers, smoking on the other end of the court-yard, briefly turn in our direction.

"That's right!" Reaper agrees. "In fact, I got to know her fairly well, even helped her with a few tasks. Very impressive woman."

"Hear she's a hard woman not to fall in love with," I say.

"Don't get the wrong idea. It was just a friendship for the cause. My heart . . ." He stops short, then leans back in his patio chair, like he's tired all of a sudden. "My heart," he says again, "belongs to someone else."

"Who?" Anna asks.

"A girl I met in Atlanta. At a party. About five years before the war. She was brought there by her cousin who was trying to introduce her to the more bohemian social circles within the city."

"How old was this girl you were so smitten with?" Anna asks.

"I think sixteen at the time," he says. "She had this magical quality to her. She had the allure of a siren except . . . sirens lead men to their death, whereas with this girl . . . just being in her presence gave me the feeling of being reborn."

"A Negro girl?" Anna presses.

Reaper's mouth slides into a wry smile. "You think I would have flirted with a white girl out in the open . . . in Georgia? Do you take me as the suicidal sort? I guess I can't be surprised if you did. I can be rash."

I crane my neck up to look at him. In this moment, I'm like a little kid in awe of some big kid's spirit and swagger.

"But yes," he continues, "she was, is, one of us. Most beautiful girl in the world of any race. We ended up talking for hours. Her parents didn't like her spending much time with the opposite sex, so she snuck out to meet me for the next four nights in a row. Always with an ex-cuse of—"

"Mr. Mann." We all look up to see a dark-skinned Negro in a tux that doubles for a servant's uniform. "Mr. Mann, Mr. Pinkman is here. He's brought a gift."

"Thank you, Daniel. Take care of the gift and tell him I regret that he won't be able to stay." Reaper turns back to us. "As I was saying—"

"I'm sorry, Mr. Mann, but he says there are a few matters he must inform you of."

Reaper's eyes narrow as he looks up at Daniel anew. "Why is he the only one who always seems to have complications." He gets to his feet. "I'm afraid I do need to tend to this. International trade is done by international clocks. But if you can stay a while longer, I'll tell you the rest of the story."

I shake my head real slow. Any fast move might send the world spinning again and my stomach lurching. "Love to hear it, but I think I'm done in."

"That makes two of us," Anna agrees, sliding her legs out of the pool. "Thank you for hosting. I do love your soirees."

"Ah . . ." Reaper looks more like a man who lost his dog than one saying good night to party guests. "Then . . . I'll host another party! And you'll both come. I'll be out of town next weekend, but the Friday after—"

Anna wags her finger at him. "That's when Hattie's having her birthday celebration."

"I see . . . The following weekend, then. And, Charlie, how about I take you to lunch this week? Introduce you to a good restaurant."

Anna pats her feet dry with the towel before forcing them back into her heels. "Before we part, tell us quickly, what happened with the girl?"

"We only had that one week, although God knows we both wanted more. There is nothing more important to me than finding her again, making her mine. It's my only remaining goal."

"Mr. Mann?"

"Yes, of course, Daniel. So good to meet you, Charlie."

Both of us, still seated on the ground, watch as Reaper follows his butler back into the house.

"That was . . . odd," Anna says.

"I'll say," I agree. "He has to take a business meeting . . . with a gift-bearing man on a Saturday night. Downright suspicious if you ask me."

"No, not that . . . well, that, too. But why did he take such an interest in us? He never gives all his time to one person like that."

"Last I checked, you and I's two people, not one." I try to pull myself together: socks, shoes, roll down my pant legs, once easy tasks that are now presenting a challenge. "But that bit about how his great telos in life is to find some mystery gal he knew for less than a week?" I let out a laugh. "Never heard such fool talk. The folks back home got more practical ambitions."

"But that's the rub, isn't it?" she asks once we're back upright and walking. "Reaper has so much money he's purchased himself the kind of impractical dreams that previously only white men could afford."

"Money makes you impractical?" There are a few others migrating to the front door, then down the front steps. I catch a whiff of hashish as one couple stumbles on by.

"My dear Charlie," Anna says, "I'm pretty sure that's the whole point of money."

It's then that a car filled with white men rolls past the house. One of them lowers his window. "Hey, monkeys! Get your zoo off our streets!"

I grab Anna's arm, ready to pull her into a run, as the other men proceed to make gruesome ape noises. But the car keeps rolling, eventually picking up speed and disappearing around a corner.

"It's just words," another guest mumbles, and he rubs his hands over his cropped curls. "No one would dare try to hurt us."

"How you figure?" I ask, hating the strain in my voice.

The man blinks. "Because," he says almost robotically, "it's different here."

Chapter 5

We were makin' puppets out of shadows.

A game not too different from the other games she and I play.

But then Pa put the lanterns out. Now the shadows got no beginning and no end. All darkness.

I ain't afraid of the dark.

But those flickers of light I see from the cracks of our cabin, I don't like that.

Flares of red, one after the other, marchin' past, burnin' color into the black sky.

What scares me is the quiet.

This silence got teeth. It feastin' on all of us. Even the big kids like Vic look like they been chomped down to somethin' small.

Mama and Pa refusin' to talk. When I tried to ask a question, Pa showed me the back of his hand, threatenin' me into silence.

I don't like her coughs neither. She won't open her mouth for 'em, she's mufflin' the sound even as they makin' her whole body jerk.

The last cough jerked her so hard she almost hit her head on the table we under.

She always coughs when she got the willies.

Pa's lookin' at her like he gonna raise his hand to her, too, just for the little noises she tryin' to swallow.

I whisper, so soft even Pa can't hear, I'm turnin' words into ghosts.

I say I'm gonna save us. We gonna be okay. I'm gonna be brave.

Her coughin' stops. That mean she's hearin' me, that she ain't scared no more.

She don't know I'm lyin'.

She don't know they comin' for us.

———

I jerk up, ready to run.

But I'm not under a table. I'm in a bed. Nothing to escape here but slumber.

I give my heart a second to calm . . . rub my eyes until the last remnants of the nightmare are gone. It's always a different variation on the same one. Every damn time I close my eyes I go back to that same godforsaken night from my childhood.

When I started having those nightmares as a kid, I'd wake up from them screaming and Mama would come running to my bedside, trying to soothe me. I loved her tenderness, but it's hard for a mother to calm a child once it's been revealed that she has no real ability to protect him.

I learned that truth way too young.

Hell, maybe that's why Mama got so religious. She realized early on that she couldn't keep her family safe and she desperately needed to believe some deity could do the job for her.

Regardless, I'm an adult now. I don't need to call on my mother to shake off a nightmare.

Except I'm not feeling too good right now. The morning's squeezing through the drapes, pounding against my temples.

It's possible I drank beyond my capacity last night.

Champagne, was it? And one-hundred-year-old cognac.

Cognac that was bottled when my granddaddy was in chains, cowering from a whip.

That brandy was served to me. In a mansion. Owned by a colored man.

I force myself to sit up, the blankets falling to my waist. I twist my body left, then right, taking a good look at each wall, wondering how much of yesterday was a delusion. The room's real enough. The sun's too real.

The path toward drunkenness is always scenic. The road back is a damn ugly mess.

I riffle through my duffel. Shirts Mama patched up a dozen times or more. Pants with threads threatening an exodus. I'm not gonna walk around a movie star's house looking like a cotton picker.

Not in front of Anna.

I grab my uniform and sneak across the hall to the bathroom, where I shower quick and thorough, brush the thirty-one teeth I got left. As I shave, I can hear voices. Louise and others. Maybe they're on their way to church.

Mama had asked me if I was planning on going to Sunday services once I got to California. I lied and said I would. I knew she was prone to worrying about the state of my soul and I didn't want her to fret over nonexistent things.

In some ways it's probably easier for her to have me out here than back at home.

When I'm not in her sight, she can pretend she raised a man with enough faith to be saved. Whereas, when we're together, she can see the way my eyes glass over whenever she asks me to pray. I don't mean to cause her pain, but I ain't never been good at hiding my feelings.

Sometimes I wonder what event led her to conclude life was a thing you just had to tolerate while waiting for heaven. Maybe it was the same tragedy that turned me into a cynic. Or maybe it was something else. Mama has so many traumas to choose from.

I run my hand over my face to make sure I got it nice and smooth. The mirror lets me know I'm looking better than I'm feeling. A low bar, but it'll do.

I leave the bathroom and find the voices in the kitchen. The scent of bacon is just strong enough to get my mouth watering but weak enough to let me know it's already gone. There's a man bent over the sink, scrubbing at some pans, while Anna, Louise, and a third woman with her back to me sit around a breakfast table studying what looks like a bundle of letters.

The woman I don't know is the one talking. "The war's over," she says, "and they're still coming. These are just the ones that came in the last month! That man is trying to destroy me!"

"Can't destroy the indestructible," Louise replies.

"It's coming from all sides these days," the woman goes on. "From the NAACP to the WAHIA. Everybody trying to take everything. Our careers, reputations, homes, everything!" She gestures vaguely around the room.

Anna pushes away from the table, looking irritated by the whole conversation. Then she notices me standing here, not wanting to interrupt but also feeling a little like an eavesdropper.

Her smile makes my headache more bearable. "Morning, soldier."

The man at the sink turns. Louise looks up, too. "You still wearing your uniform?"

I start to answer, but then the woman who had her back to me turns.

I can't move.

The most famous colored woman in Hollywood is looking right at me, taking in my uniform, my week-old haircut, my face . . .

She stands, holding her chin up. Dignified. Proper. Cold. "We haven't met yet. I'm Hattie McDaniel."

What this woman represents is even worse than what Louise does.

Still, I'll be damned if I wasn't proud as hell when I first saw the newsreel. Right there on the screen was one of ours at a podium, being honored as the best supporting actress of the year. Not best colored supporting actress . . . just best supporting actress. That moment felt downright monumental.

I step forward, offer my hand. "Charles Trammell, Charlie. Real honor to meet you, Miss McDaniel."

I don't know what she thought I was gonna say, but the relief on her face tells me she's damn grateful I said something different. She takes my hand between both of hers, all coldness replaced with warmth. "When it comes to meeting one of our soldiers, the honor's always mine."

"You worked mighty hard to support the troops," I reply. "I'm mighty appreciative."

Now she's smiling like I just told her she was up for another Oscar. "Did my publicist tell you that?" she asks, turning long enough to give Anna a wink. "But, yes, I did what I could."

"I don't believe we've met, either," says the man working the dishes. He wipes his palms dry and pumps my hand as soon as Miss McDaniel releases it. "Robert Clark. Louise's husband and manager. Sorry I didn't make more food for our after-church brunch, but I thought maybe you had snuck out while we were out praying."

The hammer starts banging at my temples again. "You've already been to church?"

"Boy, don't you have a watch?" Louise demands. "We're just thirty minutes away from noon!"

Anna giggles, which gives the rest of them leave to start laughing. I try to join in, but I can feel my neck and face heating up. I've been here for less than twenty-four hours and already got them thinking I'm a drunk. I avoid their eyes, staring instead at the papers they had been gathered around a few minutes earlier. They look like handwritten letters. I could ask about them just to change the subject, but how to do that without seeming nosy?

The sudden distraction of the doorbell is a godsend. It's Anna who goes to answer.

"You're welcome to make yourself some eggs," Louise offers. "Maybe pour yourself a glass of milk or water. But don't expect us to feed you at odd hours just 'cause you have an affinity for 'em."

Miss McDaniel shakes her head. "Hush, Louise. Didn't you tell me this young man just arrived yesterday from back east? 'Course he's tired. Probably has his hours mixed up, too."

Miss McDaniel's gotta draw to her that's a little startling. Even if I hadn't seen her movies, I'd know she was a star.

Anna returns to the room, her eyes wide.

Behind her is Reaper.

He looks fresh and energized. My memory is that I had been the one keeping up with him last night, drink for drink, even as Anna eventually gave it up. But if that's true, his constitution's a lot stronger than mine.

"Good morning," he says, addressing the room.

Silence stretches for almost half a minute.

It's Robert who first crosses to give him a vigorous handshake. "James, not sure you remember me, we met at your first party. You recall that one? You threw it just days after you moved in."

"And you've had about fifty since," Louise notes.

"You're invited to them all," Reaper says, looking a little uncomfortable now.

"Oh, we've been to a few already. But only one at which you actually spoke to us."

"I wasn't trying to ignore you. I simply—"

"Didn't see us," Louise finishes for him. "'Course you didn't. Your parties aren't exactly intimate affairs."

"Sit down!" Robert says, and pulls out a chair. Louise shoots her husband a look. Reaper takes his cue from her and stays standing.

Miss McDaniel gathers up the papers she had been bent over minutes before, folding them up neat and small until they fit in her handbag. "I really must be going."

Reaper is in the center of this kitchen, trying hard to keep his smile on as everybody else tries to avoid his gaze while eyeballing him.

Without thinking, I raise my hands to my temples, pressing down on them as if it might help. Reaper notices and I see a flash of compassion. "I came over to make good on my offer of showing you around, old sport," he says. "Can you spare the time?"

———

Outside the sky is clear and the wind's blowing fierce. I blink as bits of dust stir up, wishing I had glasses or goggles to help protect me. For a while we don't talk. I haven't even bothered to ask where we're going. I use the time to get myself accustomed to the tune of L.A. They don't have too many birds here. The background noise is the hum of auto engines and the occasional overhead plane. It's a city that's always roaring, but you only hear it when you listen.

"There are days when I think it should be Los Angeles that gets the title of Windy City," Reaper finally says as we pause to let a Negro couple pull their pretty yellow car into the drive of the house we're passing. "But at least here the wind is warm. It never snows."

White snow, stained with red, wounded soldiers screaming into a screeching wind. "I hate snow."

He answers with a nod. "The snow in northern Europe is . . . It's not something I care to experience again. Very few people around here know what it's like. I spent the latter part of the war on one of the French islands that was liberated early. The winters there were significantly better."

"You spent the last years of the war relaxin' on an island?" I laugh. "Sounds nice."

"Oh, no, it wasn't a vacation. People . . . people there needed help. *France* needed help. But once being inside her borders was no longer possible, well, I did what I could outside of them."

"How so—" I begin to ask, but then another couple comes out of the next house we pass. They're white.

I nudge Reaper.

He glances over and gives them a small wave, which the man ignores and the woman responds to with a haughty frown. "That's Francis and Mildred Smith."

"They really live here?"

"Does that surprise you?" he asks. "There are still some old money-eyed white residents around. People whose families lived here before we all moved in."

Right, Margie had said something about a white neighbor, but it hadn't fully registered at the time. "They don't make problems for us?"

"Some of them do, many don't. Probably best to steer clear of the

Smiths." He slides his hands into his pockets, relaxed. "You didn't say much about your military service last night. You must have been a tanker, yes?"

"A medic," I correct, still distracted by the idea of white folk being neighborly with our kind.

"A medic! So you saved people!"

The statement stings more than it should. "A few." I force my gaze straight ahead, as if that might help me from looking back into the past. "Nowhere near as many as I didn't save."

"The things you must have seen." I can feel him studying me.

My stomach cramps up as I wait for what's coming. The giddy curiosity that courts tales of spilled guts, the breathless mining for details of blown-off faces and dead brothers. Maybe I can turn the tables on him. Ask him about all this helping France stuff he's being so cagey about.

But then, instead of asking me a question, he surprises me.

"I'm pretty good at figuring out which questions people want me to ask and which ones they don't."

I look up at him. I get the feeling he's establishing rules for both of us.

We've reached his house and I'm not sure if he's bringing me over for coffee or what.

But then he leads me down his drive and I get a gander at the car he's taking me to. A silvery-white two-seat convertible with a tan interior. Never seen anything like it. Not even in the magazines. I let out a low wolf whistle.

"It's a Triumph Roadster. First one to roll off the factory lines this year." He lets his fingers slide over the hood. "I have Daniel wax it daily. Pretty things should never be neglected." He looks up and the boyish expression he's got on almost makes me laugh. "Shall we go for an early lunch?"

My stomach ain't at its best, but I've been in this state enough times to know that a little grease and protein will help me along. "Can you recommend a spot that serves up eggs at this time of day?"

"I can," Reaper says with a giant grin. "You'll love it."

Unlike Margie, Reaper has no problem with the highways, but he keeps the ride smooth and easy and my stomach thanks him for it. When we exit onto the streets, I start to get my bearings. "I think Margie drove me past here."

"South Central," Reaper says. "Fantastic area. My favorite in the city, in fact."

That surprises me. This place ain't nowhere near as fancy as Sugar Hill.

But it does look fun. We pass jazz clubs, theaters, and lounges. Tobacco shops and shoe stores. The streets are packed, Negroes shopping and socializing, families, couples, and singles, some dressed like they just came from church, others looking like they'd never set foot in the place. I spot a marquee with the words GOLDEN STATE MUTUAL printed in big bold letters across it. With its two stories, clay-tiled roof, and thick arches, it looks like the kind of business a man would be proud to link his employment to. Reaper ends up finding a spot only a few doors down from it. "There's a great restaurant at the Dunbar Hotel that I think you'll like." He gestures toward a place right across from Golden State Mutual.

"Looks posh."

"Yes, but the restaurant's casual enough." We get out and work our way through the throngs.

"Am I wrong," I ask as we cross the street to the hotel, "or is this part of Los Angeles more crowded than the rest?"

"No, you're not wrong," Reaper replies mildly.

"Why's that?"

"I don't spend a lot of time on why things are the way they are," he says, shrugging. "For me, the more important question is, do those things, whatever they happen to be, make me happy?"

It's a funny thing to say, and I'm about to ask him to further explain, but we've just stepped into the lobby of the Dunbar. It's a damn pretty place. The semicircular windows and arched bays. The Art Deco chandeliers. It looks like the hotels you see in the movies starring Bette Davis or Ginger Rogers. And once again almost everyone in here is colored. *Almost,* not all. I spy five people who are either white or white passing and one Oriental woman on the stairs.

"Nice, isn't it?" Reaper asks.

"That's an understatement." In truth, I'm on the verge of becoming emotional. The Green Book is filled with hotels Negroes can stay in, almost all worse than what's available to whites. But now we have this. It feels like an honest-to-God miracle.

"It was originally called Hotel Somerville."

"Somerville like the dentist and his wife?" I exclaim.

"They were the original owners. Good people."

I think back to the things Dr. Somerville had said about Reaper and his party. "You're friends with Dr. Somerville?"

"I just met him recently. But it only takes a few seconds to be impressed. Vada's impressive, too. Someone told me she was the first colored woman dentist in California."

"She still practices?"

"My understanding is she quit because patients preferred her over her husband. It was causing problems," Reaper says with a laugh. "The sacrifices we make for love." He gestures at the space around us. "They call this the Negro Waldorf-Astoria. Built by a Negro architect, Negro contractors, and on and on. Come, let's get some food in your stomach."

THE RESTAURANT'S BEAUTIFUL. Elegant but not fancy. The sound of dozens of different conversations happening all at once; the people eating are colored, decked out, and happy. The host asks Reaper if he wants his regular table by the window or the one he sometimes takes in the corner.

"The window would be perfect, Quincy." And we're soon sitting with a good view of both the bustling street and Golden State Mutual. Before the host can walk off, Reaper puts in a request. "Could you have our waiter bring over a club soda with some bitters and a splash of lime for my friend here? Just a water for me."

As Quincy leaves, I lean forward a little. "Sounds like you just ordered me up a hangover cure. Guess that means I'm not hiding it well."

Reaper smiles. "We've all been there."

Hard to imagine him hungover. Hell, I can't even picture him groggy. "What did you mean before? When you said the important question is not why things are as they are, but . . ." I struggle to remember his exact words.

"The bit about asking whether or not any given thing makes you happy or not?" He leans back in his chair. "We've all got the right to life, liberty, and the pursuit of happiness, and if you don't have the last, I'm not sure it's worth having the first two."

"Give me the pursuit of happiness or give me death?" I ask. The smell of the hash browns at the next table makes my nose twitch. "You think you'll get to pursue happiness in heaven?"

"Maybe. If not," Reaper responds, lowering his voice to a mock whisper, "I'll try for a hopeful path out of hell." He flips open his menu. "I'm not interested in why South Central is crowded. I just know that the energy of the crowds here makes me happy. It reminds me of Harlem and the original Sugar Hill. New York may be my favorite city in the world. New York is a city that knows what it wants to be."

Reaper's water arrives along with my hangover cure, but it's a waitress, not a waiter, who serves it. A beautiful, high-yellow girl who looks like she only just left her teen years behind. We place our orders, a chicken sandwich for Reaper, fried eggs and toast for me. This gal takes Reaper's order like it's a gift.

Reaper nods toward my drink as she leaves. "Go ahead, it will help."

I take a long sip. Not half bad. "Our waitress would like to serve you more than a chicken sandwich."

"I told you, there's only one girl for me."

"The one from Atlanta, right." I take another sip. "I still don't understand why you think she's so special. I'm sure she a dish, but--"

"It was more than her looks," Reaper interrupts. "She . . . she asked me what it was I wanted out of life. Has anyone ever asked you that question?"

Where I'm from folks are too busy teaching colored boys how to survive to concern themselves with what they might want out of it. My mama's biggest dream for me was that I might get hired as a porter so I wouldn't have to work the fields.

"Me neither," he says when I shake my head. "And when I answered . . . Charlie, she didn't treat it like I was listing off aspirations. This girl reacted as if I was stating inevitabilities. Back then I was going by James Gates and—"

"You were using a different last name?"

He startles, like he'd let a secret slip. "I . . . had been using the name of my father, as most do . . . but when my stepfather became ill, before he died, I changed my name to his to honor the role he played in my life."

The halting way he speaks makes me think this story's being made up on the spot. "Your stepfather's name was Mann?"

"Yes, yes, M-A-N-N. But I'm trying to tell you about this girl. I had known her for less than a week, But that was all I needed to know she was the only woman for me. She saw me in a way no one else ever has."

Even with the mental handicap of a hangover, I can see the flaw in his thinking. It shouldn't be a surprise that a girl you just met has a different impression of you than the ones you know well. It's that kind of pretty, feminine ignorance that tempts married men into extramarital sin; the lure of reinventing yourself in the eyes of some pretty young thing is hard to resist.

But I get the feeling Reaper isn't interested in logic. "Why was your time limited to those few days?" I ask instead, mostly out of politeness, because the only thing interesting about this story is his name change. "Is she still in Atlanta?"

"No. That night she told me her family was planning on getting out of the South. Of course, at the time, I had hoped to spend every second with her before her move. But on our last night together we lost track of time and I didn't end up escorting her home until it was after four in the morning." He pauses, then takes a deep breath, as if steeling himself for whatever he's about to say next. "That," he says slowly, "is when I met her parents."

"She had to introduce her man to her folks at four in the morning?"

"Her father threatened me with a baseball bat."

I laugh, I can't help it. Fortunately, he laughs, too.

"My intentions were honorable," Reaper insists, like I'm the one he has to defend himself to. "I just needed a little time with her parents, to convince them. I wanted to marry her."

"After a few nights of just talkin', you were ready for forever," I say flatly. "Nothing else happened?"

Reaper smiles, looks away. "If something had happened, and I'm not saying it did, I would have been her first."

"The very fact that you know that tells me what went down that night."

"If she had been with a hundred men before, I still would have been her first and she mine," he explains. "Love makes it new. Nothing sordid about it." In the far corner, a gaggle of women burst into giggles as they share some joke . . . or maybe they have exceptional hearing and picked up on the foolishness coming from this table.

"I thought I had convinced her father of that," Reaper continues. "He even said to come back in five days for a proper meeting after emotions had settled. But when I returned, the parents had packed up and left, taking my girl with them. The cousin who had escorted her to the party where we first met? Well, she was the one waiting for me in their stead. She gave me a note written in my sweetheart's hand." His eyes search the restaurant like he's expecting to find his beloved crouched behind a chair or hiding under a tablecloth. "The note said that she'd always love me."

Our food arrives and I dig in right away. The eggs, the toast, the club soda with bitters and lime, it's exactly what I need. "So, how'd you get to know Josephine Baker?" I ask between mouthfuls, taking the opportunity to shift the conversation to a subject more compelling.

I think I see a flash of irritation from Reaper. He wants to continue bemoaning his heartbreak. But blessedly, he lets it go. "A mutual acquaintance introduced me to Josephine," he says. "She needed help getting some messages out of the country . . . She was part of the French Resistance."

"I heard rumors about that, wasn't sure if it was true. Wait." I'm talking with my mouth full, I gotta slow down. "Did you join the Resistance, too? Is that why you stayed in Europe? Killin' Nazis for the French? Is that why they call you Reaper?"

"No one calls me that."

I look up from my food. He hadn't spoken those words so much as growled them.

"No one," he repeats. "If they did, they'd have a problem."

Everything about Reaper has changed. His eyes have gone cold.

No, he looks more than cold. He looks dangerous, a stone-faced killer.

"Right, sorry." I hold up my hands in a half-assed surrender, hoping to lower the temperature. "It was a bad joke. Meant no offense." Will he ask me where I heard it? I can't rat on Anna.

Reaper's face softens with my apology. He waves his hand as if sweeping my blunder away. I watch as his posture relaxes, his friendly smile returns.

Can't say I've ever seen anybody do that before, go from kind to threatening to kind in the time it takes to light a match. It's disconcerting, but I force myself to let it go. Maybe I'm imagining the mood shift. It happened so fast.

"I don't know if I can fully consider myself part of the Resistance," he says, going back to our conversation. "But I certainly helped those who were."

I wait for him to further explain, and when he doesn't, I let out a laugh. "You're a real mysterious fella, you know that?"

"Am I? Well, I guess we're all entitled to a few mysteries."

I'm not sure what to make of that, but we both welcome the silence that has settled between us, giving me space to heal myself with sustenance.

Once I finish off my plate, I bring Reaper's attention to the window. "My cousin's husband, he works over there at Golden State Mutual."

Reaper straightens the pieces of his silverware and then follows my gaze. "You're referring to Terrance Lewis."

"You know him?"

"Of him." When I raise my brows, he waves his hand as if trying to clear away the intrigue his comment left in its wake. "He occasionally takes meetings at the Dunbar. I've noticed him when coming in for lunch or when I come here for the nightclub. But we've never spoken."

"But you know him by sight?" I ask, confused.

"I think someone at some point must have pointed him out to me. He's very successful. Well regarded within the community." But I pick up just a hint of disdain in his voice. I can tell he doesn't think too highly of Terrance. "And you were saying his wife, Marguerite, is your cousin?"

"We went to grade school together, before her family moved away."

"Had you been close?"

When Margie's family left town, I cried like a baby over the loss of my friend.

The tears kept coming until Pa got fed up and beat the rest out of me.

But I don't tell Reaper that part.

"We'd go to class between harvest seasons, seein' as most of us children had to work the land before learnin' to add and subtract." Outside the clouds shift, creating new shadows. "I think I was on my way to becomin' a hardened six-year-old." Reaper's eyes crinkle and he leans forward, inviting me to share more. "But Margie, she didn't harden. She was the kind of child who inhaled dreams and exhaled optimism. For her, every bit of bad luck was just a plot point in a fairy tale, somethin' we could triumph over in the end. Even after her baby sister died, she found a way to wrap it into a story."

"Her sister died?" He looks real concerned, like he knows the family or something.

"Yeah, she actually lost a few siblings. Sadly not uncommon in the big families we come from." I shrug, trying to make horrors sound like mere inconveniences so neither of us have to think too hard on it. "But it's lil' Cellie I'm referrin' to."

"An odd name," he notes.

"Short for Celestine . . . Uncle Morris got himself an affinity for French names after his fighting in the Great War. Cellie started coughin' up blood right after her third birthday, lost control of her bowels, nothin' pretty about that child's end. But you wouldn't know it talkin' to Margie." I glance toward the window at the sound of brakes screeching, a motorist narrowly avoiding some kind of tragedy. "Accordin' to lil' Margie, Cellie just heard too many stories about heaven and got curious. So she made a birthday wish for the clouds to get low enough for her to grab 'em and gather up those floatin' wisps so she could craft 'em into wings. Then she strapped them on her back and flew up there early, to spend eternity ridin' the wind with the angels."

"That's . . . beautiful." Reaper has got the look of a child mesmerized by a magic show. "Your cousin has an extraordinary mind."

I'm inclined to agree. Margie's games of pretend had been like toffee and chocolate in a life full of bitter herbs. She held the key to a prettier world, one that didn't actually exist, but she made you feel like it did and with her you could be a part of it.

"And after she left, you kept in touch," Reaper prods.

"Not directly, not at first. My ma and her pa were siblings, there were three more brothers and another sister, too. But my grandparents couldn't afford to keep more than one child idle enough to educate, so they picked the son with the lightest skin. Figured he might be given an opportunity to put his education to work. That redbone child happened to be Margie's dad."

"So your mother . . ." He leans back in his seat, maintaining eye contact, letting me know I've got his full attention and interest.

"Could barely read or write," I explain. "Margie's pa wrote her the rare letter, always sure to keep it short and simple so she might make sense of it." *Wish I was there. I'm sorry. Be safe.* Uncle Morris sent those words through the mail again and again, as if he had a choice about leaving, as if safety came down to more than dumb luck.

But I don't tell Reaper that part.

"When Margie got to be about eleven, she took it upon herself to send me Christmas and birthday cards. Sometimes she'd write to tell me about a movie she saw. And when Uncle Morris passed, Margie wrote us with the news. Shortly before I was deployed, Margie wrote suggestin' I come join her in the city where all the movies she loves so much are made. I didn't take the offer too seriously then. But when I returned from the war, there was another letter from Margie suggestin' I come out to Los Angeles where there was work . . . and respect." I scrape my fork against my plate, wishing there was a little more on it. "The things she wrote about Los Angeles . . . I figured she was spinnin' another one of her dressed-up stories. But now that I'm here . . ." I tap the prongs against the porcelain, making a tinny sound. "Almost like she really did find a place where she can be a fairy princess and reify her dreams."

From the kitchen we hear the crash of porcelain hitting the floor, jolting us both back to the here and now.

"Are you done?" Reaper asks. "If so, there's someone I'd like you to meet."

———

Ten minutes later Reaper's paid the bill and we're at a haberdasher only a block from the hotel. It's got some of the finest men's clothes I've ever seen. Delicate, light wool suits, silk ties, and shirts made of cotton so fine it could almost pass as satin. The man working the store is a Negro around the age my pa would be if he were still around.

"James!" he cries as soon as we walk in. "You keep shopping like this and I'm going to have to open a whole 'nother store just to meet the demand!"

Reaper gives the man a firm shake and a pat on the arm. "I might just give you enough business to make that happen, Joe. Let me introduce you to my friend Charlie." As Joe shakes my hand, Reaper continues. "We need to set Charlie up with a new wardrobe."

I drop Joe's hand. "Sorry, I ain't shopping today."

"Of course you are," Reaper says. "It's a gift. My way of welcoming you to our city."

My stomach starts flipping again, but it's got nothing to do with what I drank last night. Anna's words about Reaper being shadowy are coming back to me. About how odd it was that he was giving me so much of his time. A bargain with the devil's bad enough, getting into the debt of the Grim Reaper gotta be a hell of a lot worse.

"I'm my own man." I put a little more distance between us, getting closer to the door. "I don't need handouts."

Reaper lets out a sigh. "Joe, I know it's an imposition, but would you mind getting us a couple of glasses of water?"

"Not at all, James, not at all," he says before disappearing into the back of the store.

"I mean it," I say, once I think Joe's out of earshot. "I appreciate you takin' me out to lunch, but I can't accept no more than that."

Reaper wanders from rack to rack, pinching the fabric of a dress shirt, then moving on to admire a tie. "What did you do to earn that medal? What exactly happened?"

I swallow hard and take another step back, not answering.

He smiles sympathetically. "It seems I'm not the only man of mystery around here. You don't want to talk about the war."

"I don't."

"Which means there's another reason you choose to wear your uniform . . . in Los Angeles . . . on a Sunday with nowhere in particular to go." He pulls out a jacket, double-breasted and long, examining it with a connoisseur's eye. "Do you really think I don't understand? No matter what he has in his pocket today, there's not a colored man in America who doesn't know what it's like to be poor."

I feel myself getting hot. "You're sayin' I look like a pauper?"

"I'm saying you look like a soldier and you're saying you want to be more than that." He returns the jacket to the rack and pulls out another. "Anna won't know the clothes came from me. Only that you know how to dress well."

"You're trying to help me impress Anna?" I ask.

"Is that what you want to do?"

Anna.

She seemed to like me well enough at the party, but this morning might have chipped away at my appeal. Maybe it's for the best. It's not smart to start up with a woman you live with, whether things go good or bad.

She's interesting, though. She's got a special kind of strength to her. A no-nonsense confidence she wears like perfume.

I like how she drops wisdom in the wrappings of flirtation . . .

"Look at you. Just the thought of her makes you smile," he says. "Come now, man to man, friend to friend, let me help you with *your* pursuit of happiness."

Joe reemerges with two glasses of water. "Do you want to try a few things on?" He directs the question to me.

It's just clothes. Not like he's paying off gambling debts or hiding me from the Klan. I'm not so bad off that I can be compromised by a dress shirt.

Who the hell knows, maybe they call him Reaper because he kills people with kindness.

I look at Reaper. "Yeah," I say, "maybe I'll try on a few."

Chapter 6

Anna's eyes pop open wide. "Wow, you look good!" She and the other boarder, Patty, have found me in the foyer. It's Monday and I just got off the phone with Dr. Somerville's secretary, who told me to come on in for a consultation. Fair to say the sports coat and cuff-linked button-down I'm wearing ain't necessary for the occasion.

But I also knew who I might bump into in the foyer.

"Are you going for an audition?" Patty asks.

"How many times do I have to tell you, he's not an actor?" Anna shoots back.

"You could be, though," Patty insists. "You've got a look. And you're just dark enough to play a—"

"I just got a few appointments is all," I say, cutting her off, 'cause I know she's about to say I'm dark enough to play a servant or a go-lucky slave. "First with the dentist, then with potential employers."

The only employer I have a hope of meeting with is Terrance's employer, Golden State, and that's not until tomorrow. But I know women like men with options.

"How 'bout the two of you?" I ask, bringing us to easier territory. "Y'all got plans today?"

Anna's lips quiver a little, like she's trying to keep an overeager smile from exploding onto her face. "I'm going to be looking at cars. I plan to get one in the next month or so. Nothing fancy, but new."

"Nice that one of us is making money," Patty mutters.

Anna looks at her with a combination of irritation and pity before waving her watch in front of Patty's face. "Speaking of making a living, you're going to be late for your audition."

"Oh, I've got to get going! I'm definitely going to get this one. I can feel it." Patty rushes out with such enthusiasm she doesn't remember to close the door.

Anna does it for her with the kind of smile that should be accompanied by a sigh. "She's definitely not going to get this one."

It's the first time I've been in a room alone with Anna since before Reaper's party. "I was looking for you when I got back here yesterday."

"I was at Hattie's. There're some things coming up that will need to be handled just right for the press. We worked so late I ended up staying over. I might end up doing the same thing tonight."

"How far away does she live?"

"Less than two blocks," Anna admits with an embarrassed laugh. "But I don't like walking home alone late at night."

"Not even in Sugar Hill?"

She gives me a look. "Even the gods of Mount Olympus had to take a few precautions."

"At this point it wouldn't surprise me if you said some of the folks 'round here *were* gods."

"We're all very human. Although you won't catch anyone turning away worshippers. Anyway, why were you looking for me? Anything amiss?"

The question's deflating. I want her to act as if it's obvious we'd both want to spend more time together given any opportunity. "Just wanted to see how you were doin' is all," I mumble.

"Mmm. What did you and Reaper talk about during brunch? What does he want from you?"

"Why's it so hard to believe that he's just bein' neighborly?" I ask, feeling frustrated. "I'm new here, he's relatively new here, doesn't seem too odd that he'd be lookin' for someone to talk to, particularly if the longtime residents living here treat him like y'all did Sunday morning. Clammed up and started actin' funny the minute he walked in the door. Why?"

She slips a finger between her teeth as she considers. "Have you ever been to the circus, Charlie?"

"Once, when I was eight."

"My parents took me to the circus every time it was in town. We ate salty peanuts and so many sweets I'd always end up with a tummy ache. I would get giddy watching the lion and bear tamers. And every single time I would fall in love with the ringmaster."

I shift back on my heels, struggling to find the metaphor.

Anna steps close to me so we're only inches apart. "You missed a button." She reaches forward to fasten it, and her nails briefly scratch my chest. "In the circus, the ringmaster is king, he's in control, he's adored. But no one wants the ringmaster to follow them home, Charlie. If he did . . . why, then, he would just be a circus freak."

For a split second, Anna doesn't look so beautiful. "He's a good man."

"He's a charming man. There's a difference." Anna steps back, admires the shirt. "Do you have plans tomorrow night? Hattie is having a strategy session at her place. She asked me to invite you."

"What needs strategizing?"

"Right . . . you probably don't know yet. Of course you wouldn't." She takes a deep breath, suddenly uneasy. "It's about a lawsuit that's been filed by some of the white neighbors."

"What?" But then I note the clock on the wall behind Anna. "I gotta go . . ."

"Of course. Be ready to come with me to Hattie's at six. I'll explain it all then." She starts her retreat, but then turns back once more. "If you do meet with a potential employer today, try to talk like a rich fellow from a novel, perhaps more Dickens than Twain."

"A Dickens character, okay." I stuff my hands in my pockets so she can't see I'm clenching them. "Would that be before or after Pip abandoned his roots?"

That earns me an eye roll. "You know what I mean."

"Yeah. You tellin' me I gotta lose the Southern drawl? That my throwing in the occasional *gotta* and *ain't* has people here looking down on me? Maybe if I came up with my very own portmanteau, that would be better for you folk?"

Anna's eyes twinkle with amusement. "I'm saying that in certain settings using words like *portmanteau* might serve you better than an actual portmanteau."

She's a lot harder to trip up than Terrance.

"The way I talk ain't got nothin' to do with my intelligence or my education. It's a marker of where I'm from. As my mama always says, only the most vacuous and ignominious of men try to act like they're from somewhere they ain't."

The corners of her mouth twitch. "Your mama says that?"

"No, 'course not. My mama probably thinks *vacuous* is the latest model of Hoover. But I'm trying to make a point."

Her laughter lights up the room. "Look here, I'm only trying to be helpful. But regardless of how you speak during your interviews, please don't lose the drawl or colloquialisms. I don't think I've ever had a Southern voice whispering sweet nothings in my ear. I'm hoping to correct that . . . maybe sometime soon."

I step outside knowing I've been insulted.

First time an insult ever got me revved up and smiling.

"Appreciate you fitting me in like this," I say as Dr. Somerville looms over me with a miniature mirror and what looks like a torture device.

"It's no longer my habit to attend to my dental practice for more than an hour or two on Mondays," he says as I open wide. "In fact, I've stopped taking new clients. But Marguerite has been a very good friend to Vada." After a minute he pulls his hands out of my mouth. "It appears you lost this tooth recently and the one next to it is damaged as well. How did it happen?"

"At the hands of the enemy."

"The war?"

"No, stateside." I don't want to talk much about it, so I give him the short version. "Some folks thought I was acting too uppity after I returned home, so they gave me a warnin'."

Dr. Somerville sighs. "You must be from the South. I failed to detect the regional accent."

Ha, I wish Anna was here to hear that. In my head I'm saying, *Yes, guvnor, I was indeed brought up in one of the Southern states,* as if I'd just fallen off the pages of *Great Expectations.* But he's got his hands in my mouth again, so the best I can do is grunt an affirmative.

"There are so many Negroes in Los Angeles who speak with Southern accents that I periodically forget it's not a local dialect," he goes on, then takes a second before asking, "Are you old enough to remember when lynchings were common?"

Is he talking about yesterday? "My clearest childhood memory is of a lynching."

"How old were you?"

"A few weeks shy of my eighth birthday."

"I heard stories as a boy, back in Jamaica," he says.

"You're from Jamaica?"

"Born and raised. I was a proud subject of the British Empire." Dr. Somerville turns, sizes up his various dental devices, each one looking more evil than the last. "The stories of American lynching . . . white men with torches, the dismemberment of Negro men, white children coming out to watch as if it was a carnival, the unheeded screams of colored mothers . . . We took them for tales analogous to ghost stories. Fanciful tales people tell children to scare them."

I didn't see the things he's describing except for the torches, and even those were nothing more than flickers of orange outside our log cabin home. I didn't hear any screaming, either.

What I saw was darkness.

All the lamps in our home out.

Not so much as the glow of a candle.

I felt the underside of the table we were hiding beneath, touching it with the tips of my fingers, wishing the wood was a shield.

I heard breathing. Coughs coming from behind closed lips.

I heard whispers and sniffling.

Me, whispering a plan as one of my cousins walked unsteadily to the door. Me, claiming I could save us.

Me, knowing I was lying, feeling shame over my helplessness, over my pa's helplessness.

"It never occurred to any of us in Jamaica that anything so barbaric might actually be true, not in the twentieth century," Dr. Somerville says. "Not in civilized Western societies."

"When it comes to the white man? Nothing's too horrible to be true."

He smiles without humor. "My dear man, I do believe you're a cynic. Fortunately, the NAACP has taken us out of those dark times. They're the reason lynchings are a thing of the past in this country. I'll have you know I founded Los Angeles's first chapter of the NAACP. A stellar organization."

If lynchings are history, this is the first I'm hearing of it.

"Come back the same time Wednesday . . . no, that won't work, same time Thursday," he says, putting away his instruments. "I'll put a new tooth in for you. No one will be able to tell the difference."

"I don't have a lot of money right now."

"Just this once, it's on the house." He laughs at my surprise. "It's something I occasionally do for uppity Negroes."

"I appreciate that." I get up, put on my jacket. "Getting a new tooth . . . does it hurt much?"

"Significantly less than losing your old one," he replies.

Now it's my turn to laugh.

As I move to leave, he says, "I hope you realize it's different here."

I turn to face him.

"Don't get me wrong, I've dealt with my fair share of discrimination. My entire class at USC threatened to transfer out if I wasn't expelled on account of my race. I was surprised to find such ignorance in a place of higher learning. But except for one ignoramus from the South, they all came to appreciate my intellect and work ethic. It takes effort and time, but the Caucasian population of Los Angeles can be reasoned with. It's why, unlike every other major city in this country, Los Angeles has never had a race riot. It's highly unlikely we ever will. You're safe here."

He's the third person to tell me we're safe here.

He's also a man who thinks lynchings are a thing of the past.

Chapter 7

Tuesday morning. I get to Margie and Terrance's place just as Terrance steps out. He's got on a smart suit clearly tailored for him. "Right on time, I see." He looks up at the position of the sun, as if he uses that instead of a watch. "Actually a few minutes early. Are you ready?"

"I'm ready." I cross my arms over my chest. "Someone suggested I might want to change the way I talk for this interview."

"Why?" Terrance smirks. "Because you talk like the backwoods country boy that you are? I'm not trying to recruit another vice president. You're interviewing for a sales job. People buy insurance from people they aspire to or people they relate to. You'll be the latter."

"I see, so you sayin' I got a shot at sellin' insurance to all the other *déraciné* country boys out here."

"Um . . . yes, that's what I'm saying." Got this son of a bitch again.

Margie comes skipping out of the house. "Oh, Charlie, look at you!" She fusses with my tie although I know I tied it right. "You're going to give Terrance a run for his money as the most handsome man at Golden State!"

Terrance laughs and wraps his arm around her waist. "Even if that were true, and it's not, you'd never attract a woman who sparkles like my Marguerite. No such thing." He catches me looking at his car, a Cadillac that looks both well polished and well used.

"Nice, isn't she? Sometimes I drive around after work for an hour or so, just to hear her purr. A little like a woman that way."

"Really, Terrance." Margie pulls away from him, giving us a pout. "There's no need to be vulgar."

"It's only a joke," he says, clearly not pleased with the reprimand. "You have to learn to let a man have his fun."

I get the feeling he's saying more than he's saying.

Maybe Margie thinks so, too. Those sparks in her eyes look like the ignition of rage. But instead of responding, she turns and heads back into the house.

"And tell Gertie I want dinner ready at seven," Terrance calls after her, but she slams the front door behind her, leaving us alone out here on the drive.

"Everything all right between you two?"

"Yes, yes." He exhales, his eyes stuck on the space she just vacated. "Your cousin's a good woman, but she sometimes needs to be reminded to be grateful for the lavish life I've given her." He shakes his head as if clearing it, then turns back to me. "I'm not sure I want to arrive at Golden State with you before the other executives get there. It might not make a difference, but on the other hand . . ."

Terrance keeps droning on, but as he speaks a white couple walks out of the house directly across this narrow street. Probably would have noticed them no matter what, but the glare the man is giving us buys him my full attention. The woman is blond with a buxom build and careful eyes. She seems to be deliberately walking a few steps behind her man.

Pa always said that when a woman walks a few steps behind her man, it's because she's been trained. And you could only train a woman to be like that through violence. He also told me that a white man who hits his wife will jump at the chance to kill a Negro.

To me, the question of whether to show up early at Golden State is answered in that white man's glare. We should go now.

But Terrance? He ain't rushing. "Les!" he exclaims.

"You know it's Lester," the man corrects, then adds with emphasis, "Make that Mr. Nolan."

"Right, right, and Mrs. Nolan," Terrance continues cheerfully. "So good to see you both. This is my wife's cousin, Charles Trammell the third."

The man called Lester Nolan spits on the ground in our direction.

"You know what you need, Les?" Terrance asks, his smile getting real big. "A good spittoon. I'll check the antique stores for you. I bet I could find you one as old as your house!"

"This house was built for my grandfather in 1878." Nolan's tone leaves pointed icicles on each word. "This entire neighborhood was built for us. And people like us."

"Terrific," Terrance booms. Mrs. Nolan presses her lips together as if holding back laughter. "I'll bet your grandfather was an accomplished man. And because of his accomplishments, look at what you have!" He gestures at his neighbor's house, and as he speaks, I realize it's a little smaller than the one Margie and Terrance have. The paint on the trim is peeling in several places. The iron gate's got rust spots. "I wish I had a grandfather like that," Terrance goes on. "Why, everything I have, this house, this car, my wife's jewelry and furs, I had to earn it through accomplishments all my own. It must be such a relief to not have the burden of accomplishing anything to have . . . what you have. I congratulate you on your fine bloodline." He raises his wrist and taps his watch as he turns his eyes back to me. "Now we should go."

I can't believe what I just witnessed.

But the white man doesn't raise a fist, or advance, or take out a gun. He's just standing there as Terrance and I get in the car and ride off, his wife behind him, grinning like she just saw the best show on earth.

That felt . . .

. . . *good.*

So, so good to see that white man shamed. In front of his wife.

The men who had insisted my pa call them sir but refused to do the same for him. The men who told us to lower our eyes when they spoke. Who expected us to step off the sidewalk to make room for them. Demanded that we publicly humiliate ourselves in front of our women and children. That we, in a million different ways, give weight to their feelings of superiority.

Lester Nolan is all of them.

The fighter in me regrets not joining in by adding a few zingers of my own.

But the survivor in me knows Terrance should have kept his damn mouth shut.

"Margie's home all day with your child," I finally say, once we are several blocks out of the sacred Sugar Hill.

"Her name's Marguerite," he corrects.

"You might have put her at risk."

"Hmm? Is this about Les?" As if the exchange is a distant memory rather than something that happened three minutes ago. "Don't worry about it. He's the kind of coward who uses lawyers to do his fighting. He wouldn't dare lay a hand on my wife. Although," he adds with a wink, "I wouldn't mind laying a hand on his. Rest assured, your cousin Marguerite was an innocent when we married. Pure as the driven snow. But Les's wife, Dolores? You get the feeling she may have picked up a few fun tricks before settling down. You ever been with a white woman, Charlie?"

I ignore the question. "What do you mean he fights through lawyers?"

Terrance's smile finally wavers. "He and some of his friends in the West Adams Heights Improvement Association are trying to get the racial covenants in our deeds enforced. Of course, he'll lose."

A sudden rush of cold shoots through my veins. "The house you're in wasn't supposed to be sold to a Negro family?"

"Just some outdated paperwork on the property." But Terrance's voice, which normally comes straight from his gut, has moved to his throat. "Something about how it can't be inhabited by Negroes, Chinese, and—I can't remember who else they wanted to deny—Jews maybe? If they were thinking straight, they would have included actors." He lets out a laugh, but there's no energy to it. "Imagine having a prohibition on actors living in decent Los Angeles neighborhoods! Now that's a covenant I could get behind."

"Terrance, if the deed to your house states that Negroes can't live in it, you could lose it. They could take it from you and give bupkis in return."

"Bupkis? They'd have to pay me a damn good sum."

"Would they?" I challenge. "The same way they had to pay those Japanese immigrants for the homes they forced them outta?"

"That was different. Japan made them into an enemy when they attacked us."

"And America made them into an example by putting them in camps," I shoot back. "When white folks get jumpy, Uncle Sam does whatever the hell he wants with the rest of us to make them comfortable."

"No one is going to kick me out of my home or anywhere else." Terrance steers us onto the freeway and speeds up until he races past the other motorists, the palm trees lining the road flying by in a blur.

"How can you be so certain?"

"Because we have a lawyer, too. Loren Miller. He'll win this for us."

"You hire a lawyer when you want to make sure laws are followed, not changed, and if the law says you gotta go, then—"

"Charlie, I told you it's being handled," he snaps. "We're even meeting about it tonight, with Loren. Look, here's our exit. Remember it, because soon you're going to have to get your own car and drive yourself. I'm not your bloody chauffeur."

It's Terrance's change of mood that lets me know how dicey the situation is.

As we enter South Central I'm struck once again by how much more crowded it is here than in the few other neighborhoods I've seen in the city. Even more so today than the other day. "There's our offices. We have the second floor."

"Yeah, I came down here on Sunday. Impressive building."

We find a place to park over a block away and then we're out of the car and immediately weaving through crowds of people toward our destination. I can't resist asking Terrance the question Reaper wouldn't entertain. "Why do you think it's so crowded here?"

He doesn't answer me right away. We walk by the merchants who take up the first floor of the Golden State building: a drugstore, a law office, a few restaurants that are, even at this early hour, infusing the air with mouthwatering scents. "It's crowded in South Central," Terrance says quietly as he leads me into a small lobby between the shops where the elevators are, "because it's the only place in the city Negroes are officially and unequivocally allowed to live."

That can't be true. Just because Terrance's house got a covenant attached to it doesn't mean people like Louise and Hattie McDaniel got a problem.

Terrance is looking over his shoulder, through the windows. Glaring hard at a street that can barely be seen under the stampede of shoes and the weight of tires. "Like any neighborhood, it only has a limited amount of space . . . and yet you keep coming."

"*You* as in *me*?" I ask, confused.

"Yes, specifically you. A colored man from the South looking to settle yourself somewhere out of reach of all those hooded white men and their ropes. You keep coming, more and more and more of you. And they don't want you to live in West Adams Heights or any of the other wide-open spaces of L.A. They want you here, exclusively here. In another five, ten years the only remaining space in this neighborhood for a man to sleep will be the streets. And that's fine with them. It's all we're supposed to have." He's got a tremble now and I don't know if those shakes are coming from anger or fear. He jams his finger against the call button. "I'll be damned," he whispers, "if I'll ever settle for what I'm supposed to have."

Chapter 8

The interviews go well. So well that afterward I spend the rest of my morning at Golden State being shown who's who and where's where.

My official training starts Monday. I'm to shadow another agent named Sam Kensington, learn how it's done. They're going to start me with a base salary, then when they set me loose on my own accounts, I'll be earning commission.

I'm gonna be an insurance agent.

Mama and Pa worked most their lives as sharecroppers. That kind of labor's only a half step up from slavery.

Ma later started bringing in a little extra by working as a maid. That's a job.

What I'm being offered? That's a career.

I've got no sales experience to speak of. No college degree to brag about.

Only thing separates me from the other applicants is a friend named Terrance Lewis.

Terrance is the reason I'm gonna be the first in my family to have a shot at an honest-to-God career that doesn't involve shooting foreigners overseas.

When my office tour is over, Terrance has his secretary give me instructions on how to take the streetcar back to Sugar Hill, since he has to work a full day.

I walk out of the offices of Golden State.

I want to run. Fists high in the air, bellowing out victory.

Two weeks ago I'd been at a general store in my hometown. I'd declined to give up my place in line for two white schoolboys who came in right as I was about to make a purchase. Two days later the daddies of them boys found me. Two minutes after that I was on my back, the salty taste of blood in my mouth, my tooth wiggling loose against my tongue.

One of them white men leaned over me, smiling like he'd just won the biggest prize while playing the easiest game. "Know your place, boy."

I had been told that before.

Those words, they follow me through cities and states. They pull at my moments of confidence, put a tarnish on my service, nurture fertile seeds of fear.

Two weeks ago I didn't know my place.

But I'll be damned if I don't know it now.

My place is among moguls and movie stars.

My place is at Golden State Mutual, working my way up to getting my own house with a gardener and a Cadillac.

And while Terrance might look down on South Central, I like it. It's crowded, sure, but folks have done a lot with it. I take a stroll for my afternoon's entertainment, stopping at a newsstand outside an apartment building to pick up a copy of the *California Eagle* and another L.A. Negro paper, the *Sentinel,* then to a tobacco shop to purchase a celebratory cigar before heading on over to the Dunbar with plans to splurge on some gourmet chow.

I step inside the lobby just to breathe it in. The Negro Waldorf-Astoria. Luxury with the added benefit of flavor. When I get my first paycheck, I'll bring Anna here. She'll fit right into this place, into this hotel that smells like promise.

This time there's a total of four white people in here, hanging out with us, including that woman walking through the door . . .

. . . I know her.

Dolores. Terrance's neighbor. Lester's wife.

The lobby's got lots of nooks and crannies, and I step behind a nearby bay arch so that I can watch her without her seeing me. She's looking for something. Swiveling her head left, right. Maybe she's plotting trouble on her husband's behalf. I knew you couldn't speak to a white man like Terrance did. Not without consequences.

And then this woman does a full one-eighty, facing the door she just came through. Her entire body relaxes. She's found what she's looking for in the man who walks in.

Terrance is wearing a wolfish grin.

He's looking at her like she's not white and he's not married.

To my cousin.

Terrance steps to the front desk; he's handed a key. Then he heads straight to an elevator. When it arrives, he steps aside to let Dolores go in first. One might think it's a gentlemanly gesture if they missed the lascivious wink he gave her.

This is more than an insult to Margie.

As the elevator doors close, I see him slide his hand around her waist.

That's how he's spending his lunch break.

Margie said that the people Terrance serves deserve fidelity. The woman knows what she's talking about! The man's got no right.

Except her argument's got a flaw.

Terrance doesn't serve. He provides.

I step out of the space where I've been hiding, hiding like I don't belong.

Like this here isn't my place.

Two weeks ago I refused the orders of schoolboys. Two days later their daddies found me. Two minutes after that, I was flat on the ground.

But it was what happened in that minute between them finding me and them beating me that I can't get over. It was in that minute that I had to do all those rapid-fire calculations.

Fight back and lose.

The first punch I threw would have felt good. But in the end, I would have lost more than a tooth. They would have stripped me naked, castrated me, hung me up, and slapped a picture of my corpse on a postcard.

Fight back and win.

If I'd managed that, it would have felt *damn* good. And I would have lived . . .

. . . for a few more hours. Until their friends came for me, my mama, and every other colored man, woman, and child within a mile radius.

Accept the blows. Accept the humiliation.

That's what I did.

And I live.

And I'm less.

I want my place to be Sugar Hill, behind my own desk at the most successful Negro-owned insurance company in the whole damned country.

I do some more rapid-fire calculations.

Confront Terrance for cheating, putting all he has and all I want in jeopardy.

I'm angry enough for that kind of spouting off to feel real good.

But Terrance ain't gonna end an affair just to soothe my nerves. And my reward for being righteous will be unemployment.

Keep quiet.

I'll keep my job. I'll survive the shame. Maybe Sugar Hill will survive Terrance's foolhardiness, too. Maybe L.A. really is different from the South. Maybe Terrance will get lucky and he'll win, which is to say he'll get to do everything he wants and none of it will come back to bite him.

And maybe, if we're *all* lucky, the rest of us won't lose.

Chapter 9

"There you are! I was worried you'd forgotten my invitation!" Anna finds me on Louise's back porch puffing at my cigar, which no longer feels so celebratory. I've been standing watching the sun work its way down the horizon for the last hour.

When I don't speak up, her forehead creases with new worries. "Did you not get the job?"

"I got it. My training starts next week."

"Charlie, that's wonderful!" She throws herself into my arms.

Every curve of her is pressing into me. It's almost enough to get me thinking good things instead of bad. But before I can make the shift she pulls back, sensing a problem. "You do want the position, don't you?"

"Most definitely I do." Then, to explain away my mood, I add, "I don't . . . have experience."

"Yes, well, I went to school to be a journalist, yet I can't even get Carlotta at the *California Eagle* to publish my latest opinion piece. Conversely, I didn't have any training at all for being a publicist . . . until I was a publicist. Now every colored celebrity wants to hire me." She places her hands on her hips, looking defiant and proud. "On-the-job training has turned me into quite the saleswoman."

"You're not in sales."

"Wanna bet? Whether you're selling a product or a celebrity personality, the trick is to do it gently." She reaches for my cigar, lets her fingers graze mine before pulling it away and taking a puff for herself.

The way her lips wrap around it fills my mind with thoughts that could get me arrested if I was foolish enough to speak 'em. "Don't push," she continues, "entice. Mold an image, create a story. If you can control the way people view what or who you represent, you'll hold all the cards. In a way, that's even what tonight's strategy session is." She pauses, sucks in a little more smoke before handing it back. "How to create power through perception."

"I'm not following."

"No one's told you about the lawsuit," she says flatly.

"Terrance was telling me about some racial covenant business this morning, but . . ." Why would Anna have anything to do with Terrance and Margie's business?

"So you have heard." She lets out a sigh. "I'm sorry. It doesn't seem fair you should have to start worrying about being kicked out of a place you've just been welcomed into."

"Terrance and Margie have been in that house for a few years, right?"

"The Lewises . . . um . . . yes, I think they purchased their place about three . . . maybe four years ago. Louise and Hattie have been here longer. So has Dr. Somerville. West Adams Heights was deteriorating before we arrived. We restored and improved every property we bought. And yet these idiots have the nerve to call themselves the WAHIA, the West Adams Heights Improvement Association. *Improvement!* I swear, there's no irony like white irony."

I got some kind of feeling rising up in me that makes my lungs work different. "Every house here has a racial covenant on it?"

"Don't worry, we'll compromise nothing. But we have to strategize and make good use of the time we have, as the trial begins on December 5, less than two months away." She glances down at a delicate gold watch clinging to her wrist. "Do you have a dollar?"

I reach into my back pocket for my wallet.

"No, hold on to it." She stills my hand with a touch. "You'll need it tonight, for the cause."

"What cause?"

She arches an eyebrow as her voice slides into a kind of homespun melody I haven't heard from her before. "The cause of tanning the hide of these rednecks . . . legally speaking, of course."

It's a very short walk to Miss McDaniel's, but by the time we arrive, I've convinced myself that I'm misunderstanding the situation, or at least missing details. Anna's far too calm for a woman facing eviction. I don't know her that well, but I do know she's a realist. If she and everybody she works for were about to lose their homes, she wouldn't put on some kind of act. She wouldn't give me false hope.

That's the logic I'm using to distract myself from my darker suspicions.

Miss McDaniel's house is a damn fine distraction. The lush trees and colorful flowers placed all over the grounds behind her gate are fragrant enough to be used as perfume. There's a shiny green Pontiac parked up against an ivy-covered wall, the bushes cut into all kinds of pretty shapes standing up against that white colonial, the wraparound porch, the grand doors . . . This woman took the money she got from playing Mammy to make a down payment on Tara.

And it's Miss McDaniel, not Mammy, who greets us. "Charlie, isn't it?" she asks. "Not Charles?" It's only as we step inside that I realize we're the first to arrive. "I'm sorry our last conversation was cut short," she adds as a maid hurries to take our coats.

This woman inviting me in is the picture of sophistication. If she were white, I'd figure her as old money. But she's dark-skinned, so her money can't be older than a debutante.

"Can Marie get you anything?" she asks, nodding to the retreating back of the gal with our coats.

"No, thank you. This sure is a beautiful house, Miss McDaniel."

"That's mighty sweet of you. But you must call me Hattie."

"You're wearing your pink diamonds," Anna says, gesturing to Hattie's teardrop earrings.

Her hand flutters up to one ear and her famous smile plumps up her face. "Colored diamonds are just a little more special than the white ones," Hattie says, laughing herself out of her formal demeanor. "You want a tour, Charlie?"

Yes.

Each room has its own theme. Her lounges have rattan chairs and are set up like she's expecting some British folk for tea. Her drawing room's more French, like she's ready to entertain King Louis. The gardenias she's got in there have the space smelling like Eden. Her dining room has an ivory table and chairs. There's a big ol' white piano center stage in her salon. And everywhere you look there're crystal figurines, antique-looking vases, and a whole bunch of other pretty little symbols of big-time success.

She takes me through her library that's filled up with books on Negro history and art. When I ask if I might borrow a title sometime, she looks at me like I just asked to name my firstborn after her.

But it's the golden statue on her mantel that arrests me. "Would you like to hold it?" she asks. "Go on now, I can see you would."

I almost drop it, it's so much heavier than my expectations. Just a smooth, blank gold face, no pupils, no eyes. Yet I feel its stare, like it's reading me.

"Winning that Oscar was my proudest moment."

Proud, yeah, we all felt proud when we heard the news. But it was a damned shame she got that honor for a movie that made heroes out of those who killed for the right to own me. Own *her.* Hattie and Louise, they're both strong colored women, making their fortune, being honored for hiding their pride from the camera. Glory in exchange for dignity.

But then, I don't recall the white folk back home offering any kind of payment for the dignity they took from me. A sale is surely better than a donation.

Carefully I place her prize back on the mantel.

"You've been here, what is it now?" Hattie looks over to Anna, as if she's better qualified to answer the question than me. "Three days? Four? Four days in and already you have to learn about this ridiculous lawsuit."

There are questions I gotta ask even though I don't think I want answers. "This house wasn't supposed to be sold to Negroes, either?"

The friendly twinkle in Hattie's eyes flares right to anger. "This house was always supposed to be mine. I'll live here as long as I please."

The doorbell rings and she moves to welcome the next batch of guests.

I can't get my head around this. Can't be that the most successful Negroes in the world are all dumb enough to buy homes they can be kicked out of. Just can't be.

Anna recognizes a few of the people coming in and goes to say hello. I think she expects me to follow. I don't.

When a servant approaches and asks if I'd like a glass of wine, I say yes immediately.

It's not long before the place is jumping. So many faces here that I know from the pictures. Ethel Waters from *Stage Door Canteen,* Ben Carter from *Dixie Jamboree.* Frances Elizabeth Williams from one of the few race films I ever got a chance to see, *The Notorious Elinor Lee*! I recognize Wonderful Smith from his voice, which I had listened to plenty of times when he was on Red Skelton's radio show in those years before the war . . . although listening to those vocal cords produce full words instead of "dis" and "dat" throws me. I spot Zutty Singleton, the jazz drummer from *The Orson Welles Almanac,* chatting with Miss Waters. And Louise and Robert are here as well.

It's not just show-biz folk, either. Men in business suits, many with primly dressed, high-yellow women on their arms, greeting one another like old friends.

But I can't help but notice those suits ain't talking to the celebrities. And the celebrities aren't talking to them, either. Like ants and bees sharing a garden, but not mingling at all.

Looks like Anna's the only one who's got a pass for both groups.

The suits come right up to her. From the bits of conversation I pick up, I can tell they know her from her articles in the newspaper. The actors come up to her, too, but all they talk about is her PR work. If these are ants and bees, she's the nectar they're all craving.

If I had another cigar, I'd give it to her just to watch her smoke it.

I turn my attention back to the Oscar on the mantel. Skin not white or black, but gold.

That's smart. No one's ever gonna deny the supremacy of gold.

There's a tap on my shoulder. "Charles Trammell, I certainly didn't expect to see you here."

NORMAN HOUSTON, the head of Golden State Mutual, although Terrance continues to insist that in practical terms he himself is the executive calling the shots.

Mr. Houston's still got on the double-breasted suit he was wearing this morning, his tie giving the illusion that he has a neck.

"Mr. Houston." It'd be great if Anna could help me explain my being here. But I can't spot where she is. Houston's shoulders are so broad they block my entire line of vision. "Thanks again for taking a chance on me," I say.

"Well, I trust Terrance's opinion on these things." He moves his briefcase from his left hand to his right. "But what brings you—"

"Norman, how are you!" Anna appears from behind him and takes my arm. "Charlie was just telling me you've taken him on."

"Ah, you're here with Anna!" His whole face lights up.

I relax a little, feeling like I just got accepted into some kind of club. "Mr. Houston was telling me how much he trusts Terrance's judgment on personnel."

"Not just on personnel," Mr. Houston says, wagging a thick finger. "He's a great judge of character and quite the sleuth. He's saved Golden State more than once." He turns to Anna. "Did Terrance ever tell you about the time that upstart company tried to poach our clients?"

"Mmm, I think I heard about that," she says, her eyes wandering to other parts of the room.

"Well, he has the right to brag. Terrance put his nose to the pavement, started talking to people, asking questions, and soon enough he exposed the owners of that company's history of fraud and salacious behavior. Put them out of business in less than a month!" Mr. Houston rocks back on his heels, relishing the old victory.

"An interesting story." Although Anna's tone suggests it's anything but. "Did Charlie tell you he's one of Louise's boarders?"

"Ah, you know Louise, too? She's quite a character." The way he enunciates *character* you can tell he's using it as some sort of euphemism. "Speaking of characters, Anna, I hear you attended the most recent party of our newcomer."

"Mmm, I'm not well acquainted with the man, but he does know how to entertain," she says evasively, as if trying to distance herself from wherever it is she thinks this conversation is going.

"Has anyone figured out what he's into?"

They're talking about Reaper, that much is clear.

"Tread carefully," Mr. Houston goes on. "Celebrity apostates are one thing. But none of us can afford to be seen having an intimate friendship with a criminal."

"We don't know he's a criminal," I mutter, wondering if white folk think *I'm* a criminal just for living in this here neighborhood.

Mr. Houston's eyes snap back in my direction. "Have you made a friend of this Reaper person?"

Do I have to speak ill of Reaper to work for Golden State? "I just moved here," I say, treading carefully. "Can't say I know anyone all that well."

Mr. Houston's mouth forms a steel-hard line. "I've been to a few of his soirees. Right after he moved in. But people with power and animus are watching now. Our follies will be their triumph."

Same's true of every colored community down south.

Or up north.

In fact, I feel like there are eyes burrowing into the back of my skull as we speak. But the only thing behind me is a golden-skinned man named Oscar.

"Is your house in jeopardy, too?" I ask Mr. Houston, hoping for a clear answer.

"No," he replies, looking a little self-satisfied, a little apologetic. "I made sure there was no racial covenant on the deed before I made an offer."

So it's not the whole neighborhood. Thank the Lord. Louise's place has got to be in the clear.

Hattie's, too.

"But," Mr. Houston goes on, sounding more urgent, "almost every other house is, including this one, your landlady's, many of your co-workers', our clients' . . . If we lose, I think mine will be one of maybe three families able to stay."

I'm getting lightheaded, nauseous.

"So you're in the clear," I hear myself say. "You . . . you're safe."

"Safe?" Mr. Houston reels back, taking the word like a blow. "How on God's earth can I be safe if my community is in danger? Our future is at stake. We have to win, together."

A bronze-skinned beauty with straight hair piled on top of her head comes up and links her arm through Mr. Houston's. "Sorry to interrupt, darling, but Loren just arrived."

"Ah." Mr. Houston turns and I follow his gaze to the door. Standing there, his coat still on, is a colored man with a Clark Gable mustache and hair that waves instead of curls. He's got a leather briefcase in his hand and a shy face. Everybody else is turning in his direction, too. Hattie strides over and gives him a hearty embrace. Behind him, I notice Terrance walking in alone, Margie nowhere in sight. He gives Hattie a look that reminds me of how Mama looks at folks who talk with their mouth full. But when his eyes land on the man Hattie's greeting, his expression changes. Whoever this fella is, Terrance has respect for him.

"That's the lawyer who's going to rescue us from this mess," Mr. Houston explains. "If you'll excuse me, I want to talk to him before the meeting begins."

Again, his words don't sit right. I've known lawyers who've managed to rescue the occasional powerless Negro from the chair. But I've never known a lawyer who could save a Negro from the rules that keep him powerless.

Everybody here is sleepwalking through the racism.

I breathe in deeply through my nose, then again, and again. My eyes start moving around the room.

"Charlie," Anna whispers, "everything okay?"

Don't want to talk to her right now. I have to focus. I breathe in the gardenias placed on the end tables, memorize the scent of the hot hors d'oeuvres mingling with expensive perfume. I need to study the details of each of the crown moldings, the polished surface of the white grand piano.

We've got less than two months before we're all cast out of Eden.

Chapter 10

"My goodness, you scared me!" Margie exclaims, as if I had snuck up on her in a deserted alley, not rung her front doorbell. "I was just putting Art to bed."

I stick my hands in my pockets, turn my head so I'm looking at the darkened street and not my cousin's curious face. "You're saying I should come back another time?"

"Don't be silly!" Margie grabs my arm and pulls me inside. "Gertie's up with him now. She'll do the honors." She helps me out of my coat, which she hangs in the hall closet. The perfect hostess.

She looks perfect, too. Her hair meticulously in place, her makeup touched up rather than removed, polished heels still strapped neatly on her feet. She's clearly not a woman who sees home as a place to let your guard down.

"Your timing is rather good actually," she adds as she leads me into the living room. "Terrance is at some meeting, so we finally have time to catch up on our own."

"Yeah, I was just at that meeting, I had to walk out early. Told the folks there I'd forgotten my ailing aunt Dottie's birthday and had to give her a call before it got too late in Virginia."

"Your aunt Dottie?" Her eyes turn upward as she tries to conjure the memory of my father's older sister. "Didn't she die thirteen years ago?"

"Fourteen," I snap. "And you know damn well nobody in our family back home has a phone anyway. But I couldn't sit there and listen to a foolhardy lawyer go on about how he can convince a white judge to change the laws to favor our people over his. This Loren Miller's acting like he's Patton when he ain't no better than the brigadier general of the Light Brigade!"

"The light . . . what?"

But I'm too busy ranting to give history lessons. "All those letters you wrote tellin' me how great everything is here, never once did you mention it was a temporary situation. You invite me in just to have me around when the white folk kick us out?"

Margie's standing across from me now, her face blank, like her inner light's suddenly been turned off. She makes a little sound like she's suppressing a cough.

But then in a blink she shakes herself out of it. "Don't be silly! All that business with the houses? That's a mere paperwork detail." She floats over to the liquor cabinet and lets her fingers dance over the tops of the crystal decanters. "Loren, Terrance, Norman, Louise, they all have it well in hand. Don't you give it another moment's thought. I certainly don't." She turns to me. "Would you like a little sherry? Lately, I've had such a hankering for sherry."

"You were hinting at this the first day I came over. Talking to Terrance about how a man's responsible for protecting his family and *home*."

"Oh, I meant nothing by that." This time the cough fully comes out, although she tries to disguise it with a laugh.

"And where would you go if you did get kicked out? Everybody around here would be in the same position!"

"Everyone here is powerful and smart." Her back is still to me, her shoulders a few inches higher than what's natural. "They'll fix everything."

"Margie, this is serious. Just living here makes us lawbreakers. And you and I both know what happens when white men think one of ours has overstepped. I still have nightmares about the night your brother—"

"Charlie, really," she says, a little too sharply. "All these legal technicalities and bureaucratic details, why, I've never had a head for it. But everyone says Loren is the very best lawyer there is, colored or otherwise. Everything will be fine." She pours a bit of sherry into two crystal glasses shaped like tulips.

"Margie, it ain't that simple."

She turns from the bar, a drink in each hand, and gives me a feminine pout. "Until five days ago, I hadn't seen you in decades. And in the short time you've been here we've barely had any time together alone. Surely we can take this rare moment of quiet to celebrate our reunion with happier talk." She hands me a glass and her eyes move to a rose sitting in a bud vase on one of the end tables. "Look at that, did you see?" She gestures for me to follow as she goes over to get a closer look. "It came from our very own bush. When I first noticed it, I said to myself, 'Why, that's the most perfect rose I've ever seen!' I made Gertie pick it for me immediately! There were so many thorns . . . poor Gertie pricked three fingers on her right hand and two on her left! But even she had to admit it was worth it."

I look at the flower and then at Margie. Her cavalier admission to bloodying up the nanny aside, I can't figure out what she's getting at.

"Every petal was such a beautiful, stunningly bright red," she goes on. "Last night I noticed it wasn't standing quite so tall and I worried that it might be losing its glory. But look! It's even prettier than before! Like velvet with those petals curling just a little and darkening at the edges."

Is she talking about Sugar Hill? How just when you think this community is weakening, it's actually getting stronger?

Except . . .

"Margie, those petals are curling because the flower's gettin' ready to die. Two more days and all you're gonna have is a bare stem with thorns."

She gives me a quizzical look. "Why, then, I'll just find another perfect rose. We do own the bush."

Now I'm not sure if either one of us has a clue what we're really talking about.

"Oh!" Her hand suddenly flies to her cheek as a new thought occurs to her. "Remember that time I made you pick those petunias from Miss Carter's yard?"

Just the mention of the memory softens me. "You told me you needed them to wear in your hair for some baptism we were all expected to show up for."

"It was baby Lizzie's baptism," she reminds me with a giggle. "You snuck into Miss Carter's yard and picked almost every petunia she had."

"I don't know what I was thinkin'," I say. "I coulda stopped after pickin' you one or two. But instead I got an armful and then went back for more."

"But on that second trip, she caught you."

"Caught me in the yard, standin', not yet pickin'."

"And you convinced her you had bravely come into her yard to chase off some rabbit who was feasting on her flowers."

"Not one rabbit, but a whole herd of 'em," I correct. "I got that woman believin' there was an army of maniacal bunnies rampagin' through the gardens of Virginia."

Margie's laughing hard now. "She came over to warn my mother! Told her to have the shotgun ready just in case they came for our vegetables. In the meantime, I was eavesdropping from my bedroom, praying she wouldn't come in to see her petunias in my hair!"

"Hell," I say, shaking my head, "by that point, she was even sure the Easter Bunny was a tool of the devil. I was a troublemaker for sure."

"You were wonderful." Margie dabs at her eyes, which had begun to water from mirth. Her sherry's half gone and has tinted her lips a deeper shade. "Always quick on your feet, never shying away from a challenge. And now look at you." She steps back and gives me a proud smile. "A bona fide war hero, a soon-to-be star at Golden State, boarding with a movie star." She takes a second as if to drink in her own words, then gives a satisfied nod before gracefully taking her seat on the settee. "You've done it, Charlie," she says quietly. "You're living your destiny."

That gets a snort from me. "I was working the fields by the time I was four and you think my elevation was somehow preordained?"

"Yes," she says simply, taking another sip of sherry. "I do."

My cheeks warm with flattery. "How did you end up explaining away the petunias to your mama?" I ask.

"Oh." Margie wrinkles her nose as if this part of the memory annoys her. "I told her Daddy brought them back for her and I couldn't resist putting them in my hair. She didn't question it, although I knew she didn't believe me. Daddy never bought flowers in his life . . . not for my mother anyway," she adds with a small grimace that she quickly wipes away. "Speaking of mothers, how's yours? Have you been in touch with her since you've been out here?"

"Again, you know no one back home has phones," I say, pretending the fact doesn't bother me. I wouldn't mind hearing my mama's voice. "And Mama can't read more than a handful of words, so letters are out. I did send her a postcard; she'll probably get it soon."

"Do you miss her, Charlie?" Margie asks.

I hesitate. "I do . . . but I think it's good to have some distance between us. Gives me the space to spread my wings and figure out who I can be without her cautioning me about the dangers of ambition for a colored man." I stare down at the floor, feeling a little guilty for speaking so critically of the woman who birthed me. "I was sorry to hear of your parents' passing, dying only two years apart, that had to be hard."

"Thank you." Her tone lets me know death is not a subject she wants to dwell on.

I try to steer her to a happier memory. "One thing I remember about your mama is that she was a genius in the kitchen."

Margie nods enthusiastically. "Do you remember the cornbread Mommy used to make?"

"Heaven on a plate," I confirm.

We spend the next thirty minutes reminiscing, Margie peppering her memories of the past with compliments about the me of here and now.

Margie was always the only one in the family who looked at me and saw more than a field hand or a future porter. I've missed having someone around who believed dreaming was essential to life.

At the end of that half hour, I excuse myself and head back to Louise's. When I get there everybody's out but Patty, who's glum from another audition that didn't pan out.

It's only when the rest return from the meeting that I realize how easily Margie was able to distract me from the looming threat hanging over all of us.

That's always been her way, making problems disappear without ever solving them. Kind of like magic.

Or, at the very least, a sleight of hand.

Chapter 11

Dr. Somerville's a liar.

Getting my tooth replaced was much more painful than losing it.

As I get up from his chair of torment, I see the pain is not the full sum of the horror. "I'm droolin'!"

I mean it as an accusation, but it comes out as a mumble.

Is it normal to feel dizzy like this?

"That's the result of the muscle relaxants," he says, amiable, as if there isn't a problem. "I also gave you a little something extra so there wouldn't be too much pain."

It could've hurt worse?

Or is that just another story he tells himself: lynchings are in the past, no one's gonna take his home, and he doesn't put patients in pain.

Bunch of downright lies.

"Wheb will ba droolin' stop?" This man has turned me into some kind of freak show.

"By the time you go to bed tonight, that part should be over. You'll still have some swelling, but by Friday—maybe Friday night—it shouldn't be noticeable. What's wrong?"

If he's asking the question, it must mean my eyes are talking better than my mouth.

The drooling is gonna go on all night? What if Anna's home? No way a woman is going to take up with a man after seeing saliva sliding down his chin.

"Check in with my receptionist on the way out," he says, too impatient to wait for me to put together a complaint. "She'll set up a follow-up appointment."

This whole thing was a mistake.

Wilma, the receptionist, looks up from her desk as I stumble out of the exam room. She's trying hard to keep a straight face. I'm a punch line.

"Will someone be picking you up?" she asks. "Or will you be taking a streetcar? Remember, you won't be able to drive for a few more hours."

Dr. Somerville had told me that, but I hadn't anticipated looking like this out in public. There has got to be another way.

Wilma is waiting for an answer.

"Can I mabe a phone caul?"

This time she can't keep her mouth from twitching. She lifts the phone and I pull from my wallet the number of the only person who might help me without making fun of me.

"Hello," I say when someone on the other end picks up. "Is Jambes Mann der?"

My first time in a limo and I got spit dripping on the upholstery.

James's chauffeur opens the door for me once we get to the mansion. James hadn't been at home when I called, but somebody reached him and this driver was sent to fetch me. Daniel, the butler, is already at the door when we pull up. Once I manage to get up the steps without falling over, he gives me a respectful nod. "Mr. Mann will be home by four. At his instruction, I've made up a guest room for you to rest. And, of course, if there's anything else you need, you should let me know."

What I need is to hide under the covers until my face starts acting right. I follow Daniel to the guest room. It's got a king-size bed, an antique armoire, drapes made of a thick velvet material that probably cost more than my whole wardrobe.

"Do you require anything else?"

I shake my head, fearful of what might spill out if I open my mouth. Daniel leaves me.

I go over to the drapes first, let my hands caress the velvet before untying them and pulling them closed. The room falls straight to darkness. I turn on the lamp in the corner.

I'm not tired. But the bed's a temptation. I gotta know what it's like to lie on a mattress that big all by myself, to have this many pillows at my disposal.

I take off my shoes and crawl in. The cotton used for the sheets might be the softest that's ever been picked. Giving in to the comfort, I close my eyes.

I've been living in the presence of luxury since I got to Sugar Hill, but now I'm cocooned by it. And for the first time, I understand it.

Luxury ain't in the gleam of a diamond or the columns of a house.

Luxury's the power to block out the sun at will, deciding for yourself when's night and when's day.

Luxury is being able to just lie here, everything touching you so soft it lulls you into a sleep you didn't even know you were craving.

Luxury, when done right, can make an alert man tired.

I'm feeling kinda tired.

———

If I close my eyes, maybe it'll all go away.

But against my closed lids, I can see the torches clear. Clearer than I can through the cracks in our cabin when I got 'em open.

Everything so twisted and wrong right now.

And she tryin' to keep her coughs quiet.

I press my hands against the table we are under, tell her I can save us.

Her brother know I'm lyin'.

He's lookin' to the grown-ups, his eyes chock-full of pleas.

But the grown-ups? They're lookin' at the floor.

I watch as he rises, forcin' himself to stand . . .

. . . and then things start shiftin'.

His clothes are changin', his white shirt turnin' green, the scarf 'round his neck takin' on a shine . . . turnin' into a dog tag.

I'll save him, I promise. And she looks at me, grateful.

But parts of him are already disappearin'.

Right where his left leg used to be, there ain't nothin' but blood.

Outside men in white sheets goose-step in time to an anthem I don't recognize.

I can't save him, won't even try.

'Cause my folks ain't got no voices.

'Cause it too dangerous to cough.

'Cause tables can burn.

The door opens. The Grim Reaper walks in, covers me up with a funeral shroud.

———

I try to rip at the shroud.

It's just a sheet. A beautiful, soft cotton sheet.

Shit.

I didn't think my nightmares had the resources to buy their way into a bedroom this grand. I didn't think I could be dragged back to that night of poverty and danger while in a place of such wealth and security.

No matter where I go, I'm never free from the worst horrors of my life. In my sleep the ordeals of my adulthood just get mixed up and twisted into that original childhood calamity of hiding under the table, my parents cowering . . . No.

I refuse to think too hard on it while I'm awake. When I'm conscious I can see what's ahead of me rather than what's behind me.

I shake my head in an effort to clear it. How long was I out? Ten minutes? Several hours? I take a deep breath, then another. I'm fine. Everything's fine.

Except my mouth still hurts. I groan, sit up, and shove my feet back into my oxfords. "My mouth hurts," I say out loud to the empty room.

I can talk again.

And I don't feel any saliva dripping down my chin.

I get out of bed. I'm a soldier. Under Nazi fire I applied tourniquets to mangled legs all while trying to convince screaming men not to surrender to the pain.

But in Sugar Hill, a dentist fixed my tooth and I had to take to bed.

There's a mirror next to the armoire. I check my swollen face, try to smooth out the wrinkles in my shirt and pants. In the reflection, I notice a charcoal drawing of a ballerina hanging on the other side of the room. I go over to take a closer look and note the signature in the bottom corner.

Degas. He has a Degas.

But then what doesn't James Mann have?

Is his lifestyle in jeopardy? Will he lose this estate like all the other residents in Sugar Hill? The trial is exactly six weeks and six days away . . .

I squeeze my eyes closed, another nightmare I won't entertain at the moment. I push down my anxiety and cross the room, inching open the door and peeking into the hall.

The electric lights on the walls are brighter than the quiet rays of gold coming through the windows. Sunset's forming.

There's a scent in the air. A mix of baked and cooked culinary temptation.

When I get to the top of the stairs I hear the muffled voices of men. One of those voices belongs to James. I descend a few steps, enough so I can make out a word here and there. James is speaking French with the accent of an American soldier. But the man he is talking to . . . Is that French? It don't sound right.

As I go farther down, I hear the front door open and close, and then seconds later James and James alone is at the foot of the stairs. "You're up!" His thousand-dollar smile looks almost cheap in this million-dollar house. "Still a bit unsteady on your feet? Let's get some food in you."

"I'm not sure I'm supposed to eat yet."

"I had my chef make up some soup and there's some soft, fresh-baked bread. I'm sure you can handle that much."

I hadn't realized he had a live-in chef.

Sure enough, when we reach the dining room, a woman is bringing out two bowls of steaming red soup with chunks of different kinds of fish floating among confetti-like bits of green and the unmistakable scent of garlic. Two glasses of white wine are already being poured. On the table is a newly baked baguette, the likes of which I haven't seen since I returned to this side of the Atlantic.

I sit and the woman places a bowl in front of me right away. "Your friend's not joining us?" I ask.

James sits across from me and cocks his head, as if he doesn't understand the question.

"The fella you were talking French to," I say as I reach for the baguette, then stop. James is looking at me like I've just sprouted horns. "Sorry, should I wait for someone to bring out a knife to slice it with?"

"What?" he asks. Then gives himself a shake. "No, no, just tear into it. Like . . . the French do."

"Guess that's just one more thing Frenchmen and Virginians got in common." I take the bread and rip off a piece. "Only, when they bottle their drink they call it Merlot, we call ours moonshine."

But I'm not feeling as light as my jests and James looks uneasy, which makes me uneasy.

"Do you speak French?" he finally asks as I take a careful bite of what might be the best baguette I ever had.

"*Arrêtez, je suis américain, parlez-vous anglais.* That's pretty much the beginning and end of my linguistic abilities," I admit.

"Ah." James relaxes back in his chair. "I'm not much better, but I try to practice whenever given the chance."

"But the man who was just here . . . was that French he was speakin'?"

"He's learning Parisian French, too," he explains. "I'm afraid it's a bit of the blind leading the blind."

"You met him at a language class or somethin'?"

"Mmm. I see you can chew."

I smile as I swallow what's in my mouth. "Bread, on one side."

"Try the soup. You can dip the bread in if you like."

The mysterious tension that was in the room seems to have lifted, which is a relief. "I appreciate you allowing me to come on over at the last minute."

"Nothing to worry about at all. Dr. Somerville is said to be an exceptional dentist. But he has so many other pursuits. I didn't know he was taking new clients."

"He's not. But he's a friend of my cousin Margie's, so he made an exception."

"Ah, I didn't know that," he murmurs, as if the information is almost sacred. "I don't believe your cousin has ever been to one of my parties."

"Oh?" I pop a spoonful of soup into my mouth. "Wow, this is somethin' else, what is it?"

"Zuppa corsa. Does your cousin not like parties anymore?"

"Anymore? There weren't a lot of our people throwin' parties back in Virginia when we were kids, so I don't know if she ever did or if she likes 'em now. Zuppa corsa . . . that Italian?"

"Tuscan." James isn't eating. He seems distracted. "It's popular in Corsica."

"And the wine?" I ask after taking a sip. "This is damn good wine."

"Yes, from the Bordeaux region," he acknowledges with a laugh. "The French turn everything into an art. Even their grapes." But his mirth's overtaken by a more pensive expression. "It was awful. Seeing people who create all that beauty subjugated by the Germans. The things they did . . . it was ugly. They say the atrocities that were committed by the Germans were without parallel."

I rest my spoon against the side of the bowl, my stomach momentarily clenching. We saw some of those atrocities. I saw them. Men, women, and children who had everything taken from them but their skeletons and skin.

"It's hard to believe that anyone could be that barbaric," he continues.

Was it, though? I knew what kinds of things people did to folks with the bad luck of being born into the wrong group, wrong race, wrong color . . . I *knew.*

And I knew it long before the army gave me a uniform.

"There's ugliness behind us." James is speaking in a hushed voice, gauging my silence. "But there's no point spending too much time looking back on it."

"You're right, gotta leave it in the past." I blink several times, as if memories were mere irritants I could clear from my vision.

"Exactly. Especially when we can look ahead. Because what's coming?" He takes a sip of wine. "What's coming is simply glorious."

His statement startles me, snapping me into the present. Glorious? Is that really a word people apply to anything outside of church? "You talkin' about the next course or the future?"

"Both," he says, placing his glass back on the table.

"You know something I don't?"

His eyes twinkle with mischief, but he doesn't answer. The maid comes back and refills both our glasses even though neither one of them is more than half empty. As she leaves, I take a long sip. "You sure do live grand."

"I built this house to impress. But I'm not certain it does."

"What're you talkin' about? Everybody's impressed with this place. How could they not be? Or . . ." I take a deep breath, broaching the topic part of me wants to avoid. "Are you afraid it's not really yours? That you might lose it?"

He's giving me a funny look. "Why would I lose it?"

"Is there . . . a racial covenant on the house?"

"Oh, that," James says, sounding almost bored.

"Anna told me you used a front man to buy it," I recall. "A white man."

"Ah, she learned about that? Well, you find the people you need to create the life you want," he says, almost more to himself than to me. But then he smiles, dispelling whatever cloud just passed over him. "There were two houses on this property when I bought it. One of them had a racial covenant on it. I think it was on the house, though, not the land. Regardless, I tore it down. What's here now was pretty much built from scratch."

"But you're not sure if the covenant wasn't on the land, too?" I press.

"I don't see it as important. This is unlikely to be my permanent home. She'll want a fresh start."

"Did you say *she'll*—"

"Do you like the style?" he asks. "Maybe it's not the right style."

Does this man have so much he can just go buy another mansion without selling this one first? "I think almost anybody's gonna like the way you have this place done up," I say. "It's different than what you'd find in Harlem, 'course. I think you did say that New York was your favorite place. Why not live there? You could buy yourself a whole block."

"There's probably some happiness to be had in Harlem." He still hasn't taken a single bite. "But I don't want to simply *have*. I want to pursue. The happiness I'm *pursuing* is here." He pauses, then says quietly, "She's here."

"Who?" When he doesn't answer right away, it clicks. "That girl you met in Atlanta? Is that the one you want to move away with?"

"She's in California," he says, as if that settles something.

Does he know how big California is?

"I'm sure she knows I'm looking for her," he says.

"Don't see how she would." I'm getting a little tired of this dead-end love story. "Did you hire an architect to design this place?"

"But how could she think I would ever stop looking for her? She senses it. We're bound to each other. Of that much I'm sure."

Now, this is a fella who talks like he just stepped out of a Dickens novel, or like one of the characters Agatha Christie likes to kill off, or Poe would drive mad. But with James, the poetic, posh talk seems natural. Like he was really born with a silver spoon in his mouth . . . although given his color that doesn't seem possible. I shrug and dig back into the food. "You might be the most optimistic Negro I know."

He laughs at that. "There's a preacher here in L.A., I've seen Hattie in his congregation. He spreads the gospel of positive thinking. You can manifest your own destiny. If you truly believe good things will come to you, they will."

If Hattie thinks nice thoughts are going to keep her in her house, she needs an asylum, not a church.

"I've always felt that way," James continues, "or no, that's not true. I've felt that since I met *her*. But to hear it preached in a church . . . optimism reshaped into religion . . . it's powerful."

"Are you sayin' that if you believe a good thing will happen, it will? This preacher's tellin' folks it's that simple?" My mind wanders back to my youth, when Mama would take us to church and the Baptist minister would tell us every problem could be solved with a prayer.

"There's nothing simple about optimism in the face of adversity," James says. "And while I know I will eventually have my love back in my life, I still have to put in a tremendous amount of effort to make it happen." He leans forward. "Take you, for instance, what good things do you want to come to you? Other than Anna."

"It's hard to want more when you're living in a movie star's three-story house with a great job offer lined up."

"Do you . . ." he starts, but then stops, as if overcome by confusion. He begins again. "You don't mean . . . Are you saying you're content? That if things stay the way they are, you'll be perfectly satisfied?"

"I'd be perfectly satisfied if things are as they seem."

The way he's looking at me is how I always imagined the Indians looked at the white pilgrims when they first showed up on these shores. Like he can't tell if I'm cursed or divine.

"What?" I ask him. "You think there's somethin' about my life that ain't up to snuff?" I keep my tone light.

"No, no," he says. "It's just . . . I've never met someone . . . from the States who's ever claimed to be satisfied." He laughs self-consciously.

"It's ridiculous, but it feels almost sacrilegious. Like satisfaction is in and of itself somehow un-American. It's not, of course," he adds quickly.

"Never thought of satisfaction as having a nationality," I muse. "But you're right. If it does, English ain't its mother tongue."

James smiles a little, still looking unsure.

I sigh and put down my spoon. "Don't worry, I'm not really satisfied. Can't be 'cause nothing here's as it seems. Not for me. Not for most people. Your neighbors are all about to lose their homes. And that means I'm about to be put out on the streets, too."

"Is that what you're worried about? I consider you a friend, Charlie. My friends don't go homeless."

This is getting to be too much. "We met a few days ago and now on top of all the clothes you want to help me with housing? Don't mean to sound suspicious, but why?"

He blanches and then takes a long drink from his glass. "I don't have many friends. I'm not sure why that is."

I think back to Anna's harsh comparison: Reaper, the circus ring-leader. It ain't right. "I didn't mean to insult you."

"You didn't." But he does look hurt. "Perhaps everyone thinks any friendship I offer will have strings attached. Maybe I deserve that, although . . . I try not to be that way. I don't want to be."

"Look, I was outta line. You've never asked me for anythin'."

"I haven't," he says quietly. "It's been a while since I've been able to sit down and have a nice conversation with someone. Perhaps every relationship has some transactional elements. But I do value your friendship just for what it is."

I insulted him. He didn't deserve that. He doesn't deserve to be considered a circus freak or a criminal. He says he's in international trade. Is that really any more surprising than a colored woman being named one of the best actresses in the country? Or a Negro running a whole insurance company or a bunch of hotels?

The moniker *Reaper* is unearned, too. I'm sure of it.

" 'Course I believe that. Don't pay me no mind. All those drugs

Dr. Somerville shot into my mouth got my brain scrambled." I try to defuse the situation by smiling wide, showing off my new tooth. "So tell me more about your girl. She got a name?"

"Right . . . I . . . You know what? I've talked enough about myself and my ambitions," he says, suddenly reluctant to dive into his favorite topic. "Tell me, if Louise keeps her house, do you believe you'll really be satisfied with your lot?"

"I suppose," I answer, dipping a spoon into the soup, inhaling the unique mixture of spices and fish. "I'll tell you one thing. Satisfaction might not be American, but if this is what they're servin' every day in Corsica? I bet those Corsicans feelin' satisfied as all hell right now."

That gets us both chuckling.

It's good to have a friend here.

Chapter 12

The agent I've been shadowing these last four days, Sam, drops a stack of papers on my desk with a loud thump followed by a second, smaller stack, which lands with a whisper. "Proof these, file those."

He strides away, arms swinging a little too fast for his speed. Only once has he spent more than five sentences on me, and that was to tell me about how he worked years to get where nepotism lifted me.

It feels funny being the one holding the unfair privileges.

I trace the outlines of the new papers, letting the edges scratch my fingertips as I tune in to the sound of the dozens of typewriters and voices sharing the floor. Only the people at Terrance's level or higher have offices with walls. My current, supposedly temporary desk is barely big enough for an elementary-school student and it's placed right next to the teacher-sized desk Sam's got.

I suspect Sam thinks he's drowning me in drudgery. He hasn't taken me to his one-on-one meetings with clients even though I'm pretty sure he's supposed to. Instead, I've been listening to his side of business calls and given piles of forms to review and adjust.

But the forms . . . those are interesting.

I've heard of life insurance before but never really gave it much thought. Never considered what it meant, that life, even life that's not bought and sold on the auction block, has got a dollar value to it. And in this place, at this time, that value ain't determined by plantation owners but by some real precise calculation between means and love. The means to pay a certain premium and the love we hold for the kin we leave behind.

I wonder what kind of policy was cut from Terrance's love for Margie.

Terrance has taken another long lunch. Undoubtedly at the Dunbar.

Not sure I like that hotel anymore.

When he waltzes in at one-thirty he looks crisp and clean. No lipstick on the collar, his shirt buttoned, tie straight. The only sign of his betrayal is the smirk on his face.

When he comes my way, I try to look even busier than I am.

"Tomorrow night, want to join the missus and me for dinner?" he says, standing over me.

I keep my eyes on the print in front of me. "I'm going to Hattie McDaniel's birthday party."

"Will she play the role of host or is she going to serve you while sporting an apron and bug eyes?"

"Hattie's a good conversationalist. Well read, too," I say, ignoring the part of me that agrees with him.

"Yes, I remember hearing that she felt a connection to the character of Mammy after reading *Gone With the Wind*. Perhaps she should read *Uncle Tom's Cabin* next." He sits in Sam's chair. "How about tonight, then? There's supposed to be a good band playing at the Club Alabam. I'll send for Marguerite, you send for Anna."

I've been hearing talk about that club from others in the office. I got enough money to cover it, assuming my paycheck comes on time tomorrow.

"Mr. Lewis!" Sam has returned, a grit-toothed smile making his narrow face wide. "How are you today!"

"Fine, just fine." Terrance remains seated, forcing Sam to stand at the corner of his own desk. "Charlie, I'm not leaving until I get a yes." His tone is jovial, but I know he's serious.

"I'll call Anna, see if she's free."

Terrance smacks his palm on the desktop in victory before getting to his feet. "We'll grab dinner first. I'll see if I can get out of here a little earlier than usual. I'm already famished."

"Didn't you just come back from lunch?" I ask, keeping my voice neutral.

"Ah, right, but due to an appointment I was occupied with matters other than food."

———

Margie and Anna meet us outside the office at five-thirty, Margie looking like a perfect ingenue, Anna a bit like a vixen. The women are in high spirits, which is enough to elevate mine.

"Is it true," Anna asks as Margie critically eyes a shoe store we're strolling past, "that the *California Eagle* is going to name Norman as businessman of the year?"

Terrance's jaw sets. "No, it is not."

"I heard from some of the staffers over there that he has it all but locked up," she presses. "And they're going to dedicate the better part of the front page—"

"It's not going to be Norman!" Terrance snaps, his face headed toward an unflattering shade of purple. Anna blinks at him, all innocence.

I think Anna knew exactly what kind of reaction that question would get her. I think her feelings about Terrance are what mine are without the complexities of gratitude.

If I'm right, it means she also enjoys provocation. I appreciate that.

"I can't imagine anyone other than Terrance will take charge," Margie coos, tilting her head to give Terrance her best starry-eyed gaze. "He's always been a natural leader."

Terrance's chest puffs, his scowl evaporating. No one knows how to soothe an ego like Margie.

We pass another store and this time Margie insists we stop as she considers a dress in the window. "It's beautiful, isn't it? Terrance, don't you think it's beautiful?"

I step away, study the business next door. It's a bar, dusty and run-down. It should be next to a smoke shop, not a dress shop. As Margie, Anna, and Terrance discuss fashion, I look through the window. It's already getting dark and the lights of the joint are dim, but past the other patrons, in the far back corner, I see a single white man. He's sitting with a Negro and is in deep conversation.

The Negro is James.

I step a little closer to the window. James looks up and we lock eyes. Just as I start to smile a greeting, Margie grabs my sleeve and pulls me back to the window of the dress shop. "You don't think that looks cheap, do you?"

"Huh? Um, no, it's nice." I should go in and say hi. James hasn't even met Margie or Terrance yet. Maybe they'll hit it off and he'll join us for dinner. Or maybe he's coming out to greet me now.

"I told you!" Margie says to her husband. A small group of Negro girl-Friday types push past, chattering with a mix of different Southern drawls, forcing Margie to raise her volume. "It's lovely. And the color would complement my complexion."

"It's a rag by an unknown dressmaker," Terrance protests. "Your next dress should make the remaining white girls in West Adams jealous. Didn't you tell me that New Yorker, Norell, is all the rage now? I'll buy you one of his designs this weekend in Beverly Hills. I'm going there on Saturday anyway to pick up a few new shirts."

"There's a great haberdasher here, right around the corner," I say.

It seems James isn't coming out.

Terrance shoots me a look chock-full of disdain. "I prefer to do my shopping in the more elite areas of the city." He pauses, then adds, "I like making them work for me."

He doesn't have to tell me who *them* is. I may be new here, but I know you have to be a hell of a lot lighter than a paper bag to work in the boutiques of Beverly Hills.

"I saw a friend of mine in there." I point to the bar.

"I hope not," Terrance shoots back. "That place is a hangout for crooks, communists, and hoodlums."

That's not intended to make me laugh, but I can't help myself. "He's none of those things. Come on, I'll introduce you." I step over to the bar's door, pulling it open.

The man James was talking to is still there, but James isn't. It takes all of five seconds to scan the bar given its size. "Just . . . give me a second." I go in alone, walking over to the table that now seats only one.

When the man looks up, I know right away he ain't American. Just something in his features and the way he carries himself gives it away. He's dressed well enough, casual but in fine fabrics, a nice watch. It's the expense of his clothes that brings the scar running down his right cheek to attention. Monied folk usually only collect the kind of scars you can't see.

"May I help you?" he asks.

Not an Italian accent. At least not from any region I'm familiar with. Maybe he's a light-skinned Arab? I don't know anything about that type of accent.

"The man you were just drinking with," I say, "James. He's a friend . . . He still here?"

"No, I am here by myself."

He says it with enough authority to make me question my sanity. I know I saw James, but why didn't I see him leave? "He's in the restroom?"

The scarred man's laugh got the edge of mockery. "You look for the company of a man in a *toilette*? You are not in the right bar."

Toilette. Maybe French? But then again, I served in France and that accent just don't fit.

"I'm not looking for anything like that." Once more I glance around the bar.

There's another door, possibly leading to a storage room . . . or out back.

Would James sneak out to avoid me?

Why?

"What is your name?" the man asks.

"Charlie." I decide not to give him more than that. "What's yours?"

"Listen to me, Charlie," he says, "people don't like it when I must myself repeat."

His English needs work. "You mean you don't like repeating yourself?"

"No, I mean to say when people do not listen to me, I make them . . . how do I say . . . I make people who do not listen to me sad. Very sad."

I stare at him, trying to figure out how much is language barrier, how much is threat.

"Did you listen to me?" The smirk on his thin face is anything but friendly.

"You said you're here alone."

A man at the bar starts swearing, but there's no one next to him to listen.

"Ah, so you see, we have no problem! No misunderstanding. I wish you a good night . . . or is it good evening? I get it mixed up."

Anna steps into the bar, shoots me a questioning look. My new companion notices her and lets out a low whistle. "God shows His love for man by making for us women like this."

I've had enough. "You've been a big help," I say before walking over to Anna and leading her back outside to rejoin our group.

I don't speak much as we continue to another block. Margie is still pining for the dress in the window and Terrance is still offering her everything short of the queen's jewels to get her off it. Anna leans into my ear. "What was all that about? With that white man?"

"I thought I saw Reaper with him," I mutter back.

She gives me one of her one-eyebrow lifts. "I haven't heard you refer to him as Reaper in at least a week."

"Here's the restaurant," Terrance says, interrupting my next thought. He ushers us into an elegant-looking spot. A welcoming, blue-black beauty waits to seat us. "I get my clothes in Beverly Hills," he says, smiling at me, "but I have too much respect to suffer through those pretentious blowhards' flavorless cuisine."

Chapter 13

I pause on the second of Louise's front steps. Anna is on my arm, looking mussed and gorgeous from a night of dancing. The music had almost been enough to get even Terrance out of his chair, though in the end he stuck to foot-tapping.

But now, more than four hours later, we're back here in the quiet of Sugar Hill. I stare up at the grand three-story house owned by a fast-talkin', poker-playin' movie star whose skin is even darker than mine.

Now that I know white folks are trying to take it away, this house has a sad kind of logic to it. When you come from nothing, it's hard to grasp what can be gained, but mighty easy to imagine what can be taken.

Five weeks and six days until the trial.

Five weeks and six days until the beginning of the end.

Anna also tilts her head up, but she's not looking at the house. She's looking at me, and her gaze chases away any threat of melancholy.

"Normally I wouldn't invite a man in after knowing him for less than fourteen days," she says. "But you seem to have me at a disadvantage, seeing as you live here, too."

A breeze picks up, casting shadows of the trees swaying in the porch light. "You don't have to invite me into your room."

"No," she agrees, "I don't have to." She leans forward and places her mouth against mine, her lips parting just enough for me to taste brandy and smoke and the sting of hot spice . . . all the things she allows inside her.

It's an opening bid.

I let my fingers slide down her arm, brushing against the curve of her hip. "Do you remember the first night we met?"

"Yes," she says.

The fabric of my shirt offers poor protection against the warmth of her. "At the time, I worried you had a crush on somebody else."

The breeze seems to shift origins, no longer coming from the sky but from the ground, gently wedging its way up and between us. "Who?" she asks. Then the memory of who we met that first night comes back to her, making her laugh. "Reaper? Ah, well, I suppose his danger and mystery are enough to infatuate most ladies. But I would never let him take me out, even if he wasn't pining over some long-gone girl. I'm too . . . I guess the euphemism would be *risk averse.*"

"And what's that a euphemism for?"

She hesitates, conveying a tinge of insecurity. "Self-interested." She whispers her answer like she's admitting to sin. "I've been accused more than once of being utterly self-serving. I'm not sure that's true, but it's not an unreasonable charge."

"Okay, I hear you. But I got a thing for beautiful survivors." I trace the line of her jaw with the tip of my finger, up to the spot right below her ear, then down again to the curve of her chin. "And you can't be a survivor without bein' a little self-interested. If others don't get that, the hell with 'em."

Her teeth sink into her lower lip. That look she's giving me got the pull of a riptide. "Charlie." She's touching me, her breasts against my rib cage, every breath presses us closer. "I'm inviting you in."

Chapter 14

"So how do you know Hattie?" he asks.

Clark Gable has just asked me how I know Hattie McDaniel.

I'm at Hattie's house, with a beautiful woman on my arm, a woman whose arms I *woke up in,* and *Clark Gable's right here talking to me like we're equals*!

I swear to God, Sugar Hill's got more shocks than an electric chair.

Hattie's entertainment tonight is Duke Ellington.

Duke goddamned Ellington.

Anna nudges me. I'm taking too long to speak. "I'm her neighbor," I reply . . . *to Clark Gable.* He looks just like he does in the pictures. Mustache trimmed, not a hair out of place, not a speck of lint on his jacket.

Yet he's got flaws the camera can't see. Flaws you can smell.

"Charlie moved into Louise's," Anna explains. She seems completely calm. Like all of this is normal.

"Oh, you know Louise, too!" A deadly odor rides the force of his laughter. Like some poor creature was given its last cigarette, then shot dead in his mouth. "I ran into her last week ringside at a boxing match. Have you played in one of her infamous poker games yet?"

"No, not yet," I manage.

"I don't recommend it. I've played her once and I'm lucky to still have my shirt," he goes on as I take a discreet step backward.

"Clark!" A striking Negro woman with rubies dangling from her ears calls him over.

"Please excuse me," he says, lighting up right away. "I haven't seen this one in a long time."

And then Clark Gable walks away to talk to her. Clark. Gable. No one back home would believe it.

I take a sip from my glass. The wine's not as good as what Reaper was serving, but still better than anything I ever thought someone would serve me for free.

Anna gestures to a pretty strawberry blonde standing near Hattie's white piano and talking to a pale-faced man a good twenty years her senior. "Do you recognize them? That's Bing Crosby and Esther Williams."

I blink a few times until I'm sure I can see the truth of it. "How does Hattie manage it?"

"Hmm? Oh, you mean how does she get all these white stars here?" Anna shrugs with one shoulder. "They love her. It's no more complicated than that. And those white gossip columnists wouldn't dare write anything critical about Hattie's parties. Not with Gable in attendance. No one wants to be on his bad side."

I watch as Esther Williams throws back her head, laughing at something Crosby said. I'm not sure I would have recognized them if Anna hadn't pointed them out. Williams, whose hair never moves on film, is wearing it loose and casual around her shoulders, and Crosby . . . that fella hardly has any hair at all.

"Does Bing Crosby wear a wig in his movies?"

"A toupee," she corrects.

I give him another look. He's puffing on a giant pipe that reminds me of one Gable used in a movie. "There's a problem with Clark Gable's breath."

Anna nods. "Gum disease. Nothing to be done. Vivien Leigh complained about having to kiss him. But that, of course, was kept under wraps. I wrote a piece for the *Eagle* a few years back on how

Hollywood tries to hide all the flaws of their white stars and amplify the flaws of the Negro ones, making a colored actress who is already a little plump wear extra padding, for example. As a result, neither group comes across as fully human. I still have it, if you'd like to give it a read."

"Sure, maybe. Does Reaper ever have white guests at his parties?"

"No," she says stiffly. Both her tone and her expression tell me I've said something wrong. "James 'Reaper' Mann is no Hattie McDaniel." When I don't respond right away, she softens, gives me a little smile. "You must be tired. You were tossing and turning a lot last night. You cried out once, but then settled, so I didn't bother to wake you."

My skin heats up with a new shame. I stare down at my shoes. I don't have to remember the nightmare to know what it was. The darkness, the whispering, the nervous cough, the flickers of fire. I've seen so much more bloodshed since that night, seen brutality, cruelty, death close up . . . yet *that's* the memory that haunts me most, the night when I couldn't even see my enemies.

Only my impotence.

Anna's studying me, her face kind. "Just be sure the dreams you're chasing are bigger than the nightmares you're running from."

I slowly raise my eyes, surprised to be so easily understood. But before she can say more, the two women who have caught up with their dreams walk over. Hattie and Louise seem like sisters, not due to any physical resemblance, but because of the clear comfort and affection they share.

"Charlie," Hattie says, giving me her best welcoming smile. "I'm so glad you came."

"Wouldn't want to miss your birthday, Hattie," I say with a smile.

"And yet you haven't made it to a single one of my Sunday poker nights!" Louise scolds. "I see you out here going to parties and all that, but somehow it's the woman providing a roof over your head that you can't make time for."

I laugh, Clark Gable's words still ricocheting in my head. "I got time for you, Louise. It's the money I might be a little short on."

"You got a job, don't you? Maybe a paycheck by now, too? And if you end up having to write an IOU, I do know where you live. My game starts . . ." She loses her train of thought as she catches sight of something behind me. "What the hell is Lena doing here?"

I turn to see Loren Miller and two women entering. One is a pregnant woman on his arm, the other is chatting with the couple like they're all family. The latter is Lena Horne.

"She's a friend, Louise," Hattie retorts.

"Is that what we're calling threats these days?" Louise shoots back. "You know that woman and Walter are why our phones have stopped ringing. They've been poisoning the well and then asking us to drink from it like it's punch."

"Walter is Walter White, the current national leader of the NAACP," Anna whispers in my ear.

"Lena's here trying to make a living like the rest of us," Hattie responds. "She's lovely."

"She's practically white," Louise growls.

"Which will only make it harder for her to land a role. I'm going over to greet her. But by all means, feel free to stay here and stew."

"Louise," Anna says softly as Hattie goes to welcome the new arrivals, "you know she's right. Lena's blameless."

"That woman let the head of the NAACP hold her up as the example of the kind of colored woman Hollywood should be casting!" Louise's girlish voice is creeping up to a higher volume. A few of the people closest to us are looking in our direction. "High-yellow gals with twenty-three-inch waists and noses narrower than a redneck's mind." Her hands fly to her hips. "You expect me not to take that personal?"

"Of course, I understand," Anna says quickly, her tone pitched to soothe. "But it was Walter who held her up as a sort of Negress Hollywood standard-bearer. All *Lena* has ever done is ask to be cast in roles that she feels are . . . are . . ."

"What?" Louise snaps. "Not demeaning like the roles I play? *Imitation of Life* was the first movie that *ever* put a spotlight on the concerns and struggles of a colored woman. *My* concerns. It was a damn groundbreaker. I'm getting sick and tired of Walter and all the jackasses of the Negro press trying to tell me otherwise."

"You're absolutely right," Anna agrees. "It was a wonderful movie, and you were wonderful in it."

But Louise ain't listening. "Think about those letters Hattie brought over last Sunday—"

"That was two Sundays ago," Anna corrects. "Charlie had just moved in . . ."

"All those colored servicemen chiding and insulting her for the roles she plays! You know it's Walter who put them boys up to it. While Hattie was feeding colored servicemen in her home, Walter was doing his damnedest to turn those very men against her. You can't tell me that his best friend, Lena, didn't help with that."

"I can tell you that and I have told you that. At least fifty times now." Anna's somehow expressing fatigue and agitation all at once. "For God's sake, Louise, you and I both know there is only one kind of character the studios want their colored actresses to play, and Lena doesn't fit the type! She can't play a maid or a slave and her singing's more seductress than minstrel. Almost every scene she's filmed has been left on the cutting-room floor. No one's offering her any work!"

"Yeah? Well, that's something she and I have in common these days, isn't it? Hattie's right, everybody's trying to take everything! The whites are trying to take my home and these high-yellow turncoats are trying to take my livelihood!" Her soprano shifts into a trembling screech. "Let me tell you, they picked the wrong woman to mess with. It took a lifetime of blood, toil, and tears to get here and I'll bury the lot of them before I let them drag me back down. And that includes that flat-assed, no-talent, Mata Hari bitch!" She gestures violently toward Lena before turning and marching off to the bar.

"Huh." I glance over at Anna, nonplussed. "Louise not getting roles these days?"

"No." She is watching Louise cross the room, her stomp easing into gentler steps as another actor approaches for conversation. "During the war," Anna continues, "things were looking up for all the colored actors. Perhaps for the men more than the women . . . but still. Eleanor Roosevelt actually wrote a letter to the studio heads asking them to cast Negroes in the kind of roles that might inspire a colored man to want to serve his country. They needed Negro enlistment and they planned to get it through showing their colored talent a little respect."

"Sounds good to me. What happened?"

"The war's over, soldier." She takes a drink, emptying half of her glass. "They don't need us anymore."

The words land with the familiarity of a boxing-ring punch.

As field hands we raise our voices in song for relief, then rejoice when landowners say our sound's pleasing, that we might try our luck as musicians . . . only to have our notes stolen and wrapped in white. Then we're told we're only good for fighting. So we turn into weapons and follow them into war, fighting for their freedom, hoping they might share some of it with us when peacetime arrives.

And then we come home and they rip off our uniforms, spit in our faces, and point us back to the fields.

Colored folks are always trying to mold ourselves into the tools needed most by white society, only to be told what we've become ain't got no more use.

"But that's why they pay me, isn't it?" Anna's eyes are unfocused, her voice hollow. "To create that need. To make the public ask for the actors they're trying to discard." She gives herself a little shake, as if trying to rid herself of a mood. "It's a party. Let's do try to focus on the good." Then a sly smile pulls on the edges of her lips. "Like last night. That was *very* good."

That gets me grinning again, too. "I'd add another *very*."

"Ha, well, we'll see if . . . Oh my God, that's the entertainment editor of the *Los Angeles Sentinel*. Was she standing close enough to hear Louise going on about Lena?"

I look over at the woman Anna is eyeing. She's standing no more than a dozen feet away. "Maybe? I didn't notice."

"Shit," Anna whispers. "I'm sorry, I've got to do damage control." Then she plasters on a smile, raises her volume, and puts on a lilt. "Janey! I didn't even see you! How are you?"

I observe as she approaches the editor in question. I do love the way that woman moves.

I wander off toward the bar. Duke Ellington is between sets and mingling with this glittering crowd. Clark Gable and Ella Fitzgerald are clinking glasses. Hattie's Oscar gleams from the mantel, exalted, watching us all.

At the bar I find Loren, now separated from the women he came with and talking to another Negro man, who I think I recognize from the movies. "I hear you're representing Barron on those narcotics charges," the actor says.

Loren nods. "Yes, I just agreed to take on the case yesterday."

"Any chance that officer had legitimate reason to arrest him?"

"Please." Loren releases a sound that walks the line between a scoff and a snort. "Officer Stovall would arrest Helen Keller for eavesdropping."

Loren turns as he hears me laugh, his nose creasing at the bridge. "We've met, haven't we?"

"I was here on a Monday," I acknowledge. "Anna introduced us."

"Oh, that's right! You had to leave early to check in on your aunt, right?" Loren lets out a relieved sigh. "I'm not always great with faces. Not uncommon for me to embrace strangers or mistakenly ignore those who should be friends."

"For me it's names," I say. "Particularly names I haven't heard before. When I was overseas, I had to resort to referring to everyone as their nationality, which is a problem when you've got five Frenchmen in the same room."

"Ha, I had the same trouble while touring the Soviet Union."

"You were in Russia?"

He covers his mouth and lets out a few raspy coughs. "Over ten years ago now."

"What were you doing there?"

"Falling out of love with communism." He pauses to light up a Lucky Strike.

This is a man with a story, and I'm dying to hear it. But when I turn my head, I see Reaper walking in the door.

He's alone, an unopened bottle in his hand.

"Several of us were invited to Russia to take part in what was supposed to be the first truly great interracial film with international distribution." From the corner of my eye, I see Reaper beckoning me over. "A whole troop of colored actors and writers and dreamers went over there by way of car, boat, and train . . . I'm sorry, but I believe that Mr. Mann over there is trying to get your attention," he says, cutting himself off with a smile.

I feel my cheeks burning even though it's not me who's embarrassing himself by waving my arms around all while refusing to walk on over and say hello. "If you'll excuse me for a minute?" I reluctantly leave Loren for Reaper, who is taking a few tentative steps into the house. "Didn't expect to see you."

Reaper's busy sizing up the room, looking anxious. "Are Marguerite and Terrance here?"

"James," Anna says, and I turn to see her beside me, creases of skin puckering the delicate bridge of her nose. "What a surprise. I didn't know Hattie had you on the guest list."

"It's a party," he says, still apparently searching the room for something. Is it fear I see in those darting eyes? Anticipation? "There are lots of people here who aren't on the guest list."

"Hattie's parties aren't quite as freewheeling and raucous as yours," she counters.

"Are Marguerite and Terrance here?" he asks again, more insistent this time.

"Of course not," Anna says, exasperated. "You know their crowd doesn't mix with this one."

That heavy cloak of intensity he was wearing drops to the floor, making him lighter. "Here, I brought this for the birthday girl." He hands Anna a bottle of Moët & Chandon.

Anna hesitates, then takes the bottle from him with both hands. "Hattie *has* been missing real champagne." I can see her making some kind of silent calculation. "You're right. This is a big party. I'm sure all are welcome." Then her head whips to the right as she notices Janey from the *Sentinel* heading in Lena's direction. "I'll give this to Hattie," she mutters before rushing to head Janey off.

"I'm glad to see you, old sport."

Thinking of the strange foreign man from the day before, I keep my response to a nod.

"How have you been?"

This time I answer with a shrug.

Reaper won't give it up. "What's on your mind?"

I cross my arms over my chest. "I'd like to ask you a question you might not want to answer."

"Ah, yes." He unbuttons his sports coat, then immediately thinks better of it and buttons it again. "I suspect I know what it is. But please, ask. I'd like you to ask."

"Did you slip out the back of that bar to avoid me?"

He clears his throat. "That's why I'm here. I was hoping to apologize and explain."

"Explain why you snuck off or why your white friend threatened me?"

"'I hear Hattie has a great backyard, might be a little quieter." He slips his thumbs in his pockets. "Shall we get ourselves a glass and take a look?"

———

I hadn't noticed that some guests brought their children along until I walk out into Hattie's backyard. Adolescents, colored and white, dancing up a storm. The faint notes of jazz coming through the open doors and panes of glass as Ellington presses his fingers to the ivory keys.

"So." Reaper is tapping his foot against the grass, moved by either the fast melody or high nerves. "How was your first week at work?"

I give him a look, already losing patience.

"Right, sorry," he says, a little shamefaced. "And I'm sorry about yesterday. I'm certain threats were not Michel's intent. He's a business associate of mine."

"Your business being international trade," I say dryly.

"Quite right." He looks away, his eyes refusing to bear testimony to his words. "English isn't his first language, so most likely a few things got mixed up, lost in translation."

"Would you like to tell me the truth about why you snuck out the back door before I could say hello?"

His tapping foot changes motion long enough to kick at a pebble. "It wasn't you I was hiding from."

The question he wants me to ask is obvious, so I keep quiet, forcing him to tell me the rest without prodding.

"I was hiding from the woman I love," he says, real quiet.

Hadn't seen that one coming. "You tryin' to tell me you're here for Anna?"

"What? No! Anna is yours!"

"Damn right she is." Across Hattie's courtyard a Negro boy of around twelve tries to teach a white girl of similar age how to do the Lindy Hop. My heart accelerates to hummingbird speed, almost bolting across the yard to stop that boy, hide him.

Then I remember where I am.

That boy ain't gonna get lynched for teaching a little white girl to dance.

"It's easy to understand why you've fallen for Anna."

I nod but keep my eyes on the kids, trickles of sweat making their way from the back of my neck down the length of my spine, my body unconvinced of the safety promised by this new city.

"She's smart. As beautiful and sophisticated as a rose," he goes on. "But my girl's a different kind of flower . . ." He pauses, takes a deep breath. "My girl's Marguerite."

That gets my attention.

I stare at him, waiting for him to say he's joking or that he's misspoken.

But he says nothing. His expression is somber.

"Margie?" I ask, still hoping he'll contradict me.

His Adam's apple bobs up and down, adding a visual punctuation mark to his reveal.

"Sweet Jesus, James. She's why you're here? You built *that* house 'cause of her? She's married!"

"She doesn't love him," he replies with more certainty than I think he's got a right to.

I take a gulp from my glass, wishing the wine was whiskey.

"He's not faithful," he continues. "The man has no respect for her at all."

That part's harder to argue with. "Their marriage is their business."

"He's making a fool of her, Charlie. A beautiful, intelligent, vibrant woman. That girl, who was your only childhood friend, is being played for a fool."

We stand there, mute for several minutes, watching the children dance without fear. Eventually I ask the only other question I can think to pose. "Why do you love her?"

"Because I do," he says firmly.

"You gotta do better than that. She's pretty, that's for sure. And she's fun. But you knew her for all of five days."

"I . . . I've traveled," he begins as the music of the band switches from fast to slow. "More than most. I know what the world is capable of."

Where's this heading?

"I've seen . . . things happen to people I cared about. Sometimes . . . often, it feels like tomorrows are . . . they're lottery prizes won by chance."

More guests wander into the yard, some laughing. I catch a whiff of the woodsy smoke of cigars.

"When I kissed Marguerite for the first time I tasted the future." I watch his back straighten, his chin inch up toward the stars. "Tomorrow, next week, next month, next year, they were all right there, beneath her lipstick, just waiting for some man bold enough to uncover them. Waiting for *me*."

A minute ago, I had looked at this guy and seen a criminal . . .

"She's more than a girl. She's the essence of possibility."

. . . now he's a goddamned poet. How many cheap, sentimental novels have you got to read to learn to talk like that?

"You're a colored man," he says to me, "from the South. And you've been to war." He changes his position so we're standing eye to eye. "You know how precious and rare it is to believe you might have a future. If someone could give you that, tell me you wouldn't move heaven and earth to be with her."

I take in a quick breath, but exhaling's hard.

"She may not remember you," I say at last.

She may not love you.

That part I keep quiet.

"I was hoping that you would set up a meeting."

A bitter laugh splits open my lips. "This is why you've been so nice to me."

"It's why I started a conversation with you," he admits. "It's not why I've come to think of you as a friend. I know that may be hard to believe. But I'm asking you to do what's hard."

"You think believing in friendship's the hard part?" I shake my head in disbelief. "You want me to set up a secret meeting between you and my cousin . . . who happens to be married to my boss."

"Terrance doesn't have to know," he insists. "Look, I've been throwing these lavish parties hoping she might stop by. She never does. And the more time that passes, the clearer it becomes that I was wrong, a party is not the right setting at all. Our reunion should be more intimate. More private. Maybe on an evening when Terrance has to work late." He lets his lip curl on those last two words, implying that

Terrance's occasional late nights got nothing to do with insurance. "You could ask her to take a stroll, and the two of you could happen by my house—"

"You gotta stop acting like a lovesick schoolboy," I interrupt, "hatchin' plans to get the prettiest gal on the cheer squad to go to some dance. I can't help you. Not with this."

Again, we fall quiet. The kids on the lawn are attempting to tap-dance now, like they're Fred Astaire and Ginger Rogers. Except if Fred Astaire looked like this child, the Klan would have strung him up just for tapping his toe within five feet of Ginger.

Watching these kids is like witnessing the impossible turn real.

"Champagne," Reaper says.

"What?"

"It's what I import. My international trade. Michel helped me smuggle champagne and wine out of France during the occupation. We sold it on the black market."

I stare at him in disbelief, but he's redirected his gaze to his shoes.

"I told you I took part in the French Resistance. I did it for the right reasons. But I also profited off the endeavor. The growers, the French-men who owned those vineyards, they shared in our profit, too. But it was obviously not the priority of the Allies . . . selling wine. It would have looked . . . bad. And some might have suspected we were aiding the Nazis, selling their commandeered commodities abroad, but I promise you, the Nazis didn't get a cent," he says with a certain amount of force. "Resistance through commerce. You can't get more American than that."

"Why're you tellin' me this?"

"My dealings with Michel . . . There have been times when we had to be secretive. Smuggling, even for a good cause, isn't exactly legal. But that's over. I'm turning all those wartime underground ventures into an aboveground enterprise. It's a complicated process, but as you can see, it's going well. There has never been such demand for French goods, and my supply lines were up and functioning before most. Plus, I've invested wisely." It's now that he finds the courage to look me in the eye again. "I know they call me Reaper behind my back. It's because they heard an associate who attended one of my parties refer to me as such. Someone who knew someone who knew the appellation from my past. But I didn't earn the name through violence."

It's me who looks away this time.

"The name Reaper . . ." And now he falters. "It's because of the way I was able to sneak in and out of the country, the way I, a Negro man, was able to slip past Nazis with the spoils, as silent as death, they said."

"And so they called you Reaper." He nods even as he grimaces. I don't blame him. Reaper is an ugly name even if earned by doing something good. I suddenly feel ashamed that I ever used it to refer to him.

"I would never, ever expose Marguerite to any kind of danger. I would protect her with my life." And here his voice breaks. "I want her to *be* my life."

How does a man who claims to have trudged through the worst of the world manage to have done so without breaking his rose-colored glasses?

But then when I look at these kids, even I can see the night's got a little rose in its hue.

I want to believe in what I'm seeing.

"Help me," he says.

If comfort is luxury, then there ain't nothing more luxurious than delusion.

I don't want to be the man who rips James's delusions away from him.

I want to share in them.

Or, at least, I'd like to have enough money and security to buy a couple of delusions of my own.

Chapter 15

"I knew it!" Anna says. "I knew he wanted something from you! Don't even think about setting up that meeting!"

The sharpness of her tone can't cut through the soft beauty of the morning. It doesn't change how pretty she looks tangled up in my sheets or the way her brown skin glows in these youthful hours. I watched her face slide from curiosity to surprise to shock as I told her about last night's conversation with James.

She wears her emotions like sequins on a dress, each one catching the light just a little different than the last, but they all got sparkle to 'em.

"He is right about somethin'." I let my fingers slide down from her shoulder to the crook of her elbow. "Terrance isn't faithful."

She rolls her eyes. "Oh, golly, stop the presses. Didn't anyone ever teach you that two wrongs don't make a right?"

"I would never cheat on you," I whisper.

She arches her left eyebrow. "Are we exclusive?"

I pull back, alarmed.

"Don't worry." She reaches over and gives the tip of my nose a playful tap. "I'm not seeing anyone else at the moment."

Hardly a forceful statement of commitment. "Terrance is humiliating my cousin."

"That's not your business."

"He's not cheating on her with just anyone," I go on.

"I know." Anna sighs and touches the silk scarf woven tightly around her straightened hair. "He likes white women. Everybody knows that."

"Everybody? Damn, he really *is* humiliatin' her!"

"An old beau cheated on me with a white woman once. Somehow, I managed to survive it. Want to know how?"

"Come on, Anna, can we stick to what matters? Margie's important to me."

Anna goes still. In her silence, my attention drifts to the motion of a long-legged spider making its way up the wall behind her.

"Fine," she eventually says, pulling back, adding an inch of space between us, "we'll cut to the silver lining. The colored elite will tolerate those within their group who have white mistresses, not white wives. And, trust me, no one is more obsessed with social standing than Terrance. But what Reaper is suggesting? He's not aiming for a fling."

"I know that."

"Anyway, Terrance can have a wandering eye and still be in love with his wife. One does not preclude the other."

"It's not just any white woman he's seeing."

She sighs as though she finds my concern for my cousin exhausting. "Is he still with that redhead married to the banker? The one with the Irish last name who denied him a loan? Admittedly not ideal, but in the highly unlikely event that her husband happens to wander into one of the Negro establishments Terrance likes to take his women to, the worst that will happen is there will be a fight, a divorce, and the cuckold will continue to refuse Negroes loans for the rest of his miserable life."

"I don't know nothin' about a redhead. I've only seen Terrance carrying on with his blond neighbor, Lester Nolan's wife."

Anna stares at me, as if she didn't understand what I just said. "No." She blinks several times, fast, like something's in her eye. "Terrance is too smart. He wouldn't."

"Lot of smart men get stupid when it comes to women." Maybe I'm one of them. Why am I sleeping with a gal I board with if she ain't promising to keep other suitors at bay?

"Did someone tell you this?"

"I saw them together at the Dunbar. They embraced right in the middle of the lobby."

"It was someone who looked like her," Anna says, sounding desperate. "Blondes like Dolores Nolan are a dime a dozen in L.A. Interchangeable. You mistook her."

"Anna, I didn't. It was her."

Clutching the sheet to her chest, she sits up, presses her back against the headboard. "Lester Nolan is one of the lead plaintiffs in the racial covenant suit against all of us."

"I know . . . Hold up, you think Lester's doing it because he knows about Terrance and his wife?"

"If Lester knew about Terrance and Dolores, Terrance would be arrested on some trumped-up charge . . . he'd meet some unfortunate accident in jail before he ever had the chance to see a judge."

Images of those children dancing the night before tumble into my mind. "L.A.'s not the South."

She lets out a bitter laugh. "Do you know what the difference is between the North and the South?"

I shake my head.

"The California police do quietly what the Southern Klan does loudly." She glares up at the ceiling fan as if it's her personal enemy. "Did Terrance happen to mention that Lester's brother-in-law, as in the husband of his sister, is a captain in the LAPD?"

There's a new turbulence in my gut, the sting of being force-fed something rotten.

"There are so many idiots here who act like the green in their wallets make them untouchable." She squeezes her eyes closed, causing puckers down the bridge of her nose. "They refuse to admit that green has never been the color of invincibility. Not unless it's mixed with white!"

I don't want to vomit in front of her. But it's a real possibility.

"You and I both know," she continues, "that the kind of damage Lester could inflict could easily spill over to the rest of us."

"What should we do?" I know there's no good answer. When she doesn't bother to make one up, I feel my respect for her break through some of my fear.

Under her breath she says, "He really is a fathead."

I prop myself up so that we're both sitting against my headboard. "Maybe I *should* arrange for James and Margie to meet."

"Oh, is that how you dismantle a bomb?" she asks dryly. "By adding gunpowder to the mix?"

"It might get Margie away from Terrance," I suggest, "and outta Lester's line of fire."

"Marguerite is not going to leave Terrance for Reaper, Charlie."

"Maybe not, but that doesn't mean she's not entitled to the choice."

Anna turns her face toward mine. Her features, hardened with frustration only a second ago, soften, then quiver. "What will happen to you then? What will Terrance do to you?"

"Don't know." I touch the lobe of her ear. She has perfect ears. "If it's the right thing to do, maybe I shouldn't be worrying about the personal costs."

She's leaning forward, taking from me a kiss so gentle it tickles. "I guess you haven't been here long enough," she whispers before pulling away. "You still haven't discovered the secret of Sugar Hill."

I watch as she slips out of my bed, dresses, and then disappears through the door.

———

"Charlie, how lovely to see you!" Margie exclaims as I approach. She's standing in her front yard with her boy and his nanny, Gertie. My goal was only to go for a walk to clear my head, but I was drawn to the route that brought me here. She points up at a tree at the very edge of her property. "We've discovered a nest," she explains.

"An owl nest!" Art pipes in. "Hoo, hoo!"

"That is the sound an owl makes," Gertie says. "But we don't know that's what this is."

"Oh, but it could be!" Margie declares. "How sweet to have one's very own owl! There were lots of owls where Charlie and I grew up, isn't that right, Charlie?"

Margie and Art have the same childlike joy. "Do you remember," I ask, "when we found that hole in the tree way back when we was young'uns?"

"Yes!" She brightens even more. "We were going to use it to store secret notes. I'd leave you one, you'd retrieve it and then leave one for me."

"But it turned out to be a woodpecker's nest," I say, now laughing.

Margie is giggling, too. "They gave me the fright of a lifetime!! That mama bird bopped me right on my head!"

I catch a hint of her old drawl and it brings me further into that pristine moment tucked inside those swampy years. "You told me I needed to try to catch one so you could kiss it, see if it would turn into a prince like them frogs did in them fairy tales!"

"Well, seein' how ugly ol' frogs always turn out to be princes, it seemed logical that a bird would turn into somethin' even more special. A king maybe. And you did try, which got that mama bird to start hasslin' you instead of me!"

We're both laughing hard now. Art and Gertie look at us like we might have lost our damn minds.

"And then your brother came 'round and tried to convince us that to calm that bird, we had to go catch it some worms!" I go on, laughing still. It takes me a good ten seconds to notice the mirth in Margie's eyes had turned into pain.

I shouldn't have mentioned her brother Vic.

"I'm sorry," I say, "I don't . . . that was insensitive . . ." But she waves off my fumbling apology with a hand gesture that indicates it's not a bother and a smile that asks me to shut up.

"It's not a woodpecker," Art says forcefully, clearly irritated now. "It's an owl! Hooooo."

"Of course, darlin'," Margie says when she collects herself and gives him a distracted pat on the head. Then she focuses in on him, as if sizing him up. Her broad, toothy grin has been replaced by a wistful smile. "They thought we were born laborers," she says quietly. "But we insisted on being children."

She's right. For a handful of years we managed to be kids.

But it was a childhood shortened with an axe.

If it wasn't for Margie, I wouldn't even have had that.

Art rubs his hands against the tree trunk. "Maybe we can climb the tree and see . . . Ow! Mommy, Mommy, I got an owie!" Tearfully he holds up his hand to reveal a splinter lodged in his palm.

Margie blanches and looks up at Gertie. "Go take care of that for him, will you?" she asks. "Darling, Gertie here will get you cleaned up and bring you back happy. Promise!"

As Gertie leads Art into the house, Margie turns back to me. "How was Hattie's party?"

Has she heard about James? That he was there looking for her?

"I did so want to go," she goes on, "but Terrance simply won't have it. Is it true that Clark Gable was there? Oh, I think I'd just swoon!"

Across the street, I hear a door open and close. Dolores Nolan's coming out of her house carrying a small suitcase.

Is that anger I see on Margie's face? But no, I must have been seeing things. There's nothing there now but a polite smile.

"Hello, Dolores," she calls out. "What's the suitcase for? Don't tell me you're moving out of our neighborhood."

I have never seen Margie intentionally antagonize another human being. Maybe it's a skill she picked up from her husband.

Dolores looks over her shoulder toward the house, nervous. "I'm visiting my mother this weekend."

"How lovely. Does she live far?"

But Dolores is done talking. She puts her suitcase in the trunk of her car and is out of the drive and down the street in less than a minute.

"She and her husband are absolutely horrid," Margie says as she watches the retreating car. And after it disappears around the corner, Margie continues to stare, as if she expects that empty bit of pavement where Dolores's car had just been to sprout a new one. "She's pretty, though."

I look up at the nest of the unknown bird. "Not my type."

"I thought blondes were every man's type." The comment's delivered with a light touch. If you didn't know Margie, you'd think she was being playful. That she's not hinting at something dark.

Then again, maybe she's not. Maybe I *don't* know her. I don't know what this woman, Marguerite, wants for herself or which compromises best serve her.

She fiddles with the skinny little belt she's wearing over her dress, pulling it a little to the left, then bringing it back to the right. "Never mind me. I get a bit cockeyed when Terrance is away."

For the second time today my stomach cramps into knots. "Terrance is not here?"

"When *is* he here these days? Always taking meetings at all hours or just indulging in his aimless, after-work joyrides. Why, you'd think his office was his home and his family his part-time job!" She laughs to let me know it's a joke even as she wraps her arms around herself, giving herself a hug. "This weekend he's meeting with some of the out-of-town Golden State agents. He'll be back Monday."

Now I'm the one glaring at the spot where Dolores's car last was. What I'm feeling isn't the kind of rage that I tapped into on the battlefield. It's worse. There's no approved outlet for this.

You don't gotta be a man of God to learn from the lessons of Adam and Eve. You don't need to be no minister to know that if you're in the Garden of Eden you can't be fooling with the temptations of a snake no matter how juicy that apple's looking.

An image of my fist smashing into Terrance's nose flashes through my mind. But I can't afford to do nothing like that.

My rage has to find a compromise.

"Margie, do you still think Ingrid Bergman should have run off with Humphrey Bogart instead of the fella who played her husband?"

She looks at me quizzically before piecing it together. "Oh, you're talking about *Casablanca*? Yes, of course I do. Although in the movie she didn't have much of a choice." She sighs, hugs herself a little tighter. "The story would have been so much better if she had just been given a choice."

It's exactly what I needed to hear. "How about you meet me for an evening stroll tonight, cousin?" I suggest. "There're some things I've discovered in this neighborhood I'd like to show you."

"Such as? Don't tell me Bogart just moved in," she says with a giggle as I shake my head. "Really, Charlie, you've only been here two weeks, and now you want to show me around my own neighborhood? Goodness, you've become an even bigger know-it-all than Terrance!"

"We go way back, Margie." I smile up at that nest. "Indulge me."

Chapter 16

"This is the house you wanted to show me?" Margie cranes her neck up, as if studying the roof. "Did you really think I could miss it?"

It's just past seven, late enough for the sun to be gone, but not so late that the dark's got weight. "You know anything about the man who owns it?"

"I hear they call him Reaper. I've never seen him, but he had the whole neighborhood abuzz when he first moved in. He throws giant parties that you can hear from blocks away." She lowers her voice to an excited whisper. "They say he's a criminal of some sort. It's rather exciting . . . or it would be if he lived elsewhere. Sugar Hill is more suited for the scandals of the stars than the underworld."

I slide my hands into my pockets, wondering if I've made a mistake. "Maybe the rumors ain't true."

"Rumors rarely get things completely right . . . or completely wrong. Of course, it all drives Terrance mad. He says it's bad enough we have to put up with the Hollywood glitterati, but now we must deal with colored gangsters, too." I can't tell if she's laughing because she agrees with that assessment or if she's taking pleasure in her husband's consternation.

I should have listened to Anna. But when I told James I'd be bringing Margie by he practically threw himself at my feet.

"I met him," I say.

"Who?"

"The man who lives here. James Mann."

"James? I've always had a fondness for that name."

"Have you known anyone who goes by that name?"

She laughs. "It's not exactly like being named Tutankhamun, now, is it? Or even Marguerite for that matter."

"I mean anyone special. Someone who gave you your fondness for the name."

She sniffs, pulls on the lapels of her coat. "Really, Charlie, what are you going on about? It's getting cold."

Above us somewhere there's the low roar of a small aircraft. I silently remind myself that on this side of the Atlantic, the planes don't have payloads to drop. "I was just asking if you ever knew someone special . . . Margie, you blushin'?"

"Enough." It's the first time I've heard her voice go hard like this. "We're not children anymore, don't tease."

"James was the first to show me 'round South Central. He even helped me out when I needed a new suit for my Golden State interview. I was hoping to introduce you."

"What, now?" She gives me a queer look.

"Seeing as we're here, it seems as good a time as any."

She's staring at me hard, like she's trying to work a puzzle.

"Come on." I urge her through the gate and up the stairs to the front door. "If you don't like the look of him, we'll turn right around. But I suspect the two of you are gonna hit it off."

"It almost sounds like you're setting me up on a date," she says with a laugh, but by the way she's eyeing me I can tell her jest is really a question.

The feeling of guilt comes out of nowhere. Terrance has been good to me. He's given me a chance at a fancy new life I would have never dared wish for.

But he's fucking white women while telling Margie that her wish to go to a Hollywood party is somehow immoral. That is probably the real reason she wasn't at that meeting at Hattie's. He's sidelining her. Forbidding Margie to stand with allies while he runs around bedding foes.

He's hurting her.

The guilty feeling is gone. I ring the bell.

It's the butler, Daniel, who greets us. "Mr. Trammell," he says, stepping aside and making way. "Mr. Mann has been expecting you."

"Charlie?" Margie asks, nervous, not moving from the doormat.

I take both her hands. "I know it's been years since we lived in the same town. Maybe we don't know each other as well as we used to. But we're still family. You can trust me."

She hesitates and then tentatively steps inside James's home.

"He's in the study," Daniel says. "This way."

We follow him through the house, Margie openly ogling her surroundings.

"How does he manage it?" she whispers.

"I . . . think he imports champagne and French wine." But this explanation still rings slightly false.

Daniel opens the door to the study. "Mr. Mann will ring me if you need anything," he says before leaving us.

We remain in the hall. Everything about this situation feels explosive.

Finally, Margie bites her lip, raises her shoulders in a nervous shrug, and steps inside.

And then she gasps, her hand flying to her mouth.

He's standing in the center of the room holding a giant bouquet of pink roses and white daisies.

"You came," he says.

"My God." Her voice is muffled, struggling to reach through her fingers.

"You're finally here." When she doesn't move or speak, he swallows hard and scratches at his neck. "Charlie, could you give us a minute?"

"No," she says quickly, still frozen in place, "Charlie, stay."

James nods his head. "A lot of time has passed. And you're married. I know that. But . . ." He pauses.

There's so much emotion on his face it feels like I'm violating his privacy by just looking at him.

"I've been searching for you. Everywhere."

Margie's hand drops back to her side. Her mouth closes even as her eyes stay wide. "All these years . . . you've been looking for me?"

"Yes."

Her head starts swiveling this way and that, as if she's trying to figure out where she is. "All this . . . is yours?"

"Yes."

"But that can't be." Her whole body's trembling. "It's a fairy tale. Make-believe. This house . . ."

"Do you like it?" he asks. "If not, I'll buy another. Anywhere in the world."

She lets loose with a startled laugh. "But you don't mean it. No one can just snap their fingers . . . and buy another . . ." Her voice trails off, her eyes drawn back to the finery around her. "It can't be possible. None of this is possible." But this time she doesn't sound too sure.

"For you, I can do anything," he says. "All that I have and everything I've become, it's for you."

She takes in a sharp, gasping breath, like a drowning woman who has managed to surface for air.

And then she takes a step in his direction, so unsteady you'd think she was balancing on stilts instead of heels. "Our last night when I . . ." One more step, then two, then three, like being compelled by a hypnotist. "You . . . we . . ."

"That night," he says firmly, "I fell in love with you."

Again she freezes. "Oh." She's just close enough for her fingers to brush against the petals of the bouquet.

He watches her. Waiting. When she doesn't speak, he presses. "This isn't the first time I've told you that. Nothing's changed. Not for me."

She gawks at him, at the mahogany furniture, at the antique vases that balance on the handcrafted end tables. And then finally her gaze settles . . . on her wedding band. "You were so strong, ambitious, capable, and . . . I told my parents about the promises you made, I told my friends that you were my prince, my future. But . . . they told me that men . . . that *you* . . . you couldn't have meant it. They told me that 'I love you' are just words men say when they . . ." Now her voice is quivering, too, giving her a pretty vibrato. "Men say it to get what they want."

James's nostrils flare. Without moving, he grows larger, managing to take up more space, more air.

Anna had described James that first night I met her. She had said he looked dangerous. I hadn't agreed.

But I see it now.

"Listen to me." He puts down the bouquet, moves in closer, using his hand to tilt her chin up so she can't look away. "No man of sound mind could hold you in his arms and not fall in love."

Her trembling stops.

They remain like that, quiet and still as statues. As if Rodin carved his lovers out of onyx instead of marble.

"Margie," I say, making sure my voice is just loud enough to be heard, "if you want to leave, I'll escort you."

The only sound is from the second hand of a grandfather clock, pressed up against the wall. Ten seconds, fifteen, twenty, twenty-one, twenty-two . . . And then to the rhythm of that clock she finally speaks.

"Go home, Charlie."

"You sure?"

"Go home." Her voice drops down to the octave of command. I move to leave.

"Charlie," she calls out, stopping me. She's got her hand placed over his heart. "Don't tell anyone."

Negroes have known dark clouds and ill winds for generations. They don't panic us anymore . . . Sometimes it's the ill wind that blows the dark clouds out of the sky.

—Langston Hughes, *Chicago Defender*

Chapter 17

The next morning James came to thank me in person, just stopping by, unannounced, on his way to church, where he would thank God for the same sin.

He called that afternoon to express his gratitude again. He called me at work twice the next day, swept up in waves of appreciation that crashed down on me like an avalanche of rocks. I apologetically confessed that I had told Anna I'd arranged the meeting between him and Margie, but instead of being mad he had appeared excited that another person was in on the secret. Like he wanted the world to know. I found myself in the position of lecturing *him* on the importance of discretion.

On the flip side, it's been six days since I arranged that fateful rendezvous and Margie still ain't said shit.

But I know from James that she sees him every chance she gets. While Terrance is away, at work or busy with less sympathetic activities.

The two of them need a divorce. It's 1945. No one would be slapping a scarlet letter on them. They should divorce and go with the person they really want.

But if Terrance wants Dolores . . .

The thought gives me a headache. Four weeks and five days remain until the trial. If Terrance's affair with one of the plaintiffs' wives is revealed, it will surely be used against all of us. How can Loren convince a judge that his clients are good neighbors if one of them is breaking up homes?

Tangled webs and land mines, that's what Sugar Hill is made of. I use my lunch break to go for a walk. I stay far away from the Dunbar just to keep from running into Terrance and his white poison.

I walk by an establishment, the kind of place that looks like it doesn't open until the moon is on the rise. The sign outside says LA FÊTE in lights that aren't on. The door's propped open and I hear someone inside say, "Let me clear something up for you, history doesn't have collateral value. Pay your premium or lose your policy."

It's Terrance's voice. Seems I haven't avoided him after all. I peek inside, trying to be discreet, but he's standing too close to the door and spots me immediately. "Charlie! Getting a little breathing space from Sam? I know he's a pain, but you won't be shadowing him for much longer."

There's a fella standing behind him, a mop in his hand, beads of sweat along his hairline despite the cool winds blowing from the outside. He's got on dress pants and a long-sleeved collared shirt that flops loose at his wrists due to the absence of cuff links. His curls have been oiled and flattened into a conk. "Terry," he says, "I got a new hustle. I've been payin' off my debts. I'll have enough to pay off my premiums, too, if you can give me a little extra time—"

"I run a business," Terrance interrupts.

"Minnie's pregnant again. Did I tell you that? I just tryin' to have a little security for the kids is all."

"Says the man who's always hiding from bookies," Terrance replies with a disappointed shake of his head.

"That's what I'm tryin' to tell ya. As of last week, I've got all those bookies paid off. If you could give me a little longer to pay *you,* I won't have nothin' to apologize to Minnie for. Come on, man, you know if our situations were reversed, I'd help you out."

"If our situations were reversed?" Terrance repeats disbelievingly before letting out a mean, laughing howl. The man cowers from that sound.

"You and Anna will be joining us at the Somervilles' tonight, yes?" Terrance says to me, no longer interested in the pleading man. "I don't know about the food, but Lena will be there, so the scenery will be good." He gives my arm a friendly slap before calling over his shoulder, "It's all due on the first, Pinky, along with interest from the missed payments." And with that, Terrance is gone.

Unthinkingly, I turn to the man he called Pinky, feeling like I should apologize for witnessing his humiliation. He straightens under my gaze and holds his arm out so the mop is farther from his body. "Janitor called in sick. This ain't my job."

"I figured as much," I say stupidly, doing what I can to help him salvage his pride. The whole place looks like it could use a pep talk, with its scratched floors and the weak fragrance of soap trying and failing to cover up the smell of the previous night's spent cigarettes and spilled liquor.

"I'm not sayin' it's beneath me. I ain't tryin' to act like I'm above nobody," he says, scratching at his neck. "Just that this ain't my regular gig. See, I'm the manager of this place." When I don't seem suitably impressed, he adds, "I used to be the owner."

Odd, bragging about how you were once better than you are.

"I've seen you," he says, his eyes narrowing, "or do I know you? Have we done business?"

The way he says *business* gives me the sense he's not talking about anything legal. Suddenly I don't feel so sorry for him.

"We haven't." I turn to leave.

"Wait, I saw you at Reaper's!"

That stops me. "You know James?"

"Yeah, Reaper! Man, that guy's somethin' else, ain't he? Got more lettuce in his wallet than a whole cabbage patch. Generous, too. He set me up with a little work." Warmed up by the subject, he reaches forward and offers me his hand. "Colson Pinkman at your service."

The name Pinkman rings some kind of bell, but I can't place it. "Charlie Trammell," I say.

The man has a firm, friendly shake. His air of insecurity gets smothered quick by a sudden show of jollity. "You know ol' Reaper well?"

It's a question I've been asking myself a lot lately. "Sometimes I think I do, sometimes I think I don't." I pause so as not to be drowned out by the impatient honking of a passing truck. "Even to his friends he's a bit of a mystery."

"Tell me about it!" Pinky scratches at his forearm as he chuckles. I get a glimpse of a few veins on his arm that are popping out blue. "My cousin's friend knew him from his Chicago days."

"James had Chicago days?"

"Sure did! Back when he was a young fellow doing his speakeasy thing. He got in the game before he even hit his second decade of life. They say he's so bad even the Italians didn't mess with his operation."

"You hear all this from your cousin's friend?" Outside, another motorist discovers his horn, a pedestrian answers with a loud obscenity. "He knew James back then?"

"Yeah, well, in fact he said it was his uncle who knew him. But he got the whole story."

"Your cousin's friend's uncle." This is better than a game of telephone. "What kinda work did he set you up with?"

"Aw, he just helped me land a few odd jobs is all. These days it's hard to make it on one paycheck." Pinky taps his mop. "A man can't be too proud to roll up his sleeves every now and then and do the kind of work others might look down upon. Rich as he is, Reaper respects that kind of work ethic. I like him. But I'm careful with him, too! They say back in the day crossing him was the same as inviting death home for dinner. That's why they call the man Reaper!"

"Uh-huh." I glance at my watch. It hasn't told time in years, but it works well as a prop. "I gotta get goin'."

"'Course, calling him Reaper is easier than trying to remember all his names," he goes on, ignoring my attempt to leave. "Didn't go by

Mann back then, I think he used Howard, and I don't think that was his real name, either."

It stops me.

James told me he had changed his name. That part's true.

So what else might be true?

"I have to go," I mumble. I step outside just as the clouds move aside, exposing the sun. The cause of the honking is a rusty old Ford that broke down in the middle of a lane. Throngs of people push past, rubbernecking at the two colored gentlemen and the Chicana gal trying to push it to the curb, laughing and cursing as they do. All these different kinds of brown here, a chocolate melting pot, bitter and sweet. James had said he likes the energy of the place. I like it, too.

James probably told a lot of people he changed his name. It's not a secret. That man Pinky knowing about it doesn't mean a thing.

They call him Reaper because of his work in the French Resistance. He's not perfect, but he ain't dangerous.

I would never reunite Margie with a criminal.

I wouldn't be able to handle the guilt.

Chapter 18

The Somervilles' house is not like Hattie's and it's nothing like James's. The soft overhead light in the dining room makes everybody's brown skin bronze while we cast shadows over the lamb being served on each plate, plump and juicy. Served by a wife, not a maid.

A wife who, due to her degrees, is affectionately called Dr. Vada by many in the community.

Anna's to my right and underneath the table's dark wood she pushes her foot against mine. I like the pressure of it. I like the way her perfume smells sugary and the food smells rich.

Lena is talking to Loren Miller, who sits across from her, shoulder to shoulder with his very pregnant wife, Juanita. "I think it's a travesty," Lena says. "Write a book or poetry. Don't turn your back on your childhood dreams!"

"Hear, hear," Margie chimes in, smiling at Loren. She and Terrance are sitting to the Millers' right. "It's positively unthinkable that a man as brilliant as you would limit himself!"

"You'd prefer me as an unemployed writer than as a working lawyer?" Loren retorts, flashing Lena a mouthful of tobacco-stained teeth.

"Of course not," Lena says. She's got one of them long ballerina necks. When she arches it to the side, you get the feeling there should be an orchestra accompanying her. "I'm simply suggesting you be an unemployed writer *and* a working lawyer! Who says one can't have it all?"

That gets a laugh from the room and a small smile from me. The Somervilles are hosting nine of us, including Norman and his wife, Edythe.

"What about you, Lena?" Juanita asks, slicing into a lamb loin, watching the red ooze out of it. "Are you living your childhood dreams?"

"I did always want to be a performer." Lena curls long, slender fingers under her chin. "But I'd hoped to be a performer who could get a little more work."

"It'll come," Norman says, but he sounds like a man trying to placate rather than convince.

"How about you, Marguerite?" Vada pipes up. "What did you dream you'd become when you were a little girl?"

"Oh, goodness, what a question!" The diamond on Margie's finger catches the light and sends rainbows across the table. "Charlie, you knew me back then, did I dream of becoming anything of use?"

"You were gonna be a princess," I remind her.

Again, voices join in laughter. But it's the polite kind, not the rowdy joy I've become accustomed to hearing in Louise's card room as she fleeces another poor soul at poker.

"And what does that entail?" Edythe asks.

"Being a princess? Hmmm . . . well, having pretty things and being *very* glamorous." Margie contorts her face into an expression of exaggerated snobbery. "It entails having a knight in shining armor to keep you safe and sheltered from enemies who would do you harm or bring you low." But some of the lilt in her voice is gone. Her chin, which had been playfully lifted, descends to a more pensive position. "It entails being respected and . . . adored. Princesses are adored." She catches herself and, once again fully aware of her audience, widens her smile until it hints at jest. "Of course, that was when I was just a silly little girl. Now that I've grown up, I aim to be much grander than a lowly princess."

Again, polite laughter. "And what's grander than a princess?" Dr. Somerville asks.

"Perhaps she's the queen to my king," Terrance says.

"Or an empress," Anna suggests, ignoring Terrance's effort to insert himself into the story.

"Why stop there?" Lena chews thoughtfully on a piece of meat before adding, "Personally, I'd like to try my hand at a benevolent dictator."

It's that line that gets the first real raucous laughter of the night.

When it dies down Terrance uses the lull to take the reins of the conversation. "Loren, when are you and Juanita going to come join us in Sugar Hill? You should be living among other intellectuals of achievement. Not slumming it with the east-side communists and homosexuals."

"You'd be surprised," Loren says with a chuckle. "Those communists and homosexuals are some of the most intellectual people I know."

"You're representing us"—Terrance's voice got some gravel in it now—"as our lawyer. When you allow your image to be soiled by a bunch of radicals and deviants you put all our reputations in jeopardy."

"You know I'm not a religious man," Loren replies, "but if I were, I might point out that Jesus kept the company of prostitutes and was himself a radical. Is he not a good representative?"

Terrance stabs at his dinner as if he is killing it himself. "If Jesus had been a colored man in America, he would have had to tell the prostitutes to find other company, otherwise no one would have even bothered to take him down from the damn cross!"

Vada shoots her husband an alarmed look. Margie places one hand on the edge of the table, the other rises to cover a nervous cough. Her eyes flit desperately toward the door, like she wants to flee from even the mention of anything ugly still breathing in her world.

She coughs again, murmuring a barely audible apology about her throat having gone dry. It gets Terrance's attention. He reaches over and takes her hand so tenderly, folks might mistake him for being a man in love. "I'm just saying we need more people like you in our community, Loren," he explains, the abrasion in his tone packed away, "and fewer idiots like America's favorite mealymouthed maid, Louise, Ben 'Uncle Tom' Carter, and Scarlett O'Hara's Mammy." He shakes his head in disgust. "It'd be nice if you could convince one of them to sell you their house and have them move into yours. Better your circumstances while bettering ours."

"Now you really have gone too far," Lena snaps. "Hattie's a gift to every community she's in."

Edythe and Norman exchange glances. It's clear they don't share Lena's opinion.

Dr. Somerville releases a tired sigh. "Lena, the roles you've chosen—"

"Not chosen." The cords in her neck are straining, making the delicate look strong. "We *all* can only take the roles we're *given*."

"I only mean to say," Dr. Somerville continues, undeterred, "that while standing before the camera's lens you've conducted yourself quite differently than Hattie, Louise, Ben, and most of the other colored actors who live among us. And while I respect that we all must make a living, there are more noble routes to success than the ones they've chosen. Everyone at this table is evidence of that."

Loren shakes his head and rubs his eyes like he's tired. "You are blaming actors for the actions of studios."

As they argue, I study Dr. Somerville's so-called evidence at the table.

All these folks whose financial success is apparently noble are lighter than either Anna or me.

Anna and I are also lighter than every Hollywood Negro I've met aside from Lena.

It doesn't take a genius to figure out what's going on. High yellows like the Houstons and the Somervilles are seen as being sophisticated. Educated. Light-skinned girls with slender legs and curves that whisper instead of shout . . . girls like Lena . . . are alluring, beautiful.

Seen that way by colored folk, that is. White folk got no use for 'em at all.

Dark-skinned Negroes who got meat on the bone are seen as oafish, ugly, comically dumb.

And that makes them damn useful to the white folk.

This is why Louise was so offended by the head of the NAACP insisting that Lena was the kind of Negro woman Hollywood should be casting.

This is what Hattie meant when she said Lena being "practically white" would only make it harder for her to get acting work.

While the Negro business world might not be fully welcoming of their darker-skinned brothers, Hollywood has little interest in coloreds who don't look fully African.

And the reasoning of both groups makes my stomach churn.

"Give me a break, Loren," Terrance is saying. "My neighbor Les is doing everything he can to force us out. And you want to know why? It's because he thinks none of us are better than the dirty stereotypes he sees on-screen."

"Well, I don't know if you can blame Hattie for the Nolans," Vada says. "If those two are taking their cues from the movies, it's probably because they're too illiterate for books."

"That's definitely true of Les," Terrance agrees, smirking. "His wife's not so bad."

Margie finishes off her glass by tilting it to the ceiling in a quick motion.

"But most white people are more like Les," Terrance continues. "Which is why we have to diminish the influence of the idiots who make us look bad. And I'm not just talking about actors. That Reaper guy, he's a problem."

"I disagree," Margie says mildly.

"What?" But Terrance doesn't give her time to answer. "You don't know what you're talking about. Trust me, I know trouble when I see it."

"He does," Norman agrees. "Remember Douglas Watts? That account manager we had at Golden State?" He turns to me, his eyes lighting up with a memory. "Terrance told me right away that he was the sneaky sort. I thought he was being paranoid. But Terrance kept at it, and sure enough, Watts was embezzling money." To Margie he says,

"Your husband can get a read on a person better and faster than anyone I know."

"Not this time." Margie picks up her napkin and daintily dabs at the corners of her mouth. "You know, I just recently met Mr. Mann at the grocer. Isn't it impressive that a fellow of his means would do his own shopping? Why, Terrance hasn't been to so much as a fruit stand in years."

Terrance's nostrils flare.

"I do believe," Margie continues, "James Mann is more humble than he appears."

"Humble?" Dr. Somerville chortles. "I think you can buy half of Jamaica for the price of that car he drives."

"He likes nice things. We can all relate to that." Margie leans forward, addressing her next remarks to Norman. "Mr. Mann imports extraordinarily expensive wines and champagne from France and even Chiantis from Italy. I'm dying to try them."

"He told you that's how he makes his fortune?" Norman asks.

"You know how much people will pay for all the things we were deprived of during the war. He simply took advantage. It's the American dream. Really, there's not a single reason to worry about him. In fact"—Margie turns her beaming smile to her husband—"he's having a party next weekend. Let's go, shall we?"

"You can't be serious!" Terrance demands.

I'm having the same thought. I can't figure out what Margie's playing at.

"Maybe you should go, Terrance," Norman muses.

Terrance is turning red. "What?"

"Ask the man a few questions," Norman explains. "If Marguerite is right, great! I'll be able to sleep a little better at night. But if she's wrong . . ."

"I'm not," Margie insists.

"But if she is," Norman continues, directing his words to Terrance, as if this subject is too consequential to bother debating with women, "it would be helpful to know. Let Marguerite introduce you, and then give me your impression."

The request's got the sound of an order. Terrance's red is deepening to purple.

But Norman pours balm on that anger before it can sizzle. "Everyone in this room, with the exception of the two of you, has been to at least one of Reaper's parties and none of us has learned the first thing about him. But you, Terrance, you have a talent."

Terrance hesitates; he's listening.

"Every time someone has tried to take advantage of Golden State you've been the one to sniff out the grift. Why not go to Reaper's party and see if he's someone who might sabotage Sugar Hill? Use your talents to protect our homes."

"Oh, for goodness' sake, James is not an enemy soldier. He's our neighbor!" Margie protests.

"Sure," Terrance says, his tone now striking a note that hovers between smugness and kindness. He smiles at Norman. "Let's go to this party of his."

Chapter 19

The Houstons offer us a ride home, but Anna and I take advantage of the mild weather and walk. Last night the winds had been blowing so hard I half expected the streets to be littered with fallen palm trees. But all that was blown away was the smog, giving us a view of the welkin spattered with stars. I keep looking up. I like being reminded that behind ugliness there's still beauty worth seeing.

I also like the smell of Anna's hair. I keep getting little whiffs every time she tilts her head in my direction.

And I like that we're holding hands. Not like new lovers, but like we're familiar. Like we got something going on that goes beyond the bedroom.

"It was a nice evening," Anna says.

"Yeah." I tune in to the sound of her heels clicking on the pavement, cars roaring on the streets farther down the hill, an owl hooting up in some tree. "Still, sometimes the things those folks say rub me the wrong way."

"They're just scared is all. Just like the rest of us. Trying to protect what they've earned, although Terrance might want to try a little harder at that." She takes a deep breath. "Do you think if Marguerite announced she was running off with Reaper, Terrance would try to win her back?"

"Maybe. Or he might go public with Dolores just for spite."

"He wouldn't . . . would he? Please tell me his brain is bigger than his ego. Oh, for God's sake, what am I saying?" She shakes her shoulders and looks down at her handbag. "That would make him Einstein."

I manage a small smile, acknowledging the joke, but there's one thing I have to correct her on. "You shouldn't call him Reaper," I say quietly.

"Oh, not this again."

"He's got nothin' in common with the Grim Reaper," I insist as we carefully step over a tree root that's upending the sidewalk. "He loves life and he's probably the most optimistic fella I know."

"Come now, Charlie. If the Grim Reaper didn't love life, he wouldn't keep taking it." She releases my hand and pulls a pack of Old Golds from her bag, then starts rummaging for something else. "And there is nothing more optimistic than Death. *Death* always gets what he wants. Eventually." She lifts her face up to me, looking a little dejected. "I think I left my lighter at the Somervilles'. Do you by chance . . ." When I shake my head, she sighs and drops the cigarettes back in her bag. "If I had gotten what *I* wanted when I was very, very little, I'd be an acrobat right now. That was my dream."

"Are you good at gymnastics?"

"Can't even do a cartwheel." She returns her hand to mine. "After that, I wanted to be a writer, and finally I just wanted to get the hell out of Missouri . . . which I did. I suppose that makes me a success story."

"I always knew you were special."

"Maybe I am. Today, Carlotta, that editor I keep talking about at the *California Eagle*? She said she's going to publish my article, Charlie. I suppose this particular piece is a little controversial. She gave me a lot of pushback, but she's given in. It'll be in the paper next Friday!"

"That's great, Anna!" My God, I love it when she smiles. In bed she always smiles, right before her mouth forms into that perfect O.

She nudges me playfully. "And you? What did you want?"

"When I was little?" I look up at the stars again. Five shine brightly, while the others seem to struggle to compete. "I wanted to be white." The childhood secret flies out of me. Thought I had it locked away good. But the peace of this night, the wine that is still warming me, the woman by my side, together unlocked the box. "Turnin' white is the only thing I remember wishin' for as a boy. I could've wished for safety. Or opportunity. Or the respect of my fellow man. But what'd be the point when bein' white could've gotten me all that and more? If I'd found a magic lamp, one wish would've worked just as well as three."

Anna is quiet for a minute. Maybe two. We walk under a streetlight that briefly brightens up the world around us before we step back into darkness. "God made you a Negro for a reason."

"Hard to believe a girl as rational as you still believes in God."

"Oh, I'm more than rational, I'm downright cynical. It's exhausting to see this world through such a clear lens. By the time Sunday comes, I'm aching for God." Her voice has gone thin, barely loud enough to be heard over the city's low rumble. "Going to church is like crawling into the most comfortable bed in the world after a day of hard labor."

"Bed's where you go for sleepin'."

"No, a bed is where you go for dreaming." She briefly touches her face, almost like she's dabbing at a tear. "Was your atheism handed down to you by your parents or did you come to it on your own?"

I've never explicitly said I was an atheist, but the label isn't a bad fit. "My mother was a Southern Baptist like everybody else I grew up with. And when life got ugly, she assured me death would be beautiful. In heaven, God would make it up to us."

"I take it she wasn't too convincing," Anna says with a wry smile.

"By the time I was eight, I realized there were things that can't be made up for. Not even by God. And if there really was a God, He would know that." I roll back my shoulders, trying to keep my posture straight under the weight of sad memories.

"That's not an unreasonable conclusion," she concedes. "I've often wondered why God doesn't kill off the evildoers before they can cause suffering. But He has reasons for everything, even if we don't always understand." I think she's about to lecture me like my mama used to do. But then I see her teeth gleaming through the darkness in the form of a smile. "I believe God had His reasons for making you a colored man. Perhaps not the least of which being that those beautiful lips would look completely bizarre on a white face."

It's while we're laughing that I spot, in the distance, coming in our direction, the firefly light of a cigarette. Someone weaving like they might be sauced. But it's not until we walk another full block that I can see that the man is Lester. Walking south toward his place while we walk north toward ours.

When he sees us, he stops. Watches us while puffing away.

I pull Anna tighter to my side and keep moving.

When we're close enough to see the red covering the whites of his eyes, Lester speaks up. "You scared of me?"

His slur brings up recollections of what a drunken white man can do.

What America allows him to do.

Yet my answer is "No." Spoken clear and firm.

And we keep walking, even though he is right in our path. I slide my thumb back and forth over the inside of Anna's wrist. I feel her pulse jumping.

But the pace of our steps is steady.

"You're not? So it's true then?" he calls out.

I don't answer. We're only a few feet away. In less than ten seconds we'll be past him.

The smell of tobacco, whiskey, and vomit on his breath stretches the distance between us. "If you're not scared, then it's gotta be true," he says as we maneuver around him. "You niggers really are stupid."

Words.

Not violence.

He doesn't turn to follow us home.

And so I hold my tongue and keep us moving. It's the best way I know to keep the peace.

But as we walk away, I gotta ask myself . . .

What would Terrance have said? Terrance, the blowhard.

Terrance, the strongman who cuts his enemies down with a viciousness served up with a smile.

Terrance, the man who sleeps with married white women without an ounce of fear.

Terrance, that no-good, blustering, grandiose, libertine motherfucker.

Being Terrance's friend is a mixed bag.

But *being* Terrance must be *amazing*.

Chapter 20

Terrance is staring up at James's impossibly high ceilings, then to the curved staircase with the iron railing. The laughter and voices of what has to be hundreds of revelers ricochet off the walls, coming back as echoes that just add to the din. Under my right foot, the marble floor's sticky with expensive champagne spilled before we arrived.

Terrance finally brings his focus back to Margie, Anna, and me. "There is no way in hell this was all paid for with French wine."

"He has other imports, too," Margie assures him. "Come, we're in the way."

There are more and more guests filtering in. I'm looking for faces I recognize. I spot a few of the actors and musicians from Hattie's gatherings.

But mostly it's strangers.

"Where do you think they all come from?" I ask Anna. If they're not from the neighborhood, it might explain some of their carefree smiles and careless intemperance. They aren't burdened by the fear of a looming trial.

Anna lifts an eyebrow and a shoulder. "All over the city? It's not hard to convince people to come to a mansion to drink another man's liquor."

Margie whirls to face Anna. "So now we're judging him for being popular? Is there anything the man can do right in your eyes?"

Terrance is standing behind Margie, so she can't see the way he's studying her: like a cop who thinks he might have stumbled onto an impending heist.

I'm trying to remember why I agreed to come to this thing.

"Ever since we were kids, you were always one to see the best in folks, always liftin' 'em up," I say to Margie, hoping she'll hear the warning under my cheer. "But you've only met him once. You're not in the best position to judge." I straighten a little and turn to face Terrance. "That said, I've spent a good deal of time with him. He's become a friend, a good one at that."

It's the best I can do. I can't call a man who would sleep with a married woman trustworthy. I can't say I haven't seen signs of shady dealings, either. Yet, despite it all, I still don't fully buy that James is an actual criminal.

Maybe that's 'cause he don't fit the mold. The colored men I've known who break laws for a living are pimps and hustlers making just enough to scrape at the bottom of America's middle class. But James is out here living a Bugsy Siegel kind of life.

That in and of itself feels like some kind of racial progress.

"I just want us to focus on the right things," Margie says, straining to be heard over the man a few feet to our left, serenading his friends with an off-tune drinking song. "Mr. Mann is a very impressive individual. I'm sure you'll see that."

"You're impressed by him?" Terrance asks.

"Everyone is," she replies.

A waiter with a tray filled with flutes of champagne stops by our little group and we all eagerly take a glass.

"Isn't it gorgeous?" Margie gazes adoringly at the bubbling gold. "Of all the things we had to sacrifice during the war, it was the loss of champagne that was saddest for me."

All three of us gawk at her as she continues to admire her drink.

And then Terrance laughs. Howls as if he's just heard the funniest, most delightful thing in the world.

I'm not laughing.

The memories play like a sped-up newsreel. Friends fighting, dying, severed limbs, nonstop gunfire, bullets splintering bone, blood bursting from men like oil wells.

For Margie, the biggest loss was champagne.

"Well, then, let us toast," Anna says, lifting her glass, "to peace." Then she looks at me more pointedly and adds with a touch of kindness and compassion, "May there be peace."

"Hear, hear!" Terrance tilts his glass until half his drink has slipped down his throat. "Damn, maybe this *is* good enough to make a man rich."

"It's certainly enough to make a man happy," we hear someone say. It's our host.

He reaches for Terrance's hand. "I don't believe we've met. James Mann."

"Terrance Lewis." Terrance shakes James's hand, a look of wary curiosity on his face. "You have an impressive home here."

"It's a little grand, but it's great for parties." James glances back at me before going on. "I take it you're a good friend of Charlie and Anna's?"

"I got the man his job," Terrance says, pointing his thumb in my direction. "Think that makes me a friend *and* benefactor."

"Any friend of Charlie's is a friend of mine. And Mrs. Lewis." The smile James turns on Margie is no wider than the one he's given to the rest of us.

But it curls different.

"I'm so glad you and your husband were able to make it."

Margie sips delicately at her cherished champagne and thanks him for his hospitality.

"I've been trying to get to know as many of my neighbors as possible," James goes on.

"We're almost a mile from here," Terrance notes. He pauses as a few people jostle past him, one of them looking like he's about to interrupt to introduce himself to James, but Terrance gives him a look that keeps him moving. "I'd say," he continues, "that puts us on the edge of the dictionary's definition of neighbor."

"A mile is nothing in a city the size of Los Angeles. Allow me to show you around the place," James says, then to Anna and me, "You're welcome to join us, but since you've been here, a tour might be a bore. If you're interested, Billie Holiday will be performing soon in the courtyard."

"You hired Billie Holiday as the entertainment?" I ask, but the enthusiasm I would normally feel ain't as strong as it should be. I keep thinking about Margie and her so-called sacrifice. How it reminds me of the Southern white women who bemoan not having enough hats in front of their Negro maids, who aren't even paid enough to feed their families.

"Yes, I've always been a fan of hers." James takes a flute from another tray that passes by. "And she's a fan of my imports." He turns back to Terrance and Margie. "We'll start with the library."

Anna and I watch the three navigate the crowd, a private group that ignores the pleas for attention from the other guests they pass.

"She's my cousin," I say quietly as they disappear around a corner. "There was a time when I considered her my best friend." I look out at the menagerie of brown faces, then through them into my own past. "I want to be able to still like her."

I get a nice shiver as Anna gently runs her fingers up and down the nape of my neck. "If you need your friends to be perfect angels, you're going to have to wait 'til you're dead to have any." She turns, facing me, drapes her arms over my shoulders. "Have you figured out the secret of Sugar Hill yet?"

"Maybe you better tell me."

"You're a smart guy, it'll come to you." She looks over her shoulder in the direction that James has led his impromptu tour. "Your cousin has options and she's weighing them. That in and of itself tells me she *does* know the secret. There, that's your hint. Let's go find Billie."

Almost forty minutes pass before James, Margie, and Terrance rejoin us, although if Anna hadn't checked her watch, we never would have known. Anna and I were completely taken by the magic of Holiday's performance. The music of the band charts some kind of path through the voices of the party guests, skipping over the clinking of glasses, ducking under laughter, finding its way unmolested to me.

"She's astonishing, isn't she?" James asks.

"No one's got a voice like hers," I agree. "Like she poured sex, beauty, and pain into one bowl and blended it into song."

"Looks like our lawyer isn't the only frustrated poet in our group," Terrance jokes. But the jab isn't delivered with that chuckling brutality I've come to think of as his signature. He returned from James's tour different somehow. Like the attitude that normally defines him gotta overcome an anxiety he's just getting acquainted with.

Margie forms her lips into a teasing pout. "I'm crazy for poetry, but I've no talent for it. Will it do to simply say that you have marvelous taste in music, Mr. Mann? And that dress she's wearing! I wish I had one just like it. It's positively divine!"

It's true. There's not a jewel on Holiday, but the fit and slink of her gown outshines the whole crowd.

"You see?" Terrance exclaims triumphantly. "That's the kind of gown one can buy in Beverly Hills!"

"She bought it yesterday," James says mildly, "in South Central."

Anna erupts in laughter.

The mere hint of mockery gets under Terrance's skin. I can see it in the twitching at the corner of his eye. From somewhere behind me I hear the clinking of glasses as strangers from another group shout the word *cheers*.

Billie Holiday slides into a new melody that moves several around us to step forward, turning the pavement into a dance floor. Margie watches with longing.

Terrance sees it and considers a moment before extending his hand. "Dance with me."

The offer startles her, then lights her up with a whole new glow.

They, too, step forward, footsteps falling in sync, swaying and twirling away as James's mild smile twists into a grimace.

"One dance won't matter," Anna says.

Both James and I turn, waiting for her to explain. Across James's courtyard I can see the spark of cigarettes lazily move back and forth, embers or fire under the control of inebriated people, making me think back to our run-in with Lester.

"Men like Terrance will only attempt grace if it's in an effort to win some sort of competition. But there is no competition, really." Anna looks James in the eye. "There are lots of titles in this world. CEO, VP, Lawyer, Wife. Whatever one's title, one wants to hold it with the best firm possible." She taps a red-painted nail against her crystal champagne flute. "For a woman like Marguerite, your firm is superior by a mile."

She's coming dangerously close to calling Margie a gold digger.

"If you were to lose this house tomorrow, would you still be able to support Marguerite in the style to which she's become accustomed?"

"I would," James says definitively. "Better, in fact. I've told her as much."

"Well, there you go," Anna says with a shrug. "That's certainly more than her current husband can promise."

"Margie isn't like that," I say, and look at James, thinking he might take offense, too.

But he doesn't appear offended. He looks like he's in thought, like Anna planted some new ideas. Small sparks of anger threaten to capsize my mood. "Even if she was like that, and she's *not*, that's not the outcome we're lookin' for," I say, glaring at James. "None of us want to see people 'round here losing their homes."

"No, of course not," he says, a little too quickly and casually for my taste. He turns back to Anna. "She hasn't introduced me to Art yet."

"How could she possibly introduce her lover to her son?" I ask, appalled by the thought.

"He's part of her," James explains. "I love everything that's part of her."

I've seen Margie with Art. She seems to like him well enough. She might love him.

But I wouldn't put money on it.

"Terrance is not a good father," Anna offers. She moves to the side as a couple pushes past us, laughing too hard to watch where they're going. "Still, he does have legacy to consider. Perhaps some sort of compromise can be arranged. Regardless, you can definitely take Marguerite from him, unless . . ."

"Unless what?" James asks urgently.

"Unless your money comes from a source a little more scandalous than wine. That she won't go for. But don't worry," she adds with a warm smile. "Some will try to convince her you're up to nefarious activities, but one can't prove a lie."

He shakes his head, dismissive. "I'm not sure I even know what lying is."

I feel my forehead scrunching up as I try to parse that one out.

"I meant to tell you," James continues, leaning forward as the sax moans out the opening notes of Holiday's "Trav'lin' Light." "I read your most recent article in the *California Eagle*."

Anna beams.

Shit!

"It was smart," James says. "Brilliant, actually."

Damn it, damn it, damn it!

I *had* started that article. Brought it to work with me to read on my lunch break, which I took at my desk. It was about Negro advancement being best achieved through reinvention rather than reform . . . or maybe it was personal advancement? Norman had called me into his office before I'd finished the first paragraph to tell me he thought I was ready to handle my own accounts. I was so excited I'd called James with the news, informing him that the next time we went to lunch I would be the one paying. Then I had hustled out to make some sales calls, ready to reel in my first commission.

I had completely forgotten about Anna's article.

I could *tell* something was bothering her last night. Like she was waiting for me to say something. So I had complimented her dress, asked if she had styled her hair differently.

Now she's blushing at a compliment I should have given her but didn't.

"They almost didn't publish it," she says. "The editor thought it might be a bit too esoteric."

"What kind of cockeyed nonsense is that?" James asks with a laugh. "What is America if not a complete reinvention of what came before? I can't imagine there are many people who would struggle with the concept. And yet they won't necessarily consider it on their own. After reading your piece, they'll start thinking." He nods at me. "Charlie here is the one who brought it to my attention. He insisted I read it, and now I understand why. Simply brilliant."

She turns her flushing smile on me. "I didn't know you read it."

"I brought it to work with me," I say, picking my words real carefully.

She's looked at me with longing before.

But this is the first time she's looked at me with adoration.

Like she loves me.

I glance over at James, expecting a wink or some kind of a secret gesture, him wanting credit for helping me out. That's what Terrance would do.

But James is too busy watching his lover dance with her husband for anything like that.

"Oh my God," Anna says, sounding horrified. "Is that who I think it is?"

Behind us is a happy crowd of Negro men and colorfully dressed women streaming down the steps to James's courtyard. And in the middle of them is one white woman in an all-black dress. She has a saucer hat angled and perched on waves of blond hair.

She looks so beautiful it takes me a minute to realize it's Dolores.

"You didn't know she'd be here," I say to James, needing it to be true. "You didn't invite her. You wouldn't do that."

He sips his champagne. "I like to get to know my neighbors."

"Jesus on the cross," Anna spits out, "you cannot be this stupid!

Her husband is actively looking for ways to ruin us! The trial is less than a month away. Sugar Hill cannot afford a scandal right now!"

"Certainly no one can fault us for extending Mrs. Nolan an innocuous invitation to a party. Her husband apparently is at a boxing match this evening. This way she's not bored."

As Dolores walks through the crowd, others stop, laughter turns to gapes and frowns. They distance themselves, creating a path for her like she's got some kinda magic power.

"This is going to get back to Lester!" Anna exclaims.

"Which one of these colored party guests spends their time gossiping with their racist neighbors?" James asks mildly.

I look back at the dance floor and see Margie still in Terrance's arms, her back to the stairs. She seems to be watching Billie Holiday over her husband's shoulder.

But Terrance's eyes are on the stairs.

He stops dancing. The hand he had placed flat on Margie's back moves to curl around her arm. He's pulling her off the floor, marching over to us, his stare filled with the kind of fire Dante described finding in hell.

"Charlie, I want to go home," Anna whispers, but I'm too damned stunned to move.

Dolores is now about forty feet away, painted red lips advertising her smile. She's got the practiced walk of a fashion model. A few more drunken couples stumble out of her way. She's coming in our direction.

If Margie notices, she's not showing signs of it. Instead, she looks back at Billie Holiday, and when she does, Terrance locks eyes with Dolores from across the courtyard.

Some glares merely express displeasure.

The glare Terrance gives Dolores is a threat.

She freezes, then takes three backward steps, starts fidgeting, first with her necklace, then with her small evening bag. Anna tugs at my sleeve, but still I stay put. Across the courtyard the sparks of cigarettes look like beady-eyed demons.

The second Margie turns away from Holiday, Terrance redirects his focus to James. "You put on quite a show." His usual blustery voice has chilled right down to ice. "I'll find a way to repay you for your hospitality."

"Terrance, what on earth—" Margie says, but before she can finish, he starts to drag her away.

James moves in front of them with a smile.

"I think you've had a bit too much to drink, old sport," he says. "As one should at a party. But you may not be aware that you're manhandling your wife." He takes a step closer to Terrance, using the several inches of height he's got over him to his advantage. "You really don't want to give her so much as a bruise. That would be quite unfortunate for all involved."

"Charlie, please," Anna says. But I find myself shushing her. Somewhere behind me I hear a glass drop and shatter. Minutes ago, I heard music, now I'm struggling to distinguish it from the commotion of stomping feet and the slurred speech of the drunks surrounding us.

Margie looks anxiously from her husband to James, then back again. And then, coming to some kind of tactical decision, she bats her lashes and throws out a giggle. "Silly, he's not hurting me! You would never, would you, Terrance?"

Terrance doesn't take his eyes off James for a second. "If I hurt someone it's not going to be a woman."

"Of course not! I was just telling Terrance how . . . how I was feeling a bit dizzy. He's just escorting me out so I might get a good night's sleep." Margie bites down on her lower lip as she smiles up at James. "But it was a beautiful party, Mr. Mann. An utter success. I'm positively in awe."

An utter success. Yet the way she said it, the way she's looking at him, it's as if she meant to put a *you're* in front of that sentence.

James smiles back, and this time it's hard to miss the familiarity, the affection. "I told you to use my Christian name."

"We're leaving," Terrance says.

"We're leaving, too, Charlie." Anna's voice has gone firm, she's no longer asking.

"Yeah, you're right," I agree, and empty my glass. As I look for a place to put it down, Margie and Terrance stride away.

But before they can get too far, Margie calls over her shoulder, "Thank you again for your hospitality . . . James."

Even from a distance I can see Dolores slump as she watches them leave.

Anna and I follow them out, but I make a point of keeping our pace slow because I don't want to end up in step with Terrance and Margie.

Before we leave the courtyard, I look back one more time and see James moving through the crowd, exchanging brief pleasantries with unsteady guests as he slowly but deliberately makes his way over to Dolores.

Chapter 21

"Where is he?" I ask Daniel. It took him an unusually long time to answer the door. I'd had to ring twice.

"I'm afraid Mr. Mann can't see you right now—"

"The hell he can't." I force my way in. Several servants are busying themselves cleaning up last night's mess. One works to remove crumpled napkins from an expensive-looking vase, another wipes off lipstick that somehow ended up on the wall. The floor beneath my feet is still wet from mopping.

"As you can see," Daniel says, "this isn't a good time. But I can tell him you stopped by."

"Where is he?" When Daniel doesn't answer, I stride on ahead, going for the library first, the butler close at my heels.

"Mr. Mann doesn't entertain guests the mornings after his soirees." Daniel's voice has moved to a higher note. I fling open the library door. The only person in there is another servant, sweeping broken crystal into a dustpan.

"He still sleepin'?" I ask. "Hung over?"

"If you'd only let me take a message, I'm sure he'd happily meet you at a later time!"

I'm already on the move again. Through the dining room, where someone is vacuuming the area rug. From the kitchen there's the clattering and clinking sounds of dishes being cleaned.

Then, through all the commotion, I hear someone speaking in what sounds like French . . . or some bastardized version of it.

No, not speaking, yelling. Someone's being bawled out real good.

I move toward the voice.

"Mr. Trammell," Daniel pleads.

When I get in sight of the patio, I can see the doors leading to it are open. I can see that white foreigner from the bar out there, red-faced and standing over James, who's seated, ankle over knee, watching his hollering friend with the kind of casual irritation of a man watching his dog bark at a squirrel.

When the man takes a breath, James answers him in slow, halting French. I can pick out bits and pieces of what he saying, like *pas de problème*, but the rest is gibberish. The tone he's using, though, that's clear enough. James is telling that man not to snap his cap. He's telling him that whatever they're talking about has been handled.

Daniel brushes past me, stepping onto the patio. "Mr. Mann, I'm so sorry to disturb you, but Mr. Trammell is here, and he refuses to leave."

Both James and the foreigner look up and see me, still inside the house, but now in their full view. James's eyes widen then narrow as he turns back to his other guest. "*Ne t'inquiète pas. Il ne parle pas français.*"

I do understand the *ne parle* part.

The white man responds by spouting off more French-sounding words. Then he turns on his heel and marches in my direction. He comes to a stop less than two feet in front of me. "*Écoute, nègre de merde—*"

"Enough, Michel," James growls, switching to English. "Don't drag him into this."

Michel's lip curls up into a sneer. But he doesn't argue. I keep my feet planted as he storms away, his steps thudding like a bass through the off-tune melody of a house being vacuumed and scrubbed.

"Mr. Mann," Daniel says, his voice quivering, "I did try to tell Mr. Trammell this was a bad time. I did try to stop him."

"Why don't you get Mr. Trammell a cup of coffee, Daniel, or . . ." He turns to me. "Would you prefer to join me in espresso?" He gestures to a small cup sitting on an end table next to a folded-up copy of the *Sentinel.*

"I don't need anything," I say, still not moving.

But James ain't having it. "Have some coffee made up for him, Daniel. Make sure it's brewed fresh."

Daniel gives a quick nod, then takes off for the kitchen.

"Take a seat," James says.

I step onto his tiled patio. It's got a view of the courtyard, where a servant is trying to fish out what looks like a strip of dark gauze from the pool. I choose the chair on the other side of the end table so that's there's a solid object separating us as we both look out at the grounds.

He picks up his espresso cup. It looks ridiculously small in his hands. "One, just one, of the several dozen employees I've recruited for our operation isn't quite working out. It's put Michel in a foul mood and he's taking it out on everyone."

"Your operation being the importing of wine," I say. The servant manages to hook the thing in the pool; it's someone's nylon stocking, taken off and thrown away in undoubtedly drunken circumstances.

"Yes, that's right. Wine and champagne. But I doubt you're here to talk commerce, and you're apparently not here for coffee." He throws back the whole of his hot drink in a single, gentlemanly gulp. "Would you like to tell me what you *are* here for?"

I'm here to give him a piece of my mind.

But something about that last run-in with the foreigner has taken the wind out of my sails, changed my mood and my thoughts. I run my hand over my chin, my palms too calloused to be scratched by my morning stubble. "I'm here to thank you."

His head swivels hard in my direction. "For what?"

"You told Anna I recommended her article to you. You didn't have to."

"That's what you want to thank me for?" He laughs. "Charlie, that's honestly not worth mentioning. I'm sure if we had been spending time together you would have brought it up to me. But prior to last night, I hadn't seen you in over two weeks." He puts his cup down. "You've been hard to reach."

"I wasn't." Down in the courtyard I see more servants on cleanup duty. One collects dirty plates left in odd places, another pulls a long scarf from a bush.

"I've called several times since you first brought Marguerite over, and when I do get you, you always cut our conversations short. The only time you've called me is when you got the promotion."

"I mean I wasn't gonna bring up her article. I couldn't 'cause I forgot about it. I didn't read it."

"Oh."

"I knew it was important . . . to her. But I got distracted. Meantime, she was waiting around for me to comment on it. That throwaway lie of yours saved my ass."

"Oh," he says again, not sure what it is I'm looking for in a response. "Well, think nothing of it."

"It *was* a lie, though," I go on. "When you said you don't know what lying is? Well, now you do. It's telling Anna I talked to you about something I didn't."

"I don't see it that way."

"No other way to see it."

"I was stating what I expected to happen." He glances upward. The sky's blue is muted by a thin haze of brown. The mechanical growl of the vacuum's louder than any chirping bird. "So, no, it wasn't a lie."

That doesn't make any sense. But I let it go. "You've been a good friend to me. The best I've had in a long while."

"And you to me."

"You're going to get us all killed, James."

He laughs as if I'm joking. When I don't smile, his amusement slides right into bewilderment. "What are you talking about?"

"Nah, the better question is, what were you thinking? Bringing that white woman 'round here? If you want Margie to know Terrance has got other women, all you gotta do is tell her. You don't gotta make a show of it."

"I've tried to tell her," he assures me. "But she won't let me talk about him. Whenever I so much as mention his name, she flinches."

"Uh-huh. And why do you think that is?"

"It's obvious, isn't it? She hates him."

The wind shifts and I catch a whiff of something foul. Like maybe someone got sick last night and the servants have yet to find and clean it.

"She's unhappy, Charlie. Do you know that when I asked her to come to my next party, she told me Terrance would never allow it? He won't allow her to go to a party, but he can sleep around with anyone he wants?"

"Did Margie know you were invitin' Dolores?"

"What? No, of course not. Marguerite thinks she is bound by her vows to stay in her prison." The trees below us are swaying, their leaves abandoning branches and taking up residence in the pool. "But if she's confronted with the truth, irrefutable truth that *he* has broken *his* vows . . . she'll be free."

Daniel reappears with a cup full of joe on a saucer. I take it from him politely even though he's looking at me like he's still mad. When he's out of earshot, I put the coffee down untasted next to James's empty espresso cup and unread paper.

"The racial covenant trial is less than a month out. Did you know that Dolores's husband is one of the plantiffs? Did you know he's got connections with the PD?" I ask. "If news of that affair gets out, Lester will use it in his effort to level this whole neighborhood. We'll all end up homeless, and that includes Margie."

"I will *always* keep Marguerite safe." The man looks downright wounded that such a thing ain't obvious. "As beautiful as this house is, I won't hesitate to move and take her away. Maybe to Harlem. Or Paris. Marguerite would thrive in Paris. I can't wait to bring her."

"You serious? Your plan is to leave us?" Acid gurgles in my gut, then shoots up to burn my lungs. "Abandon us all here in a pile of goddamned ashes from a fire *you* fueled while you're off taking pictures in front of the fucking Eiffel Tower?"

"I won't let you get hurt either, Charlie. Or Anna."

I jump to my feet and stretch myself tall just to make room for all this new rage.

"Please sit down."

There's a coil of silver hair in his head of cropped black curls. It looks like a string, and for a second I imagine pulling it until he unravels.

"I said, sit down."

The change in tone is so sudden it stills me.

His whole face has changed, too; in just those three seconds it's hardened to armor. There's a cold brutality emanating from him, like he could execute a man without effort or care.

That bit of silver ain't string. It's steel. The country club manners, the old money style of speaking, it's not fake . . . not exactly. It's decorative.

A pearl handle on a tommy gun.

I sit down.

"I've spied Terrance at the Dunbar, with Dolores, more than once." He's speaking with the mechanical pacing of a ticking bomb. "I've seen him kiss her in public. She's not the first. He flaunts his white women like they're spoils of war. And what does that make Marguerite? A medal to be displayed? Or simply a lesser conquest?" His jaw shifts slowly to the left, signaling dangerous levels of outrage. "The last time I saw them at that hotel, I waited in the restaurant. He took her up to a room and then he left the hotel, alone, less than an hour later. But I didn't leave. I waited for her."

"What for?"

"To talk to her, to find out what kind of woman she is."

"We already got an answer to that. Dolores is the kind of white woman who cheats on her husband with Negroes. Plenty of her kind in the South." In the South those women usually get caught.

Then they cry rape.

Then people die.

But they say things are different here.

"I eased into a friendship with Dolores," he says, as if I hadn't spoken. "She shared the names of a few party caterers she fancies, I've allowed her to come over and pick out a few bottles of wine to take to her Junior League meetings. She's a good person, just lonely and in love with someone else's husband. I've always shown her respect and in exchange she trusts me . . . The fact that our social circles don't overlap has made me a convenient confidant. And what she's confided is that Lester beats her." From the courtyard the voices of servants rise and fall, too distant for words to be distinguished. "The fear Lester was using to keep her in line has fermented, turned into desperation. Desperation *has no lines.* No borders, no rules."

"What are you sayin'? What's she gonna do?"

"She's going to throw Terrance in Lester's face. She hasn't said as much, but I'm sure of it."

I bury my face in my hands. "What are *we* gonna do?"

"Control the timing," he answers simply. "Let Marguerite confront Dolores and Terrance while surrounded by colored friends, not white racists. Then, later, if things get ugly between Lester and Terrance, Marguerite and I will already be gone."

"James, everybody 'round here is gonna pay the price for this game you're playin'. I'm talkin' about your community."

He shakes his head, exhales through gritted teeth. "You're assuming the worst of everyone. Maybe it's more realistic to assume the best of a few."

"You want me to assume the best of you after what you pulled last night?"

"Not me, then. But maybe of Judge Thurmond Clarke, who will be hearing the racial covenant case. I know the corrupt judges in this town, and Clarke is not on that list—"

"Wait a minute, you got a *list* of judges?"

"What I'm saying is that you shouldn't assume Clarke is going to throw justice aside and decide the case based on Terrance's extramarital affairs rather than the existing law."

"The existing law is enough!"

"Well, that's not my fault, is it?"

I stare at him, marveling at how someone so successful can be so naive. If the law's debatable, and it just might be in this case, you don't want the judge thinking that ruling in our favor is the same as setting a bunch of nefarious Negroes loose on a town full of wilting white lilies. That's why we've all gotta do our part in keeping Terrance's indiscretions discreet. How can he not see that?

"And another thing," he goes on, "a man like Lester isn't going to want the judge, or anyone in his circle, to know that his wife is cheating on him with a colored man. And if everyone in *our* circle finds out about it, then it only means that every Negro around here will be able to hold it over his head."

"You're fooling yourself."

He slams his fist against that little table so hard my hot coffee splashes onto the *Sentinel*, causing the black ink to blur into the brown liquid. The paroxysm startles me, puts me on guard.

"Why must you persist with this pessimism?" His words come out in a baritone snarl. "Why must everyone spend so much time worrying about things turning out the way they *don't* want them to, when so frequently they turn out the way they do?"

"You think so." It ain't a question. My heart is hammering against my chest like a jackhammer on pavement. "You wanna know how I got my Silver Star?"

James looks at me, surprised. "All right, if you want to tell me."

"I got my medal for savin' three men."

"Three? That's incredible—"

But I hold my hand up to stop him. "That's what the army would tell you. I tended to 'em under enemy fire. Even doubled as a stretcher man for one of them. Mortars dropping to our left and right as we carried that man to safety."

"My God, Charlie." His voice is hushed now, bravado replaced with admiration. "But don't you see, you did it. You proved my point. You proved that even in the worst circumstances, you can change your fate, change your destiny . . . and not just for yourself but for others!"

My lip curls in disgust. "You need to take a look at your dictionary.

Fate can't be changed, and destiny got itself decapitated alongside Marie Antoinette."

"Come now."

"Just shut up for a second and listen. The first of those three men I supposedly saved died four hours after I left him, died before the doctors at the field hospital even had time to tend to his wounds. The second had the courtesy of lasting a full seven days before expiring. And the third?" My eyes are tearing up despite myself. I know he sees it. I slam my fist into my thigh. "Damn it, this is why I don't talk about this shit!"

"Charlie—"

I hold up my hand again. "The third." I take a deep breath, regain some composure. "He made it through. But he did so with two legs and three fingers less than what he started with."

"You still gave that man his life."

"I wrote him, the survivor. Wrote as soon as I found out he had made it stateside. He wrote back. But you know what he said?"

"Thank you, I assume."

"He said I shoulda left him on the battlefield to bleed out. Said he'd be better off a dead hero than a live liability." I twist in my seat so I can better look James in the eye. "The army wants me to feel good about that day. Proud. They poured a few ounces of the same precious optimism as yours into a mold and fashioned a medal out of it. And I wear it 'cause I need the reminder that I at least tried to do good. But things didn't turn out the way anybody wanted them to, did they? Not for the dead men or the live one. There is no *fair*. No tidy, happy endings. And, James? Justice ain't never gonna be blind, not as long as judges have eyes."

"War . . . it changes the equation," James allows. "It's ugly, it has to be. But this is peacetime."

"There ain't no peacetime for the American Negro."

"The hell there isn't! Look at where we are, Charlie! Look at what I have!" This is the first time I've heard him raise his voice. "I've traveled the world. But this"—he jabs his finger toward the ground—"this is the land of opportunity, no matter your color. This is where every-thing's possible."

"And once you get what's possible, you take it to Paris?"

That breaks through, startles him.

"All right." He throws his hands up in mock surrender. "You got me there." We fall into a few minutes of quiet. A bird chirps, a vacuum roars. I can feel our tempers cooling with the breeze. "There's not as much opportunity in France," he finally adds after a spell, "but the food's better, so it won't be a total loss."

The quip is a kind of olive branch. "You're downright certifiable."

"There's not much advantage to staying sane in a crazy world," he replies.

I get back up on my feet. The circular course of our conversation is exhausting. It's time to go.

"I promise you," he says, "things will turn out as they should. For Marguerite, you, Anna . . . Everyone will be fine."

For a man whose world is so big, his definition of *everyone* is mighty small.

"Look, we're less than two weeks out from Thanksgiving." He gets up to see me off. "Why don't you and Anna come over for the holiday? I have a bottle of Bordeaux that came straight from the vineyards of Napoleon Bonaparte himself. We'll enjoy it over a meal cooked by one of the best chefs in the city."

"Anna and I are going to Terrance and Margie's for Thanksgiving."

"Oh." He stuffs his hands in his pockets; I can tell by the way the fabric is bulging that he's got them clenched. "Well, that will be a monu-mental event. The last Thanksgiving she'll ever spend with her traitor."

It's ridiculous to feel sorry for this man. He lives like a king. His only problems are of his own making, and he's reckless enough to make just living near him a risk.

But I do feel for him. I don't know why. But I do.

"Maybe we can grab lunch next weekend, before the holiday," I suggest.

His smile practically takes up his whole face. "So, you understand? Things are going to turn out all right."

I find his relief both heartwarming and frustrating. "I understand that you're a good friend," I say simply. "And I understand that you're gonna get us all killed."

And then I turn and leave . . .

I leave, thinking hard on the lethality of optimism.

Chapter 22

In the ten days that follow that bizarre Sunday visit with James, I sign up fifteen new clients for life insurance—even with two of those days being a weekend and the tenth day being a half day on account of the approaching holiday. It doesn't come easy. I go all over town hawking golden bits of security. I shake hands with restaurateurs and their waiters, with doctors who perform surgeries and the hospital janitors who scrub blood from the floor. When I was trailing Sam, he told me that for every fifty people you talk to you're lucky to sign up one.

I talked to fifty-seven people in ten days and I signed up fifteen. Norman says he's never seen anything like it. He applauds me for being active, mobile, for not just sitting at my desk making cold calls.

Of course, he doesn't know I have reasons for not wanting to be doing my business in the actual offices of Golden State. Reasons that have more to do with guilt than money.

I don't want to be around Terrance and his questions.

"But surely you haven't been able to avoid him entirely," Anna asks as we roam a local grocery store the Wednesday night before Thanksgiving, picking out the ingredients for sweet potato pie.

"No," I admit, dropping a bag of brown sugar into our cart. "I came in to file some newly signed contracts and he cornered me as I was coming out of the men's room. Wanted to know why James would have invited"—I glance around and lower my voice—"that blonde to the party. What did he expect to happen, is how he put it."

"And what did you say?" she asks. A couple of white women walk by us, chatting about recipes. I recognize them from around the neighborhood. One nods at us, friendly like; the other looks away.

Most of the people in this store are white.

I lower my voice even further. "I acted like I didn't know that woman had a connection to Terrance beyond being his neighbor, and seein' as he didn't want to explain, it ended his questioning."

"So you lied."

"It was a bathroom, not a court of law."

We move farther down the aisle until Anna spots the flour and shortening. "Did your family back home have any Thanksgiving traditions?" she asks as she peruses the brands.

"Last I checked, Thanksgiving is a holiday celebrated by consuming extra food, whereas my family always considered the days we had *just enough food* to be an achievement. So, no, we didn't celebrate Thanksgiving."

Anna opens her mouth, as if on the verge of conveying her sympathy, but then stops herself. I think she knows that pity isn't a sentiment I welcome. "We don't have to go to Terrance and Marguerite's tomorrow," she says instead. "Hattie says there's still room at her table."

"Terrance is my boss. Norman will be there, too. I can't skip out on a Thanksgiving dinner to break bread with a woman my bosses hate."

"Terrance hates," Anna corrects with a sniff. "Norman just disdains."

We move to the spice aisle and spot a Negro neighbor who gives us a sociable smile and another white neighbor who doesn't.

"You don't want to be dodging Terrance's questions for the length of an evening," Anna presses. "And Hattie's Thanksgiving is going to be a blast, a star-studded affair. She's invited half the cast of the last movie she wrapped."

"What movie was that?"

"*Song of the South.* Disney will release it at the end of next year."

"Is it an improvement on the roles she taken on in the past?"

Anna purses her lips, her eyes flitting to a box of Aunt Jemima pancake mix.

"We can't go to Hattie's," I say, definitive now.

"But what if it's her last?" she blurts out.

I look at her, not getting it.

She glances around, making sure no one's in hearing distance. "The trial is two weeks away."

"You told me we're gonna win."

"And I believe that." Her head drops and she fiddles with the delicate gold band of her watch. "But . . . it's possible I'm refashioning wishful thinking into belief."

I study her face for a second, then reach over her head for the nutmeg. "If that's the case, keep up the wishful thinkin', at least for the next two weeks. Fourteen days of being happy and confident—"

"Well, look what the cat dragged in!" It's Margie. She's pushing a shopping cart that's near overflowing, little Art toddling along beside her. "I swear, there's no place better to see and be seen than a market the day before Thanksgiving!" She gives Anna's hand a quick squeeze and me a kiss on the cheek.

Art looks up at us with a very serious expression. "Mommy needs cinnamon and flour and eggs and a whole bunch of stuff! She's going to make the biggest, bestest dinner ever!"

I smile down at him. "We were just talking about how much we're looking forward to having Thanksgiving with y'all."

Anna releases a sigh so small I'm sure I'm the only one to hear it. There will be no more argument about where we're going.

"I got the cockeyed idea that I could cook Thanksgiving dinner all by myself, so I gave Gertie the holiday off." Margie pulls a miniature notepad from her purse and shows us the multiple pages of her grocery list. "Honestly, I don't know what got into me!"

Another white woman comes into the aisle. *Mildred Smith.* The one who gave James a snooty glare when he waved hello during what was my first weekend in Sugar Hill.

I glance back at Anna and notice she's got goose bumps on her arms. I take off my jacket and wrap it around her shoulders.

"Of course, Terrance used to say I was an ace chef," Margie goes on as she searches the shelf full of spices. "I just don't do it very often anymore."

Mrs. Smith passes right by us. "Are you just going to leave that on the ground?" she snaps.

I look up, surprised that this woman would even talk to us. Then my gaze follows hers. Seems a matchbook fell out of my jacket pocket when I took it off.

"Sorry, didn't notice." I crouch down to pick it up.

"You niggers are such dirty people," she hisses, "trashing the whole neighborhood."

Anna clutches my arm, but the glare she gives Mrs. Smith is unflinching. Margie starts to hum a peppy tune as she continues to peruse the shelf full of spices, keeping her back to all of us.

The absence of a verbal reaction doesn't seem to satisfy Mrs. Smith, and with a huff she disappears around the corner of the aisle.

"Mommy," Art says, his voice meek, "did you hear what that lady said?"

"Hmm?" Margie finds the cinnamon and tosses it lightly into her cart, clears her throat of some irritation. "Don't be silly, darling. I didn't hear that lady say a thing."

"Margie," I say, maybe a little admonishingly. "I'm not so sure denial's the way to go here."

"What?" She blinks her eyes at me. "I truly didn't hear anything. By the way, what dessert are you two bringing? No, wait, don't tell me. You know how I love surprises. Tomorrow is going to be a gas!" She grabs Art's hand and walks off toward the register.

"It's rather breathtaking," Anna whispers once we can no longer hear the click of Margie's heels. "She's taken a childhood game of pretend and turned it into a way of life."

Chapter 23

Anna and I are the last to arrive at Terrance and Margie's Thanksgiving celebration. That's by design. I want the protection of a crowd.

Everybody's in the parlor. Norman and Edythe, Dr. Somerville and Vada, and a man who's introduced as Sidney Dones, along with his daughter, Sydnetta, a pretty young woman of refreshingly dark complexion. Art's here, too, dressed to look like he tiptoed off the pages of a Frances Hodgson Burnett novel.

"I was beginning to fret you'd forgotten the way!" Margie says, once introductions have been made. "Art, you haven't said hello to Anna and your cousin Charlie!"

"Hello," Art says brightly. "I got taller yesterday! I got measured and—"

"Your mother said say hello, not give a speech," Terrance chastises.

"Oh, don't be a drip, it's natural for a boy to brag about his height! He's going to grow up to be tall, dark, and handsome, just like his daddy." Margie looks down at what's in my hands. "Anna, is this a sweet potato pie?"

"It's Charlie's recipe," Anna says blithely. "He did most of the work."

Terrance laughs. "She's really got you tied to her apron strings!"

The pie is still warm from baking, but it's nowhere near as warm as my face is getting. I consider telling him I got the recipe from the army cook at Camp Hood, but I know that won't be any help.

Margie doesn't bother addressing the insult. "We were just talking about Val Verde," she tells us, smiling over at Sidney.

"The Black Palm Springs," Sidney says proudly. He a big man, tall and broad, with meat on the bones and a smile that makes it hard not to reciprocate. "Norman and I bought up the land decades back, about a thousand acres in the Santa Clarita Valley. Since then I've developed it into a real oasis."

"It's true! Sidney created an utterly beautiful oasis. He's both a genius *and* an artist! But we haven't been in ages." Margie sighs. "I was learning tennis there, and rode horses. It's where Terrance first took up golf. Oh, let's go back soon, Terry," she says, using a nickname for her husband I haven't heard her take up before. "Why, we could go next weekend! Let's go and I'll wear my new dress to one of the club's receptions! Charlie, did I tell you that Terrance bought me a dress just like the one Billie Holiday wore at James Mann's party?"

"Maybe we'll go after the trial," Terrance replies, sticking his hands in his pockets.

"Oh, you're always finding a reason to put off having fun." Margie pushes her lower lip into a pretty pout. "Let's just—"

"Maybe we'll go after the trial," he says again, this time edging a warning into the words. Margie narrows her eyes, letting a rare flash of anger blaze into public view. I can't tell if Terrance notices or if he even cares.

"Come on, little lady," Terrance says to me, "I'll show you where in the kitchen you can put that."

"Watch yourself, Terrance," Norman warns. "You're talking to our rookie of the year. Do you know how many clients he's signed in the last few days?"

But Terrance's insult smarts more than Norman's compliment soothes.

"Charlie had the courage of a thousand men by the time he was eight," Margie says, her singsong voice hardening a bit as she stares down her husband. "Even when the bullies outnumbered us by a hundred, even when my own brothers didn't have the capacity to look out for me, even"—the words hiccup out of her, pain breaking free from iron restraints—"even when I was so frightened I would curl up and hide under a table. Even then, he always found a way to keep me safe. He always protected me."

An intense chill runs through me, but no one notices me shudder.

"By a hundred?" Sidney repeats, a teasing glint in his eye. "How many bullies did your hometown have?"

The room erupts in light laughter.

"I mean it! He was my protector!" she cries, just inches away from a full-throated yell.

The room goes quiet, startled by her change of tone.

She stills, seemingly unnerved by her own outburst. Under the scrutiny of her guests, she gracefully glides back into playfulness. "Really, haven't any of you ever read an adventure book? There are always hundreds of bad guys and only a single hero to slay them all. Why, one need only look at him to see my cousin fits the bill as the hero!"

You can almost hear the entire room exhale. Terrance nods his approval like a coach proudly observing his athlete correct her form.

Margie is known as the cheery, unserious girl. A gal who brightens rooms, never darkens them. She's loved for it. It's her role. And her assignment.

"Well," Norman says, now relaxed and grinning, "he's certainly a hero at Golden State."

Again, everybody laughs and this time Margie joins them. They all go back to their conversation.

Terrance gestures impatiently at the kitchen, demanding I follow.

But I can't move. Not at first.

There was only one time when Margie and I were outnumbered by one hundred. Just one night when I promised safety while her brothers refused to add their voices to the lie.

One night that I've been forced to relive again and again in my nightmares.

But it wasn't bullies we needed protecting from, and the only thing that kept her safe was luck.

"Charlie!" Terrance snaps, again indicating I'm meant to follow him. I look back at Margie, but she's talking to Vada about some new topic. Story time's over.

The scent of turkey, potatoes, and melting butter rushes forward to welcome me as we enter the kitchen. So much of the counter space is covered by bowls of food waiting to be served that it is a challenge to find a place for the pie. I rearrange the dishes to make room, my thoughts still on the horror Margie so unexpectedly referenced. Terrance heads to the pantry.

"You've been busy this week. I knew you were going to end up as one of our best agents," he says, pulling out a bottle of red. "Goes to show, I still have a real eye for talent. Every man I've brought into the company is a success. Never made a mistake."

That's enough to break through and get a smile outta me, albeit a wry one. Terrance's greatest talent is his ability to turn every single compliment he gives back onto himself.

He puts the bottle back and pulls out another. "Your friend Reaper is after Margie."

I manage to squeeze the pie between a bowl of mashed potatoes and a platter of dinner rolls. "What makes you say that?"

"The way he was looking at her and . . . the way she was looking at . . ." He closes his eyes, squeezes them tight. "No. That part I imagined."

But by the way he says it, I can tell he knows he didn't imagine a damn thing. Terrance hasn't accumulated as much wealth as James. Delusion's a luxury he still can't afford.

"Margie loves you like a brother," he says. "That means you're a brother to me, too. We're family, Charlie."

He makes the word *family* sound like a call to arms.

"I need you to keep your eyes and ears open when you're around Reaper. Help me figure out what he's up to, why he invited Dolores. Was it a warning to me? Or meant as a reveal for Marguerite?"

There's a housefly on the edge of a bowl of cranberry sauce, contemplating contamination. I keep my eye on it instead of on Terrance. "What does Dolores got to do with you and Margie?"

"Marguerite," he says, his eyes still closed. "Her name's Marguerite."

I press my fingers down into a small empty space of countertop. I knew her before him, when her name was quick and easy on the tongue. A familiar name for a knowable girl.

What starts as a pause stretches into a silence. I turn back to see he has a bottle of Cabernet cradled in his hands.

The bottle's trembling.

"Women, they're not wrong when they say we're all alike." He directs the statement to the wine. "Goes back to biblical times. Samson was tempted by Delilah. Herod decapitated a man because he got worked up from watching his stepdaughter dance. We're all a bunch of dogs." His laughter's contaminated by drops of fear. "It's simpler for women—who they love is who they want. At least that's true for girls like Marguerite. Do you know when I met her, she had never let another man kiss her?"

"Why does that matter?"

Terrance finally does look up with an expression of genuine surprise. "Every man wants what other men can't have." Then something registers on his face. Again, he drops his gaze. "I didn't mean to imply . . . I think Anna is a fine girl. I wasn't trying to insult her."

It takes me a second to fully absorb what he's implying. "Fuck. You."

"I didn't mean it."

"Fuck you again, you did. I don't give a damn that Anna's been with other men. I got no interest in romancing a nun."

"Good, great." Terrance puts the wine back. "I'm just saying that Marguerite, she's as rare as . . . as the Dresden Green Diamond."

"And what's Anna, a lump of coal?" Terrance opens his hands, his apology in the form of a shrug rather than words. I try to shake it off, let it go. "Okay, I think what you're trying to say is Margie's—"

"Marguerite!" He says the name so loudly at first that I think he's calling her. He presses the heel of his palm against his brow, like he's pressing his frustration back into his head. "Your uncle Morris told me why he gave such a sophisticated French name to his little girl." He's speaking slowly, like he's remembering more than explaining. "A girl named Marguerite would be out of place working the fields. He told me that a man of wealth and ambition would know that a woman named Marguerite is a rare thing, meant for a high-society world. *My* world. Marguerite is mine. That's not changing."

"Then why are you worried about James?"

"I recognize him." His words are almost spoken in a whisper.

"You know him? From before he moved here?" Even the fly seems surprised by that one, vacating the cranberry sauce for a better view on top of a roll.

"No. I never laid eyes on him before he came to Sugar Hill. But I . . . I recognize what's in him. A threat." He's looking through me instead of at me. When I stifle a cough, he startles as if surprised by my presence. "As for Marguerite," he says, returning to his previous demeanor and focus, "all this business with the court case and threatened evictions, it's getting to her. No telling what foolishness a woman will get up to when she's frightened."

"What does Dolores have to do with this, Terrance?" I ask him again.

Finally, he holds eye contact long enough to read me, to see my anger. His chin lifts, as if my unspoken accusation should be responded to with pride instead of shame. "It's perfectly natural for a man of my success to have a little something on the side. Call it a bonus on top of my regular salary. Although," he adds with a laugh, "making a fool of Les right under his nose without his being the wiser? That's a *big* bonus. I take pleasure in that."

"He hits her, you know," I say. "I could see that the minute I laid eyes on them. The way she stands in his shadow like she's getting ready to cower. If he finds out she's cheating, she might not survive the revelation."

"That's one way to look at it," he says, breathing a little deeper, his frown a little wearier. "But if all she has is him, survival will be little more than torture."

This son of a bitch really wants me to see his infidelity as a good deed? "I'm like a brother to *Marguerite*," I remind him, putting a sarcastic emphasis on the name. "And she's like a sister to me. That makes it my job to protect her from men who would hurt her."

He raises himself up, tries to cow me.

But it ain't working. Just once I'd like to actually be the protector Margie tells me I am.

Uncertainty creeps in, etching new lines around his eyes and between them. "I didn't take you as the puritanical sort."

Again, I say nothing.

"All right, all right, I'll end it." Terrance's hands fly up in the air; he's acting like a parent who's been pestered into turning the radio dial. "I was beginning to get bored with her anyway."

"End it tonight."

"Come on, Charlie"—he gestures around the kitchen—"we're a little busy right now. And so is Dolores. She's with Les, having dinner at the home of his sister."

"His sister who's married to a police captain?" I'm not asking a question. This here's an accusation. This is a demand: *Look at the danger you invited. Look at the sword you got hanging over our heads.*

"Captain, deputy . . . some brute of the sort." I can't tell if he's putting on an act or if he really doesn't understand the gravity of the situation. "Tomorrow, I'll tell Dolores I'm done with her. I'll do it because I know it's important to you, and we're family."

He's lying.

"Now, will you help me get information on Reaper?"

"Why me? Everybody in town knows him. From the Somervilles to that Pinky fella you were giving a hard time to last week. Ask one of—"

But Terrance puts up a hand to stop me. "Pinky? Colson Pinkman? He knows Reaper?"

The look on Terrance's face makes me wish I'd kept my mouth shut. "I think he did some janitorial work for him."

"Wait, he's on Reaper's payroll?" He shifts his weight back on his heels. I hear the buzzing of a different kind of nuisance behind me.

"Pinky said he'd just paid off his gambling debts . . . I hadn't believed him, but if he's working for Reaper . . ."

"Nah, I don't think it's like that." I shake my head fiercely, like I can shake away another man's thoughts. I've got the strange feeling I've betrayed my friend, revealed some secret . . . although I have no idea what that might be. "He's probably one of the fellas who comes in to help clean up after James's parties."

Terrance's mouth is slightly open, his eyes up and to the side, like he's working out some kind of math problem. "Pinky has always ingratiated himself with the wrong people."

"Ingratiate? He just picked up an odd cleanup job or two."

"Right . . . right, of course." Terrance gives me a big, worrisome smile. "They probably barely know each other. That's why I need your help, Charlie. Lots of people have met Reaper, but you've gotten closer to him than most. Keep me updated on what's going on with the man. Who else he's giving odd jobs to. It's a small favor to ask of a cousin, isn't it? Not like I'm asking you to give *me* a job." His smile gets even bigger, all his teeth are showing.

This son of a bitch.

"Yeah, okay." I slip my hands in my pockets, lean up against the counter. "I'll see what I can find out."

The words are easy to say. I don't even blink.

Because that's what families do . . .

They lie.

Chapter 24

"I haven't been here in ages!" Anna squeals, throwing her arms up in the air as if she needs to make herself taller just to absorb all La Fête's got to offer.

I made the decision to bring her here two nights ago, right before we sat down to Thanksgiving dinner. But as far as Anna's concerned, we're here to celebrate, seeing as we drove here in her new car. She bought it just the day before. The first she's ever owned and bought with her own dough.

Now that we're here, I have to check the signage just to make sure we're at the right spot. The words LA FÊTE are lit up and blinding. Gone is the worn-down, melancholy place I'd wandered into a few weeks before. The scratches on the floor are camouflaged under polished heels and spiffed-up loafers. The live band has got an energy, vitalizing everyone and everything in the room. A tobacco-flavored haze casts the space in a soft light. Jive bombers are on the dance floor, tossing their ladies around, and at the bar it's nothing but happy colored folks sipping on whiskey and wine.

Anna grabs my arm. "Let's get a drink first," she says, without bothering to explain what comes second. "They make the best martinis here." She pulls me over to the bar and squeezes us between a giddy couple and a group of young women with lines neatly drawn down the back of their legs to imitate the stockings they either can't find or can't afford.

This ain't the Sugar Hill crowd. No diamonds here. But no poverty either. These are people like Anna. Like me. People who've gotten themselves five good steps up the ladder but still got plenty more room to climb.

Anna attempts to flag down the bartender, but the competition is fierce. "I must be losing my touch," she says. "Perhaps I should take a few lessons from Marguerite on getting men to be more solicitous."

The remark pulls me up short. "That's not fair. Margie ain't a flirt." When Anna gives me a look, I add, "She just got a habit of liftin' up the people around her. Some might take that as flirtation, but really, she's just free with her compliments."

"To men," Anna says with a laugh. "Your cousin uses flattery like Svengali used hypnosis." When she sees me blanch, she catches herself. Her expression softens. "Ignore that, I've been a bit on edge is all. I'll be nicer after a drink." Then she leans into me. "Anyway, the only man I want to flirt with is the good-looking fellow standing right in front of me."

I gently place my lips against hers, keeping my eyes open just a sliver in hopes of spying the man I'm looking for.

"Honestly, this is just what we need," Anna goes on, "getting all decked out for a killer-diller night at the club before everything gets . . . well, more serious."

Community meetings to prepare for the court case are scheduled for late next week, then it's the trial itself in eleven days, then the loss of everything. Yeah, things are gonna get more serious.

Anna waves at the bartender again and this time succeeds. "I'll have one of your famous martinis and . . . Charlie, do you want one, too?"

"Sure, why not?" There's a man around Colson Pinkman's height with his back to me. He's talking to a couple with skin the color of night and pointing to the bathroom as if giving directions.

Within minutes Anna places a glass in my hand. A swirl of lemon rind floats in the clear liquid. "We have to toast!"

"What are we toasting to?" I ask. The man who was pointing to the bathroom turns enough for me to see his profile. It ain't Pinky.

"To tonight! To Henry Ford! To our first real date!"

That gets my attention. "We been on lots of dates."

"We've had double dates with Marguerite and Terrance," she says. "We've been to Hattie's parties and Reaper's . . . and spent the whole night engaging with him. But this is the first time it's been just you and me."

I laugh. "Anna, look around, it's you and me plus a hundred."

"We're a party of two that just happens to be inside a party of a hundred," she corrects, as if that's a real distinction. "It's more intimate that way."

"If you say so." I clink my glass against hers. "To our first date, then."

It's as her glass touches her red-painted lips that I find who I'm looking for. "That's him," I say, more to myself than to her.

"Who?" She turns around to see. I wave my hand in the air to get his attention.

It works. He notices me and flashes a big, generous grin.

"Oh, look, it's Cole," Anna says, waving at the man who is slowly pushing and squeezing through the crowd in our direction. I know she doesn't realize I'm the one who first called him over. "He's the manager here. You'll like him as long as you don't make the mistake of scratching too deep beneath the surface."

When he reaches us, it's me he greets first. "Well, well, well. Seems we got a whole bunch of friends in common! Terrance, Reaper, and this beautiful creature." He lifts Anna's hand and gives it a gentlemanly kiss.

One of the women in the group standing next to us must have told one hell of a joke 'cause they all crack up, laughter floating on the smoke of Old Golds.

"Wait, you two know each other?" Anna asks.

"Charlie was in here with Terrance the other day," he explains, sniffing like he's fighting a cold.

"Ah, right, I forgot you knew Terrance. He sold you a policy, yes? Back when . . ." She falters, and even in the dim light, I think I can see a little color rising to her cheeks like she's made some faux pas.

"Back when I owned this place," he finishes for her. "You can say it. Between the Depression and the war, I'm grateful to have held on to this place as long as I did. And I'm still here, ain't I? Keeping things buzzing."

"So you know Terrance from Golden State?" I ask.

"Come again?" He leans in. The festive commotion of the room requires all conversation to be conducted in yells.

"Did you meet Terrance through his work at Golden State?" I repeat loudly. "I got the feeling you two knew each other from before."

"Oh, yeah, we did." I see a flicker of hesitance, of regret. "Terry's a sometimes friend, if you know what I'm talking about. Sometimes he gets in a mood, like he was when you saw us talkin'. When that happens, we ain't friends." Cole laughs good-humoredly. "But then he gets his head back on straight and starts acting right. Just this morning he took the unprecedented step of calling me up and apologizing for his behavior."

Anna nearly spits out her martini. "Terrance apologized? Terrance Lewis?"

"See, that's what I'm sayin'! I'm tellin' you, hell got cold today!" Again, he laughs. "But it's cool, it's cool. Two of us go way back, we like family. Heck, maybe we are family . . . with mothers like mine and Terry's, who's to say for sure we don't got the same daddy?"

"And we both know James," I begin, directing my words to Anna. But then I stop as a man trying to get to his friends walks between our small party of three, jostling my arm just enough to make the liquid splash from my glass. "Cole was telling me he got some work with James . . . Was it cleaning work?"

"Cleaning? Nah, I told you that's not my thing . . . not that I'm above it." Cole takes a handkerchief from his pocket and dabs his nose. "Reaper tell you he in international trade? He got me a piece of that action."

My heart's beating faster than the drums on the stage. "What are your duties?"

"Oh, I got all kinds of duties. More on the sales side of things. I'm doing pretty well for him, if I do say so myself. I'd wager that in another month or so he's going to want to put me in charge of a few things."

Cole has a manner to him that gives life to all sorts of bad suspicions. "So that means you'd be in charge of a sales team?" I ask, hopeful. "Maybe you'd get to pick which restaurants and liquor stores to sell the wine and champagne to?"

It's only then that the corners of Cole's mouth drop, flattening his smile to a stare. "Wine," he says. He's watching me closer now. Then he nods, sniffles again, and takes another step back. "Yeah, I'd be figuring out where to sell the wine. Look, as much as I'd love to chat, I gotta stay on top of this place. Make the rounds, check up on the staff, and the like."

"Oh, come on," I protest, trying for casual. "Hang out with us for a spell. I'll buy you a drink."

"I don't drink on the job." Again, Cole brings his handkerchief to his nose. "What I gotta do is walk the room, make sure no ladies are being manhandled without their invitation. Really good to see you, Anna."

"You too, Cole." Her voice sounds flatter than it did a minute ago.

I watch as he squeezes his way back into the crowd, this time moving away from us quicker than he came.

"What was that about, Charlie?" She's holding her martini glass against her heart.

"Before Thanksgiving dinner, I let it slip to Terrance that Cole was working with James," I admit. "And when he heard that, he started acting funny and I felt like . . . I don't know. That I had given away some kinda secret."

She's got her cheeks sucked in between her teeth in a way that makes her mouth pucker into something meaner than a pout. "Is that why we're here?"

I shrug and nod. "Figured if I could find out exactly what kind of work Cole did for James, if I could just reaffirm that there ain't nothing worth hiding, I could stop worrying."

"I see."

"I know James got his flaws," I go on, "but he's a friend. I don't like the idea that I mighta put him in a bad spot." I look at her, hoping to find relief there. "You don't think I did, do you?"

Anna places her glass on the bar. "I think I'm too tired for dancing."

The revelation comes outta nowhere. She was full of pep a minute ago. "We can just stay and listen to the music, then? It's a great band."

"It is," she says, wavering.

"Come on, we'll have a few drinks and . . . sway. We'll stand here and sway." I move my body from side to side for emphasis.

That makes her laugh. She reaches back and touches my hand without holding it. "Is that what you really want?"

"Sure! It'll be fun. Plus, I want to see if I can get a little more outta this Pinkman fella. Make sure I didn't put my foot in my mouth."

She takes her hand away, pulls a cigarette from her bag.

"I really am very tired, Charlie."

I want to argue, but the look she's giving me lets me know her mind's set. I sigh, scan the room one more time for Pinkman before escorting her out to the car. The engine's still warm from when we arrived.

Chapter 25

It's only Monday and I've already signed my first new client of the week, signed while my breakfast still had me filled up and satiated.

I'm creating success with smarts and charm and powers of persuasion. Featherlight tools that won't add a single callus to my palms.

I stroll into the Dunbar for lunch feeling good. Feeling like I can sell the waitresses a policy, the host, the front-desk clerks, too. The people I'm selling to are all young and healthy. I'm out here convincing them to write checks four times a year over the course of what I hope are long lives. Only the bereaved profit off death.

But as soon as I'm in view of the restaurant I see her: Margie, sitting by her lonesome at the table closest to the lobby and a few yards behind the host's stand. She's looking right at me, an uneasy smile adding a dollop of mystery to her beauty.

"Margie," I say as I walk up to her. There's no steam coming from the bowl of corn chowder sitting in front of her. It's either been served cold or she's been here a stretch. "Are you meeting someone?"

"Hmm, oh, no, no, please sit!" She gestures at the seat across from her, although I get the sense that my showing up has her off balance. "I just had the afternoon free and I always liked this restaurant, so." She smiles again, but her eyes flit behind me. I turn to look over my shoulder and realize she's got a full view of the front entrance of the hotel.

She's not here to eat. She's here to catch, although I'm still not sure which woman she expects to catch Terrance with. "The big brass at

Golden State are in meetings all day," I say, crossing my feet at the ankles, then untangling them again, trying to make myself comfortable in an uncomfortable conversation. "They're all takin' lunch at the office."

She registers this, taps her fingers against her water glass. "Terrance, too? You're sure?"

"I just checked in with him and Norman a few minutes ago."

"And here I was hoping to surprise him." She removes her napkin from her lap and drops it on the table like a soldier dropping a white flag.

"Can I ask you a question?"

She nods in response, still distracted and irritated by her husband's absence.

"Did you try to lose your accent or did you throw it away? 'Cause if you lost it, I can lend you some. I got enough drawl for the both of us."

That gets a laugh out of her, which is what I was going for. But my question is not entirely in jest. "Honestly, though, when did you start talkin' like a high-born New York debutante? That had to take work, right?"

Her smile fades a little. "Oh, all that moving around I did as a child . . . I had plenty of accents to choose from, a little like deciding what kind of girl I wanted to be," she says with a shrug. "How about you? I remember the impersonations you used to do, of our teachers, of the men we'd hear on the radio. And you're easily the most well-read man I know with or without a college education. You're perfectly capable of taking on any accent, any pattern of speech. Why do you insist on talking like a country boy?"

"I guess it's 'cause I came here already bein' the person I want to be."

"Oh . . ." Margie blinks at me, looking flustered.

"I'm joking. Who I really wanna be is Jack Johnson in his prime, but genetics had other plans."

That's enough to get her laughing good now. Like back in the old times when we were best friends and could tell and ask each other anything.

Maybe we're still like that.

"Here's the truth." I rest my forearms on the table as I try to come up with a way of making myself understood. "I spent most of my life havin' white folks back home tellin' me in a bunch of different ways that I'm three-fifths of a man. More primitive by nature with a proclivity toward violence if not controlled by their rules. And I did live by those rules for a long time . . . but when I came back after the war, I couldn't go along with it no more. That's how I lost my tooth. And I coulda lost a lot more if I'd stayed. I chose relocation over martyrdom."

"But, Charlie, that's all behind you," she says with a flutter of lashes. "You're here now."

"Exactly. I came to Los Angeles 'cause a bunch of white rural Virginians kept tryin' to tell me I ain't good enough on account of my color. And now I'm here. And I'll be damned if I'm gonna let a bunch of Black Angelenos tell me I ain't good enough 'cause I'm from rural Virginia. There are only so many shapes I can twist myself into, Margie. I'm done with that."

"Ah, I see." The corners of her eyes light up with what I suspect is pride. "Good for you, Charlie, taking a stand. You always have been a hero."

"A hero . . . about that . . . can I ask you somethin' else?"

"Anything."

Maybe I shouldn't bring this up. But I can't let it be. "Last time I saw you, at Thanksgiving, you brought up that night when we were kids," I begin, a tinny taste in my mouth. "The night when you and your family came over to celebrate Ma's birthday—"

"Charlie, that was such a long time ago—" she says, her eyes suddenly unfocused.

"The night they took him—"

"—no real point in rehashing it."

"—the night the Klan took your brother Vic."

She stills. For a moment I can't even tell if she's breathing. "Vic," she finally manages, "he ran out of your house that night on his own accord. We don't know what happened to him afterward."

"Of course we do. They left his body—"

"We never had the opportunity to identify . . . I don't think it was him."

I fall back in my chair, stupefied. I'd think she was making a joke, but even someone with the most macabre sense of humor couldn't find humor in this horror story. "Margie," I say carefully, "your parents didn't identify him 'cause your family picked up and left that very night. The Klan—"

"Please," she whispers, her eyes lowered to the table, her shoulders quivering, "please, let's just think of them as bullies."

The floor rumbles beneath us, the earth being moved by the force of some truck passing on the nearby street.

"What I remember"—she speaks slowly, deliberately now—"is that I was scared. And you told me you'd keep me safe. I believed you." Finally, she meets my eyes. "I still do. You're my hero, Charlie."

"Tellin' lies don't make me a hero. If anything, it makes me small. If it was my neck they were comin' for, I might have tried to make a run for it, same as Vic."

"No." The word comes out with the power of an order. "Your strength of will would have given you other strengths, too. But in the end . . ." She pauses, takes a deep breath. "It doesn't really matter, does it?"

"It doesn't matter?" I say, stunned. "They murdered your brother."

"That's what they want us to think. They want us to be wretched and frightened. But there's simply no need for it. Vic got away. Why, he's probably in Mexico right now, lying around on some beach."

"What? He . . . what?" What she's saying ain't just absurd, it's delusional. "You're sayin' he's off in some other country but never thought to send you so much as a postcard sayin' he's alive?"

"Oh, you know Vic, always fun, never responsible. Maybe if we shared a mother, he'd have thought to write her, but with his mother long gone and his relationship with our father so strained . . . no, I wouldn't expect him to stay in touch. But I'm sure he's fine."

"Margie, come on."

"What matters is you saw that Vic, my other brothers, my parents, you saw that none of them were up to caring for me in that moment and so you stepped up to the task, even though you were just a boy yourself. You've always been a force, Charlie, you're just too humble to see it." She reaches forward, lets her fingers rest on the back of my hand. "As far as I'm concerned, that's the only part of that night worth remembering."

I don't know what to say. I've got a jumble of feelings I've no idea how to sort through.

"My soup's gone cold," Margie says, wrinkling her nose at her bowl as she pulls her hand back. "I can't say I have much of an appetite anyway. All my plans seem to be destined for failure today. It's quite vexing."

The non sequitur makes it clear as day. She doesn't want to talk about it.

And why would she?

Why shouldn't she hang on to the fantasy that Vic pulled off some kind of Houdini feat if that's what soothes her? Who am I to judge how another person holds their memories?

Maybe if I could fool myself like that . . . maybe I wouldn't have so many nightmares.

Maybe her way's better.

"The day's still young," I say softly, trying hard for a smile. "Plenty of time for spontaneity to take it somewhere good."

"You're right." She spreads her arms wide and grips either side of the table. "Let's go somewhere . . . the weather's lovely."

"You mean like to a café with a patio?" I ask. I'm trying to picture Vic on a sunny patio, the sound of waves in the background. I'm trying to scrub away the image of his mangled corpse.

"No, no, more interesting than that . . . If I had Art with me, I'd take him to the merry-go-round in Griffith Park . . . oh, I know! The Griffith Park Zoo! Have you been?"

The absurdity startles me into a soft chuckle. I'm in awe of her. The way she always chooses joy. "I don't think I've ever been to a zoo of any kind," I manage.

"Oh, then we must go! Right this instant!" She waves to the waiter, signaling for a check.

"Margie, I'm workin'. After lunch I'm supposed to go 'round to Negro businesses, hunting for clients."

"Well, then consider it a business trip! I'm sure there're a few colored zookeepers who need life insurance."

Again, I can't help but laugh and start to shake my head. But it's then that she reaches forward and seizes my hand once more, this time tightly. "Please, Charlie." Her voice has gone thin, almost like she's afraid. "I need my friend today."

I've never been able to say no to Margie.

Chapter 26

While in the army, I overheard an officer talking about his adventures in Alaska. He went on and on about the polar bears with their glowing white fur, beasts so beautiful you almost want to touch them, until they start roaring, showing off a power and might that would make the bravest man tremble.

The thing Margie and I are looking at can't be the same breed of polar bear. Its fur is matted and so darkened by dirt he looks like he's auditioning for a black-bear-faced minstrel show. He takes a few steps, each one heavy and listless. The smell coming from behind the barbed-wire fence reeks of neglect.

"He's gorgeous," Margie says with breathless felicity. "How wonderful it must be to lounge around all day, protected and admired. Why, he doesn't even have to hunt!"

"Must be nice," I say, because disagreeing with Margie seems useless.

She pulls me along the paved path, stopping when we reach some despondent monkeys in a cage.

"Isn't this nice?" She clutches my arm. "Returning to childhood just for one afternoon?"

Whose childhood is she talking about? Not hers, not mine. I pat her hand and hope it will do as an answer. "I'm surprised you invited me," I say. "I thought you were spending all your free afternoons with James."

It's the first time I've brought him up to her. I half expect her to slap me for it. But she just nods, as if I'd asked any other question.

"He was called away on business. And I was so looking forward to spending the day with him. Do you know he bought me the same dress Billie Holiday was wearing? Now I have two!" She laughs lightly.

"But it's not just the gifts, right?" I ask, treading cautiously. "The person he is under all the riches, that's the man you want?"

"Oh my goodness, yes! Every girl loves to be spoiled, but it's much more than that. Honestly, I don't think I realized how low I've been these last few years before he showed up. But James . . . when I'm with him he makes me feel like . . . like . . ." She looks up at the overcast sky, searching the clouds for words. "Like I'm Helen of Troy! Have I got that right? The one from Homer's stories? The kind of girl gallant men readily fight wars over." She leans her head against my shoulder as one of the monkeys curls into a defeated crouch. "Of course he was quite distraught about having to cancel our afternoon plans, too. He hates that I can't sneak away more to be with him. I'm sure it's no fun feeling like *the other man*."

I stare down at the woman-child on my arm. "He is the other man, Margie. You're married to Terrance."

She snaps her face up so I get a full view of her glare. "How sweet of you to remember, because there are times when I'm quite sure Terrance has forgotten."

She pulls me on, this time to a giant tortoise that's doing absolutely nothing. "Have you ever noticed that white vase in James's library?" she asks. "The one with the gorgeous tigers painted on it?"

"Think so." The tortoise stretches out his neck like he's contemplating walking, only to think better of it.

"It's of the Qing dynasty. Worth an absolute fortune." She releases my arm, uses the index of her right hand to trace a circle around the wedding ring she's wearing on her left. "It positively takes my breath away. But when I asked James about it . . . why, it was like he had forgotten he even owned it! Isn't that funny?"

There's a strain in her voice. "Are you all right, Margie?"

"Did you know your mother was my daddy's favorite sister?" She steps closer to the tortoise's prison, lightly touching the chain-link fence. "He would bring her up all the time to Mommy. He'd say, that sister of mine, she knows how to keep a man. Even when things are tough, her husband can always count on her to greet him at the end of a hard day's work with a smile and a hot meal."

Her comment sends me into a state of confusion. We were share-croppers. My mama couldn't have greeted Pa at the end of hard days with warm meals because our hard days didn't end.

"He didn't think Mommy was quite as good at it."

When had Margie replaced the soft, familiar cotton of *mama* for that cold, gold-plated word *mommy*? When had she replaced her childhood Southern drawl for something more rich and less real?

Had she answered that question? Not really. But then Margie never had much use for questions that didn't have pretty answers.

"Sometimes she would give him lip or she wouldn't have dinner ready on time. Then Daddy would bring up your mother as the woman Mommy should aspire to be. And just to be sure he was making his point"—she pauses, the wind whips up, blowing a leaf into her hair— "he'd punish her."

"He hit her?" I'd never noticed bruises on Aunt Henny. But then I was only a youngster when they left.

"You don't have to hit a woman to hurt her." Margie draws away from the gate and ushers me to walk with her. "Rather he'd flaunt some woman in front of her," she says as we pass a man with a large sketch pad, using his pencil to create a giraffe that looks a lot happier than the one modeling for him. "One time," she continues, "he brought a woman to the house, sat her right down at the table, and told Mommy to serve us all dinner. He even had the audacity to give that harlot a big sloppy kiss in front of all of us before the night was done."

Her words are like ice on my skin. Mama adored Uncle Morris. She was devastated when he moved away, inconsolable when he died.

It never crossed my mind that he might be cruel.

"After that dinner my daddy turned to Mommy and said, 'I could leave with that pretty lady tomorrow, if that's what you'd like. I could leave with her tonight!' And Mommy, why, she just broke down in tears and asked him to stay." We come to a stop in front of a llama, tall enough to look us both in the eye, a baby llama huddling close to her legs. Margie bends down to study the child. "Mommy learned to be the kind of woman who could keep a husband. I once thought I was pretty good at it myself. But what if that husband can't provide the life . . . the *security* he promised? And what if . . ." Here she stands up, her attention on me. "What if it's the husband who must learn to be the kind of man who can keep a wife?"

The mother chews her cud, bored with our display. Personally, I'm just confused. Margie's trying to make a point with this story, but is it that she wants to stay with Terrance? Or leave him?

"James loves you." I shove my hands in my pockets, my sense of what's right twisted and tangled. "You're the only woman in the world he wants. Just you."

"Mm-hmm. Terrance felt the same while he was wooing me. But I suppose that's beside the point." She pulls me along and we walk without speaking until we reach an exhibit with a tiger lying idle in a makeshift cave, resentfully glaring out at the world of the free. "Oh, it's just like the tiger on that pretty vase James keeps forgetting about!" She laughs and gives the cat a little wave. "Ambitious men are so peculiar, aren't they?" she says, directing her words to the bitter beast. "They never love what they have as much as what they want."

Much evil is based on fear. Much fear is based on the apprehension that somebody else may get more than you possess.

—Langston Hughes, *Chicago Defender*

Chapter 27

It was quiet the night of the lynching. Margie's coughs, Vic's sniffling, my own whispers. Then our fear stopped even those small utterances until our home grew as silent as the Confederate statue that lorded over the town square.

I can't hear silence without thinking about locked-away screams.

It's silent here in Louise's living room. The meeting doesn't start for another forty minutes, but already there are twenty-one of us here. Two real estate agents, five doctors, four movie stars, one composer, three business moguls and two of their wives, one publicist, one rookie insurance agent, one boarder who's trying to break into Hollywood, and one husband, trying to hold the hand of his wife, despite her disinterest.

Titles seem more important than names right now. Because everybody in this room has a status we climbed to despite the weights Uncle Sam strapped to our ankles. We fought for the things we stand to lose.

That's true of Terrance, too . . . his title: Vice President of Golden State Mutual. He sits with his arm confidently draped over the back of an empty chair. A chair Margie should be in but isn't.

If there is a hell, Terrance would probably be on his way there. He's got no right to cheat or belittle others. But he did earn the power that allows him to do it.

"Six days." Hattie's whisper scratches at the quiet. I try to remember if I've ever seen her speak so softly on-screen.

"Only way they getting me out of here is if they shoot me dead." Louise projects her girlish voice to a volume that rips the quiet to shreds. "And then you damn well better believe I'll be back to haunt any white bastard who tries to so much as take a catnap in my house."

Again Robert (title: Her Manager, Her Husband) tries to hold her hand. Again, she outright ignores him.

"That colored man on Central who shot those police officers trying to evict him . . . Was that five years ago? Six?" The question comes from Vada. She toys with her bracelet of jade and gold, twisting it slowly around her wrist. "His name was . . . Marley? No, Farley . . . George Farley. It was in the papers. He paid for his house in full, but neglected a fee . . ."

"For street paving." My beautiful publicist places her hands on her knees as she fills in the story's gaps. "I do remember that. Farley couldn't afford it at the time and so they took his house."

Vada's got the glassy gaze of a woman digging through the wreckage of memory. "I recall that the police . . . didn't identify themselves when they broke in. Weren't even in uniform. They entered his home and started removing things, never uttering a single word."

"And Farley took up a gun and shot 'em," Ben Carter adds, the actor looking much more defiant than any of his roles allow.

Another two people arrive at the house, joining our group, a couple, Mitchell (title: Oil Producer) and Mabel (title: Wife).

No one greets them. Everybody's too busy eyeing the past and projecting its image onto the future.

"Loren's the one who got Farley off," Hattie notes.

"No," Norman contradicts. "Farley's in prison."

"But he could have been sent to the electric chair," Dr. Somerville points out. He sits tall, chin up. "Loren's use of the insanity plea saved Farley's life."

"Great," Terrance scoffs. "What you're saying is Loren's version of success is not getting his clients murdered by the state."

"I can see myself going insane like that." Ethel Waters (title: Singer, Actor, Broadway and now Hollywood Star). "Everything I've worked for? They're going to try to multiply all that by zero? They're gonna do something like that and still expect me to keep my hands folded in my lap, pretending I don't know how to shoot?"

"Nobody here inherited nothin'," Louise growls.

"That's true," Mitchell agrees, catching the thread of the conversation.

"We earned what we have," Hattie echoes, "with blood, sweat, and . . ."

"Humiliation," Terrance fills in.

Hattie's eyes narrow, her lips press into a warning.

"You actors humiliate our race for your fortune," Terrance shouts, his emotions uncharacteristically explosive. "All the *dis* and *dat*s in those scripts, what were you all thinking?"

For a moment no one speaks. Vada's sitting closest to Terrance, and she shifts her body a little farther away.

It's Dr. Somerville who finds his voice first. "As difficult as it may be to hear," he says, his expression hovering between apology and condemnation, "Terrance does have a point. It's because of movies like yours that we won't have the luxury of telling Judge Clarke who we are; instead, we'll be forced to prove who we're not."

"That's not fair," Edythe chides. Both Terrance and Dr. Somerville stare at Norman's wife, surprised by the source of the challenge. "It's not!" she insists. "What is it you expect of Hattie anyway? That she demands to play the part of an erudite professor? You might as well ask me to perform dental surgery. Let her play what she knows and leave the poor dear alone."

If Mammy had given Scarlett the look Hattie's giving Edythe now, Scarlett would've abandoned Tara and gone straight into hiding.

"I don't think that man Farley was crazy," Ethel mutters with apparently no interest in the argument that has broken out around her. "So they sentence you to death for murdering a bunch of thievin' cops.

Who says it's reasonable to hold on to your life when you ain't got no place to live it?"

There's not much advantage to staying sane in a crazy world.

"Hope it's all right that we just let ourselves in." Sydnetta and her father, Sidney, make their entrance and plop themselves down on a love seat. "The door was open."

Her property-developing father eyes the room, sniffing the metaphorical gunpowder. "What did we just walk into?"

"Have you ever heard anyone utter that . . . that most hateful of racial slurs in a single movie I've ever made?" Hattie asks. Sidney looks at her blankly, trying to catch up. "That's me who had that word taken out of those scripts. Me who beat out all those white women for that Oscar. I made things better for her!" She points at Patty. The aspiring actress immediately cowers, having hoped to be neither seen nor heard. "I made it so a woman with her color can get a damn job in this town!" She stares pointedly at Patty. "How many roles have you gotten since you've been here?"

Patty sends Anna a desperate look, pleading for rescue.

"Don't look at her, I'm the one talking to you. You tell them about the doors people like you can walk through because of people like me!"

Patty loosely wraps her arms around herself, a bird folding its wings. "I was in one movie," she says. "Since then, I've been cast in two speaking roles . . . Both parts were cut." I can't see her eyes with her head so low. "My agent says we've gone out of fashion."

The Oscar winner takes that in with a blink, then turns away.

Out of fashion.

They think our existence is a fad.

It's Anna who moves to Hattie's side and places her slender hand over hers, careful not to touch the gemstones on her client's fingers.

"This is Walter White's fault." Hattie spits out the name of the head of the NAACP with exceptional venom.

"Hattie dear," Edythe says, "Walter's just doing what he can to make things better for the new generation of colored actors. You should reach out to him, hear what he has to say. I'll personally call him and insist he make time for you."

"If Walter makes time for *you*," Hattie replies, "it's because he respects the way you use your assets."

"My . . ."

"You heard me. You may not have any accomplishments of merit, but at least you were able to find a skirt short enough to show off those high-yellow legs and get yourself a wealthy husband."

With that one tug, Hattie pulls off Edythe's sympathy, exposing her much more tolerable feelings of hate.

And Edythe's got the right to be angry. That particular attack was unfair and, as far as I can tell, unfounded.

"My wife has plenty of accomplishments," Norman snarls, his chivalry snapping into place.

He's right to defend her.

But despite myself, I'm sitting here rooting for Hattie.

"*We* have never demeaned our people," Norman goes on.

I run my tongue along my brand-new tooth as I listen to Norman saying many of the things I've thought about Hattie before. But looking at her now, all that fury and pain hanging off her . . . she's like me. Just another Negro, born into quicksand, who got out the best way she could, her choices determined more by her dark pigment than her bright intellect.

She sure as hell shouldn't have to apologize for making art out of survival.

"Everyone knows Edythe and I have made it our life's work to improve the lot of our race," Norman concludes with the air of a man who thinks he's finishing a conversation.

"Oh, you think you're a tribute to our race?" Louise demands. She leans forward, staring Norman down. "It would be interesting if we could do some kind of side-by-side comparison."

"What on earth are you talking about?" he asks, his anger already melting into exasperation.

"A comparison of the impact your work has had on the world and the impact mine has." Louise stands but doesn't advance, looking for all the world like a raging storm hell-bent on destruction. "Why don't we get the studios to put on a double feature: *Birth of a Nation* followed up by my film *Imitation of Life*. Watch 'em back-to-back. *Then* you try to tell me I haven't improved the depiction of Negroes in Hollywood. And while you do that, I . . . Why, I could go to one of the segregated cemeteries 'round here and look to see how much fancier the headstones have gotten since brown folk started getting that Golden State money. That's your fucking contribution!"

Norman is flustered.

But Edythe, she's focused. "Tell me, Hattie," she says, "how was the premiere for *Gone with the Wind*?"

Anna inhales sharply.

Hattie grows rigid.

"It must have been amazing," Edythe goes on. "You, in a starring role in the most successful movie of all time! Oh . . . but wait . . . I forgot. You were barred from attending. Only white cast members were allowed in the theater. But still"—her lip curls into a vicious sneer—"congratulations on the award. Oh, and on convincing the studio to not outright call you a nigger."

Terrance lets out a bellowing laugh, Vada fiddles with her jade and gold bracelet, Sydnetta kicks her legs back and forth, running without moving.

Hattie stands, ready to either come to blows or march out the door.

"Sorry I'm late." Loren bursts in, his suit crumpled. He's breathing at a pace that would imply he rushed from his car. "I had to deal with another client who got himself in trouble." He claims a seat and yanks at his sleeve, revealing a pearl-faced watch. "Ah, I take it back. We're not scheduled to start for another fifteen. But I wanted to arrive earlier. Anyway, I know more are coming, but seeing as we only have six days, let's jump right in. I've decided to propose that Judge Clarke tour your neighborhood and homes."

"You can do that?" Ben asks.

"Will that help?" Ethel questions.

"I want him to see how well you keep them," Loren explains, "the repairs and renovations you've made."

"In that case," Norman muses, "maybe the tour could start at Hattie's? Hard to imagine that won't impress him."

I do a quick double take, surprised by the casual compliment directed at the woman he and his wife just finished tearing apart.

"No." Hattie sits back down. "We don't want to be flaunting wealth. Let's show him a good family home. Maybe we could get him to start with yours, Terrance, or John and Vada, your house would be a good choice, too. It's got a nice wholesome feel."

This flip-flop in attitude . . . I know what's motivating it, but knowing isn't the same as understanding.

"Yes, but we should also bring him to Hattie's," Edythe insists. "You can't look at her grounds and not be dazzled. But maybe don't lead or end with it."

I press my fingers to my temples. I'm listening to the tin notes of pragmatism in the absence of rationalism. The melody's there, but it doesn't sound right.

"Hattie, do you still think you can get some of your fans to show up at court?" Terrance asks earnestly.

Is this what it was like when Roosevelt's and Churchill's people met with Stalin's? Two groups jerking back and forth between attack and alliance?

"I certainly hope so," Dr. Somerville agrees. "We want the judge to see that this is a community that is cherished. That we're here for one another."

But then again . . . maybe . . . this is normal?

It'd been a white Southern staff sergeant who'd issued me a gun, wishing me luck in our mutual fight for the rights of man . . . even though surely, in a different setting, he'd demand my disarmament, deny my rights, and call me *boy*.

"Norman and John know a lot of other prominent figures in the colored business community," Louise chimes in. "Could we have those folks come out, too?"

You don't have to like your allies, but you do have to support them . . .

. . . until you don't.

Chapter 28

One day before the trial.

December nights shouldn't be like this, dry and warm, inviting earth's creatures to take strolls in the dark. I sit with Anna by my side, Terrance and Margie next to her, surveying my cousin's backyard, listening to rustling leaves whose shapes I can't quite see. We could have walked, but Anna and I drove here, the Ford's forward momentum feeling almost rebellious in the face of forced regression.

Margie tilts her head up as the sound of her son and Gertie laughing makes its way out of the boy's second-story window. "It's rare to see so many stars in the city sky," Margie says.

Anna smiles a little. "When I was still a charge of my parents, I used to tell my father he should count those stars as chaperones. Who better to watch over me than Orion the hunter? Who could be more protective than Ursa the bear?"

"And what was your father's answer to that?" I ask.

"He took away my astronomy books."

Terrance barks out a laugh.

Margie rolls her head to the side, dreamy and sweet. "That's the lovely thing about living on a hill. You're closer to the stars." She closes her eyes, breathes in the moment. "I don't think I could stand living so much as a foot lower than this."

"You won't have to," Terrance reassures.

"I believe you're right," Margie agrees with a little sigh. "I won't."

Does she mean that the house will be saved? Or that she will simply give herself more fully to her lover, who can raise her higher?

"Loren's a good lawyer," Terrance offers. "Better than I gave him credit for at first. He'll get us out of this."

Margie gives him a sharp look. Anna shifts in her seat so she's facing his profile. "I thought the goal was to try to keep us in this."

"I meant he'll finish the fight."

"The only way the fight ends is if we lose," she counters.

"Oh, it's such a pretty night." Margie reaches up her arms as if she could hug the air. "It's almost like a painting! Don't you think it's like a painting, Terrance?"

"We won't lose," Terrance says, still talking to Anna, "but even if we did, Loren will appeal."

"If we lose, Loren's appeals will be nothing more than statements of principle," Anna shoots back. "Because by the time our case is taken up by another judge, the police will have already kicked us off our own property."

"And if we win?" I ask.

She answers with her signature one-shoulder shrug. "They'll appeal and we'll have to keep fighting to stay here. But they will never, ever stop trying to take."

"Oh, Anna, you're so pessimistic," Margie says with a giggle. But her laughter's fake, a demand for levity rather than the expression of it. "I for one have no intention of fighting to the end of my days. As a would-be princess I believe I should have other concerns."

"That's right!" Terrance slips his arm around her, kissing her forehead. "As your king it's *my* job to fight to protect you, and your job is to keep looking pretty."

"You think I look pretty?" she asks with a teasing smile.

"My dear, you outshine the stars."

Two days ago, I spotted Margie leaving James's home. My first thought was that she was losing her discretion, maybe because she was preoccupied with everything going on.

Or maybe it's because she's planning on leaving her marriage.

"Pretty helps," Anna says, giving her new handbag a pet. "People have more sympathy for pretty people. Tomorrow in court? I want to be stunning."

Margie narrows her eyes and studies Anna more closely. "You know, I have a lipstick that would look absolutely divine on you. Oh! And a hat I've been dying to wear, but I don't have anything that quite matches it. But you do! You have that beautiful light gray suit! Why, if you walked into court wearing that suit, with my hat and my lipstick, the judge would fall in love with you on the spot!"

Somewhere in the darkness an owl hoots just as Anna begins to laugh. "I guess you better show me the hat and lipstick then."

Margie claps her hands and leaps from her seat, ridiculously eager.

It's not fashion that's got her alight. I think what animates her is the chance for distraction, something to busy herself with other than contingency plans for if, or when, tomorrow goes wrong.

The two women disappear into the house, leaving Terrance and me alone. He lifts his chin and stares up at our celestial chaperones. "Odd times we're living through."

"Are they?"

He pauses, then shakes his head. "Fair point. What we're going through is par for the course. But we'll win, wait and see." He leans forward, placing his forearms over the meat of his thighs. "I'll win everything."

The wind makes a nervous whisper through the trees.

"You talked to me about getting dirt on James Mann since Thanksgiving," I note.

Terrance doesn't even bother turning in my direction. "Do you have anything useful to tell?"

"Depends on what you consider useful. He's talked to me about his time with the French Resistance, how he got his start smuggling wine outta France during the occupation . . . how he met some of his European friends who helped him set up a legitimate business right after the liberation."

It's true, James had talked to me about these things. I don't know what truths are being hidden or how much is just bullshit, but I hope . . . or like to pretend . . . that the only scandalous secret James could possibly have is that of his affair.

Regardless, I'm ready for Terrance's questions; I've thought through every redirect, every innocuous thing I can point to.

But all Terrance says is "Everyone has stories. The ones they birth and the ones they bury. Right now, all that matters is tomorrow."

The owl speaks up again, only this time there ain't no laughter to accompany it. "I know you're confident in victory," I say, picking my words real carefully, "but, for the sake of preparedness, have you thought about where you and Margie—I mean, Marguerite—would go if we lose?"

The amount of time it takes him to answer has me worrying I offended him just by implying losing's a possibility. But when he does speak again his voice is far gentler than I'm accustomed to. "When I asked for Marguerite's hand, I promised her and her father that I'd provide for her. I never explicitly promised to be forever faithful, although whether she assumed that or not, I can't say. But I did promise to provide her with a certain kind of life."

"You can't think Marguerite only married you for your money."

"You need to listen better, Charlie. She married me for my promises. If I break them . . . even if I lower myself by asking her to stay, it's unlikely she will."

I open my mouth to protest, to tell him that the threat to his home isn't his fault. But while it's true some of the residents of Sugar Hill didn't know about the covenants until after they bought their homes, Terrance did. He gambled.

"By now Marguerite's probably complained to you about my occasional after-work joyrides," he goes on. "Her words, not mine. You probably think that I'm using that time to see other women."

"Thought crossed my mind."

"It's not true. They really are just drives. I never get out of the car."

"Where do you go?"

"Skid Row."

I give him a sideways look, wait for the punch line. But Terrance's face is completely sober.

"Skid Row, the place I was born and raised," he says.

It takes a second for the revelation to sink in. That this blustering, egomaniacal success story of a man was born into squalor.

"Skid Row is where my drives take me every time," he continues. "And as soon as I get there, I roll down my window so I can smell it."

"Smell what?"

"Despair. It's the scent of cheap whiskey and gin, hashish, urine-soaked sidewalks. It's the smell of people whose only escapes lie at the bottom of bottles or in the barrel of guns. And then do you know what I do, Charlie?"

I shake my head, repulsed, riveted.

"I leave. I simply roll away from the stench. All it takes is the slightest pressure of my foot on the pedal and it's behind me again. As easy as raising a staff to part the Red Sea." He leans back in his chair, eyes still staring into the dark. "The minute I met your friend Reaper, I recognized what makes us alike. Just like me, he's a refugee of his history. And like me, he knows there are enemies who would like to deport him right back to it."

"I would think a man of James's means would have lots of enemies," I note.

"He does. But they haven't figured out how to ruin him because they don't understand him. Those other men, they're not like him." His lips spread open, baring his teeth in a predatory smile. "They're not like me."

Anna returns with a hat in her hand and a new color on her lips, Margie at her heels. "I don't know what I'm going to have to face tomorrow," Anna says as the two women reclaim their spots, "but it seems I'll look damn good facing it."

"You should wear the dress I got you last weekend," Terrance instructs his wife. "It will be perfect for the courtroom."

Margie stares at him, eyes wide. "But . . . of course I won't be going to the courthouse."

"Yes, you will," Terrance says, not harsh, but in a voice that doesn't invite argument.

Still, Margie argues. "Darling, I simply can't! I have so much to do. Art needs me to . . . Well, I swore to him I'd take him to . . . to the zoo! He'd be devastated if I didn't keep my word."

"I'll tell Art he'll have to wait for another day to go to the zoo. Loren says it's important that every one of us is there."

Margie's face is like a flip book, moving fast from smile to frown to open-mouthed plea. "I can't. I simply can't."

He takes her hand, holds it between his. "You can. And you will. We'll get you some tea with a little bourbon beforehand to soothe that nervous cough of yours." She sways, raises her hand to her throat as if that, not tea, will soothe it.

"Accessorize the dress with diamonds," Terrance says, kissing her hand. "There's no reason for you not to shine."

"Oh, dear," Anna says, the loud volume of her voice giving away her discomfort, "my rhinestones won't be able to compete." When neither Terrance nor Margie responds she fiddles with the hat, then pats gently at her hair. "So what were you boys talking about while we girls were off playing dress-up?"

"Things that were promised," Terrance says, "and things that are owed." He glares up at Orion, his arrow pointed threateningly into the universe. "I am owed."

Anna leans in closer to me, her fingers fumbling with the clasp on her handbag before she manages to get a hold of her cigarettes.

Margie seems to have grown calm. No, she's gone blank. Like she's not fully with us. She follows her husband's gaze, turning vacant eyes to the sky. "The stars tonight," she says, "I simply can't get over how pretty they are."

Chapter 29

The way Anna and I made love tonight was different from all the nights before. I couldn't find the gentleness. I don't think either one of us wanted it that way.

Tonight that ferocity felt right.

She's pressed against me now, her cheek to my chest, the panting and growls she had indulged in during our sex replaced with deep, even breaths.

"I like your anger," she whispers.

The words are jarring, pulling me from the pleasant haze of the aftermath. I lower my chin to try to check her expression, but all I can see is the top of her head. "I ain't angry," I say.

She pulls herself off me, props herself up on one arm, amusement wrinkling up the corners of her eyes, making mockery look kind. "Is it fear, then?" she asks. "Because that can be attractive, too."

"You like your men scared?"

"I like my men a little out of control. Rough." Her fingers slide up and down the middle of my chest. "Happiness doesn't bring that out. But fear and anger can . . . in the right setting."

"The bedroom?"

She grins, nods. "It's the only place I feel safe not being safe."

"That's backward."

"Why? Because someone told you the worst things that can happen to a woman happen between the sheets?" I feel, rather than hear, her sigh. "Maybe for white women, who are apparently so weak they can't handle a lascivious wink from a Negro. Personally, I'd rather take my chances with a violent man in the privacy of my chambers than a violent society in a public square. I'm more likely to survive one than the other."

I stare up at the ceiling, at the few bubbles of plaster that didn't smooth before drying. The mood's broken. "Where are you gonna go if Louise loses this house?"

The fingers that were playing with my chest hair begin to twitch, spreading apart as if to make space for something that ain't there.

"You see, that's the kind of danger that scares me."

"They say they aren't so hostile to us on the east side," I offer. "Maybe you and I could go looking next weekend. Maybe . . . maybe we could go in on a place together."

She pulls her hand from my body, takes a cigarette from the night-stand, lights it without a word.

"A one-bedroom apartment," I continue. "Between your wages and mine we could make it work, maybe even save a little."

"And what would we be saving for?"

"I don't know . . . a house of our own maybe."

"So we should put all our money into a house some white home-owners association will take away from us a few years later?"

"We'll buy where they don't do that sort of thing."

"And where's that, Liberia?"

"Come on, Anna."

"Are you asking me to marry you, Charlie?"

My stomach grips and lurches. "Do you want me to ask?"

"No."

I wait for the relief of that *no* to set in. But the only feelings I can access are ones of confusion.

"Thank you, though," she says, "for asking about my plans. It's the first time you have." I watch as she blows out streams of white smoke from her pursed lips, watch as the shape of it melts into a tobacco-rich fog. "So it's not knowing where you're going to end up that's got you on edge?" she finally asks. "That's the source of all that invigorating fear I just benefited from?"

"I'm not afraid." When she doesn't respond, I persist more forcefully. "I'm not! If I gotta pay to sleep on a couch in someone's South Central apartment for a few months it'll still be a hell of a lot better than nodding off in an army-dug trench."

"You never did change your speech, did you?" she says. "Not even at work."

I don't respond.

"It's a bit in contradiction with my piece, the one in which I argued for reinvention. But, of course, you know that, seeing as you liked it enough to recommend it to others. Tell me what about my article spoke to you?"

I won't let her draw me down a road I don't want to go. "Did you do any reinventing? Are you who you used to be?"

She stares at her cigarette, waits until it's dangerously close to dropping an ember before bringing it back to her lips. "I used to be a Negro girl from Missouri."

I laugh. "And now you've reinvented yourself to what? White?"

"Don't be stupid."

"All right, I'll bite," I say. "If you were a Negro girl before, who are you now?"

"Anna." She stretches out one arm, strokes the headboard before slipping her hand between her head and the pillow. "When people talk to me, they now know they are talking to Anna Caldwell. Me specifically. A woman with a name."

I get it. I know what it means to be just another Negro boy from Virginia.

To be just another one of 'em niggers.

To be just another expendable, colored soldier.

It's only since I've arrived in Sugar Hill that the world started treating me like I had my own name.

Individuality is like fashion. It only matters if people see it.

"What did you and Terrance talk about when I was off with Marguerite?" she asks.

"We talked about James." An involuntary shiver shoots through me as I recall the exchange. "Terrance is aimin' to hurt James. Maybe not physically . . . but it's gonna be bad, Anna." The shudder moves to my voice. "I can't even warn James 'cause I don't know what's coming. I don't know how to protect him."

"With everything going on, you're scared . . . for Reaper." I feel Anna's mood shift again, bringing East Coast winter into this California night.

She gets up, seemingly unconcerned with her nakedness. She taps her cigarette against the ashtray on the dresser, giving me a full view of her.

Venus is a brunette. "You're the sexiest thing I've ever seen."

"Why, Mr. Trammell, I do believe you're in love."

I let my eyes roam. "I certainly love what I'm seein'."

"With Mr. Mann. You're in love with Reaper."

The shock of her words momentarily paralyzes me. No one's ever accused me of nothin' like this. "Anna, I'm not a homosexual."

"Did I say that?" She rolls her eyes, stifles a small yawn. "No. I doubt you'd engage in anything as crass as sex with Reaper. You have me for that. But he's the one who moves you. It was fear for him that caused you to make wild love to me." She takes a deep drag from her smoke. "I get your body, he gets your heart. Guess I should thank him for sharing."

I let my head loll against the pillow. The white walls of my room have turned golden under the electric lights, giving everything a cinematic glow . . . everything except for this conversation. "I don't understand you."

"I think you do," she answers, her voice suddenly contained in a whisper. "I just don't think you're fully interested in the subject matter."

"That's not fair."

Her mouth sets into a new line of determination. But it's the curve of her hip that draws my eye. "I think you understand me just fine, but I *know* you don't understand *him*. You're a man bewitched by a mushroom cloud."

"I don't know what that means."

"That's my point." She stubs out her cigarette and then leans forward, putting her arms on the foot of the bed, letting her breasts swing, before she places her knee on the mattress, too, then the other one, crawling over me slowly. A lioness, positioning herself before launching an attack. "You're a fool."

I feel the heat in my neck rising to my face. "You're making me angry."

"Am I?" She lowers herself, tugs gently at my earlobe with her teeth. "I'd like to feel that. It would keep my mind from wandering to tomorrow." She presses that jagged nail into my chest. "Or should I go over to Reaper's? Try to seduce him? At least he's clearheaded enough to know who and what he wants. And he's not infatuated with his betters."

I grab her and flip her over onto her back. I'm holding tight to her wrists.

"That's right," she whispers. "Let's see if your anger is more forceful than your fear."

I *am* angry.

And I'm so grateful to her for giving me an outlet. For allowing me to lay my fear against her skin.

Chapter 30

I've never been here before, but I know that this courtroom ain't never seen this much color. I'm surrounded by dresses of pink, gray, blue, red, white, orange, yellow, tan, purple, green, turquoise, as if a rainbow got bored of its seven hues and asked God to throw in a few more. There's stylish turban hats made of silk and pillbox hats made of mink. The men are wearing navy, black, and tan suits, but their ties are splashes of bright-colored pride against white button-down shirts. And the faces . . . they're every shade imaginable. White to bronze, copper to ebony. It's standing room only. Reporters line the walls, mostly white but with a sprinkling of black, all of them holding notebooks and pens that won't stop moving. Above those reporters hang portraits of presidents. Washington on one wall, Jefferson on the other. Men who preached freedom and enforced bondage.

This ain't one of Hattie's parties. Here the races have no common ground. But if insults are being thought, they aren't being spoken. The order of the court's got a check on their tongues.

Lester and Dolores Nolan are near the front with Francis and Mildred Smith, sitting so close their shoulders touch, Francis to Mildred's, Mildred's to Lester's. Only Dolores leaves herself an inch of space, as if she, unlike the others, doesn't need the safety of white numbers.

And sitting less than a half foot from Francis is a couple whose skin is as black as night.

The oppressors gotta share a bench with the oppressed.

It doesn't work that way back in Virginia.

What's worse? Being confined to the back of a room among your own or having to sit within touching distance of people who want you dead?

Across the aisle from the spectacle of the Nolans and the Smiths and their black bench-mates are Hattie, Louise, Edythe, and Norman, looking for all the world like a united front. Less than half of the colored folk here live in Sugar Hill; the rest are mostly Hattie's admirers, their focus trained on the back of her head rather than the proceedings. Our brightest Negro star, the woman who raised herself up in a film that brought all of us down. But she's still ours. Our pride if not our hope.

But Hattie isn't looking at her fans. Her focus is on the opposition's lawyer. That white man up there, making his opening statement.

Terrance is watching him, too. He's sitting two rows behind Hattie and five rows ahead of me. I can see his head move every time the lawyer moves, a mouse who can't afford to take his eyes off the pacing cat.

We're all mice right now.

Margie, she's a mouse looking for an exit, turning her gaze to the windows, then rummaging through her handbag, then twisting her neck to get a look at the door.

Every three minutes or so, she raises her hand to cover a cough.

That nervous cough from our childhood, the death knell from my nightmares.

Anna's scratching at her purse where her cigarettes are, she's got the whole bench vibrating with her trembling.

I look behind me to see if others are reacting with the same kind of nerves. I spot Ben Carter in the corner sitting next to a couple of guys I don't know; he's pulling awkwardly at his tie. And there's Louise and Dr. Somerville and Vada, and . . .

Oh, wow.

I nudge Anna. "Look, standing in the back, two o'clock to the door."

Anna turns and takes in a sharp breath of air.

James Mann has entered the room, his presence a show of support for the very community that calls him Reaper.

I look forward just in time to see Margie turn and see him, too.

Her whole being changes. Love brightening her up like lightning against dry leaves.

Or maybe that's wrong. Maybe she ain't looking at him like a lover.

Maybe what she's seeing is a personal savior.

Then the room goes quiet.

For a second, I think everybody in the courtroom is on the same page. That we've all, at the exact same time, noticed James "Reaper" Mann.

And then I realize it's quiet because the opposing counsel has finally shut up.

"Mr. Miller." I turn as if the judge has called my name instead of the name of our would-be hero. "You may proceed with your opening statement."

Loren stands, brushes off his lapels. "Your Honor," he says, "here's the evidence I'm going to be presenting during this case." He pauses, crosses his arms over his chest, and looks down as if trying to remember. "I present to you . . . nothing."

A shocked murmur takes over the court, the kind that might cause the judge to bang his gavel if he wasn't himself too shocked to do it. Terrance partially rises from his seat like he's about to tackle Loren, a linebacker ready to stop the opposing team from scoring.

"Nothing," the judge repeats. I'm pretty sure he isn't supposed to talk right now, or at least he didn't talk to the other lawyer during his opening. But he clearly can't help himself here.

"That's right," Loren confirms. "I submit no evidence to support my case."

Hattie starts looking around, as if she might find an explanation in the crowd. She catches Terrance's eye and he gives her a bewildered shake of his head, too flummoxed to remember how much he hates her. He's not paying attention to Margie at all.

That's good, because Margie only has eyes for James.

"I also move," Loren continues as the room quiets down, "that the opposing counsel be denied the right to submit evidence."

The judge sits back, dumbfounded by the Negro lunatic-at-law before him. "The opposing counsel just wasted over an hour of the court's time listing evidence he apparently thinks gives his clients the right to thumb their nose at the Constitution. But, Your Honor," Loren says, finally stepping out from behind the desk, "there can be no evidence that allows any one of us to do that. Either the Fourteenth Amendment is to be enforced or it's to be ignored. I don't need ten minutes, let alone ten days, to explain that. There's obviously only one right answer. So I humbly suggest you toss this meritless case out so we can all move on with our lives."

The courtroom has gone from murmuring to an unnatural quiet . . . like everybody in here's holding their breath, and that includes the robed man behind the bench. Terrance is hunched over, his head in his hands.

Loren lets the moment stretch, then smiles and tosses up his hands. "Look, if you want to see if there's any truth at all to this baloney about my clients lowering the property values, I invite you to tour the neighborhood. This very afternoon, if you'd like. If that would give you peace of mind, *that* is a worthy use of time. Far worthier than hearing evidence that doesn't have bearing on this case."

"You want me to just walk around the neighborhood, Mr. Miller?"

"Absolutely! Or at least if it so pleases the Court. After all, the only other plans we had were to spend the day cooped up in here."

I continue to observe Terrance as Loren continues. The way his shoulders are trembling, he might be crying.

The plan had always been to get the judge to walk around the neighborhood, but not like this. Not without making a damned case. That's plain crazy.

We're gonna lose. We're going to lose everything.

"Your Honor." The opposing lawyer stands up. It could be my imagination, but he looks a little more confident than he did a few minutes earlier, his ruddy white skin crinkling up in a smile. "I don't know what they're teaching students at the Negro law schools, but I think we can agree that afternoon strolls aren't part of the judicial process."

"Oh, interesting, I'll be sure to let Washburn University know that they've now been designated a Negro institution," Loren quips. "It should be a fun surprise for all the fraternities who denied my membership."

"But look," the lawyer goes on, ignoring Loren's interruption, "if you want to do this walking tour, we can. You'll see what's at stake. It just seems like an odd request from an attorney who says he doesn't like wasting time."

"But it might be helpful for me to get a sense of the area and determine its present status," Judge Clarke muses. "And if I'm going to grant *your* request and not allow any evidence to be submitted at all," he goes on, looking at Loren, "which I'm sure even you would agree is on the radical side, then I *really* need to know exactly what we're dealing with." The judge nods to himself, clearly having made up his mind. "Let's do it. Counsel representing both sides will join me in my chambers to coordinate a tour of the neighborhood later today. In the meantime, court is adjourned until nine a.m. tomorrow."

It's not a murmur this time, but a rumble. Reporters look at one another, trying to gauge if everybody else is as confused as they are. U.S. courts don't break for field trips.

Margie looks to the back of the courtroom again, and this time Terrance notices and follows her gaze.

But James is gone.

Chapter 31

It took all of two hours after getting home from court for me to finally decide to go over and see James. Better that than staying at Louise's, where the entire household is waiting around on some judge to stroll by and tell us if we're good enough for our habitat. If we're human or an invasive species.

I can't be there watching as Anna moves from snappish to muted anxiety.

I can't watch as Louise, always boisterous and loud, sits nervously by the window like a taciturn mouse, as her husband beside her stares at the wall, a sickening new reality sticking to him like tar. They're both sure Loren has lost the case on the very first day.

I can't take the silence.

I only make it a block before spotting Margie. She's with Gertie and Art. Art's skipping along like he don't got a care in the world, yanking on Gertie's sleeve every two seconds. But Margie . . . she's walking beside the other two, facing straight ahead. I can tell she's not seeing anything outside of herself. Her focus is on whatever thoughts are running around in her head.

It's Art who spots me and starts poking at his mama's arm, letting her know I'm walking in their direction.

"Oh," she says with a vacant little smile. "Charlie, how are you?"

A humorless laugh slips out of me. "I guess about the same as everybody else around here. What the hell was Loren thinking? What the hell are we gonna do?"

"Mmm." She watches blankly as Art pulls Gertie a few feet ahead to get a better look at a bunch of ants swarming through a crack in the sidewalk. "Where are you off to now?" Her voice sounds hollow. "It's such a lovely day for a stroll."

I stare at Margie, trying to figure out if she didn't hear me or if she's truly intent on ignoring what I've just said. "I'm headed over to see James."

Suddenly, her attention snaps back. "I can't . . ." She looks over at Art and Gertie and then in a furtive, almost desperate whisper says, "Terrance is expecting me back in a few minutes, I can't come with you."

"Uh, I didn't expect you to."

"Yes, but . . ." She shoots another anxious glance at her companions, then steps up to where they are, briefly touching Gertie's back to get her attention. "Gertie, why don't you and Art go on ahead, I'll catch up in a minute."

"Of course, Mrs. Lewis." Gertie takes Art's hand and pulls him along.

When they're out of earshot, Margie turns back to me and grabs my arm. "Tell him I haven't been able to stop thinking about him all day and . . . um . . . oh, oh, wait, I know!" She opens her handbag and starts digging through it, pulling out a tiny notepad and a pen. Turning her back to me, she scribbles away before facing me again, tearing off the paper from the pad and folding it up. "Give him this," she says, holding it out to me.

I stick my hands in my pockets without taking it. "I need to ask you a question."

She looks over her shoulder at Gertie and Art, watching them move farther and farther away, before looking back to me with an impatient frown.

"Margie, are you . . . did you start up with James because he doesn't have to worry about losing his house?"

"What? Is that really what you think of me?" Her eyes widen with hurt. She presses the folded note against her heart. "Charlie, you must know, this is so much bigger than any house."

"I'm sorry." My head lowers with the weight of fresh shame. "I do know you better than that. The trial's got me talking crazy." I shift my gaze over to those swarming ants. "It is gonna be okay, though . . . even if you choose Terrance and he loses the house . . . if we all lose, it still gonna be okay."

I don't know what I'm saying. If what's happening right now is okay, then the word *okay* doesn't have any real meaning.

Her face fills up with a tender pity that makes me wince. She reaches out again with the note. "Pretty please?"

And this time I take it, stuffing it in my back pocket.

I watch as she turns to chase after Gertie and Art, returning to her husband.

Daniel is leading me through James's home, to the library again, but this time James is there alone. A glass of scotch in one hand, he runs the fingers of the other over the books that line his shelves. He doesn't greet me or so much as acknowledge Daniel when he takes his leave. He seems tense, aggravated.

"Have you read Shakespeare?" James asks as he pulls out a book with the Bard's name written in gold. The binding looks like it is days away from giving up and letting the pages fall free.

"I've read two of his plays." I stand to his side, feeling too antsy to sit.

"Let me guess, *Hamlet* and . . . *Macbeth*?"

"*Hamlet* and *Romeo and Juliet*," I correct.

James releases a sound that is close to a growl. "One play about a bereaved, highly indecisive man who literally drives his betrothed insane, and one about star-crossed lovers who mess things up so badly they end up killing themselves." He places his glass of whiskey down on the bookshelf, dangerously close to the edge, and starts flipping through the book impatiently, moving from the last pages toward the first. Somewhere outside the room I hear the ring of a telephone. "I'll never understand why societies insist on putting misery on a pedestal. As if the most romantic thing about love is its loss." His lip curls, revealing a glint of white enamel. "There is nothing romantic about loss."

Daniel comes into the room. "Michel is on the line again, Mr. Mann."

James doesn't look up, his fingers savagely working the pages as if daring them to rip. "Tell him I can't talk right now, but that everything's under control."

"So," I say as Daniel retreats, "you don't like Shakespeare, then?"

"I prefer his romances and comedies." James's hand stills on some print he apparently has some affection for. "*The Winter's Tale,* in which a king discovers that the unrelenting force of his affection is strong enough to raise his lost love from the grave. Or *Cymbeline,* a story of jealousies, anger, and violence that ends with the reuniting of lovers and the demise of those who tried to keep them apart. Or . . ." And here he smiles and holds up the book so I can read the title as he recites it, "*All's Well That Ends Well.*"

"I know the expression though not a lot about the play."

"It's my favorite." He turns the book back to himself. "It's about a woman who is rejected by her husband. But she goes to great lengths—even deceit and trickery—in order to be with him. To make love to him. And when he realizes the lengths she's gone to just to have him . . . he becomes smitten. Her determination is what convinces him that they're meant to be." He closes the book. "At his best, Shakespeare teaches us about the nature of love. He understood that love is when you long for someone the moment she's no longer in your presence. When she doesn't leave your thoughts for an instant. It's when you're . . . you're . . ."

"Obsessed. You're describing obsession."

"Obsession." James frowns. "An ugly word for a beautiful thing. I wish they'd come up with another."

"Why did you come to court today?"

He finally looks at me directly. "I was curious."

"That's all?"

"No, not all. I need to be ready, Charlie. If Terrance does lose his house, I need to make sure Marguerite and her son can quickly settle with me."

It's the wrong answer.

"So that really is what you're hoping for? That the case is lost so you can swoop in and save Margie?"

"I would give Terrance my house and everything in it if he would just let her go." Again, a phone rings. James looks at the door. There's something in his face that isn't kindness or menace. Something a lot more common than longing.

Desperation. I think what I'm seeing is desperation.

He says, "If he would just relinquish his hold on what's mine."

"She doesn't belong to you."

"But her love for me does. It's the same thing."

Even Romeo would see this man as a sap. I pull out Margie's note and hand it over. "From her . . . written less than twenty minutes ago."

"And you waited this long to give it to me?" He snatches it from my hand, holding it so I can't read it.

But I can see the way it makes him smile.

Daniel comes back into the room. "It's Michel again. He insists on speaking to you."

James whirls on his butler, his smile scorched by a sudden blistering rage. "Tell the bastard I've got it handled!"

This is only the second time I've heard James raise his voice, and I sure as hell haven't seen him breathe fire like this before. His hands are shaking so badly you'd think he was on the verge of a seizure.

Daniel meekly backs out of the room.

We both just stand there, James watching the door, now closed. And me watching him.

I open my mouth to ask what the hell's going on, but my throat's gotten too tight to squeeze out the words. I don't want to pull back these curtains.

Because . . . because I'm not sure I care. I don't give a shit.

We're all sitting on pins and needles, on the verge of losing our homes along with our vision of tomorrow. So I don't care about Michel. What I care about are my friends, my community.

I care about me.

"What do you want the verdict to be, James?"

There's only one answer I can tolerate. One answer that will keep me from marching out and siding with Terrance, condemning James as the enemy. One answer that will keep me from going back to calling him Reaper.

"I don't need to see Terrance lose anything other than his marriage," James finally says. His voice has got an echo to it, like he's turned his mouth into a hollow cave.

"So you haven't even thought about how much easier it would be to take Margie from Terrance if he loses his home?"

"Oh, for God's sake, yes, of course I've thought of that. For me, a favorable ruling for Sugar Hill is a risk. But, Charlie . . ." He takes a deep breath, glares at his hands, mastering them, forcing them to cease with their trembling. Then his eyes focus in on the note he's still holding, registering it once again like he forgot it was there.

Slowly, with newly steady hands, he folds it once, then twice, before gently slipping it into his breast pocket. "Charlie," he repeats, the echo gone, kind tone resummoned. "Negroes in Sugar Hill are living their American dream. That's . . . It's beautiful. I want that for everyone."

My whole body wilts, suddenly overcome by some force of feeling. I stagger to a chair, clutching at the armrests as if they're handrails for a crumbling staircase. "This can't disappear."

"Charlie." He says my name softly, surprised by my collapse.

"I need to believe in something." I'm crying. It's embarrassing. But I'm crying. "I want to believe in this."

"In what?" He's kneeling by my side, staring up at me with those black eyes. He no longer looks desperate. Just compassionate.

But the answer's too big.

I can't explain that on the night of that lynching I didn't have to see a rope put around a man's neck in order to witness a murder.

I bore witness.

In the darkness, while huddled under that table with Margie, I had raised my hands in the air like I had seen people do in church. I waited for the silence to be broken by the sound of angel wings, waited for God to send one of His messengers to save the innocent and smite the wicked.

Instead, I heard . . . I *felt* God's pulse . . .

. . . stop.

I bore witness.

The silence took the shape of a divine corpse. I was still weeks away from my eighth birthday, but that torch-bearing mob gave me the wisdom to understand:

There had surely been a crucifixion. Just not an Easter.

A German philosopher said it first . . .

. . . God's dead.

But heaven? That's a whole 'nother story.

I bear witness.

I see the salvation that wraps around the columns of Louise's house. Relief is woven into those velvet curtains in James's guest room. The promise of some kind of reward after suffering? That promise is sitting on Hattie's mantel in the form of an idol named Oscar.

And to think the preacher says it's prayer that will save us.

Every Sunday Margie and I saw lil' Barbara Flynn in church, praying so hard we thought she'd be raptured right there on the spot.

Barbara, who was raped, who was murdered, whose father's store was burned to the ground.

They say it's different here. And I want to believe.

I need that faith the way a soldier needs his gun.

I want it the way James wants Margie.

I relax my hands, stroke rather than clutch the armrests. I hadn't known leather could be this soft, almost like a hard silk. For a second, I'm sure I hear a quiet, rhythmic pounding.

Wealth's got a heartbeat.

My tears stop. I close my eyes. In the darkness I've made I see

Hattie's Oscar. I see it staring back at me with golden eyes that aren't there, hearing those earthbound prayers, standing regal on a mantel that could've been an altar.

I bow my head.

I ask to be saved.

Chapter 32

Déjà vu.

The courtroom looks the same. The people look the same. All that's different is that this time Anna and I are standing in the back next to Terrance and Margie. We arrived in court as early as we had the day before, but others arrived even earlier. So we stand with the press, men who see the coming judgment as a one-day headline rather than the possible annihilation of decades of accomplishments, the aerial bombing of a hard-earned future.

"I read in the *L.A. Times* this morning that this trial might go on for more than a month," Margie says, her breath coming shallow and quick. "I couldn't bear that. How could anyone bear that?"

She says it like a month and change is the same as forever. But to me it seems short.

I'd rather spend a year in this new purgatory than to be so quickly dumped back into a familiar hell.

"Did anyone else see the judge yesterday while he was touring the neighborhood?" Anna asks, sliding her hand into mine, perhaps more for comfort than affection. "He walked by Louise's so quickly. He barely glanced at the place."

"I saw him," Terrance says. "Loren and the other lawyer were standing by while he stopped for a friendly chat with one of my neighbors."

"Which neighbor?" Anna asks.

"Lester. He was talking with Lester."

I look up toward the front. There's Lester, talking animatedly to his friends Francis and Mildred. Dolores is sitting quietly by his side, her head low.

Lester looks happy.

Anna's palm begins to dampen. Margie starts coughing.

I should buy a camera. Take a picture of every house, of every Negro living in Sugar Hill. In the years that follow I can remind myself of how convincing a mirage can be.

"Mind if I join you?"

All of us but Terrance turn at the sound of James's voice. Margie's cough quits and she sways forward. For a minute I think she's gonna fall into his arms, ask him to carry her away, but she checks herself just in time, before her husband sees her inclination.

"I'm surprised they're still letting people in," Terrance says, addressing James while keeping his eyes on the front of the room, "considering how packed it is."

"They cut it off after the woman behind me," James replies. "I got here just in time."

The look of gratitude on Margie's face suggests she's reading more into the statement than its surface meaning. The corners of James's mouth inch up just a fraction. He sees it, too.

"All rise! The court of the honorable Judge Clarke is now in session!"

The judge walks briskly to his bench, then waits patiently as everyone settles themselves. He eyes the attorneys, then allows his stare to creep over the court, settling briefly on a few of the white reporters, lingering on a few of the colored ones. Can't tell if he's glad of the media attention or if he's wishing it away.

"After investigating the character of West Adams Heights," Judge Clarke says, projecting enough to make his voice sound loud and full even to those of us in the back, "it is clear to me that the plaintiffs' complaints . . ."

I wince as Anna digs her nails into the skin between my knuckles. Out of the corner of my eye, I see Margie inch a little closer to James.

". . . present insufficient cause of action under the equal protection clause for this court to continue proceedings."

The people in the courtroom are looking around at one another.

"What is he saying? What does it mean?" I hear Margie whisper.

But none of us answer. None of us are sure.

"I am thereby granting the defense's objection against the introduction of evidence or testimony."

He pauses and is met with a sea of blank looks. No one understands.

Or, more accurately, no one can believe.

He clears his throat and goes on. "Other judges who have had similar complaints brought before them have avoided the real issue. They should not and this court *will* not. It is time members of the Negro race are accorded, without reservations and evasions, the full rights guaranteed them under the Fourteenth Amendment."

Again, he pauses. Again, he's met with a room full of mouths that gape but don't speak.

But being quiet ain't the same as being still. Heads are swiveling as folks check to see if others are hearing what they're hearing. White hands are clenching, black hands are rising, some to the sky, some to a heart like they're ready to burst into the Pledge of Allegiance.

"Certainly there was no discrimination against the Negro race when it came to calling upon its members to die on the battlefields in defense of this country in the war that just ended."

The room's spinning. Or maybe it's the whole country that's doing that. I had to pack away my uniform to avoid the wrath of white Southerners. And now I'm sitting here, in court, listening to this white judge tell the world that my service has meaning. That I got a right to be proud.

Judge Clarke keeps talking, explaining why racial covenants are unconstitutional, why this case has no merit. He keeps talking and talking, speaking pointed justice into excited silence.

And then he stops, leans back in his chair, before finally saying,

"That's it. That's my decision." He smiles a little, shakes his head as if he was expecting more from his audience. "Court is adjourned."

The gavel falls.

And the court *erupts*.

Cheers.

Curses.

Laughter.

Screams.

It's like six hundred different instruments playing four different tunes. It's the melody of all that colored happiness playing fiercely over the drumbeat of white rage.

People are dancing to it. Dancing in the aisles of this very court-room like it's a New Orleans jazz club.

Anna is in my arms, her happy tears smearing on my cheek. I see Lester, dragging Dolores through the crowd. His normally white face's gone crimson. At first, I think that expression he's wearing is one of anger.

But when he passes, I see the truth. That man's downright scared.

This is a damn beautiful day.

I look over at Margie, just in time to see her pulling away from . . .

. . . James.

James. The man she instinctively embraced upon hearing that ver-dict is James.

Terrance won't lose his house, but still for Margie it's James.

And this time Terrance sees it.

By the look on his face, it's real clear he understands exactly what he just witnessed.

But it's hard for me to fret too much about that.

The most important fight is won.

For the first time in decades, I am within reaching distance of some kind of faith.

———

The weather is almost too perfect as we walk out of the courthouse. Blue sky, the kind of puffy white clouds children place over drawings of square schoolhouses with triangle roofs. The kind of clouds you could make wings out of.

Nature itself wants to join in this story of miracles.

We've got to maneuver through the people, many clustered around Hattie, who's standing on the top step talking to a reporter.

"Words cannot express my appreciation," I hear her say as the five of us push past. I only get a glimpse, but I do note the pink-colored diamonds sparkling on Hattie's earlobes. And I see Louise and Robert, hands linked, looking like a couple of newlyweds who've just said their vows. I see Norman and Edythe laughing with Ben Carter like they're all the best of friends.

Terrance leads our group farther down the sidewalk, where we've got some breathing room. "That was a triumph," he says.

"Yes," James replies. "I do feel like a victor."

Terrance gives him the kind of smile you make when you're marveling at the audacity of another.

No, not marveling . . . that ain't it. Terrance is looking at James the way big-game hunters must look at a lion.

With respect.

And with a thirst for the kill.

"Did that really just happen?" Anna asks with a laugh that's much lighter and less worldly than I know her to be. "I'm not dreaming? Oh my God. Oh. My. God! It's so big!"

For once, Anna has not picked up on the tension building around her. I can tell by the way she's bouncing and giggling that she completely missed seeing Margie embracing James. For once she's not a cynic. She's not the pragmatic, cut-the-bullshit publicist I know.

She's just happy.

"How about we celebrate with champagne?" Terrance asks, his eyes on his rival. "You have plenty of that. Come by my house this evening with a few bottles for us to toast with."

"Yes! And, James, we'll pick you up in my car!" Anna announces. "We'll all arrive together."

"That wouldn't exactly be convenient for you," James says, flashing her a bemused smile. "I'm eight blocks to your west, Terrance and Marguerite three blocks to your east."

"Oh, I don't care, I don't care!" Anna says. She's radiating delirium and joy. "I just want to drive my new car to every beautiful Negro-owned house in Sugar Hill and laugh in the face of every ugly white neighbor who tried to be rid of us. I just want . . . I want to dance!" She does a twirl right there on the sidewalk and I feel my heart pound in time with her new rhythm.

"Very well," Terrance says, steady, cool. "James will bring the champagne and you'll bring James. Marguerite and I will take care of the rest." He wraps a possessive arm around his wife. "Won't we, princess?"

Margie nods. She's as uncharacteristically quiet as Anna is uncharacteristically bubbly.

Roles are being switched up and reversed.

This should be the happiest day of all our lives.

I hope James's smile survives the night.

But if it doesn't, I'll be there for him. I've got the strength for that.

Right now, I've got the strength for anything.

Ours is the truest dignity of man, the dignity of the undefeated.

—Ethel Waters, in regard to the whole Negro race

Chapter 33

The pop of the cork makes Anna squeal and clap. Margie stands beside her, subdued, her nerves having shrunk her smile down to Mona Lisa size.

James carefully fills the five flutes Terrance provided. A fire crackles in the living room hearth. Art's rowdy laughter leaks through the floorboards of his second-floor bedroom. A child heard but not seen.

"I think it's obvious what we should toast to," James says as we raise our glasses.

Terrance clears his throat, the sound of an engine revving to race. "To the strong," he says.

"Hear, hear!" Anna's enthusiasm practically lifts her right off the ground.

But Terrance isn't done. "To those of us with the courage and grit to fight the men who try to take what's ours." His hand slides along Margie's lower back until her dress wrinkles from him gripping her waist. "To those too strong to be beaten."

James hesitates, then nods. "To the strong."

We tilt back our glasses.

Anna's eyes go wide with appreciation.

"It's Dom Pérignon," James says, noting her reaction.

"You do have a taste for the expensive." Terrance takes a seat on his sofa. "Although maybe some of the company you keep is on the cheap side?"

James looks confused at first but then notes Margie's stricken expression. The fire pops and dances as if changing with the mood. "Who exactly are you suggesting is cheap?"

Terrance raises his hands as if to beg pardon. "Don't get touchy. I keep cheap company, too, sometimes."

"Tell me who you're referring to. Say it."

James's tone is sharp enough to finally cut through Anna's giddiness. Her wide grin closes into a line.

"Terrance," Margie whispers, "now is not the—"

"Pinkman," Terrance interrupts, directing the name at James. "We both have associations with a man named Colson Pinkman. The fellow who was arrested yesterday."

The room gets real quiet. Anna surrenders to a frown.

"Colson Pinkman," James repeats. "The name does sound vaguely familiar, but I'm afraid I can't place it." His voice is steady, his forehead just slightly creased as if he's trying to remember.

If he hadn't paused a second too long to speak, you might not know he was lying. "That makes sense," Terrance says jovially. "Most days I like to pretend I'm only vaguely familiar with him, too. He and I came up together. Did he tell you that?"

"Like I said, I don't know the man—"

"Skid Row. That's where Pinky and I were raised." He crosses his ankle over his knee. "Our mothers were friends, sharing booze and johns. And we both found our way out, me through the world of insurance, he through the world of nightclubs. The two of us were the rare success stories to come out of that place. I still am. But he fell off."

"I'm sorry to hear that." James sips his champagne, posture relaxed, eyes alert. "I didn't know you came from such humble beginnings."

"Humble!" Terrance barks out a laugh. "There's a word for it. I bet you came from *humble* beginnings, too. I rose above mine."

"As did I."

"Did you?" Terrance asks. "Or did you jump?"

James glances at me, but I'm lost, too. There's a trap being laid, but I can't pinpoint the bait.

"There's a difference between jumping and rising," Terrance explains. "You can't rise from filth with dirty hands. You've got to leave all the muck behind you. The neediness, desperation, and subservience as well as the excessive drinking, the gambling, the violence, and—" He breaks off for a second, leans forward, places both feet firmly on the floor. "The narcotics. Can't take 'em, can't sell 'em. If you don't leave the dirt behind you, you haven't risen, you've simply jumped. And when you jump, you fall. Right. Back. Down." He lets his words hang there a bit, relishing the moment. "Pinky, he jumped. Jumped pretty high, too, but he let the bad memories of childhood get to him. It kept his feet from finding purchase. So he got into drinking, dope, and gambling, vices that left him too addlebrained to see the acceleration of his fall."

"What are you going on about," Anna moans, falling petulantly into an armchair. "Sad stories don't pair with champagne."

"Precisely." James raises his glass to Anna in agreement. "And without a personal connection to the man, his plight doesn't hold a lot of interest."

"Oh, that's right." Terrance scratches his chin in an exaggerated way, making a mockery of pensive thought. "I'm the only one with a personal connection to Pinky. Your connection is professional."

"I don't know what you're talking—"

"Of course you do!" Terrance happily interrupts again. "You helped Pinky get some work! You and that Corsican friend of yours."

Corsican.

A place where the locals speak French . . . but with a different accent.

I think of yesterday, those phone calls from Michel, the rage that hit James, lighting him up then disintegrating into a greater storm.

"Those Corsicans are a smart bunch!" Terrance continues. "In New York they gotta sell their poppies to the mob, and the mob then turns around and sends their wops out to sell them for five times what they paid. But colored labor's cheaper than Italian, isn't it, James? Men like Pinky won't need nearly as big of a cut. Corsicans can run the whole operation and make more than they ever dreamed. But, of course, they still need an intermediary. One Negro to oversee the niggers."

Jesus, is this true?

No, it's not. It's too ugly, too extreme. My judgment can't be that flawed. "Stop it," Anna whispers.

"Yes, stop," James agrees. "You're being both offensive and ridiculous." He looks over at Margie, hoping she'll back him.

But Margie has her neck bent over her glass, the heel of her left palm pressing into the side of her head as her eyes dart back and forth, absorbing information she's not ready to hear.

A flash of panic in James's eyes that's quickly bottled and hidden. He stands with his profile to the mantel, half his face lit up orange and red, the other simply black. "Marguerite," he says, his tone confident, calm, "rest assured none of this is true."

"I've reconnected with Pinky," Terrance says as if no one else is speaking. "I've reclaimed my role as his adviser and confidant."

"Whatever advice you've given your friend couldn't have been very good, seeing as he's in jail." James continues to look at Margie, who looks at no one.

"Yes. It's a pity that happened. Almost as if someone close to him tipped off the police."

I can't tell if James is breathing. He's gone so still one might think he caught sight of Medusa.

"But maybe that's for the best," Terrance suggests. "We can't have criminals in our midst, causing trouble, giving ammunition to racists, bringing us all down. Besides, Pinky was bound to be caught eventually, one way or the other. He's charming enough to gain people's trust, but discretion? Not really his thing. Cunning and weak, those are the Pinkman trademarks. Just the kind of bastard who would turn rat in exchange for a lighter sentence. You know what I mean?"

"What you're saying is meaningless," James manages, his eyes still fixed on Margie, silently pleading with her even as he speaks sharply to her husband. "You're telling tales."

"About what? Pinky turning rat? Oh, that's just an educated guess on my part. All I know is if he had dirt on me, I'd get out of town. Immediately." Terrance shrugs, lifts his glass, takes another sip. "I gotta hand it to you, Reaper, this really is excellent champagne."

Reaper. He called him Reaper to his face.

James turns to Terrance, moves in his direction, away from the fire, from the warmth. "This little performance isn't about some man named Pinkman. You're angry because now, after years of betrayals and infidelities, you've finally lost her. You're jealous because you've finally figured out that Marguerite loves me."

James isn't facing Margie anymore, so he doesn't see her flinch.

But Terrance does. He releases an exaggerated sigh, puts his glass on the coffee table. "And here I thought you were smart."

"Marguerite," James says, his veneer of calm weakening.

"You were a backup plan at best," Terrance says. "Even I can see that. She was scared I'd lose the house, and you promised security. But the game has changed. There's no more use for you."

"Marguerite," James says again, urgently now, "it's time for us to come clean. Tell him you love me."

But Margie doesn't respond. She can't.

She's in the middle of some kinda transformation.

It can be seen in her expression, her posture . . . a feathered fan turning into an iron shield. Terrance sees it, too, and slowly rises to his feet, his eyes glued to her.

"You heard what James said." Her words somehow both quiet and loud.

"Yes, that's right, you heard!" James triumphantly exclaims.

At the same time Terrance asks, "What are you getting at?"

"It's love." She holds the word *love* in her mouth like a cutlass between her teeth.

"Oh, for God's sake," Anna snaps. "Charlie, the entire neighborhood is celebrating right now. Can we please go join them?"

"Margie," I say carefully, "do you want me to stay?"

Margie shows no sign of hearing me. "I don't need to heed your warnings," she says. Again, Art's laughter finds its way to us. Margie takes an advancing step toward her husband.

It's that step that shocks me. Margie stepping in to controversy rather than running from it. "I could leave with James tomorrow."

"But you won't," Terrance retorts.

"I could leave with him tonight."

James looks downright exultant.

Terrance folds his arms across his chest, forces out a chuckle. "You'd be miserable." Then he says to James, "If you really knew Marguerite, you'd know that your criminal lifestyle, the ugliness, the constant threat of being found out . . . it would kill her. Like taking an orchid into a blizzard."

"Don't be silly, Terry. I'm a much stronger flower than that. I'm a fucking rosebush."

Anna actually gasps. Even James looks startled. We don't know this voice, this woman. James opens his mouth to speak, but she doesn't give him the chance.

This woman ain't about to let this be a conversation between men. "There are so many gardeners who would petition for my care. I'm coveted." Margie pauses, shrugs her shoulders, forms a smile that's as beautiful and cold as the crystal flute in her hand. "Any man blessed enough to have me had better work hard to keep me. Because, you see, I could have any man I want . . . and we both know that now, don't we, darling?" Her voice drops an octave, her stare lancing through the once impenetrable wall of his ego. "I know what I deserve."

Terrance draws in a sharp breath through his teeth, while James puts his hand on her shoulder and whispers, "Yes, my love, that's right. You know I will always treat you as the princess you are."

James heard what he wanted.

But Terrance? He heard what was said.

"I'm the one who drove us here," Anna says, brushing her hands together, getting to her feet. "And now I'm leaving. Charlie, you can come or stay. Up to you."

"You should all leave," Margie says.

It's the permission I've been waiting for. I start to follow Anna out.

"James, you should go with them," Margie adds.

That stops Anna and me in our tracks.

"Marguerite?" James's face is a blur of confusion, fear.

"Oh, that was quite rude of me, wasn't it?" she says, her voice suddenly lilting again. "But I just need to talk to Terrance alone." She takes James's hand and brings it to her lips for a kiss. It looks like a romantic gesture.

Then again, she's done the same with me. It's nothing more than affect.

But James doesn't see that. The kiss gives him the strength of hope.

"I'll wait right outside for you," he suggests, "while you pack some things. And if he gets out of line, for even a moment, all you need to do is call for me."

"You're such a dear!" She smiles, cups his cheek. "But Terrance isn't going to be any trouble. I must insist you let Anna drive you home now. It's rude to make a girl ask twice." She flutters her eyelashes, coquettish and sweet.

I look to Terrance, expecting some kind of explosion. But of course that doesn't happen. He doesn't explode because he hasn't lost the battle or the war.

He's only lost his advantage in an impending negotiation.

And James . . . for the first time ever, he looks small. Like a child. He doesn't get it. But I do.

The woman James has pledged his life to is using him. She's always been using him. First as an insurance policy, now as a weapon. She's holding him up like a grenade, threatening to pull the pin if others don't get in line.

Maybe Margie didn't transform just now. Maybe she's been revealed.

Anna tugs at my sleeve. "Now."

James looks at me, hapless and unmoored.

"Come on," I say quietly. And he follows us into the night, looking over his shoulder several times along the way.

The streetlight is out and there aren't enough clouds in the sky to reflect the lights of the city. Our eyes struggle to adjust to the dark.

"Perhaps we should wait a minute," James says, looking over his shoulder once more. "She's bound to come out soon."

Anna doesn't say a word, simply walks straight to the car.

I gently take him by the elbow. "Let us drive you home."

"I doubt she'll take more than a few minutes," James says, but allows me to direct him. I hate his confusion, hate what Margie's done.

He gets in the back seat and I take the front. Anna turns on the engine and flips on her headlights, making a U-turn from our parking spot to get us going in the right direction.

And when she does, her headlights flash over the Nolan house, sweeping over their front door, where Dolores is standing, her shoulders heaving, her face black and blue . . .

Is that what I saw? It was so quick. I turn back to get another look as Anna speeds off. But the streetlight is out. All I can see is darkness.

Chapter 34

The car idles in James's drive as Anna and I watch him climb up those broad, curved stairs to his estate. Behind him he casts a shadow, stretching back to us as if reluctant to move forward with the body it belongs to.

"Maybe I should stay with him."

"There'll be no comforting him," Anna notes. "No peppy words to make any of this right."

"He needs a friend."

"What he needs is to leave here and start anew." The glow from James's outdoor lights is powerful enough to illuminate the interior of the car, but just barely. As Anna talks, I can see her profile, but not the little lines that crinkle when she smiles or the creases at the bridge of her nose when she frowns. "He has no future here. And if what Terrance said is true, you only put yourself at risk by associating with him."

"I'm going to stay with him." I reach for the door, but Anna grabs my arm to stop me.

I turn to look at her, impatient but waiting.

"Some secrets aren't really secrets," she says.

"What?"

"They're just . . . uncomfortable facts. Fundamental truths that no one has the stomach to say out loud."

"Anna, we gotta save the philosophizing for another time . . ."

But her grip tightens. "Every Negro in Sugar Hill will tell you they're a champion of their race. They'll volunteer for the USO for colored soldiers, they support their local chapter of the NAACP." She briefly closes her eyes, I can hear her swallow. "Hattie has never turned down a well-paying role that she knows is demeaning. Norman doesn't cut his clients breaks on their dues when they hit hard times. Somerville founded the Negro Waldorf, not a free housing complex for those fleeing Jim Crow. There are no Marcus Garveys here. No Harriet Tubmans. No one is going to risk their fortunes, let alone their lives, for a cause."

"Where is this comin' from?" But she's got my attention, put my urgency to rush to my friend on hold.

"The people here are aspirational, not inspirational, figures," she goes on. "The secret of Sugar Hill, which is not a secret at all, is that to be truly successful you have to put your own interests first. Even if that means others get hurt."

I look up at the stairs to the estate. James is already inside. "You talkin' survival of the fittest?"

"No, idiot, that's fascism." She releases my arm and gives it a slap. "No capitalist is stupid enough to annihilate the weak, not when they can exploit them."

"Jesus, Anna." The motor of her idling car continues to purr. We're not moving, but nothing is still.

"Figure out who you can underpay"—she breaks off briefly, rubs her right thumb into her left palm—"or what prejudices can be twisted to your benefit. Burglaries, pickpocketing, those are crimes for the poor. But the wealthy? They rob others of their power. Your cousin Marguerite gets it. She's stronger than your pal in there. She'll get what she wants, using flattery as bait, getting every suitor hooked on the drug of denial. And if you're going to get what *you* want, you're going to have to start paying a little more attention to who you need to ally with—"

"You mean use," I snap.

"—and just as important, who you need to avoid," she says, refusing to acknowledge my commentary.

"And what exactly do you think I want?"

"To rise instead of jump." Even in the dark I can see her eyes twinkle as she notes the quieting effect those words have on me. She takes a second to pull out a pack of cigarettes from her handbag. "I gotta hand it to Terrance for that one," she says as she lights up. "That was pretty good."

"James ain't sacrificing for a cause," I point out.

But Anna only shakes her head. "He's turned love into his cause. He'll die for it."

It's too much. "I'll see you back at Louise's later. Right now, I'm gonna be with my *pal*." I get out of the car as she mutters some curse under her breath.

I hate her cynicism.

Hate it all the more because I suspect she's right. About everything.

I take the stairs at a pace just short of a run. Somewhere nearby I hear an owl hooting; another answers from not too far away. Sounds that remind me of a place I'm always trying to escape: home.

It's James, not Daniel, who answers. James with a wild hopeful look that slams into me before crashing into disappointment.

"You thought it was going to be Margie."

"She'll be here soon." He waves me inside.

I step into his foyer. He's already pacing away from me by the time the door closes.

"There's some truth to it, isn't there?" I ask.

He's pacing in earnest now, his eyes jetting all over the place. "I should go to her. I shouldn't have left her with Terrance. I should drive back there immediately."

"Truth to what Terrance said." I lean back against the wall, trying to absorb its hardness, its strength. "You work for Michel."

"With him, I work *with* him." He glances at the door, his feet still moving from one side of the room to the other. "But I'm gonna take a break from that. Start again. With Marguerite. For Marguerite."

"Michel's a dangerous man."

James doesn't seem to hear. "I helped him. He helped me. Proven myself."

Is that a hint of a Southern drawl I'm hearing? "And Colson Pink-man?"

"Pinkman's not a problem. No matter what Michel says."

"Michel? I thought we're talking about what Terrance said."

"Pinkman's just a man who's done some odd jobs for us. Nothing more sinister than that. I made sure he won't be a problem. Michel . . . he's emotional. But when he has more time to think, he'll remember I've proven myself. Time and again, damn it. He'll remember he can trust me. When he calms, he'll see that everything's been handled. And he knows I gotta step away from all of this."

Is he having some kinda breakdown? This frenzied movement, re-petitive, fast sentences composed in uncharacteristically unpolished speech, talking nonsense like it's wisdom. "How have you proven yourself?"

James shakes his head again. "Marguerite will be here soon, any minute now."

"Have you sold drugs for him? Helped him establish some kinda L.A. crime ring?"

"I'm in international trade. I've made my fortune in wine. Margue-rite and I will go away together to Paris. It'll be beautiful."

He's trying to turn words into a kind of incantation. A wish he thinks he can make true by blowing out a handful of candles.

"You gotta tell me if you're dangerous. Are you some kinda cold-blooded killer? That why they call you Reaper?"

He stops so fast you'd think he banged into an invisible wall. "Reaper." He says the name like he's hearing it for the very first time. He finds a chair, sits. The frenzy that just possessed him is abruptly and alarmingly gone.

I cross my arms over my chest, not to show defiance but as an in-stinctive gesture of self-protection. One thing I know, the only thing more dangerous than a man determined to sow chaos is a man who becomes chaos.

"I've changed." His jaw shifts left as his eyes briefly close. "I've tried to build a life that won't just dissolve into nothing. I've tried. But I'm always running into someone who knows . . . a dead version of me. Or someone who knows someone who knows someone who knows the name . . . that goddamned name." He shakes himself as if trying to cast off a dark memory. "If you understood the purity of the love I have for Marguerite, you'd know . . . nothing that beautiful could exist in a bad person."

His chest moves prominently with each breath, his posture's rigid, like a man strapped to a chair awaiting electrocution.

Seeing him like this, it's got an enervating effect. I want to crawl up the stairs to his guest room; at least the nightmares I'll find there are ones I understand.

"You're not bad. I don't got it in me to believe that." I rub my eyes, as if that'll help them see. "Not 'cause you think the best of Margie, but because you think the best about the world. And you've been a true friend to me right from the start."

"And you to me."

"All right, then, friend to friend, you gotta get out of here."

"I can't yet."

I want to smack him.

And yet part of me gets it. When Margie's parents took her away, James went off and made something of himself. Fattened up his pockets thinking it'd be enough to buy a ticket back to that place where he and Margie were possible.

And I enlisted because Jim Crow took a lot from me. And I guess you could say I made something of myself, too. Got a medal for the postponement of two deaths and the prevention of one. I still can't figure out if I'm proud of that or wounded by it . . . maybe both. But I did think that medal meant something, after all. I thought it meant I could go home to that same place I left and things would be different.

It didn't work out that way.

I let my gaze wander the room, thinking about all those servants who were here scrubbing this place down after his party. How many times have these walls been wiped clean? "Nobody gets to go back, James. Best any of us can hope for is to move the hell on."

He's motionless, deep in a trance.

"I don't care what you're trading in," I go on. "I've seen men turn peaceful through dope and violent through wine. As for the law, well, you and I both know the laws weren't written for us nohow. Not for our protection or benefit anyway. But if any of those things Terrance said are true, go. Don't wait for Pinkman to start talking. Don't wait for Michel to decide you're some kinda liability. You gotta see that there are a thousand different ways this can go bad."

"I'm staying, Charlie."

"For Christ's sake, James, there are kamikaze fighters who've got better survival instincts than you. You gotta go . . . now!"

"I'm waiting for Marguerite."

"She's not coming! Can't you see she ain't comin'?"

"She loves me."

"Okay, maybe, but not enough!"

"You're wrong. She'll come." As if to prove it he leaps to his feet and goes to the door, opening it wide to welcome in the woman of his dreams.

But the woman isn't there. Just the dreams.

Chapter 35

I get to work late the next morning bleary-eyed and off balance. When I reach the elevator, Norman is there, late himself. He smiles with a sheepish kind of joy. "Seems I wasn't the only one up late celebrating."

I nod, wishing it were true. The day is young and already it has been packed with crates full of mixed emotions and conflicting ideas.

I had never seen Louise, Robert, and Patty in a better mood. Even Anna, who had woken up irritated that I'd dismissed her warnings the night before, found herself sliding into better spirits as the coffee was poured. By the time breakfast was done, she was immersed in the joy being served at the table along with all those sausages and toast.

And why shouldn't we be happy? We're all winners.

All except for one man. A man I happen to love. Love more than my sister, who died in her youth. More than my father, who kept my affection for him in check with his fists. I can't imagine feeling this strongly about a lover, where lust muddies up intention, or to a child, where obligation does the same. My connection to James has no logic. And I don't want him to hurt.

Norman pats me on the back as we step into the elevator. "You and Anna should come over to dinner this weekend," he says, jamming his finger against the button labeled 2. "This victory's too big for only one night of revelry. I'll invite Marguerite and Terrance, too."

I try to prod my tired brain into coming up with an excuse to say no. But then the doors open and across the room, over the heads of dozens of agents and assistants working hard at their desks, I see Terrance and, inexplicably, Margie, who's in the middle of an animated conversation with his secretary. Margie sees me first and starts waving like she's hailing a cab. Terrance sets his sights on Norman and gestures that he'd like a word.

"An interesting development," Norman says under his breath as he points Terrance toward his office and goes off to meet him. Margie beelines to me.

"Charlie, my dear!" She smiles wide, sweet. "Which one is your desk? You must show me where the magic happens."

"No magic, just sales." I reluctantly lead the way.

"Anything can become magic when done well enough, and by that standard you've become Golden State's very own Houdini!" she says with a giggle. "Why, I bet every lady client you have is thoroughly entranced by you!" When I get to my desk, she claims the chair in front of it, her movements so graceful you'd think sitting was dancing.

That feels right 'cause this here's a performance. I didn't see it before . . . how her every move is choreographed, how even her laughter is music composed hastily before release. All the effort it takes to appear effortless.

She leans forward as I claim my seat across from her. "You'll never guess why I'm here."

A whole bunch of agents on the floor are talking among themselves when they should be working. It's unusual, but so is yesterday's big news. Still, there are enough industrious souls here to fill the room with the sound of typing. A few more are calling clients, practically yelling into their phones, having forgotten that they're the ones struggling to hear over the din, not the person on the other end of the line.

Unfortunately, they aren't so loud as to drown out Margie.

"Terrance is finally going to take a vacation with me! We're even bringing Art and Gertie. They're waiting for us at that lovely new breakfast spot across from the Lincoln Theater. It's pancakes and eggs and then off to Val Verde! Isn't it marvelous!"

I'm not interested in playing along. "This means you're stayin' with Terrance?" I ask. "Abandoning James?"

"What would you have me do?" Margie pushes her lower lip into a pout. "Abandon my husband for a drug dealer?"

A few desks over an agent named George bellows into his receiver, "*Trust me, your family will thank you for it!*"

This is the wrong place for this conversation, but then nothing about this conversation is right. "Just because Terrance says it, doesn't make it true."

That veneer of gaiety she's wearing scurries away long enough for me to see a glimpse of what may be a somber sincerity.

Or maybe that's an act, too.

Either way, it's in a gentle, serious tone that she says, "Before James tracked me down, I had completely forgotten my own worth."

"You've never struck me as insecure."

"But I was, you see. James will always be the man who changed all that for me. I won't forget it. Not ever." She sits back in her chair, carefully folds her hands in her lap. "You can tell him that, if you like."

"You want *me* to tell him?"

"And when you do, I'm sure you can impress upon him that it would be best for all if he . . . moved on—"

I wince, hearing words I've said to James coming from her lips.

"—from me, and from Sugar Hill. Seeing as it might be . . ." She hesitates, wiggles her shoulders a bit as she tries to summon up the right word. "Ruinous," she finally settles on. "It might be ruinous for him if he were to stay in Sugar Hill . . . or in Los Angeles for that matter. And that would surely break my heart. All I want is for him to be happy. Somewhere else."

"If you want to end it, you'll have to do it yourself."

She shakes her head, her eyes going full puppy dog. "James will need me to be as cruel and remote as possible for him to give up. Anyway, I can never talk to him again. Terrance and I . . . we've come to an understanding, an agreement. It's good. Truly it is."

"*You've worked hard! You deserve peace of mind!*" George yells. It's a wonder the man he's pitching to hasn't already gone deaf.

"Terrance will cheat on you again," I say to Margie.

"Then I'll leave. For someone better, richer, a real prince perhaps! I certainly won't be single long. But Terrance knows that, too, now, so I suspect we'll be fine." The phone at the closest unmanned desk starts ringing. Margie cocks her head in its direction. "You're a prince for looking out for me, Charlie, but please be happy for me, too. My husband and I are in love."

"That man loves you like he loves his car, and you love him like you do your mink, it's a feelin' that's got more to do with status than heart."

"Oh, you do go on. Anyway, Terrance dotes on his car and he's the one who bought me the mink, so." She shrugs and looks at her watch, a delicate thing on a rose-gold chain. "I hope he won't be in with Norman long." She exhales loudly, as if the short wait is wearing her thin. "We've already been delayed due to Norman coming in late. Gertie will be wondering what happened." She smiles at me, flutters her lashes. "Be a dear and tell Terrance I went to order our breakfast. I know what he likes." She stands, adjusting her purse on her shoulder.

"It wasn't bullies," I say, my voice low.

She looks at me, confused. "What wasn't—"

"It was the Klan. Vic panicked and ran out of the house—"

"Don't do this—"

"—and they lynched him—"

"That's enough." Her eyes are darting around, her breaths coming fast enough to hear.

"—when they found his body, it was so badly beaten it was hard to recognize, but not impossible—"

"Enough!" A couple of folks nearest us startle and look our way before politely turning back to their business. "Enough," she says once more, softer now. "I told you, I don't believe it was him. I don't know why you won't . . . why you won't just go along with it!"

So she hasn't completely fooled herself. She knows her pretty stories are lies. "Sometimes," I say, feeling frustration bubbling up into my lungs, "you gotta face things. I know how hard it was for you to lose Vic. I know what that night did to you, and to me for that matter. But no, I'm not going along with your fairy tale. I won't 'cause I know that if you refuse to look at what's wrong, you can't know what's right." I lean forward, overtaken with a new form of urgency. "Please. I need you to accept that. Just this once I need you to sit here with me and acknowledge what's real."

She's staring at me hard, unflinching. "Vic is in Mexico." She sounds out each syllable. Her tone perfectly even. "He's probably on a beach right now." She brushes some invisible lint off her sleeve, pats her hair.

She's gotten back into character.

"Enough with this silliness. I have a vacation to get to. Now, you be a dear and talk to James for me. You will, won't you?"

My disappointment is so intense it feels like pain. "No, Marguerite, I won't."

She blanches. It's the first time I've called her anything but Margie, a nickname that signals a fondness that's still fresh in its grave.

"We're not children. I can't pretend to be your protector no more," I go on. "And I sure as hell ain't gonna protect you from the problems *you* made."

In her face I see the flicker of anger, then distress, before her mask clicks back into place. "You won't talk to him for me. Even though it's for his benefit?" When I don't answer her mouth twists into a shockingly ugly glare. "I see. I suppose that means you're abandoning him, too."

I stay seated as she breezes through the room, toward the elevator. Watch as it swallows her and blissfully takes her away.

She's gone less than fifteen minutes when Terrance steps out of Norman's office and calls me into his.

I step inside his four walls and close the door behind me, marveling at how quiet it is. It's so easy for him to block out the noise of every worker in a less-powerful position. He's standing, not sitting at his desk, scribbling out some notes. He hasn't shaved or bothered with a tie. He's looking more haggard than rugged. "Did Marguerite go to meet up with Art and the nanny?"

"Gertie. Your nanny has a name." I don't move from my place by the door. "Marguerite says she'll go ahead and order your breakfast for you."

"She knows what I like."

"So I've heard."

He drops his pen with a snort, then places his hands in his pockets and stares at a framed picture on his desk. "Have you seen this?"

Reluctantly I approach as he turns the photo my way. It's Marguerite holding baby Art in a baptism gown. Marguerite looks more sultry than usual, gazing at the camera with lids half closed. But that may just be the exhaustion of new motherhood.

I look up at Terrance and see the red lines that stretch out from the corners of his eyes toward his pupils.

"I ended it with Dolores," he says.

"When'd you find time?" I turn the photo back to face him. "It's only been fifteen hours since the shit hit the fan."

"She called last night." He puts his hand on the back of his chair and slowly swivels it left and right. "Les, a nickname that should be spelled with two esses, got sauced after the verdict, roughed her up more brutal than his standard fare. She called thinking I was going to save her."

I must've misheard him. In the story America likes to tell itself, white women need to be saved from Black men, not by them.

He's chewing the inside of his cheek, his fingertips tapping the chair as he rotates it back and forth. He's revealing emotions he normally hides. "She thought I might run away with her, leave my wife and child, steal her . . . protect her, from Les." His laugh's so bitter it poisons the air. "Can you imagine having a life privileged enough to leave you that naive?"

I can see the frustration in him, the humiliation he's trying hard not to acknowledge. He may have the confidence of a champion, but even he knows that it would be a death sentence to be seen with a black-and-blue white woman, no matter who actually did the damage. He knows that even if he's man enough to save her, he's not white enough to do so with any credibility. He knows that some stories are so precious to the Anglo imagination that when you try to edit them, you die.

I don't like Terrance. But I hate seeing the limitations of his bravado. "Not like you wanted to spend your life with her anyway," I hear myself say. "She'll call a friend or a family member who will help her."

"Everyone she knows, she knows through Les, except for me. She told me I was her only hope, but . . ." He shakes his head, stares up at the ceiling. For a second, I think he's fighting back tears. But then his mouth curves into a sardonic smile. "He called her a nigger lover. First time he's ever got something right about his wife."

I almost laugh at the macabre humor. "Will Dolores be the last of them? Or will there be more?"

"White women?" He hesitates and shakes his head again. "Maybe not. As it stands, I already have the woman all other men crave." His smile turns more cheerful. "Marguerite is hoping Reaper will leave town. I hope he doesn't. Things are about to go south for that son of a bitch and I want a front-row seat. And I'd like him to see Marguerite on my arm, my ring still on her finger, knowing I won."

"Does it bother you, though?" I ask, my eyes flicking to the framed diploma on his wall. "That she had an affair?"

"An affair?" He scoffs. "Hardly. She let him woo her is all. Apparently, he tried to kiss her, but she told him she couldn't until she settled things with me. And now things are settled. The Dresden Green Diamond is mine. No other man will ever touch her. At least not outside of his fantasies."

I know how difficult it is for a man like Terrance to delude himself. And yet that's what he doing, and all for the sake of his wife.

Maybe they are in love.

"Did Marguerite tell you that we're vacationing? Last minute, but it's a slow time of year. Norman won't have a hard time holding down the fort." He tears a piece of paper off his notepad and scratches out a number. "For the resort where we're staying," he explains as he holds it out to me. "If you hear anything about Dolores's predicament, let me know."

Now it's my laugh that turns bitter. "We may live in the same neighborhood, but you know damn well Dolores and I aren't in the same circles. Unless she's taken away in an ambulance with a siren, I'm not gonna hear a thing."

"Exactly," he says, pressing the piece of paper into my hand. "I'm afraid that's the point."

Chapter 36

Throughout the morning the other agents come up to me to talk about the Sugar Hill win. Secretaries and accountants want to talk about it, too. Almost everybody who works at Golden State was either in or right outside that courtroom. They want to relive the moment they heard the verdict in the way people always want to relive the best and worst unexpected moments of their lives. Recounting exactly where they'd been sitting or standing when they got the news. Repeating the exact words of the judge like we all didn't hear the same thing. These folks don't have to live in the neighborhood to feel like the victory belongs to them, too.

By noon everyone here's given up on getting much done. Norman doesn't seem to care. He's treating this workday like a mandatory office party, giving only Terrance leave not to partake. Never seen this much joy in a room full of colored folk outside a church or a cotton club. And it's lifting me. But not as high as the others.

I keep seeing James's face. And the space inside me that used to be filled with love for my cousin is rumbling like an empty stomach.

So when, later on that afternoon, the switchboard operator puts through a call from James, I take it, eager to hear how he's getting on.

But the call does not start well.

"He kidnapped her," he says right after hello.

I lean back in my chair. "Wanna run that by me again?"

"Terrance kidnapped Marguerite. I went to their house early this morning. Terrance's car was already gone, so I knocked on the door. No one was there. Then I parked across the street and waited. Nothing. He's kidnapped her, Charlie."

I fold myself over my desk, letting my forehead rest on the wood.

"I know this is hard to hear." His voice comes through the line steady. The frenetic energy of yesterday is gone. "I know Terrance has been helpful to you, Charlie. But you also know he's a cold-blooded bastard."

"No one's been kidnapped, James."

"Why, you don't think him capable?" There's the edge of impatience pushing through. "Terrance is heartless. I spoke to Dolores after I saw Lester drive off. She has a black eye and what's probably a broken rib. Lester did that, and when she called Terrance for help . . . Charlie, he refused her."

"Of course he refused her," I groan. "Come on, you know what can happen to a colored man who's seen with a white woman when she's in that kinda shape. That right there is a shoot-first-ask-questions-later situation."

"What are you saying?" James asks, sounding genuinely bewildered. "You don't turn your back on people you care about no matter what! Someone that callous, that cruel, who the hell knows what he's done to Marguerite! I'm an idiot for leaving her with him last night. What I need is for you to find out if Terrance has any family, in or outside of L.A., anyone or anywhere he might have taken her—"

"Stop." I say the word forcefully, louder than I should. A few people overheard and are looking my way. Or maybe they're looking because my head's on my desk while talking on the phone. Either way I gotta get it together.

I sit up, hunching my shoulders, trying to make myself small as I continue in a voice just above a whisper. "I saw both Marguerite and Terrance today. They went on a family trip. It's what she wanted."

There's a long pause on the other end of the line. "James?" I say, thinking I might've lost him.

"That's ridiculous," he finally replies. "It makes no sense."

"It does." I glance around the room; people are no longer looking at me, or if they are they're being discreet about it. "James, it's the kinda thing a gal might do when trying to save her marriage."

Again, he takes a while to answer, but this time I hear breathing.

"Hey," I say, feeling all kinds of sorry for this man, "want to go out for a few beers tonight? Maybe shoot some pool, talk—"

"He must be threatening her," he interrupts. "Or Art. Maybe he threatened to take Art away."

"Even if he did, that's his right, he bein' the father and all. It may not be the best reason for her to stay, but it ain't the worst."

"I can make sure she doesn't lose her son. I just have to find her and assure her."

"No, that ain't gonna help. It's over." I look across the room and see there still is one person watching me. Norman. Even from this distance I can sense the question in his eyes.

"Marguerite isn't like her husband!" James insists. "She would never turn her back on me or anyone else she loves. That's not who she is."

"Come on, James, I'm not even sure Marguerite knows who she is." Norman is walking over. I lower my voice even more. "But she does know what she wants. That's the part you gotta accept."

I hear the click. The line goes dead.

Norman stands at the corner of my desk, watching, as I put the receiver back in its cradle. "Everything all right, Charlie?"

"Yeah." I shuffle some of the papers in front of me. "Just a confused client who mistakenly thought he had insurance on something that never really belonged to him in the first place."

I end up staying at the office late. I enjoy talking about yesterday's trial with coworkers, who will keep their talk to what everybody considers public knowledge and aren't interested enough to ask why some of my laughter is followed by sighs.

The streetcar that takes me away from South Central is packed, people practically leaning out the windows for air. But the chaos grounds me. Every time I hear the cry of an impatient child and the scolds of his mama, every time I'm jostled or forced to shift my position to make room for more, I'm reminded of what exists outside of the petty romantic dramas of my friends. It reminds me that I'm headed somewhere: Sugar Hill, where the rich Negroes live. The ones who don't stand down when white men like Lester try to take what's theirs. That's where *I* live.

I'm a man with a future.

When the streetcar gets to my stop, I find myself in a much lighter mood than when I boarded. I have to walk a little uphill, but even that feels good, that slight strain in the back of my calves reminding me that I'm climbing.

Instead of going straight to Louise's, I stop at a Sugar Hill spot where you can see the whole city below, twinkling in a way that makes me feel like I'm above the stars.

James is gonna be fine.

He's got money, he's smart, he's got a home. Whatever trouble he's gotten himself into, he'll handle, because that's what happens around here. In Sugar Hill the things that would destroy Negroes in other places . . . don't.

I spend another minute to take in the sprawl of L.A. I thought my world had walls, but there ain't nothin' here obstructing my view.

I turn and start toward Louise's. It's December, but I barely need my jacket. There are Christmas trees in some of the windows of the homes, lit up like the city beneath us. I breathe in deep, half expecting to smell those fir trees and—

It don't register at first why I'm falling forward. My brain can't make sense of it, but my body's got instincts. I catch myself, my hands taking the impact rather than my face, the worst damage being the pain in my knee, which I can't keep from scraping against the pavement.

For a second, I don't move, just wondering how I got here.

And then I smell it, both the liquor and the hate lording over me, behind me.

I twist my body and see Lester, breathing heavy like he had actually just done some fighting instead of simply pushing a man from behind like a weak schoolyard brat.

I get myself up; he doesn't move to stop me.

He's got his feet planted wide. "Is it true?" He ain't yelling the way some drunks do. The ones who yell are easier to handle. They're sloppy and unsteady. I can tell right away that's not the kind of drunk Lester is. He's the kind that just gets meaner, crueler.

He pushes back his jacket and I see what's in his waistband. Black metal against his white shirt. It's an item I got real familiar with during my time overseas when I was duty bound to kill.

"That friend of yours, he lay hands on my wife?"

A white man who hits his wife will jump at the chance to kill a Negro.

"I didn't believe it. Some funny-talking cocksucker comes outta nowhere and thinks he gonna tell me about what's goin' on with my wife?"

"Who are—"

"But then I start askin' 'round," he interrupts. His speech is slurred, but his focus is sharp. "Two people say they saw Dolores goin' in . . . in n' out of his big ol' house. You tell me, is that where she is?"

Where she is. So that's it. Two Sugar Hill women, one colored, one white, decided to abandon the men they don't want, both on the same day.

The realization feels more like an echo than a thought. I'm studying Lester's snarl. I'm smelling his breath.

And I'm thinking about the rules of Virginia. I'm supposed to cower, beg for any mercy I can get and, if necessary, point him in the direction of whatever other colored fella he's trying to lynch just to save my own skin.

I'm supposed to be impotent.

"I asked you a question!"

I look down at the gun. I know the rules of survival.

But it's different here.

I've never been a brave man off the battlefield.

That was before I knew my place.

Survival rule #1: Lower your eyes when a white man addresses you.

"Hey, monkey boy, you deaf?"

I raise my chin, look him straight in the eye. "My name's Mr. Trammell."

Lester bursts out laughing, the rancid whiskey stench hurtling forward like a chemical weapon.

"You should go home." I say it like I'm calm. Like there's more to me than a pounding pulse and cold, prickling skin. "You need to sleep this one off."

He slides his fingers over the metal handle of his pistol, back and forth, like he's petting a house cat. "Don't think you're invincible just 'cause you found one nigger-loving judge. You don't wanna push me."

The first time I laid eyes on Lester, Terrance made a mockery of him. I had wanted to do the same. But I'd been fearful.

And now he's got a gun . . .

. . . and for once in my life I'd rather die than be meek.

"I'm not trying to push you, Lester." I hear myself use his first name, after telling him to use my last. I'm scaring myself.

But when I try reaching inside to give the coward in me the reins, I find nothing but mutiny.

And so I persist. "I never spoke one word to your wife." I take a second, work to keep each breath steady. "Now you're gonna have to excuse me, I'm tired of talking."

All I gotta do is turn around and put one foot in front of the other. Walk away. But I find myself frozen, staring at Lester, who's staring back at me.

And then his lower lip starts trembling. "She's my wife."

This white man, with a gun, is really out here acting like a victim in need of comfort. Like I'm gonna give him a shoulder.

A short laugh escapes me.

A laugh. Loud and sharp, the sound smacking against his crumbling composure like a baseball bat to a stack of dominoes.

Dear God.

I just laughed in the face of an armed white man on the cusp of a breakdown.

Even Terrance wouldn't be this brazen. This bold.

I feel my spine straighten.

"I'm sorry," I say. "I truly don't know where she is."

And then I turn my back on a white man with a gun.

Each of my steps makes a sound against the pavement, a soft drumbeat, tapping out my paces, my time.

I may only have a few more seconds of future.

But if he shoots me, he'll know he's not just shooting another nigger. He'll be shooting a man with a name.

I've gone three steps, now another four, another nine . . .

Louise's door is only about eleven yards away. I don't know if Lester is still behind me. I can't look back. I gotta keep moving.

And I do

and I get to the door

and open it

and I go inside.

And I close it.

Anna comes into the foyer, sees my face. "Charlie, what's wrong?"

What's wrong.

I start laughing. It's not a normal laugh. It doesn't come out short and sharp like it did a minute ago. This laugh is wild, crazed.

I'm frightening her.

"Charlie, what's gotten into you?"

I can barely talk, I'm laughing so hard, but still I manage to gasp out three words:

"It's different here."

Chapter 37

Terrance calls me less than an hour later, apparently too impatient to wait and see if I'll call him. "Well?" he asks. "I take it you haven't heard the sound of any ambulances?"

I put my forehead against the wall. I hadn't been able to get out the words to Anna. Couldn't get myself together before she lost patience. Taking me for drunk, she stormed off to her room. I've been on my own here, wrestling with what happened, reconciling my recklessness with my inveterate instinct for survival. Trying to work out if I've become a madman or just a man.

And now Terrance wants me to put his mind at ease . . . or just give him some kind of feeble excuse to put aside his guilt, as if Dolores not being taken to the hospital means he doesn't have to worry about the situation she's in.

"I haven't seen any ambulances."

Terrance chuckles, like we're playing a game, as if we both think such a scenario's too extreme to be likely.

"I did see Lester, though," I add. "He sought me out for a conversation, brought a gun with him, too."

There's a long pause on the other end of the line. "You're joking."

"He knows you've been sleepin' with Dolores. And I think she left him. He asked if she was with you."

"And he had a gun," Terrance says, making sure he heard that part right. "How does he know about me and Dolores?"

"Apparently, people saw her going in and outta your house."

"What? Dolores has never set foot in my house. Are you sure that's what he said?"

"Yeah, I'm sure." But now I'm sifting through the memory, trying to pull from it each precise word.

"Did he mention me by name?"

"Come to think of it, I'm not sure he did." My pulse speeds up again, I don't know why.

"Did you tell him where I am?"

The question gets my fur up. "I wouldn't do that."

"Okay, that's good." He launches into another long pause. "I need you to keep an eye on the situation. Give me updates every night, even if you don't think there's anything to report. I can always extend my vacation a few more days, give Les the time to find Dolores and cool off."

"But you want Dolores free of him, right?" I ask, enunciating every word. "You want her safe. You don't want him to find her."

"I'd love for Dolores to be safe," he snaps, "but not at the expense of the safety of my own family. Not if it leads her idiot husband to think that I kidnapped her off the street. I will not deal with his theatrics."

But this is all your fault!

It's what I want to shout over the line. But something stops me. Maybe it's that I can see he's doing exactly what Anna says we all need to do, put our interests first. Maybe it's because even though I don't subscribe to that line of thinking, even I gotta ask if any colored man should put his interests behind that of a white woman. After all, there's a historic debt to be paid.

Or maybe it's because something else is nagging at me. Like there's this idea knocking on my skull, hoping I'll let it in and give it a look. And whatever it is . . . it's making me anxious again.

Or maybe that's just me, trying to get over what just happened, yards away from home. Me wondering if the threat of Lester is truly over.

"I gotta go, Terrance."

"I need daily reports, Charlie! I'm going to call you, same time tomorrow, be sure you pick up."

I hang up the phone without confirming. My eyes rest on a painting on the wall across from me, one of Louise's favorites, an angel in the process of materializing. A painting of what's almost there . . .

Lester never said Terrance's name.

He was talking about him, though. He had to have been.

But why would anyone think they had seen Dolores going in and out of Terrance and Marguerite's house? There's no way that happened. Marguerite, Gertie, Art, or at least one of them is always there when Terrance is. There wouldn't be an opportunity for Dolores to be with Terrance alone over there. Maybe someone just thought they saw her come out of the house. She lives right across the street. Someone might have gotten it confused.

Or maybe . . .

My hand finds the phone again. I dial slowly, methodically.

"Mann residence, may I help you?" Daniel says over the line.

"It's Charlie, I need to talk to James." My voice comes out raspy. I wait, feeling my throat drying, my tongue thick between my teeth.

"Charlie," James says, now on the line, "I'm glad you called. I need to apologize. I shouldn't have hung up on you this afternoon."

"That's . . . I don't care about that."

"But I do," he insists. "You were trying to keep me informed. You were being a good friend. I sure as hell didn't have the right to get cross with you."

"It's fine. It's not why I'm calling." There's more I've got to say, but my throat is so dry. Every breath scratches at it. Something is very wrong.

Or it's about to be.

James reads my silence but reads it wrong. "I know Marguerite went off with Terrance of her own volition. She's just overwhelmed. Confused. But she won't be able to stay away from me for too long. I doubt her marriage will last another week. And after waiting all these years, what's another week?"

"James, do you know where Dolores is right now?" My throat's a scorching desert. I'm choking on sand.

"Right now?" he repeats. "Let's see, what time is it . . . Right now she should be boarding a train to Canada with enough money in her pocket to get herself settled. I told her I'd send her more once I have an address, keep her afloat until she finds some kind of work."

"You sent her to Canada," I say dully.

"I drove her to the station and gave her the money, if that's what you mean. She's a friend, Charlie. And unlike some men, I don't turn my back on friends when they're in need."

"Jesus, James. You don't know—"

"Hold on a second, someone's at the door."

"Don't answer it."

"Why? It's most likely Michel. He called earlier and asked to stop by."

"Tell Daniel not to get the door!" I try shouting the words, but they come out a strangled scream, a wounded animal, a soldier crying for help while drowning in blood. Patty comes down the stairs to see what's going on, Anna right behind her.

But James is already walking away from the receiver. I can hear his voice, but it's far away. "Daniel, what's going . . . what are you doing here?"

And then his voice moves to an even farther distance. I can't make out his words, but I hear him.

I hear another voice. Lester's.

Dolores has never been to Terrance's house. But she's been to James's.

It was James who was "lurking" around on their street this morning before Lester went to work.

"Don't answer," I hiss into the phone, even though there's no one there to hear me, even though I'm trying to whisper change into the past.

But Lester can be handled. He's all bark. I've proven it. James will handle him even better than I did. I know it will be okay because—

There's the deafening blast of a gunshot and then another and another. A deep, guttural cry from someone in the background. And then it's Lester yelling, sounding desperate, angry . . .

. . . maybe triumphant.

I don't hear James at all.

Chapter 38

It would have made sense if I'd locked the door to Louise's house, refusing to go out until I knew it was safe.

Would have made sense if I'd bolted from the house and run as fast as I could to get to James, tried to save him.

But I'm walking. Not striding toward a destination, but drifting toward a vision, moving so slow time itself leaves me in its wake.

Some part of me knows Anna's yelling. I feel her tugging at my arm, trying to get me to stop, to look at her, to tell her what the hell is going on. I'd like to answer. But my tongue's fallen asleep in my mouth. Every part of me is asleep.

Even when I hear the sirens, I can't seem to pick up my pace. Even when the patrol cars pass, their lights drenching the night in red, not even then. I have a vague awareness of Anna letting go of my sleeve, of her falling back, maybe spooked by all these police cars, one, two, three . . . and now the fourth, some distance behind.

People coming out of houses, onto front lawns. Both Negro and white. Everybody with the same colorless curiosity.

Maybe they're looking at me, too. The Negro somnambulating through these here streets.

Somnambulating's one of those words I looked up in the dictionary when I was a kid, back when I thought knowing the meaning of words would help me understand the meaning of anything else.

These houses I'm passing don't look right. Their windows transformed into glowing, gold snake eyes, their grilles slits of pupils. Except the few that don't have lights on at all, those are shadows, dreams fading from memory. I could be hallucinating.

It might have gotten colder. I don't have my jacket. I do have my shoes. I have what I need to run.

I can't run, can't rush to the scene of the crime.

Can't run from it either.

Then, despite my lethargic pace, I catch up with time. It's waiting for me, coiled around James's block. The red lights of those police cars cast light on its movement, rotating in a cycle like it always does, moving us all forward, then backward along the same lines, until every horror's got an air of familiarity.

A man in uniform stands in front of James's estate, not letting anyone unauthorized on the property.

An older man I recognize from one of the gatherings at Hattie's comes out in his dressing gown. "What's happening?"

I walk past him, toward James's gate. This still could be a dream. That'd explain why all these different people I'm passing on the street seem to be speaking with the same voice. *What's happening? What happened?* Everybody's trying to figure out what tense to use.

"I know," I say, although it seems unlikely that I meant to say it to the police officer. But I see I'm standing in front of him now. That it looks like I'm addressing him, even though volunteering to talk to cops isn't a thing I do.

"What do you know?" the officer asks.

"I know what happened." I choose past tense. But could have just as easily chosen present or future.

I know this cop's studying me. I don't know if he's going to ask me another question, dismiss me, handcuff me, arrest me, or beat me. Cops are unpredictable. That's why I don't talk to them outside of my nightmares.

"Hold on a minute." He calls over another officer, tells him to stand guard, and then goes down the drive, into the house. I think he's gone a long time. But maybe that's wrong.

When he comes back, he tells me to follow. He walks me up the concrete stairs. "This place is really somethin'," the officer says as he leads, gives me a friendly grin. He's got an accent, not Southern . . . Midwestern maybe. "You niggers sure do live fine 'round here."

"My name's Charles Trammell."

But this one doesn't take it as a correction. "Mine's Officer Beatty." He thinks I'm being friendly. He's one of those white folk who thinks slurs spoken with a smile should be taken as banter.

We walk inside and everyone's here. A handful of cops, a few servants standing silent against a wall, eyes glazed. Daniel is among them, face red and puffy like he's been crying. Lester is here, sitting in a chair, an officer kneeling next to him, talking kindly.

James is here, too. His white shirt's gone red. That's not caused by the hole in his neck. The blood coming from that wound is on the floor. It's seeping, not gushing, as it must have done when the bullet first hit. His body is already learning that it's dead.

In the war I saved a fellow soldier who now says he's lost all hope on account of his lost legs. But James, I think you could have taken all four of his limbs and he'd still see promise in the future.

His hope was so strong the only way to get it out of him was to stop him from breathing.

I didn't save him.

The cop who'd been talking to Lester stands and walks over to me. "One of my men tells me you know what happened."

I look at Lester. He looks at me, then quickly away.

"Here's the thing, we know, too," the cop says. "Mr. Nolan here spotted this Negro lurking around his residence before he went to work. When he came back from work, Mrs. Nolan was gone, ain't that right, Les?"

Lester nods, staring at the ground.

"So Mr. Nolan came here to find out what was going on and this

Negro here bragged about assaulting Mrs. Nolan in the most demeaning of ways and attacked Mr. Nolan. Mr. Nolan had no choice but to defend himself. That's what happened."

"And how do you know that's what happened?" I ask. A complete sentence. There's an acidic burning in my gut.

"We know because we have a witness, don't we, Danny boy?" He looks over at Daniel. And then I get it.

Daniel's dark face ain't puffy and discolored from crying.

And Daniel lowers his eyes, says, "Yes, sir."

It's as if I did a dissection on myself, pulled out my shame and helplessness like a no-good appendix, only to find that it looks just like Daniel . . . who looks like me, on the ground, looking up at white men who have my blood on their knuckles.

"But where is she?" Lester moans.

"Now that's a question we might need some help with," the cop says, still staring me down. "Do you know what happened to *her*? To Mrs. Nolan?"

Lester looks up at me lamentingly. He doesn't appear hateful or defiant. He looks like a man who wants to say sorry but is too scared and selfish to risk such an incriminating word.

What made him spare me and kill James? Had more drinks led to more anger? Or maybe he had abstained in the short time between our confrontation and now. Maybe he's the kind who needs to sober a little before finding the resolve for violence.

"I don't know where Dolores is." There's no emotion in my voice. How can that be? "All I know is that Lester Nolan was looking for her."

"I ran into him," Lester says. "I ran into him and asked if he'd seen her. But he hadn't." His neck bends down toward the floor. "He doesn't know Dolores."

"How can you be so sure about that?" asks the cop.

I'm looking down at James. And James is looking up at nothing.

"He's got nothin' to do with this, Larry," Lester says. I can still smell the whiskey on him. "He's one of the good ones."

I wince because I know what that means. Not a troublemaker. Not a fighter. Not one of those niggers who demands dignity.

Except Lester knows better than that. He knows I got a name.

Sitting there, hunched over, trembling, he doesn't seem like a man trying to insult. He looks hapless and scared . . . ashamed even. A murderer struck by how his violence didn't give him confidence . . . by how he's gained nothing.

But look at everything he's taken.

"Okay, I trust your judgment, Les, but I'm gonna be asking everybody around here a lot of questions. You can count on me finding Dolores."

They're old pals. That makes sense. The system is a home that was custom-built for men like Lester.

James is losing his color. People always draw the Grim Reaper wearing black, but the color of death has always been white.

"You can get going," the cop says. "But we'll be talking again soon."

I look at Daniel, but he won't meet my eyes.

"I said you can go," the cop says a little more sternly.

And I feel myself sigh. I feel myself walk away from my friend.

White America has not learned what it should have learned from this war.

—Langston Hughes, *Chicago Defender*

Chapter 39

I'm staring at the bathroom mirror.

James has been dead for six days.

Been staring for more than twenty minutes now.

Or five, if you count days by hours, the tick tick of the clock.

I keep thinking these life events are going to change the outside the way they change the inside. I keep looking for gray hairs, new lines across my face, like a line you might strike across a sentence you wish you'd never written.

But I looked this way when I first arrived in Sugar Hill. I looked this way after I got my new job and the morning after I first slept with Anna.

And I look this way now.

The story of James's end has been playing out in the papers like one of those radio soap operas. Drama feeding on the drama printed the day before, salacious details piling up so high they're bound to tip over, suffocating any remnant of truth under them.

The first story printed in the *Los Angeles Times* only used James's name once. Every other reference to him was some type of descriptor: a Negro man, a colored man, a criminal suspected of kidnapping the fair-haired Dolores Nolan.

The next day it was reported that Dolores Nolan might not have been kidnapped, might have wandered off in a daze after a head trauma from the assault. This all according to the police, who offer no evidence to back up the theory. At least none the *Times* bothered printing. After all, those who enforce the laws get to decide the truth.

By the time that story hits, I've been besieged by well-wishers. Everybody in Sugar Hill knows I was James's friend. Maybe his only real one. Norman told me to take a week off work. Louise went as far as offering to make me soup, even though she's still allergic to kitchens. Even the great Hattie McDaniel paid me a call. They all commiserate with me, decrying the injustice. Tell me how shocking it is, how confounding, bewildering, earth-shattering that a white man would walk into a colored man's home, shoot him, and then somehow win the title of victim.

But I don't see nothing earth-shattering about it. It's just another unspeakably common tragedy built out of the tired clichés of a nation.

But this one hurts different.

The only folks I haven't heard from are Terrance and Marguerite. Although I'm sure Terrance has seen the news.

And then Dolores came home.

I hear about it from a neighbor before I read about it in the papers. That she stepped out of a taxicab, that Lester met her on the drive, that she threw herself in his arms.

Now *that's* shocking.

But when it's reported in the *Los Angeles Times* it's explained. Mrs. Nolan did indeed suffer head trauma and can't recall many details of her assault, but what is known, according to the police and therefore the *Los Angeles Times*, is that she barely escaped that Negro man with her life and was so frightened she ran off, out of state.

But now she's home with her doting husband, Mr. Nolan. She gives this quote to the papers:

"My husband has never so much as been in a bar fight, but he killed a man to protect me, to save me. It's as if he went to war for me. He loves me that much."

When I read that it occurs to me that maybe it wasn't Dolores's blond hair and white skin that caught Terrance's eye. Maybe Terrance has a type that don't got nothin' to do with color.

The article also says that the Nolans are moving. Clearly the neighborhood has become infested. The new residents with their criminality, loose morals, and unsavory habits are trying to drag the more established residents down to their level. The Nolans want no part of it.

I read that and put the paper down.

And now I'm standing in front of a mirror.

I raise my hand, press the back of it against my nose with my fingers splayed wide enough for my eyes to see. Now the mirror shows me the crisscrossed lines of my palm, the lines that fortune tellers say map out some kinda future.

I have a future.

I go back to my bedroom, where I spent most of the last few days.

Anna's there, perched on the edge of the bed.

"You did all you could," she says, taking my hand.

"You keep saying that."

"Because it's true."

I want to go back to the mirror. Better to study my unchanging face than the images that keep popping into my head. Those patrol cars, Daniel staring at the floor, what's on the floor. "Thing is, if I did all I could, that just means I never had the power to change anything."

"You didn't, not this."

"I'm living alongside some of the most powerful colored folk on earth, but nobody here had the power to keep what happened from happening. Nobody here could protect James, not even from himself."

"Charlie, nobody else tried."

From the other room, I can hear Louise singing some tune we've all been hearing on the radio. I can make out Patty talking on the phone, Robert laughing. Everybody here's still mostly in good spirits. They're still winners.

Anna tilts her head toward my shoulder. I bask in the way she smells.

"I'm going back to his house today," I say.

She hesitates. "Do you want company?"

She doesn't want to go, which makes her offer a little more special. I kiss her on the forehead and shake my head before rising to leave.

"Charlie . . . it's possible more will come out about James. Things that won't make him look good."

She just can't help herself.

"I know you feel compelled to go back to that house, and I want to support you, but . . . he's not there anymore and . . . it might not be a bad idea to deny association with him. At least to those outside the community."

"Should I deny him three times, like Peter?"

Her sympathy dries faster than crocodile tears. "Reaper isn't Jesus. And that was God's will."

I don't know if she means it was God's will that Peter denied Jesus or if it was His will that James should die.

———

On his dark skin Daniel's bruises aren't too noticeable, making him look more tired than beaten. His eyes aren't lowered, but they won't meet mine. I'm thinking it took no more than two blows and a threat to get him to fold. He's still wearing his butler's garb, but it's not pressed, his tie is loose, his jacket unbuttoned over his vest. As if he's trying to find the compromise between the expectations of his job and the lack of an employer to hold him to account. "The police only let me reenter yesterday morning," he says. "They've been asking questions."

The house is a wreck. Every drawer in every piece of furniture has been emptied, papers, lighters, pens, tissues littered all over the floor. "They've searched the whole place. I don't think they found anything incriminating." But I can tell he's unsure as he leads me through the wreckage.

We enter the study. There are pillows that have been slashed, feathers strewn from one corner to the other, lamps tipped over . . . The white vase with painted tigers lies in pieces on the floor, shattered markers of careless wealth.

"That statement I gave to the police . . . ," he begins. "They told me that if I didn't go along with—"

"We don't have to talk about that," I interrupt. "Probably best if we don't."

His bruises become more obvious when he flushes. I feel his parasitic shame worming its way inside me, sense the sickness of it when he speaks, like a cough he's trying to keep quiet.

"He burst in here out of nowhere and accused Mr. Mann of kidnapping his wife, of locking her away somewhere. Mr. Mann told him he didn't know his wife's whereabouts but was quite certain that wherever she was, she was significantly better off without him."

That stops me. "James said that?" And here I had thought that it was me who'd been bold.

"I don't think he would have." Daniel's voice has an unmanly quiver. "Not if he had seen the gun under Mr. Nolan's jacket."

"I can forgive you for changing your statement after the police threatened you like that, but don't go calling him Mr. Nolan," I snap. "I don't give a shit how fancy his pedigree is, he's redneck, wife-beating trash and he doesn't deserve to be shown that kind of respect."

Daniel smiles a little at that, but keeps his gaze away from mine. Swallowing hard, he pinches the bridge of his nose. "You're not the only guest here right now."

"Who else?"

"His mother."

I step back, startled.

"It's the only name from his past he ever gave me," Daniel explains. "Just a contact in case of . . . something like this."

Something like this.

But there is nothing *like* this. Only this.

Again, I look around at the mess. "I guess she'll get the house." That's a comfort. Knowing he's got someone whose fortunes he can still better.

But Daniel makes a face, taps his toe against some paperweight that's been left on the floor. "I've been told that the house isn't under Mr. Mann's name."

"What? But whose name could it be under?"

"That Corsican man, Michel Luciani." Daniel crouches down, picks up a shining white piece of ceramic, broken in a way that its edge could be used as a knife. "Mr. Luciani has told the police that Mr. Mann was nothing but a caretaker. That he was here to . . . oversee the staff. That, of course, was news to me."

There's no room in my throat for anything but the thinnest gasps of air. I don't know if James had a title, but it wasn't *caretaker*. Whatever his work was, it was much more powerful and darker than that. He was wealthy. Powerful. He didn't talk to Michel like he worked for him. He spoke to him like they were partners, peers.

But then, what do I really know about James, a man who seems to have imagined himself into existence?

What can anyone know about a man like that?

"She's in his bedroom," he says, that makeshift weapon still in his hands, "if you should want to pay your respects."

As I climb the stairs, I realize I've never seen James's bedroom before. I open the doors of four different rooms before I find it. The first thing I notice is his beautiful bay windows that look out onto his courtyard and pool. The rest of the room was clearly beautiful, too, but it's now strewn with the same glittering detritus as the rest of the house.

Standing in the middle of the room, staring at the bed holding a slashed mattress and crumpled, soft cotton sheets, is an old woman, slightly hunched, leaning on a cane. Her posture reminds me of my own mother, a woman violently robbed of the ability to hope for a better life for herself and her family. A woman who had to transfer her dreams for the future to dreams of what might come after death.

James's mother gives me no more than a glance before looking back at the bed.

"My son slept there," she says with a voice I suspect was born not too far from the Mississippi. She releases a sigh, as if speaking is tiring. "Who are you?"

"Charlie Trammell," I say. "I was a friend of his. Your son."

"You trouble?"

"No, ma'am."

"Of all my children, Jimmy got the best heart and the worst habits. The mix that make friends with trouble."

"I'm just a neighbor he was kind to."

She sniffs, puts a little more weight on her cane. "I knew he end up like this. Started off workin' with dem rumrunners back when he still a boy growin' into a man. Then all dem speakeasies. One town after another, changin' his name like other folk change clothes. He didn't think I know, but I know. A mother always know."

"I'm not too familiar with his history, other than that he fought with the French Resistance durin' the war," I say to her, although I don't know if I believe that's true.

"Yeah, he told me about that. But then the money he start sendin' got a lil' too generous. He got himself into somethin' dirty."

"He didn't assault that white woman."

"I know that. Don't you think I know that?" She don't sound angry. Just spent. "I been knowin' this day comin' since he enter this world. Since he earn himself the name Reaper."

I step forward, willing her to look at me. "How'd he get that name?"

"It 'cause they wouldn't let me into the damn hospital."

"I don't understand."

"I was goin' into labor with my fifth child. Couldn't get hold of no midwife. But I was near enough to a hospital. Only problem is, it was a white-folk hospital. Got myself turned away."

"What'd you do?"

"What you mean, what'd I do? I tried to walk home, that what! Didn't get further than the colored cemetery before he start comin'. Ended up givin' birth to that boy on an old grave marked by nothin' but a rock. Can you imagine?"

I shake my head, pretending I can't.

But I can. The image is already carving itself into my mind.

"My boy takin' his first breath on top of a corpse who don't even got the means to have a name no more? Folk found out and start callin' my Jimmy 'Reaper.'" She takes an angry swipe at her eyes with the back of her hand. "So you see, it my fault, bringin' him into this world like that." This time when she tries to inhale, she chokes on a sob. "It the bad luck I brought him, see? The seeds of his end planted right there in his beginnin'! My boy never could get more than six feet from death!"

With all the chairs slashed I content myself with slumping against the wall. "If that's the reason," I say, "every colored man in America should be called Reaper."

———

It's another day before the Nolans move out. Rumor has it they're renting a place in South Pasadena while they look for a house to buy there. Marguerite and Terrance come home two days after that.

It's a full four days before the police finally release James's body. Another two before the funeral.

The service is held in Hattie's church, and I'm surprised by how many people show up. Louise, Ben, Norman and Edythe, Dr. Somerville and Vada, Ethel Waters, Sidney and Sydnetta, Anna, who won't leave my side . . . all these folks who didn't want any association with him . . . they're all here to grieve him.

Or maybe it's just to grieve another injustice they can't do nothing about.

Either way, I can tell it makes James's mother happy to see so many people here for her boy.

She doesn't see what's missing. Michel. Terrance.

Marguerite.

It's not until we get to the Rosedale Cemetery for the actual burial that one of those missing pieces shows up.

Terrance. He jogs over to my side as Anna and I walk to where James is to be laid to rest.

"I wanted to get here for the service," he says instead of hello. "But, well, things have been busy."

I don't respond.

"Did you hear about Pinky?" he whispers. "He was found dead in his cell."

Anna makes a sound of disgust and picks up her pace, leaving us behind.

Again I say nothing at all.

"You know this isn't my fault, right?" he says, gesturing frantically at the mourners and the tombstones around us. "It's not like I said anything to Les to make him turn on Reaper. Someone must have done so, but it wasn't me."

"His name is James." I don't add that James died helping one of Terrance's women. I don't add that I think the person who convinced Lester to go after James was Michel, that he was the funny-talking stranger who put a bug in his ear, to get Lester to do his dirty work for him.

All that is just grudges and guesses, neither of which are strong ground for debate.

"Where's Marguerite now?" I ask instead. "She coming?"

Terrance looks at me askance as if confused by why I'd ask a question with such an obvious answer. "I did invite her to join me," he says. "I let her know I would be fine with that. Welcome it even, for appearances. But . . . well. You know Marguerite."

It's not true. I know Margie.

Margie's too sweet a name for a girl who slices up hearts.

The only part of Margie that lives in Terrance's Marguerite is the part that's determined to be carefree despite living in a world filled with people who desperately need care. She manages it by not looking at the ugly.

James was similar but different. A perfect representative of the nation he believed in so fervently, he invested his fortunes in the ugly, his hands dug deep in the dirt.

But his eyes weren't guided by the work of his hands. He kept his gaze as high as his hopes, up there with Orion and Ursa, those guardians humans draw from the stars.

The True History

The Sugar Hill case sparked a movement within the Los Angeles Negro community. A few weeks after Clarke's ruling, a Black family moved into a home they had purchased just outside of the South Central area that had a racial covenant on it. They were arrested and spent five days in jail. The judge in that case did not rule in their favor.

But Loren Miller and the NAACP persisted. Miller went on to work with Thurgood Marshall to bring a racial covenant case to the Supreme Court, *Shelley v. Kraemer*. In 1948, the Supreme Court ruled in their favor, making racial covenants (but not housing discrimination in general) explicitly illegal. At the time of that ruling, Miller had more than one hundred racial covenant cases pending.

In 1953, white lawmakers and landowners proposed that a planned new highway run directly through the Sugar Hill neighborhood. Sugar Hill residents again organized to save their homes, but this time they were unsuccessful. Dozens of mansions owned by some of the most successful and famous African American Angelenos were taken by eminent domain and bulldozed to make way for the Santa Monica Freeway.

The homes that weren't outright destroyed lost their value. But they still stand, and while they are in various states of repair, it's impossible to miss the grandeur of what had once been Los Angeles's Sugar Hill.

Acknowledgments

First and foremost, this book would not be possible without the real people who inspired it: Hattie McDaniel, Louise Beavers and her husband Robert Clark, Ethel Waters, Ben Carter, Loren and Juanita Miller, Norman and Edythe Houston, John and Vada Somerville, Judge Thurmond Clarke, and many others.

While some of the people and events featured in my story are real, the story itself is obviously fiction. I haven't just taken liberties with the truth, I've invented people, places, and things, imagined relationships, arguments, and love affairs.

And yet every news article I directly quote from and most that I reference in the book are both real and accurate.

It's also true that the West Adams Heights Improvement Association (WAHIA) was prevented from forcing Negro residents out of their homes by enforcing racial covenants. Unfortunately, in the 1950s, the State of California succeeded where WAHIA failed by taking the homes of the Sugar Hill residents via eminent domain, bulldozing them, and putting the Santa Monica Freeway through what had been an affluent Negro community.

I am completely indebted to the Black newspapers of the time, particularly the *California Eagle,* the *Los Angeles Sentinel,* and the *Chicago Defender*, all of which made it their business to cover the stories the "white" newspapers often tried to ignore.

I'm equally indebted to the following nonfiction works and their authors and strongly recommend them to readers who want to know more about the events and people in Los Angeles's Sugar Hill. They are as follows:

The Coveted Westside: How the Black Homeowners' Rights Movement Shaped Modern Los Angeles by Jennifer Mandel

Loren Miller: Civil Rights Attorney and Journalist by Amina Hassan

Returning the Gaze: A Genealogy of Black Film Criticism, 1909–1949 by Anna Everett

Langston Hughes and the Chicago Defender: Essays on Race, Politics, and Culture, 1942–62, edited by Christopher C. De Santis

Man of Color: An Autobiography of J. Alexander Somerville: A Factual Report on the Status of the American Negro Today by John Alexander Somerville

His Eye Is on the Sparrow: An Autobiography by Ethel Waters with Charles Samuels, preface by Donald Bogle

Hattie McDaniel: Black Ambition, White Hollywood by Jill Watts

All of these books greatly informed this novel. I particularly enjoyed reading the autobiographies and essays of the individuals featured in my novel. Most of them were written just shortly after the events I explored here in my fictional version of Sugar Hill. I stand humbly on the shoulders of giants.

Kyra Davis Lurie is a *New York Times* bestselling author and screenwriter. Her novels have been published in nine languages across six continents. Kyra was born and raised in California and lives in Los Angeles with her husband and their utterly perfect dog, Potus.